Praise for *Time and Chance*

"A dynamic novel . . . a splendid tale."

—*The Philadelphia Inquirer*

"Everybody's fantasy: what if you were given the opportunity to live the life that might have been yours—but for time and chance. A brilliant premise. Profoundly moving. A wise and wonderful book."

—John R. Maxim, author of *Bannerman's Ghosts*

"A dazzling novel. Brennert's touch is sure and honest. Events and people ring true and deep, and so the book's conclusion is not merely poignant, but movingly illuminating. It is a marvelous achievement in storytelling, a book far out of the ordinary in the craftsmanship and integrity of its execution."

—*The San Diego Union-Tribune*

"Alan Brennert has woven a spellbinding plot and created intriguing, believable characters, but he has done more. . . . There are a few rare books you continue to think about after you've finished reading them. And there are even fewer you continue to recall for the rest of your life. *Time and Chance* will be one of those I recall for the rest of mine."

—Morgan Llywelyn, author of *Lion of Ireland*

"Brennert takes a fascinating premise and breathes new life into it by means of a humane vision, well-rounded characters, strong narrative drive, and adept plotting. The book is a satisfying, deeply pleasurable read that will strike a chord of recognition with anyone who has ever felt trapped by choices made at an earlier time in life." —*Sun-Sentinel* (Fort Lauderdale)

"A playful, affecting, and well-written tale." —*Publishers Weekly*

"[Brennert] brings sparkle and realism into the story through well-crafted character interaction and detailed descriptions of the New York theater scene. Readers will willingly follow this skillfully plotted tale through sentiment and suspense to a satisfying conclusion." —*Booklist*

"An absolute joy to read, a honey of a book. I took it in large gulps, pulled along by the sheer narrative magic. Brennert does more than keep you interested; he does the more difficult thing of making you care like hell."

—Parke Godwin, author of *Sherwood*

"Without veering into bathos, it plays on the seemingly universal longing to be given a second chance in life.... [A] strong grasp of character and vivid writing...moving and satisfying."

—*San Francisco Chronicle*

"An enormously satisfying and, above all, humane novel...intelligently written, with a rare sense of ethics that draws the reader ever more deeply into the book's well-crafted and intriguing suspense." —Ken Grimwood, author of *Replay*

"Vivid and totally involving...so engrossing that I finished the last hundred pages in the middle of a houseful of people on Christmas afternoon." —*Midwest Book Review*

"The year's most satisfying read."

—*The Telegraph* (Macon, Georgia)

"Brilliantly executed...I found myself absorbed in the idea of two faces inside every person. Brennert takes you on a journey inside yourself; you will be delighted at what you find."

—Dr. Dan Kiley, author of *The Peter Pan Syndrome*

"An engrossing and disturbing novel."

—*The Dallas Morning News*

TIME AND CHANCE

ALSO BY ALAN BRENNERT

Moloka'i
Honolulu

T·I·M·E
and
C·H·A·N·C·E

ALAN BRENNERT

A TOM DOHERTY ASSOCIATES BOOK · NEW YORK

This is a work of fiction. All of the characters, organizations, and events portrayed in this novel are either products of the author's imagination or are used fictitiously.

TIME AND CHANCE

A Tor Book
Published by Tom Doherty Associates, LLC
175 Fifth Avenue
New York, NY 10010

www.tor-forge.com

Tor® is a registered trademark of Tom Doherty Associates, LLC.

Library of Congress Cataloging-in-Publication Data

Brennert, Alan.
    Time and chance / Alan Brennert. — 1st trade pbk. ed.
        p. cm.
    "A Tom Doherty Associates book."
    ISBN 978-0-7653-2952-3 (trade paperback)
    1. Life—Fiction. 2. Chance—Fiction. I. Title.
PS3552.R3865T56 2011
813'.54—dc22

                                                     2011011556

First Edition: February 1990
First Trade Paperback Edition: July 2011

Printed in the United States of America

P 1

In memory of my parents,

HERBERT AND ALMYRA BRENNERT
(1911–1984; 1918–1986)

With love and gratitude,
and apologies for the lateness of the hour

CHAPTER ONE

RICHARD

We were at the end of a three-month run, not the longest of stands in Broadway history, but for a season that saw the quick and nasty deaths of more heralded and more expensive productions, not bad; everyone agreed that it was the worst season in memory, as last season had been the worst, and the one before that, and the one before that. In other words it was a season like any other, and the passing of a struggling revival of *Brigadoon* would go largely unremarked and unlamented, save by the hundred-odd actors, singers, dancers, and technicians who had labored for close to four months to bring it to life.

There is something about acting in a musical unlike any other kind of theatrical experience; it's what we all got into this business for, the feeling we used to imagine when we sat in the audience, watching. When you're in a straight dramatic play you're always conscious of yourself, your character, your "moments"; in a comedy you work toward your laugh lines, you measure the audience response from show to show, try different inflections to milk the laugh. But in a musical...

In a musical you stand in the wings, listening, as the

orchestra strikes up the overture, as a brassy vibrato brings a shiver of anticipation, and in the pause between movements it feels almost as if your heart is beating in time to the music. In the space of a few minutes all the separate themes and songs of the play are compressed into a single prelude, each one flowing seamlessly into the next . . . and that's what it's all about, really.

Because you're not alone up there. It's not just you and the words, it's you, and the words, and the music, and the dancers, and a hundred unseen hands: the composer, the librettist, the choreographer who has to seem invisible, has to make our movements seem spontaneous, unrehearsed. The first time I saw myself on film, I thought: That's not just me up there, I can't take all the credit; it's the script, the camera, the cutting, the underscore, all working together, creating something more than the sum of its parts. It's that way in a musical. For as long as it lasts, you're all part of a greater whole; and no matter how many years later, if you're in an airport or a taxi and you hear that song you sang, or that theme you danced to, you're a part of it again.

Outside the Gershwin there was a line of people queued up at the box office, their breath fogging as they waited to buy tickets for that night's performance; a banner added to the show poster announced bleakly, FINAL PERFORMANCE—JAN. 28. I passed the line of shivering people and thought, somewhat bitterly, Where the hell were you when we needed you?—a silly thought, since the dozen or two customers who had decided to see the show before it died would hardly have extended our run by much more than twenty seconds. I turned up the collar on my jacket as I passed, but one of them recognized me and stepped out of line, instantly burrowing in the pockets of her coat. "Mr. Cochrane? Could I–?"

I stopped, smiled awkwardly, and took the piece of paper and stubby pencil she offered me. I always felt self-conscious about this; who was I, anyway, to be signing autographs? That was for stars like Pacino, not some *pisher* like me. Two years on a soap opera had done more for my public recognition than the dozen-some plays I'd done over the last decade, but when people like this woman asked me for my autograph I couldn't quite shake the feeling that I was cheating them—that I'd turn around to find Frank Langella standing behind me, clearing his throat and saying, gently, "Ah... I think she was talking to *me,* old man, do you mind...?"

Besides, I could never think of what to write. The woman was watching as I stood there blankly, groping for something clever or personal, distinctive in any damn way. "Ah... what's your name?" I asked. Barbara, she replied, Barbara Kovacks. I quickly scribbled: *To Barbara— All the best, Richard Cochrane.* Lord, what stunning originality. What epic imagination. She didn't seem to mind; she took the paper, thanked me, and I said, No, thank *you* for coming, because no actor likes to close to an empty house. And of course the moment I said it I knew that was what I should have written, but it was too late; she scurried back into line, and I into the theater.

On stage, on screen, you hit your marks, you pick up your cues; in life, unfortunately, everything is always a little too late, the right words coming too slowly, the moment passing too soon. I thought of Libby and wondered if she'd show up at tonight's performance. No reason why she should.

Backstage, every dressing table was piled high with photos and résumés. The phones were in constant use, and I thought suddenly of a Gahan Wilson cartoon I'd seen years ago: a bedraggled, bearded doomsayer carrying a placard reading, *Death means never having to call your agent.* I stopped for a moment behind Sally Marsden, who'd been the last-minute replacement for the second female lead, the promiscuous Scottish lass Meg Brockie, when Tess Canton came down with bronchitis. Sally was brushing out her hair, usually pulled back in a tight chignon but now falling freely in a style more appropriate to the play and the period; on the table beside her were half a dozen of her composites, each 8×10 page broken into four separate head shots. One had her as a *Baby Doll* coquette, another as a businesswoman in a gray suit, a third as a country girl in a plaid halter top, and the fourth, a nun. I nodded appreciatively. "If they ever make *Sybil* into a weekly series, I think you've got a lock on it."

She smiled, shaking out her long blonde hair. "I was thinking of dumping the nun. I mean, unless they're casting *Agnes of God*, what's the point?"

"You ever play a nun?"

"Professionally?"

"No, amateur novitiate night at Regine's. Of course professionally, what else?"

Sally swiveled round to face me, a mischievous glint in her eyes. "You ever hear of a game called 'The Abbess and the Penitent'?" she asked.

Sally was well cast. I cleared my throat, smiled wanly, and started toward my own dressing table. She called after me, "Richard, you're no fun at all," and I suppose she was right. Thirteen years as an actor in New York and I was woefully deficient in the prerequisites of my profession: I had never (a) engaged in a homosexual affair, (b) slept with anyone to advance my career, though I still harbored hopes, or (c) cultivated a taste for cocaine, alcohol, or amyl nitrite. What can I say? I was clearly a failure in my chosen lifestyle.

I sat down at my table and began applying the hated spirit gum to my face; at first the beard had seemed a nice touch, a subtle way of contemporizing my character, but after a hundred and six performances, a hundred and six times of applying and removing the makeup, its novelty had waned. It might've been easier to grow the thing myself, but the few times I'd tried it came out bristly, scratchy, and a bit too curly; I always looked like I should be starring in *Maciste at the Gates of Hell*. And Libby said it was like making love to a Brillo pad, though by the last few weeks of our relationship a Brillo pad might've fared better than I. I began applying the beard, piece by piece, mustache first, then sideburns.

"Evening, Richard," came a voice to my right, a voice I recognized at once as belonging to John Danker, the sixtyish actor playing the pompous Andrew MacLaren. I turned in my seat to greet him—

And started. I expected to see John, with his kindly face and graying hair, sitting down beside me—but suddenly, instead, I was staring at a blank wall; suddenly I seemed to be somewhere else entirely. I turned round quickly in my seat, startled to find myself not at my makeup table, but sitting at a desk in some small cubicle, in a room filled with other desks and other cubicles, and with the sudden clatter of keyboards and ringing phones. I jerked back, frightened and disoriented—

And I was back at the dressing table again, staring into the worried eyes of John Danker, seated right next to me.

"Richard?" he said. "You all right?"

I waited to see if the episode would recur, but the moment, whatever it had been, had passed; I was exactly where I should have been, the noise and cross-talk reassuringly normal. I tried to dismiss it as just a particularly vivid daydream. "Yeah, fine. Closing night jitters, I guess."

He nodded, starting to apply his own makeup; like me, he was already in costume, but while my character's dress was contemporary, his was period—full Scottish Highlander regalia, circa eighteenth century. "I knew one fellow," he said, "this wonderful old British character actor, who hated closings so much he'd get himself sick the night before, forcing his understudy to close out the run for him. Wasn't faking it, mind you, he just hated taking that final bow, worked himself into a case of spastic colitis every time."

I laughed, but halfheartedly, beginning to feel depressed—reminded that this was the last time I would sit here among these people I had grown to like so much; the last time I might exchange stories with John, listening to tales from a career three times as long, and five times as interesting, as mine. I'd grown quite fond of John in the past four months; he had built a career on playing stolid father figures and arch villains, but in real life he was a very fey, very sweet old man with a trunkload of wonderful anecdotes.

"It's all over tonight, isn't it?" I said.

He patted me on the shoulder. "Now look here, my

boy, I know what you're thinking and it's not true. Everyone in this business feels the same way at the end of a job: you feel like you'll never work again, it's all over, pack me up and scatter the ashes." I laughed, started to protest, but John leaned in, urgent and sincere: "Well, it's not over. Something always turns up. God's sake, look at this—" He handed me his résumé, an imposing document with credits ranging back forty years and more. "And after every show, every part, for at least the first twenty years, I thought, well, that's it, they've found me out; can't act my way out of a clamshell; might as well go into roofing, or aluminum siding."

I smiled, shook my head. "No, really, that's not it. You're right, something always turns up. If not a part, then a residual check." I paused, not quite knowing how to explain what I was feeling, finally deciding not to try. "I just get depressed at the end of a run, that's all."

Soon enough, I was standing in the wings as the overture swelled for the last time; as the wistful, plaintive strains of "Brigadoon" segued into the happy, raucous melody of "Down on MacConnachy Square," and then the bright romanticism of "Almost Like Being in Love," and on through the rest, coming full circle to the main theme, to "Brigadoon." The curtain rose, in the darkness an unseen chorus sang the prelude, "Once in the Highlands," the house lights came up, and we were on.

The nice thing about a long run—and three months, relatively speaking, is a long run—is that it gives you time to concentrate on the nuances. The first few weeks you're so caught up in the broad strokes—your physical moves, the demanding routine of being exactly where you're supposed to be at any given moment, to say nothing of simply getting your lines down—that you hardly have time to address the finer points of your performance. Once the broad strokes are down pat, you're free to concentrate on the smaller bits of business, free to play with them from show to show, changing them slightly to keep your interest in the part fresh; finding exactly which ones work best for the role. I always try to make my closing performance the distillation of everything I learned during the run ... try to make it as perfect as I can. But it doesn't always work out that way.

Act One went well—in fact, more than well; the whole cast, I think, shared my desire to make this last performance the best. And my favorite scene, in which my character, Tommy Albright, admits his love for Fiona MacLaren, started out well enough. I don't have a world-class singing voice by any means, but I've had training, I can carry a tune, and of all the songs in the play this one touched me most, and I sang it well and strong because in many ways I was singing about myself:

> *I saw a man walking by the sea*
> *Alone with the tide was he.*
> *I looked and I thought as I watched him go by:*
> *There but for you go I.*
> *Lonely men around me,*
> *Trying not to cry,*
> *Till the day you found me*
> *There among them was I ...*

I was the singer, and I was the one being sung about; of such dichotomies are an actor's life made. I finished the song to scattered applause, we went on with the scene. I held Fiona—Meredith, actually, Meredith Holt—and said, "I love you, Fiona. I guess that's all there is to it."

"I've wanted to hear ye say it," she answered, on cue, "even though it be at the last minute like this."

At this point I was supposed to hold her away from me, alarmed, and say fearfully, *The last minute?*—but just as I began to push her away, I heard, in the great vast silence of the theater, a voice—a man's voice, with a slight New England twang, his tone sharp and filled with contempt—saying:

"For Christ's sake, Cochrane, what the hell do you think you're doing?"

Instinctively, I spun around. My first, panicky thought was that I had blown a cue or a line, or that my fly was unzipped, or any of a hundred actor's nightmares. But only half a second later I realized that even if that were the case, no one—cast or crew—would ever shout something like that out loud, call me by my real name, while I was *on stage*, for God's sake.

I stood there a moment, bewildered and confused. I heard Meredith's voice behind me, nervous, but keeping in character: "Tommy...?"

I turned round again. She was looking at me with alarm, and for the life of me I could not recall what the hell my next line was. Meredith saw this in an instant and quickly covered for me: "Aye, Tommy, 'tis true. Soon now 'tis the end of our day..."

I remembered where I was and the next line came out without hesitation, as did the next, and the next; but the damage had been done. Whoever the hell that joker was, he had thrown me off. I never fully recovered from it, never shook off the fear that it might happen again, and as a result what I had hoped would be my definitive performance turned out to be one I might have managed with a mild case of the flu.

I was so angry with myself, and with whoever had shouted at me, that I barely heard the applause at curtain call. I took my bows mechanically, feeling that I didn't deserve them, not even allowing myself to think of it as approbation for three months of good work rather than a single performance. The curtains came down and my usual closing-night depression turned sour and mean.

I harangued the crew, trying to find out who had thrown me for a loop in Act Two... but to my dawning amazement no one seemed to know what I was talking about. The stagehands, the cast, even Meredith, who'd been the only other actor onstage with me... none of them had heard the voice.

My anger dissipated and I began to wonder if the voice had been all in my mind—a self-critical part of me castigating myself for not doing better. I'd never actually heard one of those inner voices speak out loud before, but they were there, to be sure, driving me, whipping me, urging me on. I suppose all creative people have them; but all creative people certainly don't hear them, on stage, in the middle of the second act.

I finally succeeded, with the aid of a half liter of wine, to put it and the odd daydream at my makeup table out of my mind; there was a raucous and pleasant closing-night party at the theater, and I was having too good a time to dwell on it. (Opening-night parties are usually held at Sardi's, when both the money and the optimism

are flowing more freely; for closing parties, tables and
chairs are set up on the stage itself, kegs of beer and bottles
of wine scattered about the still-standing set, and the
festivities held right then and there—except for me it's
always felt uncomfortably like dancing on the grave of
the fallen show.) It wasn't until the end of the evening
that my depression crept back as I sat surrounded by these
friends I had made over the past four months. I might
work with some of them again, in other shows...but that
special chemistry that makes a good ensemble, that happy
confluence of the right people, the right material, the
right time, would never come again in just this way: lightning could not be caught in a bottle twice.

John Danker looked at me as though he knew exactly
what was going through my mind. He leaned in, his voice
low amid the laughter around us. "You know what it is, my
boy? We make a home for ourselves, every time we work
on something: actors, writers, singers, building these little
nests in our gypsy souls, in place of the ones we so seldom
seem to make in our own lives. And then suddenly it's
over, and we have to start again. But you know, Richard,
we *do* always start again."

I looked at him, at the sad glow in his eyes, and I knew
that this show had probably meant more to him than to
any of us. While we were still in rehearsals, John's companion for the past ten years, Howard, had died of AIDS;
though he'd never said as much, we all quietly assumed
that John was living in the shadow of the same disease.
For a while we had thought he might drop out of the
show, but after a week off he was back at rehearsals, and
he was there opening night and every night since then.

I looked at him now—at the time-worn face that had borne many kinds of sadness—and I felt ashamed. My own troubles—failed marriage, failed relationships—hardly seemed so important in comparison. And yet I still couldn't help but wonder: "John? What is it about us . . . all of us in this business . . . that makes it so damn hard? Do we ever"—I hesitated, embarrassed even before I'd voiced the thought—"do we ever really go home?"

John laughed a small, gentle laugh. "Dear boy," he said. "Dear, dear boy." But he didn't answer, just patted me on the shoulder and poured me another drink, as the party flickered out around us and we all soon scattered, amid kisses and promises to stay in touch, into the night—as the lightning was let loose from the bottle, tracing bright, lonely arcs through the streets before returning to the dark storm clouds at the heart of our lives.

My co-op, a big, two-level townhouse on Riverside Drive, faced west; through its floor-to-ceiling windows I could see the twin towers of the George Washington Bridge straddling the Hudson, at night a crescent of blue-white lights strung between them like a necklace of stars. I first saw the bridge thirteen years ago, at the end of a long car trip from New Hampshire, as I ascended the small incline to Fort Lee, New Jersey. There in front of me was the bridge's eastern tower, a latticework of exposed girders standing ten stories high, the New York City skyline visible through its graceful steel arch. It was breathtaking; magnificent. It was the rainbow bridge, the yellow brick road, it was every magic portal to every grand and glorious kingdom I had ever imagined.

Thirteen years later, the bridge was still magical to me,

but the destinations had somehow reversed themselves. New York seemed neither Oz nor Asgard to me now, and when I looked at the cars crossing westward over the Hudson, I had the nagging suspicion that it was they who were entering a better world—a world I had left behind years before, never realizing its true worth.

In the weeks that followed I made the usual rounds—plays, TV shows, commercials. As an actor you learn early to expect only one out of every dozen auditions to pan out, but you never quite get used to the numbing tedium of the responses, all invariably alike. You sit outside the office, reading and rereading the "sides," the script scenes selected for the audition, sometimes mouthing them aloud along with ten or twelve other actors; you go in, read the lines with the casting director or an associate; if the show's director is there he may ask you to read the line a little differently, "Bring it down a few notches," "Crank it up a level," and you do it; and when it's over they all smile, and stand, and shake your hand and say:

"Very nice, thank you," or,

"Very nice, thanks for coming," or simply,

"Very nice, very nice," and you go on to the next reading, and you only hear from them again if you got the part. There was a time when all this was exciting to me, but lately it was wearing thin. I felt more and more like I wasn't really living a life, I was just *auditioning* for life. In my grimmer moments I imagined that when I died there would be this great black void, and then a deep, sepulchral voice would say, "Very nice, thank you, thank you for coming," and I'd have to start all over, without the sides.

The odd, disoriented feelings I'd experienced at the Gershwin abated for a while—only to return, in force, on my birthday. My friends had thrown a party for me; Ray and Melissa were there, Donna, Gary, Tom, even Libby had come—she'd bought me a leather datebook, pecked me on the cheek and smiled warmly, but we were still a bit awkward around one another and she hung back throughout most of the party, keeping a certain distance. She was pretty, dark-haired, in her early thirties, a songwriter and sometimes librettist; we'd dated for the better part of a year and a half before moving in together, and a relationship which had seemed to be thriving suddenly began to erode inside of six months, as had too many of my live-in relationships before this. At thirty-five, I suppose, I had become fairly set in my ways, used to living alone and, worse yet, liking it; there must be easier men in the world to live with.

I opened my presents as Tom Giani carried in the birthday cake and the rest of the group began to sing:

"Happy birthday to you . . . happy birthday to you . . ."

Embarrassed, I was only half-listening to the song, but I swear that when they got to the next bar I heard, clear and sharp and unmistakably, the sound of a little girl's voice:

"Happy birthday, dear Daddy—"

I spun round, just as I had on stage that night, searching for the voice. But it was clearly a child's, and there were none in the room; the couples I knew with children had had them fairly recently, and the babies were at home with sitters.

The group urged me to blow out the candles; distractedly, I blew out three or four on the first breath, then finished the rest with a second. Libby alone saw the worry in my eyes as I continued to gaze around the room, searching for something that could not be; she put a hand to my shoulder, her voice low.

"Richard? Are you all right?"

I wanted to say: No. I'm not. Something's happening to me, honey, and I don't know what, and I'm scared. I wanted to hold her, and fall asleep in her arms. But I said only:

"Sure. I'm fine," and then they were cutting the cake, and handed me the first piece. But it was the damnedest thing. Perhaps it was just worry and distraction; perhaps I wasn't really paying much attention to what I was eating. But as I took a bite of what was clearly an angel-food cake, I could almost swear it tasted like . . . chocolate.

It seemed clear, even to me, what was happening: the stress of breaking up with Libby, of the end of a run, of sudden unemployment, was taking its toll. I debated, for several days, going back to see my therapist, whom I'd stopped seeing over a year before out of sheer attrition; but before I had the chance to call the rest of my world fell in on me.

The phone rang at six o'clock on a Tuesday morning. There are certain times, certain moments, when you know exactly what is about to happen, what you are about to hear. You know that it is not your agent calling about an audition; you know it is not an early call to a film shoot; you know it is not a wrong number. How you know these things, I have no idea; but you do. I picked up the phone and heard the harsh whisper of long-distance static, and my heart started racing, my fears crystallizing. No voice had to get on the line; I knew what was coming.

"Richard Cochrane?"

I took a breath. "Speaking."

"This is Parkland Medical Center, in Derry, New Hampshire."

I shut my eyes. Oh God. Oh God, no . . .

"My mother," I said. "What's wrong?"

There was a brief pause, then, soft above the hiss of the connection: "I'm afraid your mother . . . passed away last night, Mr. Cochrane. I'm very sorry."

I listened, numbly, to the details: how she had been having chest pains the night before; how she had apparently taken three nitroglycerin tablets over the course of an hour, and then, when the pains had not gone away as they always had before, she called the paramedics; how the hospital had sent a mobile ICU to her home, but by the time they got her to the hospital there were no vital signs. I listened, and said something, what, I can't recall, and I hung up, my mind whirling with all the things I would have to do, the people I would have to call: the mortuary, my aunt and uncle in Connecticut, the airline. It was exactly what my mother had done, I later realized, when my father died—I had still been too stunned to do anything but wander the house in a daze, but she'd automatically begun making the necessary calls, as she had done so many times, for so many other relatives, over the years. And now it was my turn, to do for her what she had done for all of us—shouldering the pain and responsibility and the burden of thinking clearly and rationally when all you really wanted to do was mourn. I sat down on the edge of my bed and began to cry, and all I could think was, *Mama, my poor mama.* I had not called her that since I was a little boy, but now it was the only thing I could

think of to call her; *Mama, my poor mama, I'm coming, I'll
be there.* And I only hoped I could do half as well for her
as she had done for all the loved ones she had buried, all
those sad long years.

CHAPTER TWO

RICK

The baby was screaming again, waking me from what had been, in any event, a restless sleep; in moments I was stone cold awake, with no hope, I knew, of going back to sleep. It had been that way for weeks now—tossing and turning every night, some nights awakening for no apparent reason at three or four a.m.—and then I'd just lie there on the edge of sleep, never quite drifting back, until sunrise. Tonight, at least, I had a reason for being awake, and a reason for getting up.

Beside me Debra stirred, only half awake; she turned on her side, murmured, "Your turn," buried her head in her pillow, and drifted off to sleep again. I was always amazed and envious of her ability to do that. Even as a young child, it always took me at least an hour, sometimes more, to get to sleep; and I could never, under any circumstances, go to sleep during the day. Only at night.

I got up, pulling on a bathrobe, and padded to the nursery, hoping that Jeffrey's cries hadn't wakened Paige. I picked him up; he needed changing. I stripped off his Pampers, cleaned him up and slipped a fresh pair onto him; he was still crying, now more at being awake than anything else. I held him against me, his tiny head resting on my left shoulder, and patted him soothingly on the back. "Sshh, shhh," I said, rocking him gently. "It's okay, kiddo. You're entitled. Can't say I like being up at this hour myself." I continued to rock him and stroke his back, and at length his cries became less and less frequent and his eyes drooped closed. Gently I put him back in his crib, tucked the blankets around him, and stood watching him for several minutes, his small chest rising and falling, rising and falling. I had to smile. He was finally starting to shape up into an actual miniature human, after many months of bearing a stronger genetic resemblance to the sweet potato family; I could even see faint echoes of Debra's bone structure in his face.

I looked down at him, proud that I had been able to comfort him and still his cries, and thought: I love you, Jeffrey-bean. Why isn't that enough?

My mind began racing along familiar tracks, like one of the houseflies that flew inside during high summer and kept bouncing from wall to wall, searching fruitlessly for some escape, endlessly circling bright lights. For me the bright lights were in my head, and I, too, could not stop from orbiting them.

No point in going back and disturbing Deb; no reason to enrage her even more than she'd been when she went to bed. I winced, the past evening just now coming into clear relief: the restaurant; the fight; oh, shit, everything.

The fight was stupid and pointless, as most of our fights seemed to be these days. The waiter had screwed up the appetizers, delivered the wrong one to Debra; she didn't mind, didn't want to make a scene, but I began snapping at the poor kid, demanding he replace it, my irritation totally out of proportion to his mistake. Across the table Debra stiffened, her eyes glazing over with apprehension, the look that said, Oh God, not here, not again. I saw the look, recognized it, and didn't care. From that point on, every flaw in the service, every annoying distraction, exacerbated my anger; several glasses of wine didn't help any. By the end of the meal Debra was sitting coolly, trying to restrain her own anger; once we were on the road, it all spilled out: "What is wrong with you! You were acting like a spoiled *child*."

"The man had the IQ of a floor lamp! Is it too much to expect—"

"I am tired of this!" she snapped, and in retrospect I could hardly blame her. "You embarrass me, you make me want to run and hide when you're like this. What the hell is wrong, Rick, what the hell are you so angry about?"

We rode home in virtual silence as I told myself: For Christ's sake, Cochrane, calm down; she's right, you were being an idiot. I knew what I should say, but I couldn't break the silence, couldn't bring myself to admit that there was something wrong with me, something I couldn't yet face. Finally, before bed, I managed a brief, perfunctory apology, which rightfully did not placate Debra very much. She nodded, turned on her side, and went to sleep with that damnable ease; I lay awake for an hour, staring at the ceiling, wondering what in God's name was happening to me.

When I'd finished torturing myself with the memory of my stupidity, I gave Jeffrey a small kiss on the forehead, adjusted his blankets again, and went down to the kitchen, intending to fix a sandwich from cold cuts in the fridge; but when I looked up, I realized I was at the wet bar, a glass in one hand, a decanter of scotch in the other . . . and I froze.

I put the glass down, very quietly, and shoved the scotch back to the rear of the bar. Then I sank slowly into a chair, my hands trembling, leaned my head so far back it hurt, shut my eyes and wished the morning were already here.

By sunrise I looked so wretched that Debra didn't even broach the subject of last night; more worried than angry now, she suggested I go to the sleep-disorder clinic at Dartmouth and I promised to give it a try, deep down knowing that all they could do was treat the symptom, not the underlying cause . . . and I had not even admitted what that was to myself, yet. Two cups of coffee got me safely down Route 3 to Nashua, but even so I dragged myself into the State Mutual office ten minutes late. I poured myself another cup of coffee, black, and settled in behind my desk. I sat there, trying to shake the cobwebs from my brain, looking in my phone log at the dozen or so calls from claimants I would have to return; I turned to reach for the phone—

And all at once I was no longer at my desk, no longer in the busy office filled with ringing phones and clacking keyboards, but . . . somewhere else.

For the briefest of moments, I found myself seated next to a man wearing, of all things, tartan plaid—some bizarre period dress, breeches and a loose white shirt beneath a tight velvet jacket. I reared back, flinching, confused and disoriented—

And as suddenly as it had come, it was over; I was back at my desk again. No strange, graying man in period garb;

no hint that it had even happened. Jesus! I'd heard of people hallucinating from lack of REM sleep, but this was scary; slowly it sank in that I might be doing some serious damage to my body. Deb was right, I had to do something about this. I called information, got the number of the sleep-disorder clinic and determined to call them that afternoon.

Somehow I never did. I went home for lunch and rested for half an hour, wishing that I could somehow will myself to sleep, even for a few minutes; but of course I couldn't. Back at the office I drank at least two more quarts of coffee and caught up on my phone calls. I was talking to one of our attorneys about a pending workers' comp case, trying to find a way to settle this without going to the appeals board, when behind me I heard a woman's voice—not any woman I worked with, not any voice I recognized—say:

"I've wanted to hear ye say it. Even though it be at the last minute like this."

Absently, I noted that the woman was speaking with a Scottish burr, but I didn't think much of it, assuming it was some claimant talking to one of the other adjusters. But the next thing I knew I heard another voice, a more familiar one, with a hard, angry edge to it:

"Cochrane! Did you *hear* me?"

I turned round quickly. My supervisor, Hunt Bailey, stood behind me, his face red with anger; I hadn't even noticed that he'd returned from his court case. I begged off the phone conversation, hung up, and swiveled, a bit apprehensively, toward him.

"I'm sorry, Hunt, I wasn't listening."

"I said, what the hell do you think you've been doing?"

I was more than a little taken aback. Hunt was generally

an easygoing sort, very New England, reserved, not given to outbursts like this. I blinked, starting to get worried now. "What—what do you mean?"

Hunt stood there, obviously trying to keep calm. "Did you disburse the award on the O'Connell case?"

"The back injury? Yes, of course. The check was cut—" I rifled through the mound of paperwork on my desk, triumphantly produced a document, handed it to him. "Here. On the twenty-second."

He scanned the paper, nodded, handed it back to me. "And the other half of the award? The head injury?"

Something sank inside me. I started going through my papers again, trying to conceal my mounting panic; finally, after several moments, Hunt said, "Don't bother. I already know. The applicant's attorney just called to inform us payment was not received during the prescribed twenty-day period, and the court has been notified accordingly."

I went white. I stopped, turned, looked up at him. Christ, no wonder he was so upset. "Hunt, I—I don't know how it slipped by me. I just—Jesus, man, I just don't *know*." I licked my lips nervously. "The head injury was the lesser of the two judgments..."

"It was still thirty thousand! And now we're looking at a three-thousand-dollar penalty, for—" He was still angry, but some of his old reserve had crept back. "Can I see you in my office?"

Once we were alone, he sat on the edge of his desk, looking at me with a mixture of frustration and concern. "Rick, I'm not sure what to say. This isn't the first mistake like this you've made, though it is the most significant. I'll have to take some kind of disciplinary action, you realize that, don't you?"

I nodded numbly. He leaned forward, frowning, his voice a bit softer. "I know you're having some health problems. The insomnia, I mean. Maybe you need some time off. To get some help."

I looked up, alarmed. "I . . . I appreciate the offer, Hunt, but . . . I can't afford it. I mean, we've got a new baby, and—"

"I don't think you can afford not to. I don't want to have to call this a suspension, but I will if that's what it takes to get you back on track. Understand?"

I almost snapped at him, something short and nasty and totally unjustified, but thank God I had restraint enough not to. I bit my lip, nodded, and looked away from him. "I'll go to a doctor. Maybe he can give me some pills."

"That's not the answer, either," he said, more gently.

I stood, forced myself to look him in the eye. "I'm sorry, Hunt. I didn't mean to disappoint you."

He nodded. There was a brief, awkward pause, as neither of us knew what to say next; quickly I turned and left the office, hurrying back to my cubicle. The other adjusters, those who had overheard the first part of our conversation, glanced at me with either sympathy or derision; my claims assistant, Amy, stood up as I passed her cubicle, adjoining mine, and followed me inside to my desk.

"Rick?" she said. "Are you—"

"I'm fine," I said, forcing a smile.

She shifted her weight, frowned. "Maybe—maybe I forgot to remind you about the disbursement, you know? Maybe I should talk to Hunt, and—"

I was touched, but I shook my head. "No. Absolutely not. It wasn't your mistake, it was mine." Before she could say anything more, I affected a businesslike air, shuffled some paper, and said, "Would you find Peter Klein's file for me, please?"—and as she rummaged in the file cabinet I looked down, focusing all my attention on the paperwork in front of me, and fought back the anger and contempt rising within me—anger at the patronizing stares that had followed me down the corridor, contempt for work that I hated, but most of all, contempt for myself, for not even being able to handle a job I thought so little of.

I was in no mood for what I found when I returned home: my quiet house had suddenly become the crossroads of the universe. Our baby-sitter, Carol, was heading up the front walk just as I pulled into the driveway. I followed her inside, and the minute I opened the door I was assaulted by the sounds of my son, squalling his eight-month-old head off, and my daughter, bouncing hysterically around the house in a green leotard torn at the knee. *"Mom,"* she was calling up the stairs, "I can't go on looking like *this*! We've got to *do* something."

Debra appeared at the top of the stairs, holding a suddenly placated Jeffrey to her breast. "Honey, what do you want me to do, call the Joint Chiefs of Staff? I'll fix it in a minute." Seeing me enter, she smiled wearily. "Rick, can you sew Paige's costume for her? I've got a thousand things to do before we leave."

Paige looked horror-stricken. "Dad doesn't sew, he does acupuncture. I'll fix it myself." She hurried out of the foyer, around the corner, and out of sight. I looked up at Debra. "Works every time, doesn't it?"

Debra grinned. "Welcome to our latest experiment in entropy. Better get changed, we've got to leave in half an—"

There was the honk of a car horn from outside and

Paige suddenly rocketed back into the room, a needle and thread in one hand, panic in her eyes. "Oh God, they're here! I gotta go. Maybe I can fix this in the car."

"Good luck, honey," Debra called after. "We'll be watching."

Paige paused at the door, smiled a long-suffering smile. "Mom, you don't say 'good luck,' you say 'break a leg.' 'Good luck' is like a jinx, you know? But thanks." She banged out the door, hurrying down the walkway to where a station wagon of other costumed thirteen-year-olds sat, noisy and nervous and excited. I held the door open, looking at them, dimly recalling the anticipation they were feeling; then, as they roared off down the street, I slammed shut the door.

"Better hurry, hon," Debra called, already carrying Jeffrey to the nursery. I started to follow her up the stairs, Carol darting in front of me en route to the kitchen. The words came out before I had a chance to consider them, for if I had, if I'd been at all reasoned or rational, I would never have uttered them: "Deb, I had a really awful day, I may not be up for this. Why don't you go see the play, and I'll stay home with Jeff, okay?"

She stopped, and in that split second I could see her shoulders tighten and her whole body tense, and I knew I'd made a mistake, a bad one. She turned slowly, her face taut, her tone icy. "Don't you dare do that to Paige," she said. "Don't you *dare*."

"Hon, it's just a silly school play."

She stared daggers at me. "Not to her."

I backed off quickly. "Okay, okay. I was just—"

"My God," she said contemptuously, turning again to head for the nursery, "how could you even *think* of not—"

"I'll get ready," I snapped, and brushed past her to the

bathroom. Within twenty minutes I had showered, shaved, and changed; we gave last-minute instructions to Carol, climbed into the Volvo, and headed for Paige's school, riding in silence most of the way. Paige's school had been my school, once upon a time–a two-story, yellow brick building squatting on a hill at the edge of town. I glanced at Debra, staring out the side window, and marveled at how little she had changed since I met her in college: the short crop of chestnut-brown hair was a little longer, her glasses more stylish (she had never been able to wear contacts; couldn't stand the thought of having anything in her eyes), a few laugh lines and wrinkles here and there, but basically still the same bright, thoughtful young woman I had fallen in love with, so long ago. How could this be happening to us?

The auditorium was the same one in which I had languished so often in assembly; I could not for the life of me remember any of the lectures or speakers we heard during those assemblies, but I still remembered vividly those tatty red velveteen seats, the way you pushed the bottom half down to sit and how it snapped back, with a shiver of springs, when you got up. I sat down with the other hundred or so parents filling the auditorium and felt suddenly as though I were back in twelfth grade, about to be subjected to another assembly. I felt claustrophobic; trapped. I felt restless and contrary and angry for being here . . . but now, as then, there was no way out.

The play was *Peter Pan*, and Paige had the title role. I wish I could say I was proud when I saw her walk onstage for the first time in her green leotard; wish I could say how thrilled I was to hear her sing, or how nervous I became when she was "flown" across the stage, strapped into a harness and supported by wires. But I can't. I'm ashamed to admit it—I was barely able to admit it to myself—but instead of pride, or excitement, or pleasure, I felt nothing. I watched and I listened, but I felt merely numb; I smiled and applauded at all the right places, but inside I felt strangely hollow.

Afterward we went backstage along with the other proud parents. Paige was grinning, hugging her fellow actors, all of them practically jumping up and down with pride and relief that they had survived the performance. Debra gave Paige a big hug. "You were beautiful, honey," she said, a catch in her voice. "You were just wonderful."

"Thanks, Mom."

Debra gave her a last squeeze, then straightened and stepped back. Paige looked at me expectantly. I stood there, still feeling numb, and all I could manage was a forced smile and a flat, "You did fine, hon. Just fine." Her eyes hungered for something more, and I wished to God I could find the words she longed to hear.

No, that's a lie. I knew the words, they were the same words I had yearned to hear years ago, in college, when I was the one on stage; I just couldn't say them. So I stood there, smiling blandly, as the silence stretched awkwardly between us; and finally, in an effort to fill it, Paige rolled her eyes and said: "God, did you hear me at the end of Act Two? I wanted to die, I got the line *so* wrong!"

"I didn't notice," Debra said.

"You didn't?"

"You'll do better next time, kitten," I said, and instantly regretted it. Paige looked downcast; disconsolate. Debra shot me a dirty look that said: She wants to be told how well she did *this* time. I knew it, of course, just as I knew the words that would make it all right for Paige...and still I couldn't say them.

Debra ruffled Paige's short blonde hair. "You were terrific, honey. How about we go out to celebrate? Carvel's? Dairy Queen?"

Paige shook her head, managed a wan smile. "Thanks, Mom, but a bunch of us are getting together, you know? A cast party? I'll be back by nine, okay?"

Debra nodded, kissed her on the cheek. "Have a good time, hon. We're proud of you."

Paige nodded. "See you later, Mom. Dad." She gave me only a perfunctory glance—all I deserved, really—and melted into the backstage crowd. Debra straightened, turned...and I nearly lost my breath at the cold, stark hatred in her gaze. I cleared my throat. "Deb...I'm—"

"Don't say a word," she hissed, turning away from me. "Whatever you have to say, I couldn't possibly want to hear it." She stalked away into the wings, toward the exit; I winced, followed her into the parking lot.

"Debbie, please, let me explain—"

She spun round, glared at me, and I saw that her mascara was smudged, her eyes wet with tears...not for herself, I knew, but for Paige. "How the hell can you explain it? How do you explain hurting a little girl who wanted only to be told how *proud* her father was of her?"

"I am proud of her!"

"Like hell," she snapped, as other parents unlocked their cars and strained to hear without seeming to. "You're not proud of her, damn it, you're jealous!"

I stiffened, suddenly aware of our audience; I took her by the arm, tried to steer her toward our car. "For Crissake, Deb, don't—"

"Let *go* of me!" She wrested free, the tears streaming down her face now, her voice ragged. "You're jealous and you're angry! At who, Rick? At her, because you think she'll grow up to do what you couldn't? Or me, because I'm the one who kept you here, in New Hampshire?"

She tore open the car door, jumped in, twisted the key, and didn't even wait for the car to warm up, just put it into reverse and rocketed backward, nearly bowling me over as I tried to follow. The Volvo sliced through the dirty slush left over from yesterday's snowfall; I watched as the car turned left onto Clinton Avenue and was gone. I no longer cared who was watching; I snapped up a chunk of ice, hurled it onto the frozen macadam of the parking lot, and swore. I stood there, breathing hard, each breath turning to frost in the chill moonlight, and cursed myself for a fool. I couldn't even work up any indignation at Debra: she was right, everything she said was right, and after my treatment of Paige, I deserved it, the whole embarrassing scene.

I didn't notice Bill Cohen until he was right behind me. The father of one of Paige's schoolmates—and one of my own classmates years before—he tapped me lightly on the shoulder. "Rick? You, uh, need a lift?"

I turned, smiled weakly, shook my head. "No. No, thanks, Bill," I said. "It's not far. I'll walk."

"You sure?"

"Yeah, positive. Thanks."

He nodded, moved off; suddenly anxious to get away from here, I buried my hands in the pockets of my topcoat and hurried out of the lot. I made my way down the long, winding hill to Clinton Avenue, my path illuminated by the strobe of headlights passing by. I turned east on

Clinton; Montcalm Street was six blocks ahead, and that would intersect, in a mile or so, with my street, Schuyler. That was one advantage, I supposed, to living in a small town: you were never very far from home.

Walking the streets, it all came back to me, all the feelings I'd had thirteen years ago: the stifling insularity of this tiny place; the sense of claustrophobia I'd felt even standing out in the open; the people so damn provincial, the horizons no farther than the end of your block. Small lives bounded by small dreams. I'd wanted to leave, wanted more than Appleton, New Hampshire, had to offer; why hadn't I? Why in God's name hadn't I?

But I knew why, and the knowledge was no balm. I turned north onto Montcalm, passing the quaint Colonial-style houses, all so much alike and anonymous. I knew that when I got home, it would be to a house much like any one of these; and when I died, the house would be sold to a man or woman much like myself, and all that would mark my time on this earth would be a name on a deed in the county clerk's office, a notice of ownership transferred, a brief record of stewardship—stewardship of a wasted life, and lost opportunity.

My birthday party, a week later, was a stiff, dismal affair; Deb and I were still on the outs and the miasma of my thirty-fifth birthday didn't do much to improve my mood or our relationship. We took to a cool, remote sort of interaction, nothing overtly hostile, just two strangers sharing a house and family; divorce was probably on both our minds, but it was still frightening to consider, a word we were not quite ready to voice. Sometime during the week it occurred to me that it had been over three months since we had last had sex: and I found that I didn't really care.

Our living room was filled with friends and neighbors and the children of same; Bill and Louise, Sarah and Dennis, Jack and Denise, all clustered around me as Debra stood stiffly to one side and Paige carried the birthday cake into the room as they sang:

"Happy birthday to you . . . happy birthday to you—"

Paige put the cake down on the coffee table in front of me, and even she was singing; but instead of her voice, or the others, as they reached the penultimate line, I heard others—voices I didn't recognize, voices belonging to no one in this room—singing:

"Happy birthday, dear Richard—"

I spun around. No one called me Richard; no one ever called me that. The song finished, my friends applauded, and I tried to push it out of my mind. Paige cut the cake, handed me the first slice, but all I could think about were those voices, that name, and—dimly recalled—that day in the office, the hallucination, that Scottish girl and her lilting voice. I tried to concentrate on the here-and-now, on reality; someone handed me a fork, and I took a bite of the thick, dark chocolate cake.

It tasted like angel food.

CHAPTER THREE

RICHARD

My flight from New York to Boston brought me into the city close to five p.m., just as the lights at Government Center were coming on, washing the snow-covered plaza in a chill blue light. A few blocks down, the Sears' Block, too, was lit, but from within, a warmer, more inviting amber light—more light, more warmth, than I was likely to find in my mother's empty house. I blinked back tears at the thought, told myself I had a duty to perform and there would be time enough for mourning later; time enough to cry when I would awake on some distant Saturday and the day would pass without the weekly call from Elsie, wanting to know what the reviews were like on my latest play, or telling me she'd found a mention of me in some obscure soap-opera digest, and that she was sending along the clipping for my scrapbook.

I rented a car at Logan Airport, taking the usual baffling assortment of tunnels and turnoffs to the Expressway, fighting commuter traffic all the way to Route 3, north. Appleton, New Hampshire, lay midway between Nashua and Manchester, a few miles east of Route 3; not much more than a thirty-minute drive from Boston. As I drove

I glanced occasionally out the side window, at winter's hand lying heavy on the land: at fields of granite poking, like patches in well-worn broadloom, through half-melted carpets of snow; at shards of ice floating swiftly down the gray, frigid Merrimack; at rolling hills, cowled in white, studded with bare maples. There was a comforting bleakness about the landscape, the harsh reality of New England winters that formed the gray, pragmatic bedrock of New England souls. I was back just ten minutes and already it had all come back to me, all the things I had run away from thirteen years ago—the climate and geography that gave so many of these small New England towns a kind of fortress mentality, of us and them, "them" being anyone not actually born in a particular town. And yet, as the converted textile mills and factories and fish hatcheries rolled past in the dimming light, I felt calmer; comforted. I spotted the Sunoco station at the edge of town and felt a rush of warmth: I was entering familiar territory, and in each building, each business, from the filling station to the Kresge's five-and-dime, from the King George Diner to the Rickels hardware store, I found some solace and reassurance. This was home to me, once; and even if it could never be home again, it could never be truly foreign, either.

I parked in front of my mother's house on Lochmere Street, walked up the short pathway to the house, ran my fingers along the top of the living room windowsill and found the extra key my mother always left there. I let myself into the darkened house, flipping on lights as I walked through the foyer, into the living room. Everything looked normal and undisturbed: the bright orange recliner sitting in front of the console television; the marble coffee table;

the brown and white couch with the small hole in the middle cushion, where my father had absently laid his cigar one day years before. I sat down in the recliner, leaned my head back, and sighed: the breath took in a scent, faint but lingering, of smoke, permeating the upholstery—an acrid reminder of something I would rather have forgotten.

A year after my father died, my mother suffered her first heart attack—brought on, I'm convinced, in large part by her loneliness, her helplessness in the face of life without him. It was something I would never have expected, given their tense, sometimes rocky relationship over the preceding ten years; she'd talked about leaving him more than once, but never did—her life, and his, dictated more by inertia than desire. Or so I'd thought. When he died, I suppose, she came to realize how much she had loved him, after all; came to realize, too, perhaps, the wasted years spent on bickering or apathy; and all at once the gregarious, outgoing woman I'd grown up with became withdrawn and afraid and lonely. I convinced her to move closer to me, so I could take care of her if need be, and visit her more often than the occasional weekend trip; I scrounged up the down payment for a unit at a retirement community on Long Island and she closed up the house in Appleton, intending to sell it later.

But it wasn't meant to be. The van carrying my mother's furniture stopped in for repairs before starting for Long Island . . . some idiot mechanic allowed the bottom of the van to get too hot . . . and the truck burst into flames, consuming all my mother's earthly goods.

I'll never forget the phone call telling me what had happened; how I broke the news to her as gently as I could, how her shoulders hunched and her hands went to her face and she began weeping, quietly. With the phone in one hand, I put my free arm around her, trying to comfort her as I snapped at the bureaucrat on the other end of the line.

Ten days later we discovered that it was the other houseload of furniture on the van that was wiped out, not my mother's; that her possessions had, in fact, suffered only smoke damage. I rented her a houseful of furniture in Long Island until her own things were cleaned and restored by the movers, but by then it had all been too much for her: Dad's death, the heart attack, the fear of everything dear and familiar to her being destroyed. Despite my pleadings for her to stay, she moved back to New Hampshire, desperately missing her friends, her house, the comforting monotony of Appleton.

I sat in the recliner now, smelling the faint reek of smoke, and cursed myself for not fighting harder to keep her in New York; for not being able to visit her more when she was there; for a thousand and one things that had gone wrong that I could never have foreseen, but *should* have, somehow. I pushed myself out of the chair, finally, and wandered into the kitchen; in the sink a coffee cup lay on its side atop a saucer, and a half-open box of raisin bran stood on the kitchen counter. In her bedroom the bed was unmade, and amid the folds of disarrayed blankets were the small plastic containers which once held three nitroglycerin tablets. I skirted the bed, trying not to look at the containers, or at the sheets which in their folds and wrinkles held impressions, of a sort, of her last night on earth; the phone was at a slight angle on the nightstand, the receiver placed hurriedly in the cradle, the cord backward; she was everywhere in the room, her final moments etched indelibly for any who had eyes to see, but nowhere as much as in the slip of paper—neatly written script on a white sheet maybe five by seven inches—sitting on the dresser. I picked it up, my heart suddenly pounding, and read:

My dearest Richard,

   If I should die please don't let them do an autopsy on me.
   Buy me a metal coffin like the one I got for Dad.
   Call Memorial Arts and have them put my name on the plaque in the cemetery. If I'm not home when I die, please send me back home to be with Dad.

Love, Mom.

And beneath the signature, an afterthought:

Lay me out in the blue dress I bought for Diane's wedding.

Diane was my twenty-year-old cousin; her wedding was two weeks away. If the bulk of the note had been written sometime after her first heart attack, but before she moved back to Appleton, the last line must have been fairly recent; but whether it was written a week before, a day, or even that same night, I could never know for certain. I thought of her in this room, waiting for the paramedics, hurrying to an upper shelf or a shoebox or the bottom of her purse, taking the note from where she kept it—scribbling that last request, then placing it where she knew I'd find it—reaching out to me, across time, across pain, across all the years and distance between us—and I began to cry. Even at a time like that, even when she was dying, she was thinking ahead, trying to make it easier for me; and I wasn't there for her. She died alone, with no familiar face around, no one to hold her hand; least of all her son, so many miles away. I sat on the edge of her bed and cried for all the times I'd never been there, cried for all the holidays I'd missed, cried for all the things I did and the things I didn't do, all the lost chances and missed opportunities.

On stage, on screen, you hit your marks, you pick up your cues; in life, everything is always a little too late.

I stayed in her house while in Appleton, but avoided that bedroom thereafter; when my aunt came over the next day, I asked her to tidy it up, feeling foolish but unable to do it myself. The next few days I was on autopilot, trying to lose myself in the logistics of it all: picking out a coffin, floral arrangements, selecting a service, notifying her friends. I was adamant about one thing: there would be no "viewing period" the day before the funeral. When my Dad died, we had gone through the agonizing ritual of a wake, four hours in the afternoon, four hours at night, waiting for long stretches in an empty chamber until people drifted in two or three at a time, instead of all at once. They were probably the most pointlessly enervating hours of my life. No; if people were to pay their respects, they could do so before the service.

Visiting Appleton was always an odd experience, and this trip was no exception. While growing up it had been a hellhole for me, a stifling, provincial little town: my acting ambitions were largely alien to most of my classmates or their parents, who thought I was either a freak, or a fag, or both; those of us in the school drama club were a tight-knit group, united against the ridicule of our peers.

But now I came back, and everyone, but everyone, had seen me at one time or another on television; Mrs. Cracken at the Appleton Sweet Shoppe never failed to recount every detail of my short run on *Guiding Light,* and even bullies who used to jostle me in the playground now wanted to know—I mean *really* wanted to know—the sexual proclivities of every actress I'd ever starred with, and whether or not I'd scored with them. It made for a pretty schizoid experience, but I must admit, I did derive a certain perverse satisfaction from it. Sure enough, I had occasion to stop at the Sweet Shoppe to pick up some cough drops— I'd forgotten how bitterly cold New Hampshire winters could be—and Mrs. Cracken was behind the counter, her orange-tinted hair bundled up in a net, a wide smile on her crinkled face.

"Richard!" she said, her smile growing even wider. Then, remembering, her smile faded, and as I put two quarters down on the counter, she reached out and gently touched the back of my hand. "I was so sorry to hear about your mother," she said. "She was so young."

I nodded. "Sixty-seven. She should've had more time."

"Isn't that just so. And you look at some of these, pardon my French, some of these rat-bastards that just go on and on, and you have to wonder. You just have to wonder." I nodded, started to say something, but she went on: "Like that horrible Chester Winthrop, the one on your story, after all that man has done to his wife, no one would miss him for a *moment—*"

I cleared my throat. "Jack Lehrman."

"Pardon?"

"The actor who plays Chester. His name is Jack Lehrman. He's really quite a nice man."

"Oh yes, I'm sure he is. But it's a perfect example, the man cheats and abuses his wife, and *she* dies and he goes on and *on*—it's just not fair, don't you think?"

I smiled, amazed at her ability to accommodate two totally contradictory concepts; but before I could reply, I heard a man's voice behind me, saying, "If life were fair, Miz Cracken, what would Ralph Nader do for a living?"

I turned around, recognizing the voice instantly; but I'd forgotten one important thing, and had to lower my gaze quickly. There behind me—sitting in his wheelchair and sporting a wide grin—was Dave Finney. "Yo," he said, looking me over with mock-uncertainty, "I know you, don't I? Third guy on the left in the Burger King spot? Whopper with fries? I cried when you ordered it. Really cried. Shit, can I have your autograph?"

I grinned back at him. "Gimme a break, Finney, okay?" I hesitated a moment, then overcame my uncertainty, squatted down, and gave him a hug. He laughed, patted me on the back with his big hands made calloused from years of tooling around in his chair. "Cochrane, you deviant, what are you doing back in the boonies?"

I stood again, my tone quickly sobering. "You didn't hear?" Off his blank expression: "My mother died. Tuesday night."

The playfulness immediately left his face. "Oh Jesus, man, I didn't know. I'm sorry." A brief pause, then he nodded to the Dunkin' Donuts shop across the street. "Can I buy you some coffee?"

We crossed the street, and I marveled at Finney's inge-
nuity in getting up over the curb: he bumped up against
it, reached out with his heavily muscled right arm, grabbed
a lamppost, and pulled himself and his chair over the
curb and onto the sidewalk. Somehow not that markedly
different from the Finney I used to know, the one who
was always vaulting fences or riding horses or running
bare-assed down a hillside for a joke.

And yet very different. We sat there nursing coffee and
donuts and I wondered, could this really be the same guy
I grew up with? His hair was still a dirty blond, still somewhat shaggy and unkempt, and there was that old familiar
twinkle of mischief in his sky-blue eyes; but the face
surrounding those eyes was lined, written over with pain
and hardship, a signature of disappointment as well as
strength. His voice seemed softer—I always remembered
him entering a room on a shout and a yelp—and the flip,
go-to-hell attitude he'd had as a kid was muted, if not
totally gone, erased by time and sadness.

And somewhere, deep down, I knew it was my fault.

"How are Roslyn and the kids?" I asked, forcing the
whisper of guilt to a far, hollow corner of my mind.

Finney grinned. "They're great. Donnie's heavily into
track—doesn't just rush around the house, he sprints. God,
he's got legs that reach all the way to Vermont. Ruth turns
nine next month; she's a nice kid but painfully shy, can
hardly look you in the eye when she talks to you. But she'll
grow out of it."

"You still working at DeLuca & Sons?"

"Not for years. I'm teaching at the high school now."

I was startled, and must have looked it. Finney was

legendary for the number of classes he'd cut, and gotten away with; hard to imagine him anywhere near the old place, even now.

He laughed. "I know. More than the mind can comfortably imagine."

"What are you teaching?"

"Health sciences." He noted my incredulous look and gave me a lopsided smile. "Well, you don't have to look *that* surprised. I had to do something while I was recovering from the accident—must've read every book on biology and medicine that my dad could truck over from the library . . . thinking that, you know, maybe all those doctors had *overlooked* something." He laughed, and the laugh approached the boisterousness of the old Finney, but laced with a new edge of self-deprecation. "Well, needless to say, I didn't make any new advances in medicine, but it got me thinking. About something beyond getting soused, or getting laid—the two big Gettings of youth, as you may recall."

I smiled, remembering. "You remember that night you got so shit-faced that Roslyn's father turned the garden hose on you when you tried to come in after a date?"

Finney winced, good-naturedly. "Believe it or not, I don't dwell a whole hell of a lot on all that. No point to it, you know?"

Finney had been a wild sort, in those days; the kind of guy who loved a party, and if there wasn't one in progress when he arrived, made one on the spot. He spoke too loud and drank too much, but there was an endearingly loopy quality to him that bonded the two of us from the first day we met, and it had become my particular role in life to be his safety clip—to drag him off when he started to pick a fight with the wrong people, or drive him home when he'd had too much to drink.

Then I left town, and no one, apparently, filled my role; and one chilly, icy night, feeling rowdy and raunchy and higher than a kite on Cuervo Gold, Finney left a bar in Nashua, but this time there was no one to drive him home. He lost control of the car somewhere on Route 3, hit a telephone pole... and woke up a paraplegic. It was the one thing we never spoke of; the one guilt I could never voice, to him or anyone else.

He leaned forward, reading my suddenly somber expression as bereavement, which in a way I suppose it was. "Richard? When are the services?"

"Tomorrow. Ten a.m."

"I'll be there. How long will you be in town?"

I shrugged. "She died intestate, so I have to find a lawyer to handle the probate... have to break up the house, distribute her belongings to relatives, friends... Maybe another week."

He nodded and put a hand comfortingly on mine. "When you're feeling up to it... maybe next week... I'd like to have you over to the house. You, me, the family, maybe a few of our friends from high school." He smiled, shrugged. "Could be the last time you'll get back here. And anyway, at a time like this, you should have friends around you."

My throat caught; I could feel tears welling up in my eyes, and my voice involuntarily trembled. "I let her down, Finney," I heard myself say, weakly. "I wasn't there when she needed me, really needed me." I looked away, ashamed, but the hand on mine remained steady and strong.

"She needs you now," Finney said gently. "And you won't let her down."

I hope I didn't. I gave her the kind of service I think she would have wanted; the kind she arranged for Dad two years before. Even though she hadn't been to church in twenty years, she found the rituals of religion comforting. I put aside my own agnosticism and arranged for an Episcopalian minister who quoted at great length from Psalms and spoke of God more often than I cared for, but who did, very graciously, interpolate his Biblical quotations with some small tributes to my mother, to the way she held the family together, the way she picked up the pieces after disasters and tragedies—from the deaths of her mother, sister, and husband, to the flood that wiped out all of our possessions when I was fourteen. The funeral procession made the short drive to the Cemetery on the Plains. We lowered her into the ground beside Dad, Grandma, Aunt Eleanor and Uncle Nick, and I said goodbye to my mother, and wished I had told her how much I loved her. I told her now and hoped that she could hear.

The next several days were only slightly less arduous. I found a lawyer to handle the probate and a motel to stay in while my aunt and uncle helped me break up the house. I saw no harm in giving most of her furniture to Ed and Charlotte's kids, most of whom were newly married and just getting started on life. That was a strange experience, too: seeing David and Gail and Lori, all of them just toddlers when I used to visit as a kid, most of them now married and many with children of their own. I felt very old and very out of it.

As I did, in some ways, at Finney's party. I arrived about seven-thirty, the first guest, and Finney poured me a beer (he was drinking club soda) and showed me his house. If I was surprised by his teaching position, I was blown away by his library: history seemed to be a favorite subject, encompassing everything from Braudel to Samuel Eliot Morison, from Van Doren's *Benjamin Franklin* to Harry Truman's *Letters*. My eye went immediately to the drama shelf, crowded with well-thumbed editions of Thornton Wilder, Tennessee Williams, and Lanford Wilson. I squatted down, my attention caught by one slim volume sticking out half an inch farther than the rest: a rare first edition of Robert Anderson's *Silent Night, Lonely Night*. I slid it out, turned it over admiringly in my hand, then looked up over my shoulder at a grinning Finney. "You son of a bitch," I said, smiling, "you've got a better library than I do. You realize, of course, I'm going to have to kill you now, then smuggle these things out of here before the police arrive?"

"You like Anderson, don't you?" Finney said, knowing full well that he was one of my favorite authors, and this my favorite of his plays. He nodded toward the edition I held in my hand. "Read the inscription."

I sighed as I opened it, expecting to find an autographed flyleaf—maybe I *would* have to kill him—and found instead:

To Richard: Who watched over me, as friends do, and never let me stray too far from home. With thanks and affection—Finney.

I actually lost my breath for a moment, my mind a

tangle of conflicting emotions. I was touched and over-
whelmed by the gesture as well as the inscription, but
part of me was raging at myself, *It isn't true, not when he
needed you most—you failed him, like you failed* her. I fought
to keep my composure. "Finney ... this is a lovely gesture,
but this is a first edition, I couldn't—"

Finney laughed. "It's yours. I found it in a little used-
book shop in Concord; had your name on it from the
moment I saw it."

I still felt I didn't deserve it, but could hardly refuse. I
nodded, smiled, and put a hand on his arm. "It's terrific.
Thanks."

A rising tide of voices was coming from the living room.
Finney grabbed the wheels of his chair, spun it around in
a neat forty-five-degree arc, and made for the foyer. "Sounds
like we got quite a bash brewing out there. We never
missed a good party, did we, Cochrane?"

No. We never did. And it turned out to be a wonderful
party. Bill and Louise Cohen were there, and Jack and
Denise Boulton, and Sarah and Dennis McCardle; one or
two brought their kids, and all were as glad to see me as
I was them. I'd grown up with these people, from ele-
mentary school to college, something few if any big-city
kids could say of their contemporaries; they all seemed
happy and comfortable and settled. There was a stack of
oldies in the CD player, music playing unobtrusively in
the background; I paid little attention to it, reminiscing
with my former classmates, playing with their children,
marveling at the fact that we all sprang from the same
place, grew up in the same way, were exposed to the same
influences ... yet they took one turn and I took another,
and even now I couldn't say why, or how. I felt ... what *did*

I feel? Loss? No; how can you lose something you never had?

I was vaguely aware of the doorbell ringing, but too wrapped up in playing with Bill and Louise's ten-year-old son (who seemed to know every guest shot I'd ever done on episodic TV) to note who was joining the party... until Finney tapped me on the shoulder. "Richard. Look who's here."

I turned. I like to think I'm a good enough actor that I did not betray anything but pleased surprise. I knew her as Debra Aversano; I think Finney had told me she'd married a guy named Jacobs, in all likelihood the tall, bespectacled man helping her with her coat. As she shrugged it off, she turned and looked at me, the smile on her face revealing the same awkwardness and trepidation I was feeling.

"Rick," she said; then: "I'm sorry—is it Richard now?"

I nodded, got to my feet. After an awkward moment, the two of us laughed nervously and hugged, but it was a cautious, careful kind of hug, the sort I gave to fellow guests on talk shows. I stepped back and smiled. "How've you been, Deb?"

"Getting older, and more indebted, each year... at nineteen and a half percent interest." She laughed, and her smile seemed to mellow. She motioned to the man who was handing their coats to Roslyn. "Hon? This is Richard Cochrane. Richard, my husband, Mark."

Mark and I shook hands and exchanged pleasantries, and I wondered idly how much he knew about Debbie and me. Then I noticed, coming up behind Debra, a young boy—eleven, twelve years old?—and my heart began to race.

"Richard, this is our son, Eric."

I smiled, nodded, kept my fears to myself. "Glad to meet you, Eric." I looked quickly away from him, back to Debra. "What are you doing these days, Deb?"

"Me? I'm an art appraiser. In Concord." We talked a little about her job, about the lithography studio Mark owned, the limited editions he printed, and about Debra's assistance in the business; all very friendly and casual and superficial, as though Debra and my parting had not been as acrimonious as it had. All the while I kept thinking about the boy, about Eric, about who he was and might be, about who I was and could be. Then another old friend joined the party and I got sidetracked for a while, which was just as well. Finney and I were coerced into singing our famous, patented medley of the Coasters' greatest hits, and it wasn't until two hours later that I found myself with Debra again—this time the two of us, alone, in the kitchen. I was taking a Heineken from the fridge when she entered. I offered her one, and as she stood there drinking it she seemed a little more relaxed, leaning against the kitchen counter as the sounds of the party carried back through the louvred doors.

"Bright kid you've got there," I said, trying to ease gently into a subject probably best left untouched. "Asked me what kind of residual structure applies in daytime TV. If I were that savvy when I was his age, I'd probably have a hell of a lot more money in the bank right now."

Debra laughed, and the laugh was the same one that I remembered from years before; her eyes behind her designer glasses were bright and mischievous. "He's going to grow up to be either Andrew Carnegie or Charles Keating. It's a tough call."

I laughed, and in the silence that followed I looked out

in the direction of the party, then back to Debra, and could feel the pause growing tenser. "Deb," I said slowly, "is he—I mean, was he—"

Debra's eyes clouded over a bit; slowly she shook her head. "No. Eric was born about a year after Mark and I got married. Two years after you and I broke up."

And all at once, the unaccustomed feeling that had been growing within me the last two hours was abruptly, painfully quashed. "Oh," I said lamely. And then it struck me. I looked up, quickly. "But then what happened to—?"

I didn't finish; didn't need to. Debra sighed, looked at me sadly; as though knowing, somehow, the hope that had been rising in me, and knowing that she must now dash the rest of it. "I—had an abortion."

I started. "You never let on you were even considering that."

Debra shrugged. "I was afraid you'd think I was using it as a...a club. You know: 'Marry me or else.' I didn't want you to say yes out of guilt for what I might do."

There was a long, tense silence as I looked away, trying to sort out my feelings; then, quietly, I said, "It was close, Deb. It was very close. I could've gone either way."

"I know," she said.

I turned, faced her again. "I would've paid child support—you know that—I offered—"

But Debra just shook her head sadly, now as then. "I didn't want to be a single mother. Didn't want my child to grow up without a real father. So I made the decision and it was the right decision for me, at that time, at that moment; I've never regretted it. You shouldn't, either."

I looked down, self-consciously, before answering.

"I guess part of me already knew," I said softly. "I mean,

no matter how angry you were at me, I couldn't imagine you'd keep him ... or her ... from me for thirteen years. On some level, I knew you'd done something like that, but when Eric walked into the room—" I stopped, looked up, and saw Debra looking at me, trying not to show the pity that was clearly in her eyes. I felt ashamed; embarrassed. Suddenly all I'd done with my life, all the things I'd accomplished since that moment thirteen years before— all of it paled when held up against this woman standing beside me, and the phantom son I had had, briefly, but only in my mind.

I tried to meet her gaze evenly. "Deb? Why did you come tonight? You never answered my phone calls, my letters ... were you that angry with me?"

Debra sighed. "For a while. Not as long as you'd think. But after the first year or two, I couldn't bring myself to make contact again after so long and I just ... let it slide, I guess. I'm sorry." She took a swallow of her beer. "I read the death notice in the *Union-Leader*, called Finney, and he told me about the party. Mark actually convinced me to come. He said it wasn't fair to me, and it wasn't fair to you, not to."

I smiled. "He seems like a good guy. You made the better choice."

"I made a different choice," she said. "Just like you did." She tapped me lightly on the arm with the back of her hand, and nodded toward the living room. "Party sounds like it's breaking up. We'd better go."

I said my goodbyes to all of them, to Debra and Mark and Eric last of all, and then stayed behind for a nightcap with Finney and Roslyn; it was after eleven when I left, declining an offer from Ros to drive me to the Colony Inn. I felt like walking; I felt like seeing this town again, perhaps for the last time. I bundled up in my overcoat and headed up Montcalm Street toward the center of town.

It was bitterly cold and perfectly clear: there was no wind, and the needles on the spruce trees lining the street seemed frozen in time, not moving so much as a centimeter. The houses on either side of me were by and large dark, but a few were cozily lit from within, diffuse light spilling out from behind closed drapes and shut blinds.

I turned right onto Clinton, past Kellerman's Tobacco Shop, J&L Hardware, and the Kresge's five-and-dime. A light rain was beginning to fall, although the sky, oddly, was cloudless. I turned up the collar on my coat and walked on. Growing up, I had found this town confining, constraining; I chafed and raged and couldn't wait to escape from it. Now, strangely, all that I hated so as a child and young adult, all of it seemed merely quaint, and not a little charming. I turned left on Revere Street, away from the commercial district: more pleasant, comfortable homes, more sheltering trees. The rain was getting heavier now; it fell not at an angle but in perfectly vertical sheets, and the sound it made on hitting the pavement seemed . . . odd. Distorted, somehow, as though it were not quite hitting the concrete or macadam, a glassy, ringing sound. Part of me absently noted the peculiarity; the larger part of me was running over and over the last week in my mind, like a moth circling a flame. I thought of my mother, of Finney, of all the people I had left behind, all the choices I now so bitterly regretted. I thought of what I would do when I returned to New York, the same old routine—

auditions, readings, rehearsals—and realized that I dreaded going back to the ritual motions of what suddenly seemed an aimless, pointless existence.

As I turned onto Schuyler Street the rain became a torrent, and for a moment—just a moment—I felt disoriented . . . as I had weeks before at my makeup table, on stage, and at my birthday party. For an instant the rain was so thick that I couldn't see two inches in front of me, and when I finally could make out where I was, I had the odd, irrational suspicion that I was standing opposite from where I had faced before; that the houses on my left were now, somehow, on my right. My head cleared and I started hurrying down Schuyler; soon enough it would intersect with Hancock Street and my motel was only a block away from that. I picked up my pace, giving only a glance to the houses on either side of me.

But a glance was all I needed. There was only one house on the block still lit: a Colonial home with a manicured lawn, a Volvo in the driveway, and a bicycle sitting under the shelter of the porch. The dining room window was bright, the drapes open; inside, two figures, a man and a woman, were pacing animatedly back and forth, yelling at one another. I slowed, I'm not sure why, as the sounds of the argument carried outside—the words muffled by the teeming rain, but the angry tones quite unmistakable. The woman was turned away from me, the man half obscured by the drape; now she turned, and I got a good look at her face.

It was Debra.

There was no question: the same face, the same slim, almost boyish figure. I stopped, fascinated and confused: hadn't Debra said she and Mark lived in Concord, not

Appleton? And the man in the window, his voice didn't sound anything like Mark's, his build was all wrong.

I stood there, mesmerized, as the couple continued their argument, as the woman—as Debra—continued to shout. The man's hands clenched and unclenched, he made a couple of sharp, jabbing motions with them... then, disgusted, he turned suddenly, strode to the window, and stared outside, his face a tense mask of frustration and anger.

The man in the window... was me.

CHAPTER FOUR

RICK, RICHARD

It started raining as we sat down to dinner, a sudden cloudburst that grew louder and more insistent by the minute, muffling the tinny noise of the living room TV that Paige had neglected to switch off. The two sounds vied with one another for dominance: the incessant tattoo of raindrops on the roof, interrupted now and then by scratchy bursts of canned laughter. It grated on me, I did my best to ignore it, but midway through the meal my composure cracked and a volley of moronic game-show music sent me stalking angrily into the living room, then back again. "Jesus Christ," I snapped at Paige as I sat back down at the table. "It's called an *off* switch. You push it when you're finished watching something. Why the hell is that so hard to remember?"—my anger totally out of proportion, as usual, to the magnitude of her crime. She said nothing, merely exchanged suffering glances with her mother, which neither thought I saw. Paige quickly finished eating, then hurried upstairs to her room. And the uneasy truce between Debra and me that had prevailed throughout dinner erupted into open warfare.

Hunt Bailey, it turned out, had called during the day;

had told Debra of his concern for me and his recommen-
dation that I take a leave of absence to seek—goddamn it,
I could practically hear him say it—"the proper medical
assistance." Now Debra was all over me: Why hadn't I told
her about the other day, about my screwup with the
O'Connell disbursement? "Maybe I didn't want to," I said,
needlessly sarcastic. "What, I have to share all of my failures with you as they happen?"

She sighed. "Why is it always winning or failing to you?
You're ill, Rick, that's all—you're overtired, and over-
stressed, and you need help. Hunt just wants to see that
you get it."

Reasonable enough; but I was too far gone to let reason
stand in my way. I stood, began pacing. "Look," and even as
I said it I knew it was stupid, knew I should let the thought
die unvoiced, "I don't much appreciate my wife and my
boss trading phone calls, conspiring behind my—"

"*Conspiring?*" Debra was justifiably wide-eyed. "Will you
listen to yourself? We're hip-deep in paranoia here. What
is this, the Nixon White House?"

"Shut up!" I snapped, my patience gone, my hands ball-
ing into fists at my side. "I am fucking *tired* of your smart
mouth, your smartass cracks—"

I heard the fall of footsteps on the staircase, fast, light
steps on thick carpet—

"And *I'm* tired," Debra was shouting back, "of your damn
self-pity—the frustrated artist who threw it all away, gave
it all up, to marry the girl he got in—"

"I've never said that!" I yelled. "You have *never* heard me
say that to—"

"You don't have to! It's in your voice, it's in your face,
every time we go to a play or a movie—that faraway look

you get, that damned sullen silence you sink into for hours afterward! You don't have to say anything, you're still a good enough actor to—how'd they put it, back in Stagecraft 2A? 'Do it with a look'?" By now she too was standing, her face tight, her body rigid. "You *reek* of selfless martyrdom, Rick, you know that?"

"Shut up!" I was pacing in smaller and smaller circles, my fists swinging at my sides. I wanted to hit her, God, how I wanted to hit her; I could see it so clearly in my mind, the impact, a bubble of blood, the lip splitting open like the skin of a bruised fruit—

"Stop it! Can't both of you just *stop* it!" Paige stood in the doorway, breathing hard, having just run down the stairs; her face was flushed, her cheeks streaked with tears. "I wish I didn't live here! I wish I could just *leave!*"

"Go back to your room!" I shouted.

"Go to hell!" she shouted back.

Enraged, I barely knew what I was doing. I moved so fast it took both Paige and Debra by surprise: a long, quick stride with my arm upraised, one hand grabbing Paige by the wrist as the other slapped her, hard, on the cheek. She jerked her head away from me, softening the blow, but it was only when she turned back that I realized what I'd done; only when I saw my mottled fingerprints on her face, like some violent stigmata, that I realized I had finally crossed the line and gone too far. Genuinely horrified, I let go of her wrist and dropped my hand, impotently, to my side. Paige stood there, as astonished as I; the last time I'd hit her was when she was four, she'd tried crawling out the third-story window and I swatted her so hard she wouldn't go near a window for weeks after. I thought all at once of the four-year-old she had been, of Debra, of myself back then—not yet so angry, nor so bitter—and I barely recognized us, barely remembered it as something out of my own life.

"Oh, God," I whispered. What could I say? What was there to say? "Oh, Christ, honey, I'm sorry... I'm so *sorry*..."

Quickly, wordlessly, she turned and rushed upstairs again. I didn't think there could be anything worse than the betrayal and contempt on her face; but when I turned I saw in Debra's eyes not anger, not contempt, not merely that, but raw, undisguised hatred.

"Deb," I stammered, "I—I didn't—"

Debra looked at me with cold fury.

"Fuck you," she said. She turned and slammed out of the dining room, the louvred doors banging against the wall like gunshots. In helpless anger at myself I lashed out and pounded the flat of my hand against the wall. I don't know which felt worse, the stinging pain in my hand or the realization that there was still, obviously, a great deal more violence inside me, waiting to be tapped. Forcing myself to be calm, I walked slowly over to the dining room window; I stared out at the sheets of rain bouncing off the roofs and hoods of parked cars, sheathing each in a kind of corona. I thought of my wife and daughter—of what must have been going through their minds just then—and knew I had traveled further from reason, and from their affections, then I ever had; that it would take more than an apology to Debra, or a hug to Paige, to patch things up again.

They hated me, truly hated me—almost as much as I hated myself. Tears blurring my vision, I stood listening to the drum of rain on the porch overhang—part of me noting something odd about its rhythm, some eerie percussion unlike any rain I'd ever heard—and only after a minute did I become conscious of the man standing outside beneath the willow tree.

At first I thought he was just my own reflection thrown back at me in the dark glass, but then he moved, and I flinched in response. It came to me now that he'd been there, in the driving rain, for quite a while—that I remembered seeing him at least five minutes before, out of the corner of my eye, at the height of my argument with Debra. My first paranoid thought was that he was a burglar casing the house, but there was something familiar in the way the man stood, the way he held his head, shifted his weight. I switched off the dining room light, losing its bright reflected glare, and for the first time got a clear glimpse of him. I looked more closely...

And saw myself.

I jumped back, reflexively. What the hell? Maybe it *was* a reflection, after all—but no. It hadn't moved when I did, it—Christ, why was I calling him "it" all of a sudden?—*he* just stood there, looking at me through the curtain of rain that separated us... and it was only then I noticed that he was looking at me with the same stunned astonishment with which I must have been staring at him. Our eyes locked for several moments...then, screwing up my nerve, I hurried to the hall closet and grabbed my coat, shrugging it on as I rushed outside.

He didn't move. He kept his ground, even as I pounded down the steps of the front porch. I hesitated a moment, I don't quite know why—and when I started toward him again, it was slower and more deliberate, despite the heavy rain soaking through my wool overcoat with every step.

He took a step forward—still beneath the shelter of the

willow tree—and then stopped as though waiting for me. I suddenly wished I could take back the last five minutes— pretend I'd never looked out that damn window—but I was committed to this now. And, oh God, the closer I got, the more clearly I could see. It was the same face that stared out at me from my bathroom mirror each morning, the same lanky build and light brown hair, the same eyes, the same mouth...yet there were odd differences too, the hairstyle a little trendier, posture a little straighter, shoulders squared back just a bit more...Jesus, what was going *on*?

I finally joined him beneath the umbrella of the willow branches—stopping just three feet from him, no closer— and after a moment found the nerve to speak up.

"Who"—my voice cracked; I tried again—"who the hell are *you* supposed to be?"

My double just stood there a moment, looking as nervous and frightened as I; and when he spoke his voice was my voice, the pitch, the timbre, everything the same; not my voice as I heard it normally, people never hear themselves as they really sound, but the voice I had learned to recognize as mine, the one I heard on tape recordings or home videos.

"My name is Richard Cochrane," he said.

The man from the house stared at me, dumbfounded, for several moments—several *beats,* I thought, feeling almost as though I were on stage, some surreal Pinter play, perhaps, and shortly the house lights would come up and we could all go home—and then my double, my twin, broke into a hollow, uncertain laugh.

"The hell you are," he said. He looked as frightened as

I felt. God, it was *me,* from the mole on his right hand to the small, almost invisible scar at the corner of his left eye, evidence of chicken pox when I was eight years old. He was studying me as I was him, spotting the same telltale signs; like me searching for something, anything, that might expose this as a hoax, a practical joke, a dream. But the differences between us, physically—the hairstyle, the way he seemed to stoop slightly as though constantly prepared to ward off some coming blow—were far outstripped by the similarities.

I reached into my jacket—he shrank back slightly, but said nothing—and pulled out my wallet.

"Here," I said. I pulled out my driver's license, held it out to him; he took it by a tattered corner, careful not to actually make physical contact with me, his eyes going immediately and unbelievingly to my photograph . . . but then, as he glanced at the address on the right, he looked suddenly reassured, and laughed a relieved laugh.

"Sorry, man," he said, handing it back to me, "but you blew it. I've never lived in New York in my life."

I'm not sure where the thought came from, but before I knew what I was saying, it had come out.

"Not in *this* life," I said softly.

He looked shaken by that, tried to cover it up with an unfamiliar bravado . . . unfamiliar, at least, to me. "Look," he demanded, "what kind of crap are you pulling here, anyway? Who the hell *are* you?"

"I told you." I took out my Visa, my MasterCard, my Amex, and held them out to him, fanned out like a poker hand. "You want to see my credit cards? Here. Look—"

But he wouldn't look, as though afraid at what they

might reveal. He shook his head. "Anybody can get a piece of plastic. Doesn't prove a thing."

I shuffled the cards back together, thinking furiously as I returned the cards and license to my wallet. "Okay," I said. "My mother's maiden name was Fischer. My Dad's mother's name was Minnie, he had two brothers, Freddy and Warren, Freddy died when he was—"

"County records," was all he said, and God damn him, he was right.

I wasn't used to proving who I was; if anything, I'd gotten used to people recognizing me on the street, even to having to deny who I was, at times, to preserve my privacy. Even the occasional traffic cop knew my name or remembered my face from a guest shot on TV (though that never did stop them from ticketing me). Part of me wanted to walk away, turn and head back in the direction from which I'd come; to hell with him, to hell with all of this, whatever it was. But I didn't. I couldn't. I put the wallet back in my pocket, trying desperately to think of something that could verify who I was, some shared experience that might convince him.

I looked up; smiled. "I was nine years old. We were on Uncle Nick's cabin cruiser—going for a cruise up the Merrimack—and I was horsing around, hanging by my knees from one of the bunks, and I fell, smack on my head. Everyone was so panicked and upset that Uncle Nick gunned the boat all the way home, twenty-five knots, and me so upset because *they* were upset that I started throwing up—which only panicked them more, 'cause that's what happens when you have a concussion." I looked at him triumphantly. "Right?"

He shook his head and shot me down again.

"Whole neighborhood knew about that. I must've told everybody I knew; hell of an adventure for a nine-year-old. You could've found out from Bill, from Finney, from anybody."

I considered and discarded a dozen other incidents from my—our?—past, but the trouble was, he could probably say the same about virtually anything I might bring up, any incident I might've talked about with friends or family. Christmas Eves at Uncle Nick and Aunt Eleanor's, me entrusted with the solemn task of choosing a present, reading the tag, handing it to the proper person... or the time Uncle Nick drove my mother and me over to New York State, some dot on the map called Port Jervis, a trip that took hours longer than envisioned, though Nick never complained, not once... and while Mom visited relatives he took me to a soda fountain where I scarfed down a chocolate soda with vanilla ice cream...

Looking back, I realized how many of my childhood memories revolved around Nick—a big man, nearly bald with thin but curly salt-and-pepper hair, always smoking a fat Cuban cigar. No memory meant more to me, though, than that time in fourth grade when I was singing solo at a Christmas concert and Uncle Nick cut short some business meeting to slip into the school without telling anyone... he just sat in back, listening proudly to his nephew's debut performance, then slipped out again, and I only found out about it later from my aunt. So strangely, the happiest memory I have of him... is one in which I never saw him at all.

All at once, then, I knew what I had to say; didn't want to say it, but knew I had to. My look-alike was staring at me, waiting for me to make the next move . . . so I took a breath, worked up my nerve, and said quietly, "When Uncle Nick died . . . when the doctors lost him, on the operating table, during heart surgery . . . I remember how Mom was in the kitchen hanging up the wall phone, the yellow wall phone, and she was crying, just as I was coming in the house. 'I have some bad news,' she said, turning to me. 'Your Uncle Nick just died.' And I felt sad, I really did; I felt sad for Aunt Eleanor, sad because he was so young, only forty-nine. I went into my room to be alone, but I"–I hesitated; ashamed, even after all these years, to say it–"I never cried for him. I loved him, I missed him, I still miss him to this day . . . but I never cried. And I never knew why."

I had never told another human being that, and judging by the look on his face, neither had my doppelgänger. Ashen, shaken, he looked at me and I could see that for the first time, unable to deny it, he knew the truth: that somehow, some way, despite all reason, we were *both* Richard Cochrane.

He put a hand to his left arm, rubbed it as though to warm himself; then shivered, as if from the cold. He looked up at the rain falling around us, the sound of it on the pavement still oddly dissonant, and when he finally spoke all the combativeness was gone from his voice.

"Getting cold out here," he said tonelessly.

"Can we go inside?" I asked, the warm glow from the living room window indescribably enticing–but knowing even as I said it the impossibility of the request.

He smiled faintly, shook his head. "Debra and Paige–my wife and daughter–they're both still up. We couldn't–"

"No, of course, you're right. Stupid thought." I glanced

at the window, hoping at least to catch another glimpse of—what did he call her? Paige?—but saw no one.

"There's always the garage," he suggested, somewhat apologetic. "I'm sorry ... I wish—"

"Garage'll do fine," I said.

He lifted the overhead door by hand, conscious, even as I was, of the noise it made as it rattled up on its tracks, then down again, the interior light snapping on automatically. There was room inside for only one car—a Nissan Sentra, looked to be only three, four years old—what little space remained was half devoted to storage and half to a workbench chock-a-block with power tools. I wandered over to the bench, running a hand wonderingly over the vise, the saber saw, the electric drill. I'd never gotten the hang of such things; never had to, really, living in town-homes and apartments all my adult life—I once had to call a fix-it man just to find out my shower head needed a new washer. Nice to know I had the potential, at least, to be handy around the house.

My double finished closing the garage door, then turned and stood awkwardly at the other end of the room, between us a clutter of children's toys—an old tricycle, a Muppet kite with a red and white tail, a Georgian-style dollhouse. "You live in ... New York?" he said, more fear than curiosity in his voice. But fear of what?

I nodded. "Thirteen years."

He navigated the jumble of mothballed toys but seemed to draw no closer to me. Then, in a strained, quiet voice: "You didn't marry her ... did you?"

I shook my head.

He took a deep breath, let it out. "Jesus," he said. "How the hell can this be happening?"

"I don't know," I said.

"I mean, this is crazy. Things like this just don't *happen*."

I shrugged. "Who's to say? Just because it's never happened to us before, doesn't mean it never happens."

He looked up sharply. "Stupid time to be making jokes," he snapped.

A little off balance—what was he so angry about?—I quickly regrouped: "I wasn't joking. I mean, they say every time we make a decision, the potential exists, at least, for a whole other—"

He'd been facing away from me; now he turned round quickly, a sudden light in his eyes, a certain dread in his voice.

"Oh, Christ," he said softly. "That man I saw in the tartan? He was in ... costume? For a play?"

Now his attitude was beginning to make sense to me. "A revival of *Brigadoon*."

"You're an actor?" He was almost pained to say it. Envy, plain and simple. I wasn't prepared for this. In some crazy way I think I was expecting him to be happy for me, as if I were a long-lost brother who'd made good. But of course we weren't brothers and I shouldn't have expected any such thing.

He kept an edgy distance; suddenly I felt like a slug he'd found sliming across the sidewalk and couldn't quite decide what to do with. His next words were priceless.

"You any good at it?" he said, and it was clear from his tone that he'd like nothing so much as for me to say, *Naw, I'm dogshit. We can't all be Olivier.* Or at the very least, *Well, you know, it's a tough way to make a living ... hard to really make a go of it,* shrug my shoulders diffidently, and let it go at that. But I bristled at his naked envy, his obvious hope that I had not done what he'd obviously never even attempted. Maybe it was cruel of me—or maybe it was my own defensiveness and insecurity, here in this house, this home I might've made, but never did—but I told him. Everything.

I told him about starring opposite Blythe Danner in *Hogan's Goat;* about playing Billy Einhorn in *House of Blue Leaves;* about working with Jason Robards in the revival of *You Can't Take It With You.* I told him about my Drama Desk Award for *Cloud 9.* I name-dropped unmercifully, every well-known actor I'd ever worked with whose name I thought might get a rise out of him. I told him about my television work, precious little of it very satisfying to me, but unspeakably glamorous to an outsider: the notoriety, the exposure, and not incidentally, the money. I told him about my townhouse on Riverside Drive, my timeshare condo in Bermuda. And with every name, every achievement, I could see him die a little inside.

Yet when I finally finished—and after a few minutes the pleasure of it had evaporated; I felt self-conscious, silly, and childish—he didn't look sullen or hostile, just stared at me as though he'd been in the same place I just had, and said quietly: "So what are you doing here?"

The question caught me off guard. "What—what do you mean?"

He shrugged. "I don't pretend to understand how this all has happened, but there's got to be some reason *why* it has—right?" He gazed at me with eyes that seemed, suddenly, not so different from mine: reflecting different pasts but much the same sadnesses. "What is there about this wonderful life of yours that sent you here, to Appleton, to"—he hesitated, as though having trouble coping with the concept—"to the life you *might* have led?"

I tried to think of some glib and superficial answer... then realized how absurd that was. He was right: we were here for a reason. What, I wasn't sure, but it would be insanity to turn it away with a lie.

So I told him. Everything.

I told him about my failed marriage to Catlin: how we got married for all the wrong reasons, mistaking sexual obsession for love, and even now, thinking about her, I felt a stirring in my groin, a ghost of remembered passion. I discreetly skipped over Catlin's personal peccadilloes and concentrated on the stupidity of the union in the first place: we'd both known it was no good for either of us, but sometimes the most destructive relationships can also be the most seductive. I gave him a capsule summary of the many abortive relationships since then: First Joanne, a bright, sensitive actress I met while doing *Hogan's Goat;* we lived together for two years, but as much as I'm ashamed to admit it, when she won a Tony for *Loose Ends,* I couldn't handle it and the relationship fell apart. Then there was Lana, a vulgar, selfish, truly loathsome woman with whom I spent six horrible months as a kind of self-punishment, I suppose, for breaking up with Joanne. And most recently Libby—smart, funny, independent—who grew too close, I think, and so I set about frightening her away.

I told him about Mom... about Finney... about my guilt and regret, the wish that I could make it up to them somehow, though I knew I never could. I told him about meeting Debra and about the child we'd never had. And toward the end I admitted my worst fear, the fear that I would

die alone; that I'd become one of those old industry professionals who sat alone in their rooming houses—if I was
lucky, the Motion Picture Home and Hospital—surrounded
by one-sheets and scrapbooks, watching myself on aging
videos, recalling my salad days. Or worse, continuing to
go out on auditions long past the point when anyone
wanted me, sitting in stuffy anterooms, clutching yellow-
ing composites, hoping for a one-line role, a walk-on, a
silent bit in a commercial, anything.

He looked at me and the hostility, the antagonism between us lessened; his voice was soft, his gaze distant.
"Better to die alone," he said, "than unremembered." His
eyes met mine, and in that moment, I think, we began to
understand one another. When I asked him about his life,
he spoke calmly and tonelessly—too calmly, there was something spooky about it—as though he were desperately
afraid to let go, to release his anger and frustration. Why,
I discovered soon enough.

I started with the good years, because there were good
years, to start; that first one, with Debra and me and the
baby in the two-bedroom apartment on Hancock Street,
God that had been a wonderful year. Deb had been teaching a local night-school course in Art Appreciation—to a
class composed primarily of starchy New England ma-
trons who'd doubtless signed up thinking they'd be
spending a few amiable Tuesday evenings chatting about
Norman Rockwell or (at the most radical) Andrew Wyeth.
I'll never forget the night—I'd arrived early to pick Debra
up from work, having only one car between us—that Debra
showed them a slide of Goya's *Saturn Devouring One of His
Children*, and a collective gasp of dismay and disgust

floated up from the crowd like swamp gas. At least one of the ladies got up, huffily pronounced that if she wanted to see pictures like this she'd go to traffic school, and stormed out of the room in a snit. They lost two more students by next week's class, but most remained...and one even enrolled again next term!

God, she was so beautiful—standing there beside a projection of a Greek *kouros* statue, so enthusiastic about her subject, leaning in with a pointer as the light from the projector played on her short dark hair, different slides casting varicolored reflections in her glasses. Even today, when I think of her, that's how I see her in my mind—standing in front of that class, pointer in hand, making jokes or vividly recounting the history and meaning of Minoan frescoes.

I looked up to find, somewhat to my shock, that my visitor was looking at me with barely concealed envy in his eyes—just as surely and crassly as I had been looking at him five minutes before—but as pleasant and unaccustomed as it was to be envied, I couldn't let it go at that.

"The worst part," I said quietly, "is that when I think of how it was, between us, it...it all just seems like a mockery, because of what *is*. You understand?" I licked my lips, not having articulated this to anyone else; hardly, even, to myself. "It hurts, remembering the good times, because you know what they finally became. You're even robbed of that, in the end."

I told him what it was like, waking up knowing you had to spend that day, every day, five days a week, doing a job you hated, a numbing tedium that drained you of actual thought or inspiration, reducing you to little more than a marionette. I told him about Debra...how I'd come to resent her, loving her and hating her at the same time ... loving the woman I married thirteen years before, but hating the choice I'd made, the opportunities I'd passed by. I told him about Paige and my stupid childish jealousy of what she might become. I started to tell him about the fight that night, about hitting her, until I realized that he must have seen every humiliating moment of it, and I felt even more embarrassed and ashamed. And as I spoke, the shame made the inevitable sea-change to anger.

I got up from where I'd been sitting, started to pace in small circles near the workbench, something winding up again inside me; I tried to keep my hands still, but they wouldn't stop clenching and unclenching, the violence that had boiled up out of me before still simmering. I wanted to lash out: at my hands, at this stranger who was so much more than a stranger, at my life, at Debra, at—

"God *damn* it!"

I slammed my hands down onto the oak workbench, feeling the sting in my palms, the muscle spasm shooting all the way up my arms. I sank onto a stool, my fists on my knees. Suddenly there were tears in my eyes. I lowered my head so he couldn't see.

"I don't want to hurt them," I said, so quietly he may not have even heard. "I love them. I *do*."

The other me looked as though he actually understood, though I knew he couldn't, and nodded slowly. "I know. I know you do."

"I'm just afraid if I stay, I'll..." I looked up, my eyes dry now. "You ... you read about that kind of man, you know? The kind who beats his wife ... abuses his children ... takes out his own failures and frustrations on his family. And you think, Christ, how can anybody *do* something like that, what kind of creep do you have to be, anyway? And then—"

I winced. "Then you wake up one day and you realize that he's you: that you're him. It happened while you weren't looking."

My twin came over, sat beside me, put a hand to my arm. It felt strange—being touched, reassured, by yourself; wrong, somehow, narcissistic—and yet the concern was real, and in a way he *wasn't* me, in a way it was all right for him to feel for me as he might a stranger, and I him...

"You ever thought about divorce?" he asked.

I smiled ruefully. "Yeah, sure. I go to New York, try to break into the business at the age of thirty-five, and pay child support, to boot?" I shook my head. "Too late for that. By at least ten years."

I stared into space, barely aware any longer of his hand on my arm, sinking into that black depression that claimed me so often these days. I looked at Debra's car sitting a few feet away... and found myself saying something I had never dared speak aloud before.

"I have this... fantasy," I said, feeling my eyes fill with tears again, but past caring now. "Sometimes, late at night, I think about coming down here... closing the overhead door... starting the car, then just sitting back and... waiting. You know?"

He looked at me, shocked and horrified, for a long moment; and when I'd stopped crying he looked at me soberly and said, "No. That's no way out. I—" A pause, as he seemed to consider; then: "I have a better way."

I laughed a short, sour laugh. "Like maybe a shotgun?"

He shook his head. "No," he said. "Like..." He got up,

paced, but for him the pacing was not anger and frustration but a nervous, creative energy; he seemed seized, excited, by some new idea. Outside the rain continued, unrelenting, the sound it made on the roof of the garage—a wooden roof, not metal—ringing oddly inside, sounding strangely hollow, like water bouncing off the surface of a kettledrum.

He crouched down, meeting my eye level, and took a breath. "Like what's to prevent me," he said softly, nodding in the direction of the house, "from going in there... into your home... and you"—he nodded in the opposite direction—"from walking back down that street... where *I* came from?"

I started. *"What?"*

"Why else would we be here, like this?"

I got to my feet. "No. That's crazy. We must be here to, to learn, to see what we might've had, what we might've been, not—"

"And seeing what you might've been—me—does that make you feel better?"

I looked at him—wishing I could say yes, wishing I felt some epiphany, some dramatic resolution—but feeling only, God forgive me, what I felt when I looked at Paige.

I shook my head.

"No," I said. "I guess not."

"Then listen." He paced, gesturing as he spoke, eyes bright with enthusiasm. I could see why he was so successful—that fire, that energy. Did I ever have such energy and enthusiasm? Could I ever have it again?

"If you stay here," he said slowly, "you know what will happen: you'll either hurt them or you'll hurt yourself. True?"

I nodded, both terrified and excited by what I knew he was about to say...

"And if I stay where I am," he went on, "the guilt is going to eat me alive just as surely as your anger is consuming you. You want the career, the dreams you turned your back on thirteen years ago; I want the happiness that's eluded me ever since I left Appleton. Don't you see? *This* is why we're here, together, like this. What else could it be?"

Inside, a naked hungry part of me yearned to agree, but my conscious self held back. I walked to the other side of the garage. "And what if we can't get back? What then?"

"Then we live with the choices we made," he said. "Like we're living with them now. My God, man, don't you realize what we're being offered? How many people go through their lives thinking *what if*–if only I'd done this, if only I'd done that? We're being offered a chance to do just that. You'd throw that away?"

I took a short breath. "I–I can't just...abandon my family–"

"But you're not," he said gently. "We're the same person, don't you understand? We took different paths, but for the first twenty-two years of our life we were the *same man*. You won't be abandoning them to a stranger, you'll be entrusting them to another part of yourself. Just as I'd be entrusting my life, my friends, my career, to another part of me."

God, how I wanted to believe him. I thought of Paige, who surely hated me and whose love I might never reclaim. I remembered the rage I'd felt, and the bloody-minded desire to do the same to Debra. I saw Debra in my mind as I always saw her, teaching her class, the light of the projector casting red and brown shadows on her face...

and then suddenly I saw that they weren't shadows at all, but bruises—savage testimony to a pathetic man's impotence and loss—and I knew, finally, that he was right, that I had no future here but blighted hope and helpless rage.

"Your Debra," I said softly. "Did you love her?"

He nodded. "As much as you did." He stepped closer, touched me lightly on the hand. "I have things I cherish in my life, too, you know. Friends. Lovers. I'm trusting you to take care of them."

It seemed to be decided. We spent the better part of an hour briefing one another on the details of our lives, as best we could in the time remaining to us; already we could hear the rain outside beginning to slacken. We exchanged clothes, but as I started to hand over my wallet I drew it back briefly to take out a snapshot of Paige in jeans and a pink T-shirt. There would be photos of Debra in his world, but not of Paige; I would be the only man on his earth who would even remember her, but I didn't want to trust to memory. I shrugged on his coat, and I was ready.

We walked out to the willow tree; he nodded down Schuyler Street, still partly shrouded in the downpour. "I'm staying at the Colony Inn," he said. "When you get there, look up your name in the phone book. If it's not there, you'll know you've crossed over."

"And if this doesn't work?"

"I think it will." He held out a hand; I clasped it, hard. "Good luck," he said.

"Take care of them," I said. He nodded, and I knew, for a fact, that he would; better care, I thought bleakly, than I ever could. I turned quickly, before I could change my mind, and walked out from under the willow tree into the teeming rain. I walked for one full block before looking back, and when I did, the rain was still so intense I could make out only the vaguest of shapes; one of them might have been a man, standing on the lawn in front of the house, but I couldn't be sure. I walked on for another block, coming to the intersection with Hancock Street; I looked back and could see nothing and no one outside the fading memory of my home. I turned, hands in my pockets, and headed west on Hancock, toward the Colony Inn.

Appleton looked the same as it ever did and I hadn't the slightest idea whether I had, in fact, left "my" Appleton; and the farther I walked down the quiet commercial street, the rain slackening to a gray drizzle, the more the last hour and a half seemed like a dream, an idle fantasy. The closer I got to the inn the more certain I became that in my grief and guilt I had imagined all of it; by the time I entered the lobby I was convinced I would dial my own number, on the third ring Debra would pick it up, and I'd walk home, laughing at my own silliness, finding no doppelgänger, no other self, just my house and my family. I shook the water from my coat and approached the registration desk; the night clerk looked up, recognizing me.

"Mr. Cochrane?"

There. You see? All a dream. He knows me, I've lived here all my life. I stepped up to the desk, about to laugh sheepishly for being out in the rain in the middle of the night, and ask to use their phone... when suddenly the clerk looked at me with a shy, hesitant smile, pulled out a scrap of paper and a pen, and in a tone of awe and respect unlike anything I'd ever heard, said:

, "Would you mind... I mean, I know it's late, but I

don't work days, I wouldn't get a chance to ask . . . could I have your autograph?"

I stood there, too stunned to say anything; mechanically, I took the paper and pen. It felt strange, and even signing my own name seemed as though I were signing someone else's by mistake; but not so strange that I couldn't grow to like it. I handed it back to him, then borrowed the phone and flipped through the white pages, searching for my name.

It wasn't there.

I dialed my number. I awakened a middle-aged man not mollified by my apologies. He called me a turd and hung up on me; and as I replaced the receiver, the dream turned slowly real. Outside the skies were clearing, the road slick and glassy after the rain. A car passed the inn, its brights dimming as it turned the corner, a spray of water fanning out in its wake; across the street stood the Shaw's supermarket, the Colonel Sanders franchise, a small gift shop called the Bucolic Bazaar. It was all so familiar, so normal, that I had to remind myself that they were not the stores I shopped in and drove past every day; that the Appleton just outside was not my Appleton, but his; that I was now a world away from everything I'd ever known. I felt awed, saddened, frightened, elated. Later, in his—my— hotel room, I called Logan Airport, reserving a seat on the first available flight to New York; then lay awake the rest of the night, dreaming of the new life ahead of me, and mourning, in ways large and small, the passing of the old.

CHAPTER FIVE

RICHARD

I watched him head down the cobbled walk to the street, briefly passing under the willow; I saw him backlit by the streetlamps across the street, and as he lingered in the shelter of the tree he seemed to breathe for the first time since we met, taking in the wet night air like a man released from long captivity. Or perhaps that's just what I wanted to see. He left the willow and struck up Schuyler Street, hands in his pockets, head tilted up slightly; and as he walked the rain seemed to wrap around him like a cloak, taking him in, bearing him away. I couldn't tell if it was simply the storm obscuring his figure, or if I was witnessing some brief moment of eclipse—a shadow cast by the occlusion of two worlds. But almost as soon as I lost sight of him, the skies began to clear and, by the time I turned toward the house, the downpour was little more than a drizzle. On the porch I glanced back down the street, now slick and shining with reflected light. I could see all the way to Montcalm, and there was no one in sight for blocks.

I took the few steps to the door, then hesitated—feeling, understandably enough, like an intruder. I took a set of keys from my pocket: two house keys, as he'd showed me, one for the back and one for the front; a key to the Mutual office; another for the Nissan and one for the Volvo parked out front. I hefted them in my hand; they didn't make me feel any less like a burglar, but I took a deep breath, put the larger of the two house keys in the lock—

As the heavy oak door snicked shut behind me, I entered the two-story Colonial . . . and realized that I'd come home.

It was the home I'd never consciously envisioned, but the framework of which must have always existed somewhere in my unconscious, because everything I saw seemed *right:* nothing in the house, at least at first glance, seemed as though it might have been built or purchased by a stranger. It was after eleven, most of the lights were off but the few that were on—a small lamp in the living room, one in the kitchen—spilled a warm amber light over the rooms. I hung my overcoat in the closet, no longer feeling like an intruder, and wandered from room to room as though it were only right and natural.

Unlike my parents' home, which had been furnished in antique Colonial—overstuffed sofas in busy prints, Queen Anne chairs and overly ornate beds with crocheted coverlets, all of it unspeakably stifling—this house was furnished in rustic modern, at once Colonial and contemporary. Golden oak beams and rafters in the living room, with matching trim around the windows; hardwood floors in the foyer and the kitchen, a cerulean-blue carpet in the living room; modern but slightly rustic furniture with the accent on woods and brass, in contrast to the glass and chrome of my New York co-op. It was partly my taste, and partly, I assumed, Debra's; very New England without being too atavistic, modern without being trendy. I felt so comfortable that I sat down in one of the armchairs for a few minutes, listening to the tick of the brass clock on the wall, feeling very much at peace. The walls were decorated with limited-edition serigraphs and prints—a snowscape by Anita Jones Stanton; one of Joel Meyerowitz' Cape Cod photographs—again, Debra's taste, but mine as well.

After several minutes I was feeling so much at home that I decided to go upstairs and take a peek at my new life, my new family. But the door to one bedroom was closed and I was reluctant to open it and go poking my head inside just yet; the other was open, and I stood in the doorway, just able to make out Debra in the dimness, sleeping on her side as she always used to, a bunched-up pillow under her head. I had an almost overwhelming urge to step inside, to study her more closely, to see how much this Debra resembled my own; I almost entered, but a sudden fear took hold of me. What would I say if she woke up? What if I said the wrong thing, did something unnatural, something that might make her suspicious? *What if she could tell?*

I backed away, now very conscious of the sound of my footsteps and the creaking of the floorboards as I headed back downstairs. And as I stood in the dining room, looking out at the street where just a few hours ago I had been standing—as I stood here where *he* had stood, living in *his* home, *his* world—I felt what I should have felt the minute I proposed this whole crazy scheme: mortal terror. Good God, what had I done? What had I gotten myself into? Yes, we'd been the same man for the first twenty-two years of our existence, but that was *thirteen years ago.* Thirteen years of shared private moments with Debra, of murmurs in the dark after making love; thirteen years of *making* love, of those particular kinds of verbal and sexual shorthand which evolve between husband and wife over the course of a marriage. What if I touched her in the wrong places, what if my kiss was different from his? What if he always took his coffee black, and I asked for sugar and cream? And the daughter—Paige. Bringing her home from the hospital, all the funny, silly little things a baby does that only a parent remembers; her first tooth, her first report card, her first boyfriend... All *this* I had to fake, somehow? I sank into a straight-backed dining room chair, my pulse pounding, my palms sweaty. The potential for disaster stretched limitlessly before me, from the intimate to the trivial. How in God's name was I ever going to pull this off?

And even if I could manage all that, how would I repair the damage Rick had done to his marriage? It occurred to me that I might not have to worry about what to say to Debra or Paige—because neither one of them might even want to speak to me. After what my other self had done and said tonight, how did I knit together the enormous breach in this family?

I had a sudden urge to run—until I realized I had nowhere to run *to*. My life, my career, my home, all my friends and lovers, past and present—they all lived in a different world entirely. Even if I ran to New York, their counterparts on this earth wouldn't know me from a hole in the ground. Strangely enough, realizing this—that I had nowhere to go, that I had to make this work, somehow—quelled my panic a bit. Of course I couldn't run. I didn't want to run; I wanted to make this work. But how?

I went back to the living room but its warmth and coziness had pretty well evaporated. I sat in the same comfortable armchair and fought my way back to calm and deliberation using breathing exercises I'd learned at the Actors Studio. Yes; that was it. Think of it, I told myself, as an acting assignment; a role, like any other. Rick Cochrane, not Richard but *Rick:* thirty-five years old, lived all his life in this small town, married, two children, claims adjuster for State Mutual. Whenever I began a part, I wrote myself a biography of the character, imagining where he grew up, his hobbies, his taste in books, music, art—background detail that would never come out explicitly in the performance, but which anchored the character in my own mind, gave me a broader base from which to tap emotions. But I'd never played an actual, living person before; the closest I'd ever come was John Adams in a summer-stock production of *1776.* Still, I reminded myself, I did do research, consuming two biographies of him in an effort to get a sense of the man. This was no different. (Well, not much different. All right, *very* different, but I couldn't let myself think so or I'd panic and blow it.) I needed research to draw upon. The manual Rick mentioned would help with the job—after you've waited tables and learned to balance three different orders, first in your head and then on your tray, you can do just about anything—but for the home life I'd need photos, home movies, something to fill in the blank spaces . . . and Lord, were there ever blank spaces.

As quietly as I could manage I began looking through closets and drawers, praying I didn't wake Debra or Paige. In the hall closet I finally hit pay dirt: photo albums,. at least half a dozen of them. I opened one at random and saw a fading print of a middle-aged man, beer belly spilling over a baggy swimsuit, with his arm around a cellulite-laden woman with bright orange hair; beneath it was written, in my own handwriting, *Uncle Henry and Aunt Mo at Weirs Beach, summer of '79*. Debra's relatives? Must be. Good; very good. All this would help me connect names to faces. I flipped the page and had to smile at the shot of Paige—couldn't have been more than six years old—rocketing off a giant water slide, limbs askew, looking as though she truly hated this. In Debra's handwriting beneath it: *Flipper, Flipper, faster than lightning*... I nearly laughed out loud.

I searched some more, hoping perhaps for a diary, but found none; Rick would have it easier than I, thanks to my acting journals. There were a couple of carousels of slides—vacations, birthday parties—and that was about it. Still, the albums would be invaluable. I shut the door, feeling better but hardly confident. There were still too many gaps, too many potential pitfalls; I couldn't hope to avoid them all. I told myself not to worry—that even if I were to slip up, stare blankly when she mentioned a date I should have known or call someone by the wrong name, her first thought would hardly be that her husband had been replaced by an impostor from an alternate reality, but that her husband, for some reason, was acting strangely. But why? Why would he—I—be acting that strangely? What excuse could I come up with, should the situation arise?

I returned to the armchair and sat, surrounded by pools of amber light and by warm, golden oak; did my breathing exercises again, feeling calmer, hearing the tick of minutes creep by as noted by the big brass clock; and then, all at once, it came to me. My eyes snapped open. It couldn't be this easy, could it? But it was the perfect solution; the ideal catch-all. Carefully, I thought the whole thing through, trying to punch as many holes in it as I could; and when I couldn't, when I was convinced that it was possible I might actually pull it off, I got up a little past midnight, took the Volvo, and drove off down Schuyler Street to the center of town. It was all very simple, really.

As kids we used to say that Appleton was the kind of town where they didn't just roll up the sidewalks after dark, they sank 'em twelve feet under. Now, driving through the commercial district well past midnight, I saw that little had changed: even the Sunoco station was closed; passing travelers who ran out of gas here were left strictly to themselves, God, and the Auto Club. I turned left off the main drag and began the snaking ascent up Manchester Avenue to the high school, located on a high hill at the edge of town.

Years before, I remembered, the only thing moving in Appleton after eleven o'clock—aside from the occasional snowy owl, migrated from colder climes—was one of the sheriff's department's two patrol cars, slowly making the rounds of residential and business districts, rarely finding anything more insidious than a bunch of kids smoking dope in the village green. These dangerous miscreants were usually busted, with uncommon relish, by a sour, officious old fart known to us all, not so affectionately, as Mister Death: the sort of tall, bony, humorless bastard who was born to wear black robes and a cowl, but settled instead for a sheriff's uniform.

I'd heard Mister Death went on to meet his mentor some years back, but if his successors followed his patrol patterns there wouldn't be a police car anywhere near the high school before dawn; they usually swung by around eleven, then concentrated on the lowlands for the rest of the night. I parked the Volvo in the school parking lot, just below the crest of the hill—low enough so it couldn't be spotted easily from town, but high enough so I could see down from the front seat—then got out and looked down at the sleeping village.

Most houses were dark; only the streets were lit, some painted a smoky ochre by sodium-vapor lamps, others a fluorescent white. Moonlight reflected off the glassy surface of Goffle Brook, winding its way from east to west, through the center of town and out again, to join, some miles north, with the Merrimack River. The only sounds for miles were the chirp of crickets and the distant trill of an owl. I breathed in the cold night air; it tasted of spruce and white pine and a hint of impending snow. I smiled, feeling more at peace than I had for years. New York seemed a lifetime away already. Finally, after several minutes, I returned to the car; time to begin what I came here to accomplish.

I slipped in behind the wheel, the engine idling to permit the heater to work, and repeated my breathing exercises, focusing on the task ahead of me. I was already exhausted from the events of a long and very bizarre day, but as the hours crept past I did not allow myself to fall asleep; every time I began nodding off I woke myself with a start, turned on the radio to keep myself awake or got out of the car and let the chill brace me. Finally, about three a.m., I shut off the heater. By dawn I felt wasted, drained; I looked in the rearview mirror at veined and shadowed eyes. It was colder than hell, and I was sniffling and shivering—probably gave myself a cold—but if that was the only price I had to pay, it would be worth it. Down below the town began to awaken, lights snapping on, people braving the early morning cold to warm up iced-over engines; and at the bottom of the hill, a VW bug began the long ascent up Manchester Avenue. I was shivering, exhausted, and red-eyed, but the chill I felt was less from cold than from anticipation.

The VW was in the parking lot within minutes; a man in a custodian's uniform got out, started toward the school, then saw my car and began walking, puzzled, toward it. I saw all this in my rearview, but as soon as he drew abreast of me, my gaze snapped forward again. I fixed on a spot in the air about three inches in front of me, and the windshield, the dash, the town, all went out of focus.

I heard a knocking on my left, a rap of knuckles against glass. I fought the reflex to turn, kept staring straight ahead.

"Hey," came a muffled voice outside, "fella. You okay?"

I didn't answer. The voice became background noise, white sound, no more to be responded to than the drone of a radio.

"Hey! I said, are you all right?"

More white noise: the rattle of a lock as someone tried to force open the car door. In front of me the world was still unfocused. I blinked only when the sun bounced off the rolling currents of the brook, making bright wheeling spikes of light in the distance.

After a while the voice went away, but I didn't move, looking neither right nor left. When I heard the distant whine of a siren, I had to fight from smiling; moments later, a red and white ambulance sang all the way up the hill, orange lights flashing like one of the foil pinwheels I played with as a kid. By the sound of its siren I could tell it had pulled up beside me, but I kept my gaze resolutely forward, even as the side door lock was forced open. I may have blinked, but I know I didn't move. I felt so far removed from it, it might as well have been the sound of a television in another room.

"Sir? Can you hear me?"

I ignored them. I must have looked pretty ripe, eyes bagged and bloodshot, my body shuddering every few moments from the cold. I felt hands on me now, pulling me out of the car, and I relaxed my body, thinking of Michael Chekhov's first requirement for actors: Ease. Unless you are at ease, even the lightest moves or gestures will look heavy, artificial. I let them manipulate me as though I were no more animate than a sack of flour.

"Hypothermia?" someone said. I kept my eyes unfocused, saw a blurred sky swing past as I was lowered onto a stretcher—

"Get his temp," someone replied, and a thermometer was forced between my lips. The stretcher was lifted and a thermal blanket thrown over me; in moments I was inside the ambulance, now shrieking downhill again. At the periphery of my vision I could tell that the paramedic to my left was flipping through my—Rick's—wallet; he leaned forward, his face looming over me, concern in his voice. "Mr. Cochrane? Can you hear me?"

I suddenly felt like a turd, exploiting this good man's concern for my own ends, but there was no turning back now. I made no reply.

He took the thermometer from my mouth. "95.2. He'll be fine. But he's sure not responding like any hypothermic I've ever seen." He unscrewed a thermos, forced some hot coffee through my lips. "Call ahead and tell them to have a shrink on hand when we arrive."

"Ahead" turned out to be the Parkland Medical Center in Derry. I was shunted from the E.R. to a thermal bath, where I began to allow myself to focus again, my eyes moving from side to side as I took in my surroundings. By the time they got me into a bed I was responding to outside stimuli once more. A doctor in his late fifties, passing through the E.R., seemed to recognize and hurried over to my side. "My God," he said. "Rick? Rick, what happened?"

I just stared at him.

"I'm sorry," I said with absolute honesty. "Do I—?"

I didn't finish, but it had its effect; alarmed, the doctor hurried away. After they took a full range of blood tests and other exams, just to nail down that there wasn't anything terribly wrong with me physically, another doctor came back and said, "Mr. Cochrane? Can you tell me your name? Your full name?"

Tentatively, I said, "Rick. Rick Cochrane."

"And where do you live, Mr. Cochrane?"

"Appleton. 488 Schuyler Street."

"And how long have you lived there?"

I looked momentarily disoriented; confused. "I don't know," I said. The doctor exchanged grim looks with a nurse, then patted me reassuringly on the arm. "You're going to be fine," he said. "Your wife's been notified, she's on the way. I'm going to send in Dr. Sklar now."

Dr. Sklar was a shrink. Nice man, big, crew cut, glasses, bad taste in sport coats. He continued in the vein of the previous doctor, asking me simple questions about my life. I answered each one of them perfectly truthfully, which was of course the beauty of it. I told him my wife's name, but I couldn't tell him our anniversary date. I told him what company I worked for, but I couldn't give him the street address. I knew how old my daughter was, but not where she was born. I told him my age, but didn't have the vaguest idea of the last time I was under a doctor's care. The last thing I remember? That was easy. The argument. The argument with Debra. How often did you have such arguments, Mr. Cochrane? "I can't remember," I said apologetically.

He left after half an hour, and if he wasn't totally convinced that the man in this room had suffered a complete breakdown, I was willing to turn in my Equity card.

I was feeling pretty smug and satisfied about it, too, though I didn't allow it to show; the face I presented to the world was that of a broken, disoriented, emotionally shattered man. It wasn't until just after that, that the smugness vanished.

A nurse pulled open the curtains surrounding my bed— and Debra stepped up to my bedside. I stared at her, genuinely shaken; it was the first close-up look I'd gotten of her, of *this* Debra, and my heart nearly skipped a beat with the wonder of it. My God, it was her, the same woman I'd talked to in Finney's kitchen a world away from here; and yet she wasn't the same, couldn't be the same. I guess she took the astonishment on my face for confusion, because suddenly her composure cracked and she looked hurt and distraught and frightened.

"Rick?" she said softly. "Do you . . . know who I am?"

I nodded quickly. "Yes. Yes, of course."

"Are you all right?"

"I'm fine," I said.

She looked relieved; too relieved. I reminded myself why I was here, how necessary this was. So when she said, "Roger Peale called me when he saw you here," I just looked at her blankly and said, "Who?"

The relief on her face crumbled and I instantly regretted it; I hated putting her through this, but told myself I had no choice. It was scant comfort. "My obstetrician, Rick," she said, her voice very quiet. "He... he delivered Jeffrey. Don't you remember?"

Forgive me, Deb. "No," I said tonelessly. "I'm sorry."

But the worst was yet to come. The curtain parted again as the nurse showed in a young girl—tall, blonde hair, braces—and though I'd glimpsed her briefly the night before, it was from a distance, and I genuinely didn't recognize her at first.

Paige saw it in an instant; and if Rick thought that there was nothing worse than the contempt and disdain on her face when he struck her, he was wrong. She saw my blank look and tears sprang to her eyes; she started to open her mouth, then stopped, her lower lip trembling; she looked wounded beyond words, not wanting to believe this could be—her own father and *he didn't know her.* I recognized her an instant too late, and even though it helped make my act believable, even though it would ultimately help all of us, I was immediately overcome with guilt. I'd been so caught up in my little acting tricks, smugly congratulating myself on my finest performance, that I'd forgotten this wasn't a play, those weren't stage tears, and—hardest of all to accept, but I knew it now—I wasn't an actor anymore. I was Rick Cochrane, and I was part of these people's lives.

I felt tears coming to my own eyes. "I'm sorry," I found

myself whispering, sorry for reasons I couldn't tell them. "I'm sorry..."

And with that, Paige ran to me, threw her arms around me, and hugged me tight–tighter, I think, than anyone had ever held me in my life. "It's all right, Daddy," she said, mistaking my apology for Rick's, for last night. "It doesn't matter, I didn't mean it, just–" The tears started to flow again; she bit her lip. "Just get well, Daddy. Please get well..."

They left soon after, leaving me alone with my regret over this complex charade. God–wasn't this always the way? Put me in an ideal world, a world I'd only ever dreamed of, and I was already finding something to feel guilty about. No, I couldn't let that eat at me, not if I wanted to pull this off... and I had to pull it off, because really, I had no other choice. This *was* my world, now. The pretense was a necessary evil, an expedience which, with luck, would soon no longer *be* pretense, as I fell into the role–dammit, stop thinking of "roles" and "parts"–as I *lived* this *life* and it became mine. And it was mine, in a sense; I had lived it without even being conscious of it, but now I was aware of it, that's all. Think of it, I told myself, as though you were awakening from a coma: thirteen lost years, which you will now set about rediscovering, reclaiming.

Then I got my second shock of the day, one that made it easier to accept the pretense and the half-truths. I'd been transferred to a private room and I was just settling in to watch the noon news on WNEV, when I heard a voice outside and down the hall say:

"Is that it? 2311?"

And another voice replying, "Right through there, we

just moved him in," but it was the first voice I was still fixated on, a woman's voice, with a familiar New England twang, the words clipped and short—

I sat bolt upright in bed.

My mother bustled into the room, purse slung over one arm, her free hand clutching a box of chocolates. She saw me, saw the dreadful state I was in—I still hadn't slept, my eyes were more veins than pupil—and stopped short. Reflexively she put a hand to her mouth.

"Oh God," she said. "Rick? Are you—?"

My heart was pounding; I was having trouble breathing. I felt everything you could feel, under the circumstances: astonishment, disbelief, joy, relief. I wondered if perhaps I *was* crazy, if the act hadn't been an act—and then she was at my bedside and before she could do anything I was out of bed, I was embracing her, I was crying, we were both crying. Oh God, I thought, thank you, *thank* you, it was more than I could've hoped, more than I'd allowed myself to dream. Rick hadn't told me; he'd wanted me to find out for myself. Sweet Jesus, I had a second chance—a chance to be there when she needed me, to make up for all the lost days and lonely years, to be the son I should have been, but never was. I held her and cried with the joy and the wonder of it, and I suppose she was crying for joy, too—joy that I knew her, that I wasn't as far gone as she'd feared I'd be. "It's going to be all right," she kept saying, trying to comfort me. "It's all going to be fine." I stroked her back, nodded, and blinked back my tears. "I know, Mom," I said softly, almost laughing. "I know it will."

The consensus among my doctors was that I'd suffered a disassociative reaction to severe emotional stress: a

fugue state, during which time I had driven off and isolated myself in my car, with attendant psychogenic, or hysterical, amnesia. Hypnosis was a standard course of
treatment in such cases, but it seemed to have no effect
on me—how could it?—and was quickly abandoned in favor of more conventional therapy. For the next week or so
I spent at least six hours a day with a psychiatrist, getting
at the source of "my" problems. I was savvy enough not
to try and seemingly resolve them in one or two sessions,
but by the end of the week my shrink was greatly encouraged by my progress, enough to authorize my discharge
from the hospital.

He didn't suspect it, of course, but those sessions were
valuable to me in ways he could never guess. In an attempt to restore the lapses in my memory he showed me
pictures—slides and prints brought in by Debra, culled
from the same carousels and scrapbooks I'd found days
before—spanning ten years and more. Paige's baby pictures, snapshots taken on vacations to Colorado and Aruba,
birthday shots of me, of Debra, of Paige, videos of Jeffrey
at two weeks, five weeks, three months . . . Watching them,
I practiced a kind of sense-memory exercise—looking at a
slide of a picnic, for example, I would try to summon up
the smell of new-mown grass, the buzz of insects, the
taste of potato salad and pastrami, the drone of an air-
plane passing overhead, anything to give the image a tex-
ture in my own mind, to make it real, to make it mine.
And in all those photos was a man who looked just like
me, a man I couldn't distinguish from the one I saw in
the mirror; a man I could easily have been. Toward the
end of the week, one of my last sessions, I showed up in
Dr. Sklar's office, idly walking back and forth while he

finished up rounds, and happened to see a photo of me on his desk. I picked it up—and didn't realize till half a beat later that I had seen not a man with my face, but me. That's all; just me.

My third day in the hospital, Hunt—Bailey, was it?—stopped by; he seemed like a decent sort, very troubled and concerned for me, assuring me my job was secure and I could take all the time off I needed to get well. So when I finally checked out and returned home, I had several weeks to get my bearings, to acclimatize myself to my new surroundings, my new family, and not the least of it, my new job. The manual on workers' comp was slow going, boring beyond belief—but if I could memorize a three-act play I could damn well get this down, and would.

The tension that had prevailed between Rick and his family was replaced by a different sort—a walking-on-eggshell tension in which neither Debra nor Paige wanted to do anything, say anything, that might trigger a re-emergence of hostilities. It felt awkward and strained and after two or three days of it I think we all were about ready to claw our way up the walls; something had to be done to break the ice, to convince them that "I" had indeed changed. So one Sunday night after supper, as I sat reading the Arts section of the New Hampshire Sunday *News,* I suddenly looked up and said, "Hey, there's a production of *A Chorus Line* at the Hampton Playhouse. Anybody want to go?"

They both looked up, Paige from her homework, Debra from feeding Jeffrey, and stared at me with astonishment and trepidation. As though maybe I hadn't really spoken at all; as though maybe they were hallucinating.

"A Chorus Line?" Debra repeated nervously. Paige cleared

her throat: "When I wanted to go see it in New York you said—" Then she stopped, not wanting to dredge bad times up again, but I just laughed and waved a hand.

"I know what I said," I lied, "and I was wrong. C'mon, let's go, I could use some diversion after a week in the Snake Pit." They laughed at the characterization, and from that point on, the hospital was no longer the H word, but the S.P. The ice had been, if not broken, then at least chipped.

That weekend we went over to Hampton to see the musical. I'd seen it before, of course, in New York, at least three times; this was a local production, and it showed—clumsy staging, spotty casting, the girl playing Cassie couldn't sing as well as she could dance—but I enjoyed it as I always enjoyed it. *A Chorus Line* can't help but touch you in a special way if you're any kind of creative person, and it hit all the right chords again, from the sassy confidence of "Nothing" to the bittersweet goodbye of "What I Did for Love." And as I sat there, the latter song affected me in a way it never had before, the words telling of a time when you had to give up your art, without regret, without rancor, because the time had come; as it had, I realized, for me.

Debra and Paige stole nervous glances at me throughout, relieved when I laughed and cried and applauded at all the same spots as everyone else; and afterward, when in great good cheer I packed us all off to Carvel's and sprang for ice cream, they looked at one another with mounting amazement and cautious delight, as though to say, Could it be? Could it really be? We drove back to Appleton, I popped a CD I'd bought of the show in the CD player, and we sang all the way back, laughing at how far off-key we wandered. Drained and happy, we staggered into the house, I kissed Paige good night, and Debra and I turned in for the night.

We stood close in the darkened bedroom, and for the first time since I had returned home, we came together. Oddly, at this pivotal moment, this ultimate risk of exposure—what if I did something too different? what if she could tell?—I felt only passion and excitement and confidence. When I kissed her, I was kissing the woman I'd loved so many years before, the one I'd let get away; it all came back, all the ways in which we'd touched one another, the things we whispered, the cries and the pauses. I was eager, hungry, determined to recapture everything we'd shared—so determined that I didn't even care if I was found out. And that was probably the wisest thing I could have done. We made love for hours, and when I finally drifted off to sleep it was to the sound of her breathing beside me, the feel of her hand on my chest; a soft, feathery comforter covered us, a pillow of warm air lay atop that, a wedge of moonlight fell across our feet, and I no longer had any doubts or regrets. I was Rick Cochrane of Appleton, New Hampshire, husband to Debra, father to Paige and Jeffrey, and I was happy.

CHAPTER SIX

RICK

Kennedy and La Guardia were socked in by fog, so my flight from Boston—a six-engine prop job—was rerouted to Teterboro, a small airport in northeastern New Jersey. We'd been stacked up over Newark for what seemed forever, only to be told, finally, there were no runways available; it was an hour from Boston to New York, another half hour wasted circling Newark, and all the while I sat there with one hand balled into a fist, the other tapping impatiently on the arm of my seat, my anger at the delay steadily reaching flash point. At last, unable to contain it any longer, I got up, stalking down the length of the narrow cabin to confront a stewardess as harried as I was. "Do you have *any* idea at all," I said, in typically understated tones, "just when the hell this thing is going to land?" For a moment she looked as though she might reply in kind, but, keeping herself in check much better than I, said flatly, "We're doing the best we can, sir. A few more minutes. If you'd return to your seat—"

"You said 'a few more minutes' half a fucking hour ago," I snapped. This time she glared at me as though she'd be delighted to introduce me to the airport runway, preferably from a height of ten thousand feet at an airspeed of a hundred kilometers per second.

"Until you get in your seat," she said, voice sharp as broken glass, "we *can't* land. And since I don't enjoy being up here with you any more than you do with me, I suggest, *sir*, that you return to your seat."

I almost escalated the argument—then, thinking better of it, made an ambiguous grunt instead and stalked back up the aisle. As I did, I passed two teenage boys traveling together; returning to my seat, I could hear one of them—softly but clearly, audible even over the drone of the engines—declare: "What an asshole."

A short laugh, then the other, concurring: "Fuckhead."

I froze in my seat. My first instinct was to spin round, confront them, paste the little bastards in the face—

And then, quickly ashamed at the pointless violence that sprang so readily to mind, my second instinct was to agree with them.

We banked to descend on the airport, and I marveled at how once again I'd taken a mild inconvenience, a small annoyance, and transformed it into some kind of *Götterdämmerung*. An hour's delay. So what? Was that really what I was so pissed off about?

No; not really. No more than Paige's failing to switch off the TV had been. The anger was already there, like a phantom limb. An anger I'd lived with for so long that I took it with me everywhere I went, and had to create things to be angry about, to justify its existence. The life, the frustrations that had created all that rage and hostility were literally a world away; yet here I was, dutifully bringing it with me into my new life.

You fuckhead.

No. I wasn't going to do it. If there was ever a time to turn my back on that anger, to amputate that phantom limb, it was now. If I brought it with me, it would despoil this new life as surely as it had ruined my old one. I closed my eyes, trying to imagine the anger as a physical thing being left behind as we descended—a bitter cloud, dissipating in the skies above Teterboro. The last violent remnant of Rick Cochrane, failed father, unhappy husband. And the man who would emerge from the plane into the gray March light would not be Rick, but Richard—maybe not a perfect man, but a success, at least, at what he chose to do—what he'd had the courage to choose. Or so I hoped.

The airline provided a shuttle bus for those of us heading into Manhattan, another for points north or south; heading up Route 46, passing through Little Ferry, Ridgefield Park, Palisades Park, I didn't pay any of it close attention, too intent on what lay ahead of me, until we exited the parkway at Fort Lee. The shuttle swung up an overpass, revealing what we couldn't see from the highway below: the steel tower of the George Washington Bridge, its high arch looming huge and somehow magical, directly ahead—like a gateway to a city of giants.

The only city I'd ever spent much time in was Boston, but Boston is more a horizontal city than a vertical one. New York I'd visited before, but I'd forgotten the sheer immensity of it all—everything squared, cubed, magnified to sizes that went beyond mere necessity—buildings so high they seemed unreal, like stone leviathans out of Celtic legend. In New Hampshire I'd weathered enough hurricanes to be skeptical of the solidity of anything above five stories; these things were thirty, forty, *fifty* stories high. And yet I found something both frightening and faintly erotic about being surrounded on all sides by them; something exciting in the very danger I feared, as though these massive reminders of human mortality made you—made me—all the hungrier for life. Even more so when the bus let us off at the Sheraton Center on Seventh Avenue and I stood there trying not to look like a tourist, trying to look like I belonged, despite my growing delight and excitement.

The street, the sidewalks, everything was in motion: pedestrians crossing against the light, cabs cutting across three lanes of traffic to gain some brief advantage, buses exhaling clouds of exhaust as they braked to a stop. The sounds were as big, as brassy, as the environment: car horns blaring every few seconds; the gunning of an engine as one car, then another, ran a red light; a constant background noise of construction work, jackhammers and cement mixers and a deep, low whistle that seemed to sound every other minute. God *damn,* but it was wonderful. After the maddening quiet of Appleton, the predictability of each sedate, if not serene, day, this was a noisy, bustling heaven; a welcome chaos. The jackhammer, the rumble of cars as they passed, all the low bass noises seemed to reverberate in my stomach, in my groin; I felt something coming alive there as well, and as I made my way through the crowd of pedestrians pushing down the street I felt a thrill at every jostle, every passing contact with someone, male or female. I looked up at the leviathans on either side and I felt again that enticing fear, that taste of mortality that only seemed to whet my appetite for life. After thirty-five years of order and monotony, I was ready for some sweet chaos, some beguiling anarchy.

I flagged a cab, stole a glance at the address on Richard's driver's license, and had the cabbie take Broadway to the Upper West Side, thrilling silently as we passed the Palace, the Winter Garden, the Marquis. They were more now than just names glimpsed in a stage review; they had faces, I could close my eyes and I could see their marquees, their facades, the customers in line for matinee tickets. This world was slowly becoming real to me.

The cabbie turned left at 72nd Street, then right onto Riverside Drive. On our left, in Riverside Park, runners jogged up and down the esplanade fronting the Hudson; mothers pushed toddlers in strollers; a middle-aged man waited as his very tiny dog went about its business beside an indifferent oak. On our right, twenty-story brownstones alternated with old limestone mansions-turned-townhouses; to my surprise, the cabbie pulled up in front of one of the fanciest of the townhouse buildings and stopped. "Here you go," he said. A little dazed, I gave him a ten for a seven-dollar fare—no doubt marking myself as either a tourist or a philanthropist—and got out, a bit wide-eyed, taking in the building. I walked through the revolving doors—flat black panels with brass trim, flanked by elegant green marble—into a posh lobby: gray tiled floor, leather tufted couch along one wall, an expensive etching above the couch, and an elderly doorman standing beside a bank of intercom lights. He looked up, saw me, and smiled. "Mr. Cochrane," he said. Then, in a softer, more reserved tone: "My sympathies for your mother. Was she very old?"

My mother. Jesus, I'd almost forgotten. She was... dead... in this world; just as Richard had said. I hoped the doorman took my momentary confusion for bereavement. "Sixty . . . sixty-seven," I replied, feeling strange as I said it.

"Ah. Still young, then." At least compared to the doorman, who looked to be pushing seventy himself. He held up a hand, went to a desk near the intercoms, unlocked a drawer, and handed me a sheaf of mail. "I'll tell the letter carrier you're back." I thanked him, nodded when he again offered his sympathies, and as quickly as I could sought the sanctuary of the elevator. Riding up in the car—the walls a soft, tasteful velvet, jet black and lush burgundy—I took a deep breath. Christ, this felt weird. My mother was dead; but she wasn't really, not *my* mother. Mine was healthy and safe—a world away, but safe. Still, I'd never see her again, would I? So in a way, she *was* gone, but not in any way the doorman would ever suspect. Now I did feel a pang of bereavement, of loss, at the thought; but loss for me, not for her—she would never miss me, never even know I had left, because Richard was there in my stead. How strange—to be gone, and not even to be missed by those you loved . . . I'd never thought of that, never imagined the hurt it could bring.

I got out of the elevator, pushing the ache to the back of my mind as I headed toward Richard's apartment: 1409. I walked uncertainly down the hall, scanning the raised brass numbers on each door until I finally found the right one. I unlocked it, swung open the door.

I stood in the doorway, a bit taken aback by the spaciousness and style of the place; part of me, I think, had still hoped, irrationally, that Richard had not been as successful as he'd claimed. No such luck. It was gorgeous. No foyer or vestibule; I entered through the dining room—small but not cramped, at the center a glass-topped dining table, a chrome base, and four chairs with plush chocolate-brown cushions—into a step-down living room that sprawled before a breathtaking view of the Hudson River. Beige carpeting, the color of pale sand, was complemented by contemporary furniture in muted pastels: an off-white sectional couch (you could tell he had no children), a crescent open to the floor-to-ceiling windows; comfortable pale blue chairs; equidistant from both, an oval chrome-and-glass coffee table. Dazed, I wandered into the kitchen: small but fully decorated in blond pine, equipped with a stainless steel refrigerator, a cooking island in the middle, and not one but two microwaves.

And that was only the downstairs. On the second level was a library, its bookshelves crammed with novels, nonfiction, and, of course, theatrical books of all kinds. Across the hall, the single bedroom came furnished with another drop-dead view of the Hudson, a blue velour bedspread covering a king-size mattress, and a nightstand and dresser, both the same blond pine as in the kitchen.

Most impressive of all for an actor's home, there were no more than a few framed show posters and other career memorabilia—most of them tucked away in the library or in the upstairs hallway. I looked closely at one of them: STARRING RICHARD COCHRANE, ABEL GANLEY, JOANNE MC-CLOUD. I kept staring at it; it felt oddly disconcerting, like seeing your name on a book you never wrote.

I went back to the living room, gazed out at the view, then back at the apartment. I should have been delighted that this spacious, elegant home was now mine—but I wasn't. Because it wasn't mine, not really; I might've been in possession of it at the moment, but the spirit, the soul, the invisible center of this home, was Richard's. It was

Richard, not me, whose hard work and talent had bought it; Richard who had gone out there every day, making the salary to be able to wake up each morning and take in this view. No, before I could call this place mine, I would have to earn it. Until I did, I would always feel like a boarder here—a tenant, not an owner.

On the kitchen counter an answering machine's red message light blinked on and off, so many times I could barely count the number of messages stored. Cautiously I slid a switch from "ANSWER" to "MESSAGES."

A woman's voice, fluty and musical in pitch: "Richard, it's Donna. Just wanted to check in, see if you're back, see how you're feeling. I'm so sorry about your mother. Give me a call when you get in. Take care of yourself, all right?"

A man's voice, a bit gravelly, subdued: "Jesus, man, I just heard about your Mom. Hope you're okay up there. If you're checking in with your machine, you need to talk, give me a call, whenever. I'll be at the Long Island number this weekend if you call then: 516-901-7777."

Another man, higher-pitched, a fast New York rhythm and accent: "Richard? Gary. Libby just told me about your Mom. Damn. It's been a lousy couple years for you, hasn't it? First your Dad, now this. Well, listen, I've been there myself, so if there's anything I can do, just let me know, okay?"

Another woman, pleasant voice, a bit hesitant: "Richard, it's Libby. I hope you're all right... I mean, I remember when your Dad died, what you went through then, and this time you have to do it alone, and..." A pause. "I just wanted you to know someone is thinking about you. Give me a call when you get back."

There were at least half a dozen more calls, all similar;

I saved the messages, moved by their sincerity and concern, impressed by the quality and devotion of Richard's friends. Now fear began to gnaw at me; fear that somehow, these close, loving friends would spot me for a ringer on first glance—that they'd see through me instantly, demand to know where their friend was, what I had done with him. Hell, for that matter, how would I even know them if I ran into them on the street? What if I passed one of them without knowing, without acknowledging him or her? What if they confronted me, demanding, "Tell me my name, you bastard, I dare you, *tell me*"?

Even as I sank bleakly into a chair, a part of me was saying: Hold on, we're getting way too melodramatic here; let's calm down, okay? No one was going to stop me on the street, point a long finger at me and howl aloud like Donald Sutherland at the end of the first remake of *Invasion of the Body Snatchers*.

I got up, poured myself a glass of wine from the built-in wine racks in the dining room—1978 Nuits St. Georges; shame to waste such a good vintage on mere panic, but what the hell—and after a few swallows, considered my course of action as calmly, as deliberately as I could manage. An idea forming, I searched the kitchen until I found Richard's address book, then went back to the phone machine, playing back the messages one by one. *Donna*. I scanned the names and addresses, found only one Donna: *Donna Gillespie, 42 Bank St., 978-3267.* I played back the message until I knew the tone, the pitch, the rhythm of her speech well enough to recognize it should I hear it on the street or in the event she called again, then went on to the next. This one presented a different problem: no name, just a number. So I worked at it backward, going through the address book until I found the number (one of two: one Manhattan, one Long Island), and immediately to the left of it: *Ray Perelli, 83 CPW.* I did one or the other with each of the remaining messages, getting the name first, then studying the voice.

There was no last name, though, after the only "Libby" in the book; no address, either, as though both were so familiar he hardly needed a reminder. Of course. *That* Libby. The one he'd just broken up with. I paid especially close attention to her voice, but as I did I grew sweaty and nervous, my confidence waning again: what if she were to call now, while I was sitting here? What if any of them did? Once word got out that I was back in town, I'd be deluged with calls, maybe even visitors, before I was ready. Suddenly panicky, I set the machine to "ANSWER"; best to let it intercept any calls that might come in while I was still feeling my way through all this—I'd meet them all eventually, but only when I felt secure enough.

I needed time to perfect my impersonation of Richard, time to memorize names, numbers, voices. So that day I settled in to my new life, screening all calls, not returning any, letting them all believe I—Richard—was still in New Hampshire. I didn't dare even leave the apartment to go shopping; too much chance someone "I" knew might spot me on the street. I ordered my groceries from the D'Agostino's market a few blocks away and deli from Fine & Schapiro's on 72nd Street. I locked myself up with Richard's voluminous acting journals, doing nothing but read and reread them for at least three days—a dozen or more leatherbound, five-by-eight diaries, each one carefully labeled, two or three titles to a volume: *American Buffalo/House of Blue Leaves; Hogan's Goat/All Summer*

Long/Two Gentlemen of Verona. An eerie feeling, seeing things in your own handwriting that you know you never wrote, reading of events and emotions you'd never experienced; hearing the familiar cadence in the words and thinking, My God, that's just how *I* would've said that... feeling almost as though you had. It wasn't exactly *déjà vu,* I had no memory of having done any of the things he had; it was just the way he talked about them—I couldn't help but hear my own voice as I read, and after a while I could almost believe I *had* played Homer Bolton in *Morning's at Seven* or Maurice Duclos in *Fallen Angels.*

But more than just seeing how Richard approached a part—his thought processes, the acting tips which I grudgingly admitted might be helpful—the journals were invaluable because so many of the friends he'd made over the years, friends whose voices even now I listened to silently as the answering machine picked up, he had met through his work. And so I discovered how he'd met Ray, a director, when the latter had directed him in *House of Blue Leaves* at the Roundabout Stage; how Donna had played Juliet to his Romeo at the Yale Rep; how John and Rhoda and Joanne and he had played repertory together in SoHo, alternating *The Barber of Seville* with *Uncle Vanya,* certainly an exhausting double bill. I felt awkward, like a voyeur, as I read about Richard and Joanne's romance, their first night spent together, how their mutual attraction blossomed over the course of a run into love and a live-in relationship. I thought of Debra and felt a pang of longing and guilt—but the longing, I knew, was for a wife and a life that were years past, and I forced myself to retreat even deeper into the journals.

And along with them, I devoured much of Richard's

library as well: books on acting technique, working guides to the profession, theatrical biographies...most of them read long, long ago in Richard's own development as an actor, but for a relative newcomer like me, invaluable in both advice and inspiration. It was thirteen years since I'd been on the boards, and then only at a college and local-theater level. I might be able to pass without embarrassment on a stage, but what if I got an offer to do a television show? I didn't even know how to hit my marks—what the hell would I do? Yet despite this, the more I read, the more impatient I got to get out there and *do* it—to start living the life I'd come here to live.

After a week's seclusion the messages were piling up and one caller had even tried calling the Colony Inn back in Appleton only to be told I'd checked out. Regardless of my self-confidence, I was going to have to confront my fears sooner or later...so, screwing up my nerve, I dialed Donna's number, half hoping no one would pick up. But someone did, and I recognized the fluty, high-pitched voice at once. "Hello?"

I took a breath and plunged in. "Donna? Richard."

"Richard! You're back?"

My heart was pounding; my palms sweaty. "Yeah, I just got in."

"Are you all right?"

"Well as I can be," I said, "under the circumstances."

"Were your aunt and uncle there, to help?"

I hesitated a split second—she must have meant Edgar and Charlotte, but had they met Richard in Appleton? Then I realized it didn't really matter; Ed and Charl were hardly likely to be in direct communication with Donna. "Yeah, they were terrific. I could've gotten through it on my own," I went on, improvising, "but their being there helped a lot."

Liar. Faking bereavement, faking exhaustion, fake fake bloody *fake.* The harassing voice inside me threatened to crack my composure; hastily I changed the subject. "So how are you doing?" I said, hoping it wasn't too abrupt, but she took it, I guess, as someone not wishing to dwell on a grim experience and said, "Oh, well, the usual. I tried out for that new musical comedy, the one Kristen's in? They liked my delivery, hated my voice. A week before I'd been up for another musical; they liked my voice, hated my delivery. Tomorrow I'm planning on sniping at passersby from the Chrysler Building."

I laughed, not too heartily, I hoped; I had the feeling Richard would have thought of something witty to say, something to defuse her frustration without dismissing it, but nothing came to mind and the pause stretched out awkwardly. "Well," Donna finally said, "I'll let you go. You going to be okay?"

"Sure."

"Your Mom was a neat lady, you know."

And suddenly there were tears, real tears, in my eyes, as the realization that I would never see her again hit fully home for the first time. Her, and Debra, and Paige, and Jeffrey, and ...

"I know," I said, my voice trembling with emotion. "Thanks. I'll ... I'll talk to you later, okay, Donna?"

"Take care of yourself, Richard."

I hung up ... and for the first time since that night in the garage, I cried. I tried to remind myself of the violence and desperation of that night, but it seemed so far away now, its imperatives so remote. I forced myself to conjure again that terrible vision of Debra, bruised and hurt, or myself, lifeless inside the Nissan, the garage clouded with asphyxiating fumes. I knew I'd made the right choice, for them and for me; but that didn't stop me from grieving. After a while I stopped and went to the window, looking out at the sun setting over the Hudson; and felt, strangely, a bit more deserving of this view and this home. I may not have earned it by right of work, but I realized then that it had, in fact, been purchased at some cost to me: some significant cost. As much as I wanted this new life of mine, it had not come cheap.

The other calls went without major incident, save for a few awkward pauses and confusions on my part; at one point Gary mentioned a play which I mistakenly thought he was trying out for, when in fact it was something he'd done two years ago. "Shit, Gary, I think I'm getting Alzheimer's," I told him. "No," he said, more concerned than suspicious, "you've just had a lot on your mind lately." Later, talking with another actor friend, Susan, I could tell from context that she'd been in a production of *Children of a Lesser God,* but mistakenly assumed she'd played Sarah instead of Edna; I used the same excuse, and got the same sympathetic reply.

Clearly, though, I couldn't go on like this forever, so I trooped over to the Drama Book Shop, picked up a set of *Theatre World* volumes from the last ten years, laboriously went through each volume's index and drew up a master list of the plays every one of Richard's friends had appeared in—Broadway, off-Broadway, off-off-Broadway, road companies, resident theater groups ranging from the Iowa Theater Lab to the Mark Taper Forum in L.A.

And since every listing came replete with character names, I made copious notes of the various parts each had played, then set about memorizing the whole shebang—good practice, in any event, for the memorization I'd have to do in the future. I was incredibly rusty at first, but not as bad as I'd feared; juggling dozens of active insurance claims in my head turned out to have been pretty good prep.

Cautiously, I began arranging casual lunch dates with Richard's friends and acquaintances; the first with Gary, then Donna, then Tom and Craig and Ray. I was terrified the first time, had to go to the bathroom three times during the one hour we spent together, but I did it, with less effort than I'd suspected. Part of it was that every time I found the conversation drifting toward uncharted seas, I managed to steer it back to Gary's (or Donna's or Ray's or Leslie's) current or recent work. There's that old joke about actors loving to talk about themselves: "But enough about me; let's talk about *me.*" But if it's true of actors, it's true of writers, directors, choreographers, musicians, all creative people in some degree. Work isn't just work to them—the kind of numbing tedium that the majority of Americans call their jobs; the kind *I* used to call a job—it's what they love to do, what they can't stop doing. Ask anyone in show business what they're up to, I discovered, and you'll get twenty minutes of bitching, moaning, rhapsodizing, recriminations, wishful thinking, passionate debate, worldly cynicism and starry-eyed optimism, the latter two often within the space of the same sentence. I sat there listening raptly most of the time, feeling both blissfully happy that I was among people with the same passions as

I and bitterly envious at the experiences—even the bad ones—that I had yet to enjoy.

So the shop talk helped divert questions or conversation away from subjects I'd rather not have gotten into. But there was something else that made the lunches and the dinners and the after-show drinks go so smoothly; something else that allowed my impersonation to go unnoticed. Richard's friends were good friends—they loved him, cared about him, enjoyed his company, appreciated his friendship. But they weren't with him twenty-four hours a day as Debra and Paige and I were together; they didn't know what he ate for breakfast, probably never noticed whether he was left-handed or right, weren't alarmed when I ordered a Coke instead of a Pepsi, or if I took my scotch neat instead of on the rocks. And if by chance I did do something out of character for Richard—like order my steak medium-rare, where he had preferred them, say, well-done—they didn't seem worried or suspicious or baffled, as Debra surely would have; they probably just assumed my tastes had changed, and let it go at that. Even Joanne, Richard's girlfriend of years before, must've thought much the same thing; it had been a long time since they'd lived together.

It made things easier for me, but there was something sad about it, too; that a man could have such good, close friends, and be so little known to them, as well—no one who knew or cared about the pet peeves, the odd habits, all the strange and endearing things you learn about someone you see, day in and day out, for years. Part of me missed it; part of me was glad to see it gone.

I still, however, found myself avoiding getting together

with Libby; the liaison was too recent, too much chance of me tripping up. I returned her call, acted friendly but a bit remote, and when she suggested getting together I put her off, claiming exhaustion. She may not have believed me, but probably saw my reluctance as plain old emotional distance, the awkward uncertainty between ex-lovers that usually followed a breakup.

But if talking with Libby filled me with apprehension, another call was closer to mortal terror. It was my third or fourth day of seeing people, I'd just come back from lunch with Ray; I felt confident, relieved, upbeat. The phone rang, I answered, and I heard the three words I most dreaded hearing when picking up:

"Hi, it's me."

Oh, shit. Me? Me who? What did I say? Should I fake it, pretend to recognize the voice, hope to God he dropped some clue, some context I could puzzle out?

"Hello? Richard? Are you there?"

The long silence I'd let go by gave me a sudden burst of inspiration. I tapped on the mouthpiece and began repeating: "Hello? Hello, is anyone there? Who is it?"

"Richard, it's Joel, can you hear me?"

Son of a bitch—it worked. (Thereafter I always kept a piece of cellophane next to the phone, crinkling it for some instant static in similar emergencies.)

"Joel . . . hi. Bad connection."

"Want to call me back?"

"No, it's getting better. What's up?" Joel was Richard's agent; that much I'd gleaned from the address book. He sounded young—thirty-five, thirty-six?—and energetic. "How are you? How'd things go in New Hampshire?"

I gave him my by-now-standard line, well as can be expected, etc. etc.

"Did you get the flowers the agency sent?"

"Yes," I lied. "Thank you. They were lovely."

"Well, you may not be up for talking shop—"

"No, no," I said innocently, "that's okay. Takes my mind off things, you know?"

"Sure," he said. "Well, okay, we got a call for you. Voice-over, spokes, thirty-second spot. Can you audition tomorrow?"

I nearly fell through the floor.

"Spokes?" It was out before I could help myself.

"Yeah, they saw the pitch you did for Longines and think you might be right for this. You up for it?"

I almost begged off, but some wiser, bolder part of me urged me on, told me I had to get my feet wet eventually. I found myself nodding and saying, "I . . . I guess so. Tomorrow?"

"Three o'clock, Producers Sound Studio. Here, I'll put Ronni on to give you the address."

I stared at the paper on which I'd scribbled the address for several minutes before my breathing became regular again. Jesus—I hadn't been to an audition in thirteen years. And I'd *never* been to a commercial audition. What the hell was I supposed to do? What was I supposed *not* to do? How the hell was I going to make it through this thing without looking like a total amateur?

I looked again through Richard's library; one of the working guides to the profession had a brief, two-page overview of commercials, both performance and voice-overs, but nothing too helpful. So it was down to the Drama Book Shop again, where it turned out there was more than enough research—including an entire book devoted to the subject of voice-overs, titled *Your Money Where Your Mouth Is.* I was on my way to the cash register when someone stopped me: "Richard? Hi! How are you? What've you been up to?"

The man—fifty, bespectacled, thin—might as well have been asking me what the intrinsic characteristics of a neutrino were, for all that I could reply. I was terrified: terrified because I didn't know him, didn't recognize the voice, and terrified that he'd see me with this primer on commercials that Richard would clearly be beyond. I turned the book over in my hand, the cover against my thigh, and then tried to do a reasonable impersonation of happy recognition, outstretching my hand as I smiled. "Well, hi, how are *you*?"

"Fine," the man said. "I had a new reading at the Common Ground. Went very well. Good group, though not as good as yours."

Reading: okay, he was a playwright. Group: cast? And I—Richard—had been in a previous reading. "What's it about?" I asked, following my rule of thumb: when in doubt, ask about their work. He talked for a few minutes about the play—sounded pretty interesting, actually—then asked me what I was doing. I shrugged. "Nothing much. I've been out of town. I've got a commercial audition tomorrow, that's about it."

"Well, it was good seeing you. Give my best to—you still with Joanne?"

I shook my head. This part I knew. "Not for a while." We shook hands again, and within minutes I was out of there, down the narrow staircase to the unmarked entrance on

Seventh Avenue, taking in deep breaths of the crisp April air. Before I had time to consider how many more times I would have to play that same scene, before I could contemplate how I was going to find out who that man upstairs was, I propelled myself away from the bookstore, flagged a cab, and as we rattled uptown through late afternoon gridlock I was already scanning my book, hungrily devouring anything and everything that might help me make it through tomorrow's session.

I felt sick to my stomach all morning, the nausea finally easing in the afternoon, only to be replaced by a fierce case of nervous colitis. I took five Pepto-Bismol tablets over the course of two hours, praying, as I cabbed it to Producers Sound Studio, that I wouldn't have to interrupt the audition to rush desperately to the nearest men's room. I needn't have worried on that count, although my bladder did become particularly insistent once I'd entered and shaken hands with the director and the ad agency reps. "Pleasure to meet you," said the director, a friendly Britisher in his mid-forties. "Enjoy your work." The admen smiled stiffly, as though they'd been doing this all day. Then they all crammed into a small control booth as I took my place in the studio, in front of a microphone. I put the ad copy on the script stand next to the mike; earlier, in the waiting room, I'd marked the copy with the various inflections I thought appropriate, and now I looked it over one last time as the engineer's voice rasped out of the speaker: "Mr. Cochrane. Can we have a level, please?"

I nodded, read the first few lines of the copy so the engineer could get a proper sound level, and was chagrined when he announced, "Can you angle your script more to the left? You're reflecting off the paper and into the mike."

I wanted to die, but no one in the control booth was looking at me like the greenhorn that I was, so I just smiled and adjusted the angle of my script stand. My hands were trembling. I quickly dropped them to my side, hoping no one had noticed.

"All right, Mr. Cochrane," the Britisher said. "When you're ready."

I took a sip of water from a glass and pitcher nearby, then launched into the reading:

"Essence. The dictionary gives it two meanings: the heart, the spirit, the substance of a person, or an idea; and a fragrance; an ex—"

Before I was halfway through, the engineer broke in: "You're pulling away from the mike. Let's take that again."

Damn. I hadn't even realized it, but I had—I'd shrunk back from the copy, almost imperceptibly, as though it posed some physical danger to me; but that inch or two was enough to screw up his sound levels. "Sorry," I said. I glanced up; the director was still smiling, but did the admen seem suddenly fidgety?

For Christ's sake, Cochrane, get it together!

Embarrassed and infuriated at myself, I straightened, studied the lines again, and concentrated on nothing but the task ahead of me. I wasn't going to end my career before it had even begun, and I was damned if it would be stillborn at a stupid perfume commercial. The engineer nodded when he was ready, the director gave me a smooth and gentle, "When you're ready," and I launched into it again:

"Essence. The dictionary gives it two meanings: the

heart, the spirit, the substance of a person, or an idea; and a fragrance; an extract.

"Essence, from Estée Lauder, is both. Different things on different women, its fragrance reflects her uniqueness, her spirit.

"Find her Essence—or risk losing her heart."

This time I didn't stand too close or too far from the mike; didn't angle my script the wrong way, didn't make a single misstep. The director nodded, leaned in. "Very nice. Could you try it a little slower? And a bit more intimate?"

At first I thought I'd read it too fast, but the rational part of me quickly realized that he was simply asking for a different take. I obliged, the director smiled, shook my hand, and saw me to the door. "Perfect," he said. "Just perfect. Thank you so much for coming." Well, I wasn't perfect, that much I knew; but I *had* been competent, and I hadn't embarrassed myself. All the admen continued to smile stiffly, but I didn't care. Just as I didn't care when, the next day, Joel called to break the news that they'd hired someone else: "An age thing, they wanted someone older, with more authority." I tried to sound pragmatic but disappointed, but inside I was jumping up and down, screaming with relief that no one had called to tell him, *Jesus, who* was *that guy you sent over, anyway? Is this amateur night in Dixie, or what?* I'd been a professional, working with professionals; I'd done a competent if unexceptional job, and hadn't humiliated myself or my agent. Suddenly I was raring to go out there again, all fired up for the next chance, the next audition. Because next time I didn't want to be merely competent or professional; the next time, dammit, I wanted to be *good.*

CHAPTER SEVEN

RICHARD

The Sunday morning after we'd gone to see *A Chorus Line*, I awakened briefly, around six, at first light; we'd forgotten to draw the blinds the previous night and before getting up to close them I lingered in bed for a moment, feeling Debra's arm against mine beneath the down comforter we shared, listening to the long, shallow breaths she drew as she slept. There was a faint chill to the room despite a warm flurry of air falling from the overhead vent, and a lattice of frost on the outside of the window, tinted gold in the early morning light. I smiled. I felt warm, protected, secure. After a minute I got up, drew the blinds, and crawled back under the covers, drifting back to sleep.

It must have been close to seven-thirty when the knocking awakened me from a dream of snow and wind and an ice fortress I'd built when I was twelve years old. Even through the filter of sleep and memory I could tell it wasn't the front door—not a knocking on wood, but something equally familiar, familiar even within the context of my dream. A rapping of knuckles, not on wood, but on—glass? Yes, that was it: the distinctive sound of a windowpane vibrating in its frame. The ice fortress melted around me as I shook myself awake—but why did the knocking still sound as though it belonged in my dream?

Debra stirred as I sat up and saw that the rapping was coming from behind the blinds. "What the hell is that?" I said, but Debra just turned over on her side with a muttered, "Oh God, not again," burying her face in a pillow.

"Hey, Cochrane," came a voice from outside, and it, too, sounded familiar, "come out and play!"

I was at the window before it occurred to me that we were on the second floor, and what in God's name could be out there, anyway? I raised the blinds with a jerk of the cord—

And there was Finney, seemingly floating outside our bedroom window, a big silly grin on his face.

"About *time*," he said, voice muffled but ebullient through the glass. "Frigging *cold* out here. Open up!"

Groggily I unlocked the windows, swinging them open as Finney deftly pulled back to avoid hitting them—and as I looked down I could now see that he was standing on the third highest rung of a twenty-foot ladder.

Standing. Finney was *standing*.

I couldn't find my voice. I stammered something short and incoherent; Finney just grinned. "Articulate," he said, "as ever."

A blast of cold morning air shook me from my silence. "Finney... what"—I tried not to look at his legs, tried to keep the amazement from my voice—"what the hell are you *doing* out there?"

"What does it look like?" he said. "I want to elope."

I laughed, as much at the joke as in wonder and delight

as Finney climbed inside on two good legs, then did a standing jump off the windowsill onto the floor, hitting it with a loud smack. It came back to me then: how, when we were kids, Finney would never enter our house by the front door; he'd always scramble up the drainpipe to my second-story room, standing precariously on the ledge and announcing himself with a rap of knuckles against glass. Bloody miracle he never broke his fool neck.

But now he winced as he hit the floor, bending to rub at his knees. "This isn't as easy as it used to be," he admitted. Straightening, he noted Debra with her head buried in the pillows. "Morning, Deb."

Debra gave up on further sleep, turned over, and snapped up the alarm clock from the nightstand. There was more resignation than surprise in her tone. "Finney, it's seven a.m., for God's sake."

"Really?" he said innocently. "I thought it was at least nine-thirty. The party didn't even break up till four."

"Ah," Debra sighed. "And here I thought this might be a frivolous visit." She wrapped a blanket around herself like a cocoon, got up, and padded toward the door. "I might as well go check on Jeffrey. Rick, if you do decide to elope, leave me the keys to the Volvo, okay?"

Finney laughed, watching her leave, then turned to me. I was still so stunned at seeing him here, seeing him whole, that I'd kept silent during his little sparring with Deb; but what he said now caught my attention soon enough. "So is it true what they've been saying about you, Rickie?"

I hadn't been called *Rickie* in years; I was beginning to remember why. "Uh, that depends on who 'they' are and what they've been saying, I guess."

"You kidding? You're the premier topic of conversation around town. You really go after the old lady with an ax?"

"What?"

"Just kidding. Not that bad. Not that good, but not that bad. Hell," he said, sizing me up, "you don't look all that whacko to me."

I winced. I'd forgotten how far and wide bad news and scurrilous gossip traveled in a small town. I could practically trace the path of the rumor mill: the custodian at the school told the principal, the principal told a teacher, the teacher told another teacher, a student overheard and went home to tell his or her parents ... and from there the whole town would be athrob with the drumbeats of the Jungle Telegraph. I sighed. "It was kind of a ... breakdown," I said sheepishly. "Overwork. Overstress."

He looked at me, the flippancy briefly gone. "You okay now? Anything I can do?"

I shook my head. "I'm on the mend."

Debra reentered the room, looking rather bedraggled in her coat of quilted blanket, and trooped wearily toward the bed. "So, Finney," she said, sighing. "Anything I can get for you? A rope ladder, a few bedsheets braided together ...?"

"Right. Time to move on," Finney said, grinning. He looked at me with sudden illumination, real or feigned. "Hey, I know what you need," he said, moving to the window again, the mischief returning to his eyes. "A little recreation. Couple drinks, a few rounds of eight-ball ... shit, how long has it been, anyway? Say, Saturday night?"

Out of the corner of my eye I could see Debra shifting in bed, sitting up, suddenly alert.

"Finney, I don't know, I start work again this week. I ..."

"Aw, c'mon, man, just a couple drinks. I'll pick you up after dinner, you'll be back in time to tuck in the kids. What do you say?"

What could I say? I was so happy to see him, to see him well and whole that I wanted to go as much as he did, probably more. "If Debra doesn't have anything planned—" I turned to her; she was looking at us coolly, and her voice was strangely flat.

"No," she said. "I don't have anything planned."

Finney slapped me on the back, climbed backward out the window, and started back down the ladder. "Later, Cochrane," he said before disappearing below the window frame. I shook my head, laughing to myself as I shut the window . . . not really noticing the troubled frown on Debra's face until I climbed back into bed. And then it was impossible not to notice it.

"Deb? Something wrong?"

She gave me a disbelieving look. "Rick, the Amazing Spider-Man climbs two stories to our bedroom window and you're not sure if something's wrong?"

I had to smile. Even when she was angry, she was funny; it was one of the things I'd remembered best about her, one of the things that still excited me. "Oh, hell, that's Finney. When we were kids, he used to—"

"I know. Scale the trellis and knock on your window. But what is endearing in a teenager is not—" She stopped, as though she didn't even want to bother to find a punch line. She got that flat tone in her voice again. "You're actually going to go out drinking with him Saturday?"

I wasn't quite sure of my footing here; wasn't sure what relationship Rick had had with Finney these past thirteen years. But I knew this much: Rick had been there that night when "my" Finney crashed his car on Route 3. Rick hadn't failed him. And from what Finney had said, it had been a while since they'd done anything like this. So cautiously I ventured, "C'mon. How long has it been since he and I have gotten together?"

"I know, but—"

"He was my best friend, growing up, Deb," I said. "I can't just cut him loose, can I?"

Debra frowned. "No, of course not, and I wouldn't want you to. God knows I have old friends you're not entirely comfortable with." She shook her head, leaned in, and kissed me lightly on the lips. "Forget it. I'm just cranky this early on Sundays. Go out, enjoy yourselves."

I kissed her back, then, feeling over-confident, I made my first big mistake of the day. "Hey, how much trouble can a couple of old married men do, anyway?"

She looked up quickly, her whole body shuddering involuntarily—and even if I didn't know at first exactly what I'd done or said wrong, I knew I'd done something. "Married?" she said quietly. "Finney?"

She got up suddenly, went to the window, and drew the blinds before anyone could see her standing there in her slip; she looked down at the bars of sunlight that fell across the carpet, and even if I couldn't see her face I could easily read the deep and genuine distress in the way she stood, her back muscles tensed, one arm crossed and rubbing the other. I went to her, touching her gently on the free arm; she stopped rubbing it briefly. "I . . . I'm sorry, hon," I said. "I got confused. That's all."

She looked up, smiling a pained smile, considering a

moment before speaking. "It's just so easy to forget," she said. "One minute you seem fine... more than fine, you seem happy, really happy... and the next—"

"I know," I said. "I'm sorry."

"It's not your fault. You can't help it."

We stood there, neither of us quite knowing what to say; finally, I wrapped my arms around her from behind, rubbing gently at her stomach with my hands, my voice soft in her right ear.

"I still remember the good times, Deb. I still remember sitting behind this cute, dark-haired Art major taking a theater course for her Humanities requirement... how after a week and a half of trying to come up with some subtle opening line, I finally just tapped her on the shoulder, smiled, and said: 'Excuse me, but I've been trying to find some way for us to Meet Cute and I can't seem to do it. Do you have any ideas?' And she thought for a moment and said—"

"'I think you just found it,'" Debra finished for me, softly.

We laughed and I drew closer, putting my arms around her, our mouths joining. I don't quite recall actually moving toward the bed, but since that's where we ended up I assume some sort of voluntary motor control was involved. We made love for the next hour and a half, like the college students we had been fifteen years before; finally we lay nestled together, giggling and exhausted, nibbling at one another's necks...

Until two quick knocks startled us. Debra reflexively raised the sheet, I looked automatically to the window; but it was the door that swung open now, and a vexed—

though not really annoyed—Paige stood in the doorway, one hand on her hip, her head cocked to one side.

"All right," she announced, "I've been pretending to be asleep for, like, an hour, okay? But I'm hungry, and Jeffrey needs changing, and if you two aren't totally disabled by now you can come back up after somebody fixes breakfast. I mean, some of us live on food, you know?"

I laughed. Debra laughed. Down the hall, Jeffrey, possibly feeling left out, started to wail. Somehow, I didn't mind at all.

After having spent the better part of the week reading and rereading the three-hundred-odd-page *Workers' Compensation Law of the State of New Hampshire*—only slightly less compelling than the Yellow Pages, though not quite as bad as *Titus Andronicus*—I had new respect for Rick. This was a hell of a lot harder than memorizing a part. When you're doing a play there's a progression of events that propels the words, makes it easier to commit the lines to memory; there are also other players' lines to cue yours. But this—this was random bits of information, definitions, legal codes and such. There was no way I could memorize all three hundred and eighteen pages of it, but by the time I had to "return" to work I had made a sizable dent in it, as well as in the *Dictionary of Insurance Terminology* I picked up in a bookstore in Manchester. I knew about benefit levels and survivor payments, disability income riders and elimination periods; I knew the difference between Coverage A and Coverage B, and I could tell you all about subrogation, aggregate indemnity, and residual disability. It was hard, and most of it was dry and deadly dull, but Monday morning, driving down 102 into Nashua, I was confident, I was prepared, and I was actually eager to put my research into practice.

The State Mutual office was on Ferry Street, not far from the Arts and Science Center. I remembered Nashua as a rather bleakly industrial town, but high tech had made its inroads here as in most communities within shouting distance of Boston. Still, coming in from the northeast (or ass-end) section of the city, it looked like the Nashua of my youth: factories, breakeven retail shops, generic fried-chicken stores. I found the State Mutual office with no difficulty, paused outside to deal with a brief case of stage fright, then pushed open the double glass doors and entered.

It was essentially one very large room, maybe thirty by forty feet, divided into small cubicles about six feet by eight feet and five and a half feet high. Already, at nine a.m., the room was busy with the sounds of ringing phones, crosstalk and coughing, though none of it too overpowering, the fabric on the cubicle walls doubtless absorbing much of the noise. I headed down one aisle, and as I passed workers spotted me, rose hesitantly, and came out to greet me with a gentle pat on the back or a careful handshake, as though afraid if they applied too much pressure I might break.

"Rick. Good to have you back," said one, chubby, red-faced, sleeves rolled to the elbows. "Welcome back," said another, tall, big-boned, prominent Adam's apple, could pass for Ichabod Crane. "How you doin', man?" came another, young, about twenty-three, longish blond hair. "Missed you," said a black woman, mid-thirties. I shook their hands and acknowledged their smiles and greetings, stealing, not too obviously I hoped, quick glances at the Lucite nameplates on the front of their cubicles. "Thanks, Mike," I said to the chubby man; "Good to be back, Irv," to the tall one; "Getting there, Steve," to the young guy; "I appreciate that, Karen," to the black woman. It was like running a gauntlet. I was relieved when I reached the end of the aisle—only to realize once I got there that I hadn't the vaguest idea, in all these honeycombed spaces, just where my desk was.

Thankfully, Hunt Bailey emerged from his office just then. "Rick. Welcome back," he said, shaking my hand. He put a hand to my back and began guiding me down a near aisle to my desk. "Irv took part of your caseload while you were gone," he said, "so don't worry, you won't be playing catch-up for the next five months. Maybe only two." He laughed, then quickly added, "Seriously, if it gets too much, don't be afraid to let me know. Ease back into it, if you like."

I nodded. "I'll be okay, Hunt. Just bear with me if I seem... you know... disoriented at first."

We arrived at a cubicle bearing a lucite nameplate reading RICHARD L. COCHRANE. "Still having trouble, ah, remembering things?" Hunt asked, looking awkward but concerned.

"Little things, here and there."

"Well," and he outstretched his hand again, "any problems, just let me know. Good to have you back, Rick." I smiled, nodded, and as he turned away a petite young woman—about twenty-three, short brown hair, big friendly eyes behind wire-frame glasses—got up from her desk in the cubicle next to mine. "That goes for me, too," she said, giving me first a peck on the cheek, then a hug; it took me a moment, but I remembered Rick's description of his claims assistant. What was her name—Amy? Yes, of course; she'd sent me a card while I was in the hospital.

We separated; I smiled. "Good to be back, Amy."

"How are you feeling?"

"Better. I take it the company didn't file for Chapter 11 in my absence?" I couldn't help a certain internal satisfaction, a smugness, even; everything was progressing so smoothly, it wasn't going to be as difficult as I'd imagined.

"Sorry. Still solvent." She looked at me cautiously. "You ready for an update?"

"Never readier," I said. We turned, I stepped into my cubicle—

And saw, for the first time, the mountain of paper that was sitting, all very neatly ordered, atop the desk. Good Lord, I thought; is that all *mine?* In one pile there was nothing but mail, each piece already opened and paper-clipped to its accompanying envelope; there must have been forty, fifty different items there. The next stack was also mail, but segregated in some fashion I could not discern. A third seemed to be medical reports of various types; I flipped through them as I moved, dazed, around the desk. But dwarfing all of these was a stack of file folders—some tan, some green, some orange—almost two feet high, each bearing a tag with a different name. *Geller, Rose. Stillman, Elizabeth. Klein, Peter* . . .

I glanced at the open file cabinet next to the credenza behind the desk: there were at least a hundred more file folders in the four-drawer cabinet. Slowly, I took my seat behind the desk; failing to find room on the desk for my briefcase, I let it drop to the floor and stared, horrified, at the avalanche of material in front of me.

"Okay," Amy was saying, oblivious to my plight as she consulted her notepad, "hitting the high spots, there's an ENT report from the Stillman case on the top of the heap—I can't wait to hear their justification for that one—that you'll probably want to disallow. Moving down the hit parade we have an MRI on the Fergusson case, an interpreter's bill for Mr. Ribiero that's equal to our combined weekly take-home pay, and you'll probably want to pull a CYA on the McClure case, put a hold on the lien till defense deposes him..."

Suddenly, I was having trouble breathing. The kind of respiratory constriction I'd normally only felt with bronchitis, where you take in a breath, your lungs fill with air, but the tight band across your chest is so painful that each succeeding breath becomes harder and harder to take.

"It looks like Mr. Bascombe is P&S; time to apply the green hot packs. Objective residuals are minimal, but subjectively there's what his doctor calls a 'moderate' functional overlay. We could go either way on this one, fight it and call in an AME or split the difference, call it twenty-five percent..."

Half of me was trying futilely to follow what she was saying, while the other half was struggling to breathe and not let my panic show. I seemed to take in less and less air the more she talked; I had the wild, panicky thought that I would collapse here, that I would suffocate before anyone could help or even figure out what was wrong.

"We're getting close to court date on the Garman case, I'll take care of the F&S as soon as you dictate the letter to the applicant's—"

I jumped up and was halfway around the desk before she even looked up from her notes. I was going to choke,

I had the sudden irrational thought that there was no air in this cubicle, that all the air was in the aisles—all I had to do was get out there, and I could breathe.

"Rick?" she said as I hurried past her. "Are you—"

"Men's room," I managed to get out between ragged breaths. "Be right back." And before she could say anything more, I was out of the cubicle and hurrying down the aisle, drawing troubled stares down the length of the entire room. It wasn't any easier to breathe out here. I reached the end of the aisle and looked frantically about for the men's room, the exit door, any refuge at all. I rushed down another aisle, this one perpendicular to the one I'd come from, and caught sight, finally, of a REST ROOMS sign at the far end. I hurried into the safe harbor of the bathroom and locked myself in a stall, sitting on a closed toilet lid, taking in ragged gasps of air. The tightness across my chest was lessening, the panic ebbing as I told myself I was not dying, I was not suffocating—I was simply terrified. More terrified than I had ever been in my life; even worse than the time I'd had surgery for what turned out to be a benign polyp in my throat, and I'd feared the end of my livelihood, my life.

I'd just experienced the ultimate actor's nightmare: I was on stage, in front of a packed house, and I couldn't remember a single line. That was what it was like sitting there, listening to these foreign phrases, these incomprehensible acronyms, spill out of Amy's mouth—and me expected not only to know what they meant, but to act on them as well.

God! What kind of idiot was I, to think that memorizing the code, learning some terminology, was all I needed to bluff my way through? I may have known the concepts but I didn't have a clue about the process: might've memorized the terms, but didn't have the slightest inkling of the shorthand, the subtext, any of the things that actual experience brought.

My breathing was slowly becoming more regular; I was starting to think more clearly now. Part of me wanted to duck out the nearest exit—hand in my resignation over the phone, get another job, one I could start from scratch—Lord, that sounded like a *fine* idea, didn't it, just start fresh somewhere else—

But I wasn't back in New York. I couldn't just quit one job and get another, just as good, if not now then two weeks from now; that was a luxury no longer available to me. What real job training did I have, anyway, other than acting and bussing tables? Was I going to take some entry-level position somewhere, data processing, say, or retail sales, then try to support a wife and two children on an entry-level salary? And that was the optimistic scenario. What if I couldn't even *get* another job? I'd always had the freedom before of having to feed only myself, and I was always willing to make drastic cuts in my lifestyle, if need be; but again, that was a luxury I could no longer afford. What would happen to Paige and Jeffrey and Debra?

No. I had to go back out there. I had to find a way to make this work.

I left the stall, went to the washbasin, and wiped the sweat from my face with a damp paper towel. Falling back again on my breathing exercises, I felt myself growing calmer, though hardly any more confident. After a few minutes I was as ready as I was likely to get; trying to stand as straight as I could, I left the rest room, struck up the aisle calmly and slowly, and stopped in front of Amy's cubicle, where she looked up worriedly at my approach.

"Amy," I said calmly, casually, "could you come outside with me for a moment?"

She looked a bit confused, but followed me without question out the front door and half a block down to the nearest corner. I motioned her to sit on a bus stop bench while I paced nearby, my words punctuated by the occasional blare of a car horn or idling of a car's engine at a stoplight. "Amy, did Hunt—did he tell you anything of why I was in the hospital?"

She looked uncomfortable, as though she wished I hadn't brought up the subject. "He said you'd been suffering from . . . exhaustion. Overwork."

"Is that all?"

"Rick, it's not any of our business what you—"

"Amy," I said slowly, "it's okay. I had a breakdown. A nervous collapse. I don't mind talking about it. And it *is* your business, because I'm still not . . . fully recovered . . . and I need your help. I've suffered some degree of . . . memory loss."

She looked up at this, troubled by my admission, uncertain how to respond. "Do we really have to talk about this?" Very New England.

"When you were giving me the update in there," I admitted, "I couldn't understand half . . . three quarters . . . of what you were saying. All those years . . . all those skills, that experience . . . it's gone, Amy. Do you understand? Gone."

Now she was looking at me with true concern, her awkwardness forgotten as my words sank in. "When Hunt told me," she said finally, "I just assumed it'd be . . . little things, you know? Like what your driver's license number was, or phone numbers, or—"

She trailed off. I sat down beside her on the bench, looking her straight in the eyes, trying to be as honest as I could without telling the whole truth, a truth she would never believe, in any event.

"I wish I could tell you," I said, "that someday, some morning, I'll wake up and all those years will return in a flash. But I can't. I don't know if I'll ever get any of those memories, those skills, back. So I'm going to have to learn them all over again. You understand?"

She'd looked away again, but now she turned back and I was startled to see that there were tears in her eyes.

"Amy?" I said softly. "Are you all right?"

She nodded. "It's just that—" Her voice wavered. "Everything I know about this business, Rick, I learned from you."

Like a parent no longer able to care for himself, I sat before her, the parent having become the child, and the child the parent.

Gently I told her, "Then you'll have to return the favor. Give me back what I gave to you. Think of it as something you've held for me, for safekeeping, until I needed it again: A trust I placed in you, and now you pass it back to me."

And she did. She went through every item on my desk with me, showing me the routine, the process, exactly as she had been taught it. I learned how to sort incoming bills into two categories: those I'd initiated or authorized myself, diagnostic tests, rehab costs, attorney's fees; and bills or liens submitted by others that I would either approve or disallow, like the guy who'd broken his arm and tried to get us to pay for an ENT (eye-nose-throat) exam. I learned about applicants' medical exams and defense (our) medical exams; about how to set an agreed medical examiner to arbitrate any major differences between the two; about the rating-manual formula for translating "residual disabilities" into cash settlements. And if you found yourself becoming relatively numb to the daily stream of back/arm/leg injuries—as, I discovered, you had to, or you'd become so emotionally drained by every case you couldn't function, which was fair to neither you nor the claimants—every once in a while there came along a story so tragic, an accident so debilitating, that you allowed yourself the luxury of involving yourself, of figuring out ways to get him or her something a little extra, a little special.

Inside of a week I was able to handle the more routine cases myself, and felt certain that with time I'd be able to take on the more complex ones as well. Much of the job was tedious, but once in a while that intriguing case came along and the actor in me would read it with fascination, in the same way I used to absorb newspaper stories or watch people on the subway—research, grist for the mill. Even though I'd reconciled myself to the idea of not being an actor anymore, it was hard to shut off a part of me that had been so voraciously inquisitive for so long.

Toward the end of that first week on the job, on Thursday night, Debra, Paige, Jeffrey, and I took my mother to dinner at a little seafood restaurant in Merrimack. I'd wanted to go to a ritzier place I knew in Boston, but Debra reminded me of the outstanding balance on our credit cards and I acquiesced quickly. I was still getting used to the smaller income and greater overhead of being a middle-class family man; I'd grown accustomed, the last five or six years of real success I'd attained in New York, to being able to buy pretty much whatever I wanted in the way of small luxuries. Now I had to stop and think each time I wanted to buy a book or video, a small gift for Paige or Debra or Mom; had to think how much we had in checking or savings accounts, what the available credit on our Visa or MasterCards were—and more often than not I had to check the buying impulse, decide to wait for the paperback rather than buy the hardcover, or grab lunch at a Wendy's instead of someplace fancier.

But however I might have chafed at such differences, they paled—they seemed a fair exchange—for the simple joy of being able to glance into the rearview mirror and, still a little awed and dazed, see my mother sitting there. Gradually, over the past several weeks, the memory of her lying in state at the funeral home had faded, and after a while I no longer thought of her as Rick's mother but as mine. Because she *was* my mother, right down to the same little quirks of character that used to drive me batty.

In the restaurant, for instance, she ordered her usual—fried shrimp. Never an adventurous eater, my mother hadn't tasted lobster until she was sixty-three, and rarely ordered anything she hadn't tried before. "Mom, c'mon," I said, "I hear they've got great abalone here. Why don't you give it a try?"

She gave me the same answer she always gave: "If I don't like it," she said, "I won't have any dinner." She ordered the fried shrimp.

It had always been like this, growing up: my mother felt secure, safe, in routine, and so every day, lunch was at the same time, every night we had dinner at precisely the same hour, every year, with few exceptions, we went on the same vacation to the Catskills in New York. I loved my folks, but they made me crazy sometimes; even now, as happy as I was to see Mom alive and well, I was chagrined to find myself chafing at her excessive overcaution.

Somewhere between salad and entree Jeffrey became restless and colicky and began crying. Debra fed him some baby food with a spoon. He spit it out. She gave him his bottle. He didn't want it. The wail was high and shrill, and despite my best efforts to remain phlegmatic, I wasn't used to this and Jeffrey's screams began to grate on me like broken chalk on a blackboard. Debra took him out of his high chair and held him; that seemed to help, but when the entrees arrived and she put him down again so she could eat, he took up where he'd left off, with a ten-decibel howl that was beginning to draw glares from nearby diners. Debra's hand froze in midair, fork suspended over her plate; she shut her eyes with a look I had come to know well the last two weeks. She'd been shouldering the whole burden of Jeffrey, doubtless trying to ease my own stress in this period of "recuperation," but I obviously couldn't let things go on like this much longer.

"Here," I found myself saying, "let me take him." Debra looked relieved as I rose, reached down, and picked up the squalling infant. I hoped my face didn't betray the utter terror I was feeling. What I knew about babies couldn't be seen under an electron microscope; what in

God's name did I think I was doing? "Ssshh, ssshh, it's okay, it's all right," I said, holding him against me, hoping I was holding him correctly, living in terror that I might, God forbid, drop him. I kept murmuring soothing, fatherly sounds, to no discernible effect. Was there some trick to this I didn't know about, some secret paternal knowledge I had never been privy to?

I stroked his back, as gently and soothingly as I could manage. "Ssshh, ssshh," I kept repeating, but he was having none of it; he just kept wailing away. I took him into the lobby, away from the stares of diners. His head perched on my shoulder, I walked him back and forth, his scream just inches from my left ear... and out of nowhere a nasty thought leapt to mind, nasty and chilling: *What if he knew?* What if he could tell that the man holding him, rocking him, frantically trying to soothe him, *wasn't his father?*

Whole new vistas of fear and insecurity opened up before me. I was so preoccupied with them that I didn't notice at first that his bottom was wet. Perfect. *Now* what did I do? I couldn't very well go back to Debra and say, Gee, honey, your son needs changing; but my only nodding acquaintance with diapers had been a bit part in a Pampers commercial, and I hadn't even been the one changing the baby.

Steeling myself to the inevitable, I returned to our table, catching a fleeting, wistful glimpse of my dinner, still a long ways in my future. "Deb?" I said, as casually as I could manage. "Where's his diaper bag?"

She handed me a gray canvas affair, looped it over my free shoulder, and I was off to the men's room with the still very vocal Jeffrey. Inside I debated the best place to set him down, finally opting for a bed of paper towels arranged on the counter between washbasins. I gave the diaper he was wearing a thorough study, then cautiously undid the little strips of tape at top and sides; and to my great and eternal relief the diaper came undone, reverting to its disassembled hourglass shape.

I picked Jeffrey up, slid the diaper out from under him—and, as I did, discovered that when changing babies of Jeffrey's gender, you should always, *always* cover their little penises with something—anything—in between stripping off the old diaper and slipping on the new. Because if you don't, make no mistake, those tiny wangers can deliver quite a payload. Hydrostatic pressure, I believe it's called.

So after I'd toweled off the front of my shirt—this time draping a dry corner of the used diaper over Jeffrey's privates—I cleaned him up with a baby wipe, then grabbed a fresh Pamper and made my best guess at what went where. I figured the skinny center of the hourglass must be the crotch, and when I raised one end of the hourglass up to his stomach, lo and behold, it matched up with the other half in back. I taped the two sections together, and wonder of wonders, there he was, an actual diapered infant, assembled by my own hand. I was feeling pretty pleased with myself, too—heck, this fatherhood stuff was a snap—at least until a glance in the mirror reminded me of the large wet spot on the front of my shirt. Far from resembling either Robert Young or Hugh Beaumont, I looked like the class geek.

Thank God no one entered the men's room those next few minutes; if they had, they would have thrilled to the sight of a grown man, stripped to the waist, shouldering a quiescent child with his left hand while holding a wet shirt up to the hand drier with the other.

Returning to the table I put Jeffrey back in his high chair, sat down to my sub-zero crabcakes and wilting salad—whereupon Jeffrey immediately began screaming again, loud enough to be heard in Rhode Island. I looked at Debra. Debra looked at me.

"How much do you think we could get for him on the open market?" I asked.

Jeffrey's mood didn't improve much by the time we finished dessert, and by the time we hit the road Debra was afraid he might be coming down with something; so I dropped her and Paige and Jeffrey off at our place, and Mom and I went back to her house for coffee. I walked into the two-story home on Lochmere Street and felt strange, so very strange; I'd spent a week, not so long ago, in a house almost identical to this one, the same dark brown carpet, the same orange recliner and marble coffee table. Yet when I was here, a world away, the house was lifeless and still; and now each piece of furniture, each dish left in the kitchen sink, held a ghost of remembered pain and sadness for me—echoes of another reality, a sadder ending.

"Rick? Did you hear me? Regular or decaf?"

I tried to push all of it from my mind. It was a dream, that's all; just a dream that would grow dimmer over time. "Decaf, thanks." Yes—the gray-haired woman standing in the doorway, *she* was alive, *she* was real, and she was the only thing that mattered, nothing else.

But the house, and everything in it, held ghosts for her, too, I discovered. She brought out the coffee and we sat in the living room, me on the couch, she in her recliner, her ever-present crossword puzzle books on the end table beside her. She sipped her coffee and looked past me, at the hole in the couch made by my father's cigar years before.

"Sometimes," she said, as though we were picking up a conversation already started, "I wake up and I forget he's gone. Just for a moment, you know, but I open my eyes and I think, I've got to make breakfast for Bert; and then I remember. And it's terrible. Every morning, it's like losing him, all over again."

I started, having heard the very same words, the very same hurt and confusion in her voice, before. And I said, "I know. I miss him, too," knowing *I'd* said that before, feeling almost as though I were on stage, second night, picking up my cues...

"He'd lie on that couch and sleep, and sometimes we'd hardly speak a word to each other all day; but I knew he was there. After forty years," she said, "you take things for granted, you don't talk or show affection the way you did when you were young. But when he was in the hospital—" She continued to look past me, as though seeing him, even as I did, in the intensive-care ward before his surgery; he must have been frightened beyond measure but he never showed it, a man who all his life had made her crazy with his imagined illnesses, but when the real thing came he faced up to it, he found strength and calm. "I kissed him, and I said, 'I love you, Bert,' and he said, 'I love you, hon.' And that was the last thing he ever said to me."

She was crying now, and so was I. I held her, tried to

comfort her as I'd tried once before, elsewhere, elsewhen. "It's okay, Mom," I said, desperate for her to believe that. "I'm here, I'll take care of you ..."

"I know you will," she said. "You're a good son."

No, I thought. Not yet.

We cried for several more minutes, then separated. I looked at her, laid my hand on her shoulder.

"You going to be okay?" I asked.

She gave me a weary smile. "What choice do I have?"

I smiled back. "That's right," I said. "Like it or not, we go on." I paused a moment, then: "Hey. I tell you what. We'll drive into Boston next weekend ... maybe see a show, do dinner at Quincy Market..."

"Oh, I hate Boston," she was quick to say. "It's so big, and so noisy—"

Compared to New York it was a sleepy little hamlet, but I'd forgotten my mother's long-standing aversion to large cities. "Okay, well, we'll come up with something. You gotta learn to be more adventurous, Mom, you know?"

"I suppose," she said, not too convincingly.

I left her a little before ten, and as I walked down the path to the street, I turned back and looked at the small house, at the warm light behind drawn shades, so different from the last time I'd seen it. As I stood there the living room light suddenly winked off, like a candle in a jack-o'-lantern abruptly snuffed out by an errant wind, and I felt a chill, a sudden urge to run back and make sure she was all right; but then the upstairs lights snapped on, I saw her figure move behind rustling drapes, and I smiled. Back in my car, letting the engine idle to take the chill off me and the Volvo, I began thinking of the places we could take her, the things we would do together, the ways I might find to make her life less lonely. This time I was going to do right by her; this time, I really would be a good son.

CHAPTER EIGHT

RICK

AT RISE: It's nine a.m. in Steven Lindstrom's luxurious duplex on the East Side; it's impressively done up in Fifties decor, pastels and plastic, two floors connected by a brass spiral staircase. There's a jukebox on the second level, neon diner signs on the walls, and living room furniture straight out of The Jetsons. Downstage Right is a state-of-the-art computer and printer; Downstage Left, a large sprawling couch, and underneath a pile of blankets and a fan of computer paper, something seems to be alive.

Upstage Right a key turns in the lock of the apartment door, and BETH enters. She's about twenty-eight, a bit over-weight but smart and funny; she stands in the doorway, sighing familiarly at the paper and clothes and empty Pepsi cans strewn randomly about.

BETH. Steven! Steven, you up? *(No answer. She flips on the light; sighs.)* I'm not going into the bedroom again, Steven. You're not paying me enough; nurses at Ver-dun suffered less. You're going to have to come out. *(A long beat as no one replies; uncertainly:)* Hey. You even in there? *(She pauses, wondering what to do, then spots on a*

*table the sort of square rubber item people use to disarm
auto alarms. She picks it up, presses it—and immediately
there's a shrieking siren of beeps from the couch. The blankets, the papers, all of it spouts into the air as STEVEN
LINDSTROM, fully clothed, bolts upright in "bed.")*

STEVEN. Jesus! What the hell is—

BETH. *(Approaching, she flips the beeper into Steven's
lap.)* I don't know why you even have one of these.
What do you need a key ring for, much less a key ring
locator? You never go anywhere.

STEVEN. *(Groggily coming awake)* That's not true.
There's the key to the mailbox; I go down to the lobby
every day to pick up the mail.

BETH. You go down to the lobby on Saturdays, when I'm
not here. Sometimes you bribe the doorman to get it for
you. *(Off his look of surprise at being found out)* He shared
his bottle of Dom Perignon with me, one day after work.
How many Saturdays does that buy off? Thirty? Forty?

STEVEN. *(Sheepish)* Depends on the vintage.

BETH. *(Automatically she starts picking up the reams of
computer paper.)* So what are you doing sleeping out
here, anyway?

STEVEN. *(Through the following he goes Upstage Left to
the small kitchenette, starting up a coffeemaker, taking out
cups, sugar, etc.)* Well, uh, there's just a few, ah, bugs, in
the bedroom.

BETH. *(Disbelieving; disgusted)* "A few bugs"? Good
God. Is this some new aberration? First you don't leave

the apartment for three years, now you don't leave the living room? *(She crosses Downstage to the entrance of the unseen bedroom, starts to open the door.)* What are we working toward here—permanent residence in the upstairs bathroom? Or maybe that's too spacious for you? "A few bugs"—Jesus! *(She enters the bedroom, the door swinging shut behind her.)* Where's the light switch?

STEVEN. *(Nervously)* I wouldn't do that if I were—

There is a high, blood-curdling shriek from the bedroom. Beth emerges like a cruise missile, slamming the door behind her, bracing her back against it as though against some imminent escape from inside, breathing raggedly, face white.

STEVEN. *(Shrugs as he starts pouring coffee for two)* Like I said. Just a few roaches.

BETH. A few—? Steven, this is not archie and mehitabel, this is the Naked Jungle! Have you at least had an exterminator take a look at this?

STEVEN. *(Calmly brings her a cup of coffee)* Last week. I think he used, like, Agent Orange, but I'm going to have to wait a few generations for the insect leukemia to crop up. Coffeemate okay? I'm out of cream.

BETH. That's all? He sprayed toxic chemicals under your box frame and that's all he can do?

STEVEN. *(Uncomfortable)* Well, he did suggest—how did he put it—"bombing" it. They put this thing, this canister, in your apartment—set a timer, and let the gasses do their job for, oh, twenty-four hours. *(A beat)* Of course, you have to leave the apartment for a day.

BETH. *(Flatly)* And you said no.

STEVEN. I'm just not comfortable with the concept of setting off neutron bombs in my living room.

At that, something snaps in Beth; her patience is at an end. She starts backing away, her voice starting out cool and controlled but progressively becoming more hysterical as she reaches the exit.

BETH. Okay. That's it. I can't take this one minute more. You have a problem here, Steven, a serious problem, and I'm not talking about the Hal Roach Studios in the other room, I'm talking about you, you and this damned apartment!

STEVEN. Beth, c'mon, you're making too big a deal of this. I could leave here anytime, anytime I really wanted.

BETH. Could you? *(She snaps up her purse, crosses Upstage to the apartment entrance, stands there a beat.)* Then follow me out. Follow me down the goddamn street. Because it's the only way I'll keep working for you, Steven. *(She hesitates, then pulls open the door and hurries out, leaving the door ajar.)*

STEVEN. Beth! *(He rushes after . . . only to stop, precipitously, at the doorframe. He cranes his neck, calling out down the hall.)* Beth! Beth, please! *(He wavers there in the doorway, puts both hands to either side of the frame, as though he might somehow propel himself through. He starts to, starts to make a move . . . then falls back. Falls back and, very slowly, very sadly, shuts the door behind him.)*

End of Scene One.

"So have you read the play?" Joel asked, maybe an hour after the agency messenger had dropped off the playscript. Well, of course, the moment the door closed I'd ripped open the package and begun devouring the play—but would Richard have been so excited about a prospective job? I hedged a bit and allowed, "Yeah, most of it."

"What do you think?"

"Well, it's not every day you run across a romantic comedy about agoraphobia," I laughed. "But he's a great character." And he was. A successful investment counselor, attractive and intelligent, Steven Lindstrom seemed to have the ideal life. He worked at home, made his own hours; consulted with clients by phone, did all his work on his laptop, then sent it to corporate headquarters by modem. He had a fabulous apartment, great for entertaining; a business manager who paid all his bills, wrote all his checks, took care of all the day-to-day hassles of dealing with AT&T, Con Ed, Bank of America, and the IRS; a full-time assistant to run errands, cable TV delivering a hundred and forty-three channels, and subscriptions to the *New York Times, The New Yorker, Time, Newsweek,* and *The Wall Street Journal,* all of which he read from cover to cover to keep up on the latest issues. He was terrific at what he did, much sought after in his field, and derived a substantial living from it. There was just this one little problem: he hadn't left his apartment in nearly three years.

"The thing that's so meaty about the part," I said, "is this dry, witty exterior, you know, these one-liners that deflect attention from his fear, his absolute terror of leaving the house—those two levels, there, to work with—"

"Yeah," Joel agreed, "and the love story with the new

assistant, and her trying to draw him out of his shell... so what do you think, you want to go for it?"

"Hell, yes," I said. "When do I audition?"

There was a long, awkward silence at the other end of the line.

"Audition?" Joel sounded like a father whose child had just called him *Mama*. "It's off-off-Broadway, man. They're lucky to be getting you, at these prices—seven-fifty a week, but I think I can get them to throw in another two-fifty, three hundred for expenses. And of course you've got the standard out clause in case something better turns up, one week's notice—"

Feeling like an idiot, all I could do was ignore my gaffe and hurry on to other subjects: When did rehearsals start? Any idea of who the other actors were? Joel didn't know, said he'd get back to me as soon as he set the deal, and, hanging up, I castigated myself for my naivete. The idea of not auditioning for a role—the concept that actors might reach a certain level of respect and notoriety where offers were simply made—had never entered my mind. Well, all right, I knew they might not have brought Tom Cruise in to read, but I didn't think Richard had achieved that kind of status. Once again, my envy for him clouded what should have been an ecstatic moment. I'd landed my first part in my first New York production, but it wasn't as though I'd won it myself—I was still coasting on Richard's reputation.

Well, to hell with Richard. To hell with *how* I got the part—what was important was what I was going to *do* with the part, everything I always knew I could do, those long arid years in New Hampshire. I was going to prove to everyone—prove to myself—that I did have the right stuff.

And I wasn't going to deny myself the indulgence of a celebration. I threw on my topcoat and hurried out of the building, turning left on Riverside Drive toward 72nd Street. It was a clear, crisp, blustery evening, and as I turned left onto 72nd I could see flocks of people walking, rushing, laughing into the wind, some scurrying up the long stone steps of the subway station at 72nd and Broadway, others congregated around the newsstand on the small traffic island, newspapers riffling in the breeze like tabloid flags. I watched pedestrians as they dodged taxis running red lights, high-heeled women whose shapely calves would disappear, briefly, in blasts of steam billowing up from beneath manhole covers.

I hurried to join them, as a gust of wind suddenly sent me staggering sideways, taking me by surprise. God, that was what I loved about this city, about this life—every day, to be taken by surprise in some way, small or large, good or ill; so distant, so different from the numbing monotony of Appleton and Nashua. Across Broadway stood the P&G, a small bar frequented by actors living on the Upper West Side; weaving my way through cars at the intersection, I could see inside an actor I knew, one of Richard's friends I'd had lunch with. I hurried inside to greet him, wishing more than anything I could tell him my secret: aching to tell him that tonight I finally belonged here, in this bar, in this city, in his company; that tonight for the first time, I could honestly call myself an actor.

R ehearsals didn't start till the following week, giving me ample time for both preparation and celebration; more of the latter, as it turned out, than the former. Ray

Perelli was throwing a party Friday night. When I'd had lunch with Ray, weeks before, I found him vastly entertaining: a fast-talking Italian boy from the South Bronx, now a successful stage and occasional film director. He'd been dressed trendily but casually, his leather jacket just weather-worn enough not to seem as though he'd snapped it up off the rack at Bally's, a black fisherman's cap perched on his head throughout lunch. He seemed to know everybody in the business and delighted in recounting—in his gravelly Bronx voice—their virtues and shortcomings. "Walking nightmare," was how he described one of his leading ladies. "She takes meds for back pain but they make her sleepy, so she drinks about thirty cappuccinos a day to compensate. A little high-strung." Or this on a well-respected film and stage actor: "Worries every goddamn little line into the ground. 'Is this really what he means here?' 'What's the subtext to this joke?' There *is* no subtext, you'd tell him, it's just a joke. He wouldn't believe you. Took us an hour and a half to get through the first three pages." Or the anxious, first-time backer of a comedy whom he had to keep reassuring, "Look: one hundred percent of the audience doesn't have to get one hundred percent of the jokes; if eighty percent gets them all, and the remaining twenty percent gets maybe half, you're doing fine. He'd made his money in retail sales, so numbers he understood; I found myself making graphs, curves, fucking *flow*charts for him."

In short, Ray was an earthy, show-biz maven, and I looked forward to his party without the slightest apprehension. I figured, what, maybe ten or twenty people, and out of that I might have met maybe half a dozen...piece of cake, right?

Yes, well, it was more like an intimate gathering of about two hundred of Ray's nearest and dearest friends. I knew that Ray and his girlfriend, an English actress named Melissa Cullin, had an address on Central Park West; this should have told me something, but I was still too new to this town to peg geography with per-capita income. I walked into a penthouse condominium that made Richard's look like a locker at the Port Authority: sweeping views of Central Park and the Pond, and beyond that the impressive panorama of Fifth Avenue, glass and steel towering above a field of green. The high-ceilinged, three-level home was decorated in bright, stylish contemporary design; a sprawling couch overflowing with guests looked out at the fabulous view, while behind it, that same view was reflected in a mirrored wall.

Melissa greeted me at the door; thank God I'd run across a picture of her in a *Theatre World* volume and connected it to the Melissa whom Ray was always talking about. "Richard. Hi." She pecked me on the cheek, taking my coat as she led me inside. "Congratulations on getting—what is it called? *This Way Out*? I hear it's a fabulous piece."

I smiled. "Good news travels fast."

She laughed. "Only slightly less so than bad news." She pointed to the dining area, largely obscured by a horde of hungry guests. "Now past that human bulwark over there, as usual, is the buffet. The queue moves about as quickly as the Long Island Expressway, but it does move, and people *have* been rumored to have been fed, so I'd take a stab at it if I were you. Also—" She looked at me hesitantly for a moment, as though about to say something, then thought better of it and shook her head.

"Sorry. Lost my train of thought for a moment. Buffet. Diners. Bar. Yes, we've lost the bar, it seems to have vanished into the crowd, but it was last seen not far from there." Before she could point, the doorbell rang again; she turned round, called out, "Ray? Ray, can you get that, please?" But her call was swallowed up by the dull roar of conversation. "Oh God," she said, "we've lost Ray, too. I'd better take that. Good to see you, Richard." She bussed me again on the cheek, then left me to my own devices.

I took my place in the buffet line, doing my best not to look the Country Mouse as I stole glances at the opulent, showy penthouse. In contrast to Richard's co-op, where all industry-related items were discreetly tucked away, here they took center stage: the walls were festooned with posters from shows Ray had directed or Melissa had starred in; with blowups of *Playbill*s from various productions; there was even a Richard Bernstein painting of Melissa out of *Interview* magazine dominating one entire wall of the living room. There were limited editions or originals by Meekyung Jang and Rudy Fernandez—neither of whom I would have recognized had it not been for Debra's art catalogs—and, in one corner, a sleek, polished Steinway, its lid open in anticipation of someone's playing it that night; but for now, muted and comfortable in the background, a stereo system that seemed to have speakers everywhere was playing *Michael Feinstein Sings Irving Berlin*.

Ahead of me in the buffet line someone who worked for Joseph Papp was talking turkey, over Swedish meatballs, with someone from the Gersh Agency. I couldn't help myself. I felt giddy, enchanted; it was everything I had always dreamed a classy, New York showbiz party to be.

Even better, after I'd worked my way through the buffet and was wandering, plate in hand, through the party, were the people—actors and actresses I'd seen only in films or television—who came up to say hello, to ask me how I was doing. Successfully resisting the urge to ask for their autographs on my shirt cuffs, I mentioned, as nonchalantly as possible, the new play, then asked them what they were up to... making shop talk with people who, just weeks before, had been distant icons.

At one point a short, curly-haired man in an impeccably cut gray suit came up to me, shaking my hand as vigorously as I pretended to know who the hell he was. "Richard," he said, "nice to see you. Congratulations on the new play. I understand the playwright is a real comer."

"So I hear," I said, hearing it, in fact, for the first time.

"Too bad about *Brigadoon*. Maybe just a bit too starry-eyed and old-fashioned for today's audiences, but a good try." He looked momentarily distressed, as though averse to share some troubling thought with me. "In all honesty, Richard, you deserve better vehicles, better showcases for your ability. Are you"—and here he affected an even more troubled air—"are you really satisfied with your current representation?"

I think I knew what was going on now, but since I still didn't know who I was talking to, there seemed only one sensible answer. "Yes," I said. "I'm quite satisfied with Joel." Two things happened to his face, then: a brief wrinkle of disappointment, followed by a bright, fake heartiness. "Well, fine," he said, shaking my hand again, and I could tell the conversation was now over. "If you ever change your mind, please remember, I've always been a fan. I think I could move you to another plateau entirely, Richard, I honestly do. Whenever you're ready." And he melted back into the crowd from whence he came, leaving me—I admit it—jazzed as hell. Son of a bitch—I'd just been hustled! And it felt *wonderful.*

"Richard?" Ray was suddenly standing next to me. "What the hell were you doing talking with that creep Van deMeer? Last time I saw you together I thought you were going to deck him."

Well, at least now I knew his name. "Oh, hell," I said, trying to cover my gaffe as best I could, "no use bloodying up your carpet, right? What is it they say—living well is the best revenge?"

"Well, I'm heartened by this sudden wellspring of tolerance, I really am, considering who's walking in the door just now." Off my blank look he said, "Melissa didn't—?" He sighed heavily. "Melissa wimped out. She was supposed to tell you about—oh, crap, take a look."

I followed his gaze to the entrance. There was a knot of people gathered at the open door, greeting the latest arrival, and as one or two of them shifted position I was able to get a clear look at her. She was a tall woman, probably as tall as I, with shoulder-length, ash-blonde hair; she was slim, but as she slipped off her wrap I could see her shoulders were quite wide, her skin smooth and tanned, and maybe because of those wonderful, sexy shoulders she seemed to tower over even the tallest man around her. But after her stature, your gaze was drawn to her face—not a conventionally beautiful face by any means but a compelling one, the angularity of her features softened by the frame of light blonde hair.

And when she opened her mouth to laugh, it was a full, rich, hearty laugh, no holding back; almost—to risk

sounding sexist—a masculine laugh, in that there was no
feminine coyness about it. I had no idea who she was,
though she did look familiar, but even on a quick glance
I could say without hesitation that she was one of the most
beautiful women I had ever seen.

Ray was obviously trying to interpret my stare. "She's
just come in from the Coast, man, just back in town after
they canceled her series, and hell, we couldn't *not* invite
her, could we?" I looked at him, not having the vaguest
idea what he was talking about... and then something
registered. Series? Of course—that new sitcom on CBS,
what was it called? And she was the co-star, she was—

I suddenly felt myself grow short of breath.

Catlin McCandless. She was Catlin McCandless, and
she was Richard's ex-wife.

"There's no bad blood between you two, is there?" Ray
asked nervously.

I looked back at her. She was moving away from the
door now, threading her way through the crowd, all of
whom seemed to know her and offered hellos or hugs,
genuine or affected.

"Not that I know of," I said truthfully. I watched as she
turned, suddenly, and spotted me; her eyes brightened,
not with malice, that was clear, but with surprise and
pleasure. She broke into a smile and started making her
way through the crowd toward me. I should have been
terrified, should have been scared shitless; but instead I
felt only a rush of excitement and anticipation, and when
she came up and gave me a friendly hug, any thought of
fear dissipated in the warmth of her arms.

"Richard!" She pecked me on the cheek; we separated,
and when she looked at me I could see the laugh-lines

around her eyes, lines she didn't bother to conceal. "My God, look at you. You're still an E ticket, and there are days I have to spend two hours each morning working my way up to a D." She had the last soft traces of a Georgia accent, cadence mostly; I found it indescribably appealing.

"Catlin," I said, for some reason feeling immediately comfortable with her, "don't give me that crap. You're an all-day admission, and you know it."

She laughed, that full, hearty laugh I'd heard only from a distance; up close it was even better. "You are sweet as ever. Why'd I ever let you go in the first place?"

Now I was starting to feel less comfortable. Richard had told me something of Catlin, I'd read a little about her in his journals, but for some reason he'd committed less about her to paper than he had about Joanne, or Libby, or even Lana.

I quickly changed the subject. "I was, ah, sorry to hear about your series."

She waved it away with a short frown, taking a silver cigarette case from her handbag. "Don't be. The first thirteen were fun, I mean the writing was really sharp, we were all up for it—then when the numbers slipped the network did what it does best, try to fix something that isn't broke. By the end of the season we were all down on our knees, praying for cancellation. Would you hold this?" I held her purse as she lit a cigarette, taking a deep pull on it and exhaling a plume of smoke. She took back the purse. "What," she said, "no lectures?"

"Pardon me?"

"In L.A. you get used to these surly looks from non-smokers, or righteous speeches along the lines of, 'Don't you know you're killing yourself?' Or, 'What do you think your lungs look like right now?'" She took another drag on the cigarette, blew out smoke, and grinned. "I used to quote Beth Henley's line from *Crimes of the Heart:* 'That's what I like about it,' I'd say. 'Taking a drag off Death. Gives me a sense of controlling my own destiny. What power! What exhilaration!'"

By now a small crowd had clustered around us, asking Catlin about her series, about California, about her current plans. I felt relieved in one way—part of me anxious about being alone with her, screwing up some detail of her and Richard's shared history—while another part of me was pissed about *not* being alone with her, about having to share her with all these others, and why didn't they all just dry up and blow out of here, anyway?

Someone mentioned the duck pâté being served, triggering a recollection from Catlin. "We had ducks when I was five, six years old," she said. "Ducklings—nothing cuter than a soft, tiny little duckling. And no bigger nuisance than a full-grown, hungry duck waddling around the yard, quacking at all hours of the day and night. And we had *four* of 'em.

"So before the ducklings got too old, my folks told me and my brothers we had to get rid of 'em . . . but every time we'd set 'em loose at Nunley Pond, they'd march right back to our house. Well, hell, what were we gonna do? If we didn't get rid of them, Daddy would've, and they were *our* ducks—our responsibility.

"We gave it a lot of thought, trying to come up with the quickest way to do it—and finally, we just took the ducklings out back, buried 'em up to their necks in dirt in the backyard, and then, real fast, we ran the lawn mower over 'em, and that was that."

There was stunned silence for what seemed miles around. Several ashen faces; several horrified looks. Catlin took in this sudden mix of dumbfoundment and revulsion and added, defensively, "They were just *ducks*, for pity's sake. You grow up on a farm, you get used to that sort of thing. When it's your responsibility to get rid of something, you *do* it. Though admittedly we were kind of interested in seeing how this particular method might work." Confidentially, she added, "I mean, it does get boring, sometimes, out in the sticks, and we *were* only six years old."

Several of the hangers-on abruptly decided to hang somewhere else. Several women looked indignant and huffed off, one man looked rather sick and headed for the nearest bathroom. For my part I looked at Catlin, at the puzzled shrug she seemed to give before lighting up another cigarette, and suddenly felt like Woody Allen in *Manhattan:* who, as a child, had gone to see *Snow White and the Seven Dwarfs*—and had instantly and irreversibly fallen in love with the Wicked Queen.

I knew I should have stayed as far away from her as I could manage; knew I was courting disaster just being around her, when any casual comment, any offhand recollection—"Jesus, Richard, you remember when we were living in that tiny little rat-trap in the Village?"—invited catastrophe. But I couldn't keep my eyes off her, all through Ray and Melissa's party; couldn't stop thinking about her all that night and into the next day. Maybe it was because she was so unlike Debra, so unlike any woman I'd ever known... or maybe it was because I'd never known that many women, really, before marrying Debra and settling down.

You're crazy, I told myself, crazy to even consider this. They were married, for Christ's sake, there's a whole history there you have no knowledge of. But then I thought of Richard and of how he must be facing much the same problem with Debra—whom I was married to far longer than Richard was to Catlin—and I felt a sudden jab of ego. If Richard could pull it off—I had no idea, actually, if he had, but the attempt was what was important here—then I damn well could try, too. My pride now united with my lust, I found Catlin's number in Richard's address book and, taking a deep breath, called.

"Catlin? Hi. It's Richard."

"Oh. Richard. Hello." She sounded a little fuzzy, though it was well past noon.

"I didn't wake you up, I hope?" I said, suddenly nervous as a teenager asking out the most popular girl in class.

"That's okay," she said, stifling a yawn, "my own fault, should've put on the answer machine before I turned in. Couple of us from the party went dancing over at the Limelight." Her voice sharpened as she came awake. "Good seeing you again last night. You looked different."

I started. "Different? How so?"

"I dunno—just different."

Before I could panic, I said, "We didn't get much chance to talk, in that crowd . . . I was wondering if you'd like to get together, grab a little dinner?"

She seemed surprised but pleased. "Why, sure. That sounds like fun." It turned out she was free the next night, so we arranged to meet at a Chinese-Cuban restaurant, La Dinastia, near me. *"Chinese-Cuban?"* she whooped. "Are you putting me on?"

"Chinas y criollas. They've been around for ages, but they've become aggressively trendy of late."

"I *am* out of touch," she sighed. "Now that you mention it, I do remember them from before I moved to L.A., but—"

"See? Spend a few years on the Coast and you lose touch with all the latest *in* cuisines."

"This," she said, "I have to see."

I spent most of Saturday and Sunday forcing myself to concentrate on going over the script for *This Way Out,* but somehow the prospects of rehearsals this week weren't nearly as exciting as those of dinner Sunday night. Dressing for the date, it did occur to me just how dangerous all this was—what I was doing; what I was hoping to do—but I felt no panic, only that same thrilling mixture of fear and anticipation, that erotic danger I'd felt first entering New York with its stone leviathans. Flushed with excitement, I walked over to 72nd Street—another breezy April evening—and waited outside the restaurant until Catlin pulled up in a cab.

She was wearing a red suede dress, medium-length skirt with a slit up the side that revealed, as she climbed out of the cab, rounded thighs and long, long legs. This time she kissed me casually on the lips, then turned to the menu posted on the inside of the restaurant window. "My Lord, you weren't kidding, were you? Chinese-Cuban. What will they think of next?" Her eyes narrowed. "Is it mere co*in*cidence," she said suddenly in a sharp, mock-suspicious tone, "that these are two *commu-*

nist countries here? My Daddy would have a conniption fit if he thought his daughter was eating at a commie front." She laughed that deep, throaty laugh again. "Of course, Daddy would have a conniption fit if he thought I was doing half of what I am doing."

Inside, the menu proved to be as entertaining to her as her reading of it was to me. "Oh, this is a *scream*," she said, scanning the items. *"Foo yung con pollo,"* she read. *"Chow mein,"* she said, in a perfect Cantonese accent, *"de vegetales,"* in an equally impeccable Castilian accent. *"Sopa wonton!"* she laughed, breaking up into a fit of the giggles. I watched, enchanted and amazed; I'd never met anyone who could be so much fun just reading a damn menu. When the waiter came she asked him if she could have her wontons with salsa instead of sweet-and-sour sauce. He didn't get the joke, which only amused Catlin all the more.

It was like that throughout dinner—I asked Catlin about Hollywood, about living in California, and I got a wealth of funny, frequently bawdy stories about horny producers, impotent directors, temperamental actors, and *nouvelle cuisine* restaurants that served something called a fiddlehead fern. Despite which, she rather liked Los Angeles, even as she rather liked New York; growing up in the backwaters of the South seemed to have given her an appreciation for anything different, and a tolerance for it so long as it was amusing.

I laughed more in that one evening than I think I had in the previous year back in New Hampshire. The only thing that marred my pleasure was Catlin's occasional reference to "our" mutual past: to some place we'd been to together, some person we'd known. I faked it as best I

could, but I could see it was going to be a problem and I
would have to find some way to deal with it if I was going
to continue with this pursuit—and I did intend to continue it, there was no question of that.

We talked and ate for two and a half hours, and after
dinner I invited her over to my place for a nightcap. She
looked startled for a moment, but that inevitable good humor took over: "You still remember how to fix my Lynch-
burg Lightning?"

This I knew I couldn't fake. "I think I'm going to need
a refresher course."

At the D'Agostino's market we picked up a bewildering
array of ingredients; back in my townhouse, I watched with
awe and apprehension as she combined them. Half a jig-
ger of lemon, half a teaspoon of sugar, three and a half
jiggers of Jack Daniel's, a splash of lemon bitters, and—
most *outré* of all—three jiggers of Dr. Pepper. I tried to
look as though I'd seen her do this before, but in truth I
felt a bit like a worried kid watching his big sister playing
with his chemistry set, about to cheerily offer him a bea-
ker of God knew what.

When she'd finished she handed me my drink, put
hers momentarily aside, then casually took from her purse
what looked like a small, silver-plated snuff tin—though
when she popped open the lid I knew immediately that
the white powder inside was definitely not a tobacco
product. She then took out a small mirror and proceeded,
with the help of a razor blade, to cut herself a line of cocaine. I tried to cover up my surprise as best I could; this
was not something you ran across every day in small vil-
lages in New Hampshire.

She looked up; I hoped I hadn't betrayed any of my small-town naivete. "You don't mind?" she asked, a certain pointedness to her tone I didn't understand.

I shrugged, trying to be cool. "No. Why should I?"

She looked—I don't know; impressed?—and took out a small coke straw. "I take it you still don't indulge?"

I took a swallow of my drink; the whiskey and the Dr. Pepper actually complemented one another quite well, the sweet and the sour. About ten seconds later, however, I became convinced that Catlin had added some liquid nitrogen to the mix when I wasn't looking. "This," I said, managing somehow to avoid croaking out the words, "will do me fine."

"If it's not potent enough," she said with a malicious grin, "I can add another half-jigger of J.D."

"I'm fine," I said. I did feel fine, too. I wasn't quite sure what country I was in at the moment, but I felt extremely fine.

After she'd done her cocaine and I'd finished my drink, we stood close by the window overlooking the Hudson, a string of lights making its way back and forth across the George Washington Bridge, soft and distant glows coming from the small towns along the New Jersey coast. I turned to show her something, running my hand gently along her bare arm, feeling how toned but soft her skin was, smelling her hair as it brushed across my shoulder.

"Richard?" She wasn't that much shorter than I, less than an inch, so she didn't have to look up at me—she could look me straight in the eyes. I liked that, somehow, though I didn't care as much for the tone of her voice, amused yet apprehensive. "You wouldn't by any chance be making a move on me here, now would you?"

I ran a finger up the tan curve of her neck. "What if I were?"

She considered that for a long moment.

"That depends," she said, reflectively, "on whether we're looking at just a friendly roll in the hay, or–?"

She trailed off. I shrugged. "Good question," I said. "One for which I don't have an answer, just yet."

"Oh, Lord," she said. Before she could turn away I leaned in, took her gently by the shoulders, drew her to me and kissed her, long and hard. She hesitated after the first time, drew back, and repeated, "Oh Lord, here we go, here we go," but when I leaned in again she was coming forward as eagerly as I. Our mouths locked, and I was surprised and delighted by the ferocity of this second kiss; her tongue probed hungrily inside my mouth, as our faces tilted her teeth nicked my tongue but neither she nor I seemed to care. Kissing her was nothing like kissing Debra–no gentle union but rather a fierce competition to see which one of us could grab the most pleasure, which one could devour the other the quickest. And that was what the entire night was like–no sweet, tender lovemaking, just raw, impolite fucking. Not for Catlin a loving caress of her nipple with my tongue, not when I could graze the areola with my teeth, her body shuddering between pain and pleasure. I learned quickly to bite, not to suck, to clutch, not to embrace–to take, rather than invite.

We competed for the pleasures of each other's bodies in a fiercer kind of sex than I had ever known, all my aggressions finally finding a proper release; we screwed until we could barely move, hours later lying limp and drained on sheets soaked with sweat, both of us too exhausted to get up and change them. Catlin did find the energy, though, to recover her pack of Salems from the living room; she leaned back in bed, lit a cigarette, took a deep pull, and let it out with what sounded like a sigh. "Oh, Lord, Richard," she said. "Are we startin' up again, or what?"

"Jump-starting would be more like it," I noted.

"This is crazed, Richard, truly crazed; you know that?"

"That seemed to be one of the attractions, a little while ago," I said with a grin.

"Oh, yeah. It always is." She blew a plume of smoke to the ceiling. "Richard, just what in hell are we thinking of? I mean, it's not exactly like the first take turned out so hot; we really want to try a second one?"

"Yeah," I said, dead serious now. "I do."

She considered a moment.

"So do I," she said miserably. "Goddamn it." She paused, thinking it over, trying to talk herself out of it: "Richard, c'mon! You remember how it ended up last time? You remember that weekend in Bermuda, the week *after* the weekend in Bermuda, the taxi ride down to the Village—"

"No," I said suddenly. "I don't remember."

She stopped, looked at me. "Of *course* you remember, how the hell could you forg—"

"Cat," I interrupted, "can't we just pretend we never printed the first take?"

She blinked—not quite certain, I suppose, whether I was making a joke—and in her hesitation I plunged ahead. "Catlin, I'm serious. If we keep dredging up all the mistakes we made the first time around, we'll spend all our time arguing over who was right and who was wrong, and who was crazy and who was a pisshead, and, shit, pretty soon we won't have any emotional energy left for new fights on new subjects!"

She cracked a smile at that. I pressed the momentary advantage. "I want to try again, Cat. I think you do, too. But we won't be able to with the ghosts of who we were banging away in the closet, fighting long-settled fights over long-forgotten slights. I mean, hell, we were both a lot younger then, you know?"

She eyed me cautiously. "Not all that much younger, kimosabe."

"Look. You said yourself I seemed—different. Right?" I tried to sound casual, but inside I was terrified she might somehow intuit just how true that was.

She regarded me carefully, smoking her cigarette, squinting a little as though at a photograph not seen in many years, searching for some tiny detail that seemed out of place or odd. After what seemed like months she frowned, stubbing out her cigarette in the ashtray in her lap. "Maybe you are," she said at length. "And *if* you are—I can't fucking believe that we're even considering this, but—Richard, everything's got to be different. No righteous crap, no lifestyle lectures, no trying to change me, 'cause I *like* me, just the way I am, you understand?"

"I like you exactly the way you are," I said, moving to kiss her. I massaged her neck, firmly, strongly, the way she liked. "Maybe I was just too young to appreciate you before." We kissed again, and now I could feel her mounting excitement, as well; she wrapped her arms around me, her sharp fingernails running along my spine, teasing me to a hot fervor. "No talk about the past," I whispered, and I could feel her nodding, her hair brushing against my cheek. "Those are *my* terms. If you bring up anything from the first time around, I'll pretend I don't know what the hell you're talking about; I'll look baffled and blank and I won't even acknowledge it. You understand?"

She agreed, and in agreeing, took part of the enormous weight of Richard's past off me. "A new start," I said, and then we were at it again till the dim hours of the morning, finally falling asleep sometime after four a.m., sleeping in till noon. I slept through four phone calls and a buzz from the doorman—but I don't think I'd slept as soundly, as contentedly, in my life.

The excitement and exhilaration that carried me through the next few days is nearly indescribable. By the time rehearsals began on Tuesday, I was more than ready: I actually walked the forty-odd blocks from my apartment to the rehearsal hall, there was that much energy pounding away inside me. Appetites long denied were being satisfied; and the more I indulged those appetites, the greater they seemed to become. The city helped feed them, too, with its manic intensity, its unquenchable energy; all I needed to pump me up was to hit the streets and plug into the biggest goddamn electrical socket in the world.

The rehearsal hall was in an old industrial office building on the south side of 54th Street; many of the businesses were entertainment-related—costumers, photo labs, answering services—along with a few boutiques and travel bureaus. As I stepped off the ancient elevator onto the eleventh floor, I saw a violin shop directly in front of me; I paused a moment to look in its display window, at the Stradivarius on its pedestal and the tiny bowl of water to humidify the air inside the display case. On the frosted glass of the front door were the words *Jacques Français— Rare Violins*.

The rehearsal hall—one of several down the corridor from the violin shop—was a big room, maybe twenty-five feet by forty-five, with old industrial arched windows looking out at even more ancient buildings across the street, and beneath the windows, old-fashioned radiators painted a pale green. Exposed pipes, not stage rigging, hung suspended from the high ceiling; mirrors lined the east wall, while a brass ballet bar ran the length of the south wall. In one corner stood a battered old Steinway, its black enamel chipped at the edges; in another, a walnut podium not unlike a schoolmaster's lectern. The only other furniture in the room was a dozen or so folding chairs surrounding a long conference table.

The room was already half-full as I hung my topcoat on a coatrack in the corner; at its foot was a pile of those ubiquitous nylon bags actors are forever lugging around with them. At my entrance, people began to cluster round the table and introductions were made. A tall, thin, sandy-haired man in his early forties was the first to step forward, hand outstretched. "Mr. Cochrane. Pleased to meet you. I'm Jonathan Lawlor." Jonathan was the director; he wore a pair of tan jeans, tennis shoes, and an old pullover sweater. A comfortable, unpretentious man. By contrast, the young man at his side was maybe twenty-two, twenty-three—fresh, it seemed, out of college, but not just any college: Harvard, most likely, or Yale. Dark-haired, dark-eyed, he had a preppie wardrobe—chinos, navy blazer, a sweater-vest—and a certain nervous intensity. This was Evan Hazlett, the playwright; his handshake seemed a bit overearnest, even as his smile seemed an anxious one.

Jonathan then introduced me to my fellow cast members— none of whom, luckily, Richard had worked with before:

Mary Sue Elkins, the young, somewhat stout actress who played Beth; David Eisenberg, who played Steven's best friend, Larry; and Julie Crawford, the lanky, freckled redhead playing Steven's free-spirited new assistant-cum-lover, Phoebe. All in all there were about a dozen of us, and after some preliminary chatting we took our places around the conference table, opened our scripts, and prepared for the first run-through.

Even I, with my limited experience, knew that the first reading was basically just a warm-up exercise; no fancy interps, no *outré* line readings, just a shakedown cruise to get all the participants familiar with one another and with the play. So we started, me silent as Beth made her entrance, searching for Steven in the morass of his apartment, until my first line: "Jesus! What the hell is—" And off we went.

The first scene I was a little nervous, a little shaky; after all, this was my first real acting in thirteen years. And as luck would have it, Mary Sue, playing Beth, was a born comedienne; even reading the lines off the top of her head, she was funny as hell. I was lagging behind her in terms of comic effect, but wasn't worried; I figured as the reading went on, the more relaxed and comfortable I'd become with the lines.

But then after Beth's exit there was Larry's scene— Larry, a dour cynic whose deadpan cracks were some of the best in the play. David was no less accomplished in his scene than Mary Sue had been in hers, and now I started losing even more ground as David/Larry walked away with the scene. I redoubled my efforts, and for a while I think I was close to being on a par with David.

And then came Julie—Phoebe—freewheeling, adventurous, everything that frightened, defensive Steven was not—and the ground I'd gained in the last few minutes slipped perilously away from me. Julie, damn her, was wonderful. She had that rare and precious ability to make the lines not sound like lines: the talent to make even the most calculatedly witty line seem extemporaneous. In marked contrast, coming from my mouth, the lines sounded forced, artificial.

I lost my confidence in that moment and never recovered it. For the next two and a half hours I suffered the agony of saying lines I knew were wonderful and hearing them come out sounding flat and rehearsed. I was the star, the center of the play, but as I sat there and listened to Julie, to David, to all of them, I had the sad, sick realization that even the worst actors there—the cameo bits, the one-liners—were light-years better than I. All of them, I knew, had had to read for their parts; none of them had them handed to them, as I had. I was the star, I was the main attraction, and I was a fraud. When the reading ended—when it finally ended—everyone was friendly and enthusiastic, and if they had any surprise at this lame showing from the usually dependable Richard Cochrane they probably chalked it up to a bad night's sleep or the usual first-reading rough edges. Only I knew the truth: that I was an impostor, a sham; that I didn't deserve this part, didn't deserve their respect, didn't even deserve to be here, among them. And worst of all, I knew that eventually—inevitably; barring some kind of miracle—I would be found out.

CHAPTER NINE

RICHARD

Shortly before he was due to pick me up, Finney called to say he was having car trouble and could I swing by his place instead? "Sure, no problem," I said, brightly if not intelligently, because as I hung up it occurred to me I didn't have a clue just where his place *was*–the odds were seriously against his having bought the same cozy Colonial he and Roslyn shared in my world. Careful not to let Debra catch me doing it, I scanned the short list of Finneys in the phone book, stumbling across a familiar address: *Finney, David. 148 Pennacook Road, Apltn.* I blinked, thinking for a moment I'd misread it, but there it was: the same address, three miles outside of town, that I'd visited so many times in my youth; the same rambling, ramshackle house his parents had bought decades ago, intending to fix up but somehow never quite getting around to it. I knew Finney's folks had passed away five years before, but could he really still be living there? In that drafty old barn of a house, ringed by a tumbledown stone fence?

But no; maybe in this world, Finney's parents *had* fixed it up. Maybe Finney, for that matter, had renovated it himself. I put the thought aside. In the living room Debra was skimming a copy of the Christie's auction catalog and I pecked her on the cheek. "That was Finney. His car's on the fritz, he wants me to pick him up."

She smiled knowingly. "Yes, and I understand the sun's going to rise in the east tomorrow, too."

I assumed by her comment that this situation wasn't unique, but since she seemed more bemused than irritated, I kissed her again—this time more lingeringly—and smiled. "I'll take the Volvo. Back by ten at the latest, okay?"

It was a clear, cold April night, a light dusting of snow on the streets, recent enough that only a few tire treads predated mine on my passage through downtown Appleton and up winding old Pennacook Road. Finney lived only a few minutes outside town, but as children the distances had seemed so much greater to us; even now, living here again, I couldn't help but be surprised when someplace I'd remembered as being as remote as Mount Parnassus turned out to be practically next door.

But in some ways Finney's home had always been as remote as Mount Parnassus. Finney's father had been a chemist, underpaid and overworked, employed by Axton-Cross in Manchester, who years before had gotten a wild hair about buying a house in the country, growing his own vegetables, and becoming a gentleman farmer. Except he never did quite develop a knack for it. In back of the house had been animal pens, goats scuttling behind chicken-wire fences, a loud and anxious squawking erupting from the henhouse at anyone's approach. There'd been a good ten acres or so of tomatoes, potatoes, lettuce, corn, and other crops, but if the yield made any difference in the Finneys' standard of living, I never saw it.

Turning into the Finneys'—correction: Finney's—gravel driveway, I half expected to hear the squawk of chickens or the bleating of goats. But as my headlights illuminated the yard, I saw that the animal pens were long since rusted shut, the chicken wire coiled in useless loops, the fields sheeted with winter frost. All that, I suppose, I'd expected; what shocked me was the house itself.

It was the same as the last time I'd laid eyes on it, perhaps fifteen years before. Someone might've slapped on a fresh coat of paint, flat and perfunctory, a few years back, but already that was fading and chipping; the roof, as near as I could tell in the scant light from my car, was badly in need of repairs, and I could even see a few shingles, torn from the eaves by a nasty wind, scattered across the front lawn. The lawn, of course, was blanketed by snow, but the rest of the yard had always been graced by hardy evergreens—white pine, spruce, cedar—now left unattended and untrimmed, their branches sagging like the wattles of elderly men; even the deciduous trees, like the crabapple tree I fondly recalled climbing, were so thick with bare branches I wondered if they would ever return to life, come this spring or any other. Up above, the attic windows—blown out by a hurricane when Finney and I were ten years old—were still, all these years later, boarded up with cheap plywood.

But most bizarrely of all, there in the driveway just ahead of me, shining prettily in the wash of my brights, was a flame-red Jaguar XJ6—sleek, sporty, and pricey, its lines only somewhat diminished by the dent in the passenger side or the dings in the rear bumper. I got out of the Volvo, feeling suddenly rather downscale as I circled the Jag for a moment before heading up the front porch. The boards groaned unhappily as I took the steps, but I made it to the doorbell without incident and rang—half-expecting Lurch from the Addams Family to answer it. *You rang?*

But on the second ring the door swung wide and Finney stood grinning in the doorframe. "Cochrane! I saw you lusting after my car, don't think I didn't. Hell, you're lucky Mister Death's not around anymore, he'd've gunned you down without even stopping. Get your ass in here."

He stepped aside to let me enter, and it took all the control I could muster not to betray my astonishment and dismay at what I saw. I told myself that Rick must've been here dozens, hundreds of times before; but it was all bewilderingly new to me, and I struggled to keep it from showing.

"Hang on—let me get my coat and we'll be on our way, okay?" Finney was up the stairs two at a time, and as I heard him clumping about on the second floor, I wandered about dazedly downstairs. Like the exterior, the interior of the Finney home was distressingly similar to what I remembered: the same overstuffed, copper-and-red-print sofa; the same ersatz-walnut-grain coffee table, particleboard beneath the cheap veneer; the same ornate brass standing lamps, actually quite nice though I couldn't imagine they reflected Finney's tastes, just his parents'. Above the mantel was tacked a blue-and-white varsity pennant, our school colors; on either side of it were a brass soccer trophy Finney had won in our junior year and a lucite plaque naming him MVP on the school football team, the Panthers, senior year.

I wandered into the dining room. In the china hutch, next to the old but elegant dinnerware, were another handful of athletic awards, some dating back to junior high, and a permaplaque of the front page of the *Appleton (H.S.) Sentinel*'s story on the time the Appleton Panthers whipped the Manchester Crusaders, 22 to 7. In the upper left-hand corner was a photo of Number 23, Dave Finney, whooping it up postgame with his fellow Panthers.

Almost twenty years later Finney galloped down the stairs as though warming up for a marathon, and suddenly I wanted badly to get out of this house, as fast and as far as I could manage.

"Ready to roll?" Finney said, slapping me on the back. I was out the door before him and in minutes the Volvo was back on Pennacook, heading toward the intersection with Route 3.

The light snow had virtually all melted and I could take the road a bit faster than I'd anticipated, Finney noting this with a wry smile. "Not bad pickup," he allowed, "for a box on wheels."

His teasing tone told me this sparring was probably of long standing between him and Rick, so I just gave him a lopsided smile and said, "Least mine's working. What's wrong with the Jag?"

Finney shrugged. "Transmission again. The body shop up in Manchester wants an arm and a leg, and that cheap bastard DeLuca won't give me another advance, so the cat's sidelined for a few weeks."

DeLuca? Finney was still working at DeLuca & Sons, the textile plant? Not still as a night watchman, surely? "How are you, uh, getting to work, then?"

He shrugged. "Some say this is why God gave us feet."

"What time do you have to leave to get there on time, anyway?" I asked, hoping my subterfuge was not too evident.

"Five-thirty," he said, "five-forty, to get there by six p.m. If I'm a little late, there's usually someone left from the day shift to cover for me."

Day shift. Of course. He *was* still the night watchman; that was why we were getting together tonight, Fridays and Saturdays had always been his nights off. Fifteen years? Fifteen years and still—

I tried to assimilate all this at the same time I had to fake some semblance of a casual conversation. "Jesus," I said, "are all these maintenance bills on the Jag really worth it, Fin?"

Something like genuine irritation flashed in his bright blue eyes. "Oh Christ, Cochrane, don't get started on that again, okay? It was my goddamn inheritance and I could spend it any way I fucking well pleased. Give me a fucking break."

Inheritance? Good God—that Jag must've cost fifty, sixty grand, easy. I couldn't imagine Finney's parents having amassed a life savings of much more than that. I didn't know what to say, but I had to say something, so I just shrugged it off with a casual, "It's your money"—but Finney's response was no less disconcerting. "That's right," he said with a smirk, adding offhandedly, "Or at least it *was*." He laughed and I managed a strictured smile, but inside I felt a gnawing fear take root, worrying away at the edges of my perfect world. By the time we reached the Manchester bar that Finney had suggested, I was less aware of its noisy, blue-collar ambience than I was of my mounting need for a drink—anything to numb this growing anxiety within me. But at the table, when I told the waitress I'd have a scotch on the rocks, Finney gave me the strangest look: "Hey. Cochrane," he said, laughing a short, uneasy laugh. "Sure you wouldn't rather make that a Bud? Somebody's gotta drive home, y'know."

I looked at him, looked again at the waitress, and found myself asking, "Do you, uh, have Heineken?"

"Whatever you want, hon," she said.

Finney ordered a Jim Beam. "Bring the bottle, hon."

Somebody's gotta drive home.

I was staring blankly into space in the general direction of the waitress as she sashayed to the bar; Finney took my stare for something other than it was and said, "'Whatever you want, hon.'" A pause, then: "What *do* you want, Rickie?"

I looked up. "What?"

"Nothing," he said. "Debra pissed at you for going out with me tonight?"

Hoping to sound merely disingenuous I asked, "Why should she be?"

Finney laughed. "I don't know. Maybe she thinks I'm a bad influence on you." Our drinks arrived, I took a swallow of the beer but would much rather have had the scotch. No sooner had Finney downed half his drink than I looked up to find him gazing across the room at someone— his arm shot up, and that big familiar grin lit up his weather-beaten face. "Hey! Sherry! How's it going?"

I followed his gaze: a woman at the bar, mid-twenties, with dark hair and prodigious breasts, suddenly smiled and waved back. "Finney! Hi!" By the time I turned back, Finney was already rising, drink in hand, nudging me with one elbow. "Cochrane, c'mon," he said. "Lemme introduce you to someone."

I didn't have much choice but to follow him across the packed room to the bar. He and Sherry kissed hello with a bit more than casual affection. "Good to see you," she gushed, adding, just a little too earnestly, "You know, you are the *last* person I expected to run into tonight. Hallie, do you know Dave Finney?"

The woman seated to her right was also in her twenties, red-haired, freckled, and had the look of someone who is about to be slightly embarrassed. Finney introduced me to Sherry, Sherry introduced me to Hallie, even as Finney was motioning the bartender to freshen the women's daiquiris; then he sat down beside Sherry, who had casually reseated herself so there was an empty stool between her and Hallie.

The whole thing smacked of setup, but what could I do? I sat down next to Hallie. Sometime in the last two minutes Finney had inhaled the rest of his Beam, so he ordered another for himself and a second Heineken for me, though I'd barely touched my first.

Hallie and I began chatting, and I managed to carry on a pleasant enough conversation with her—nice lady, actually, a computer programmer with M-Tek—despite the fact that inside I was near panic. Good God, what had I gotten myself into here? Was this SOP for Rick and Finney, catting around in bars, Finney pimping for Rick? I hated the thought that Rick might have been cheating on Debra, hated it because if he had the potential to be an adulterer, then so did I. I felt dirty, dishonest, unfaithful, because like it or not the seed of any and everything Rick had ever done lived in me, as well.

I couldn't let that make me crazy. I couldn't dwell on Rick's flaws, real or imagined, and then worry if and when they would flower, wickedly, in me. All I could do was take charge of now, of the moment, as I had taken charge of the life Rick had left to me. It was too early in the evening to invent a reason to go home, but I came up with the next best thing: glancing at my watch, I stood and announced, pointedly, "'Scuse me a minute—my son's got a fever and I promised I'd check in on him. I might have to leave early if his temp hasn't gone down. Be right back." And I was making my way toward the men's room before Finney could utter a word; I could practically feel the anger coming off him in waves. I glimpsed the disappointment in Hallie's eyes, the irritation in Sherry's, and I regretted the necessity of lying to them, but it was either that or an even more unpleasant scene at the end of the evening.

I lingered in the men's room for a plausible interval, and when I returned to the bar the women had vanished into the ether. Finney sat slumped over what appeared to be his third drink of the evening, glaring at my approach.

"Jesus Christ," he said, disgusted, as I slid onto the stool beside his. "You know what you just threw away, man? You have any *idea*?"

"I think so," I said. "I may be stupid but I'm not blind."

"Don't look so goddamn satisfied." he snapped. "What are you so goddamn satisfied about, anyway? You bitch and moan about your sex life, about how you and Deb haven't gotten it on in, what, three, four months—"

So that was it. "That's changing," I said quickly. "Really."

"Yeah, sure." He was barely listening to me. "Just like that girl from Cambridge—Jesus, man, you had a clear shot at her, she thought you were terrific, but you, you just pissed it away—"

I was surprised but pleased: it was nice to know that

whatever his faults, Rick didn't have it in him—*I* didn't have it in me—to cheat on Debra. But then, out of nowhere, a nasty voice inside taunted: *No, of course not. You just do it with other men's wives. Small difference.*

The thought startled and appalled me. I told myself that we'd agreed to it, that he'd entrusted her to me as I had my life to him—

But Debra hadn't agreed to it, had she? I might not have been cheating on her, but I was still deceiving her, wasn't I?

Stop it, I told myself, stop torturing yourself. She was better off for the deception, all she'd had to look forward to with Rick was divorce, or battery, or widowhood. She was happy with me; I knew she was.

"Finney," I said slowly, "it's no bullshit. Really. Things *are* better between us. The breakdown, you know, it cleared away a lot of bad feelings; a lot of old hurts." He looked at me skeptically. "I appreciate what you're trying to do," I said, "but it's not necessary. Honest to God. Okay?"

I think it finally started to sink in to him, because after a moment he nodded, downed the rest of his drink, and stood. "Okay. It's your life; I hope you know what you're doing." Part of me bristled at that—coming from him, of all people—but he gave me a good-natured whack on the back and started off toward the back room. "C'mon, let's go rack 'em up."

The poolroom was packed with about half a dozen big, muscular guys who might have worked at Empire Sheet Metal down on Hancock Street or Dulac's Concrete over near Hooksett. We had to wait about ten minutes for one of the four tables. Grateful for the distraction, I picked a cue stick and began chalking it. "So what'll it be?" I asked Finney. "One-pocket, nine-ball, rotation?"

Finney gave me a funny look at first, then broke into a short laugh. "I think we'll get by fine with plain old eight-ball."

"Whatever," I said, racking up the balls. I took solids; Finney took stripes. He broke, and on the break, sank the six-ball in the side pocket. Throwing me a cocky grin, he tried for a two-cushion shot into the same pocket, but missed by well over an inch. "Shit," he snapped, as I stepped up to the table and sized it up. The cue ball was teetering near the right corner pocket, and the ball I wanted to sink was maybe a quarter of an inch from the opposite pocket. In between were two of Finney's balls, either of which I might inadvertently sink if I made the shot in a straight line. So I opted for a bank shot off the far cushion, the cue ball rolling down to the far end of the table, forming a long, graceful V as it neatly knocked my object ball into the corner pocket.

I was so engrossed in the game, so happy at this welcome respite from the emotional turbulence of the last hour, that I completely failed to notice at first the amazement, then the irritation that flickered across Finney's face. I just went on, oblivious, with the game: first a three-cushion shot, sinking my object ball in the far corner pocket, then a combination shot, deftly skirting two of Finney's balls in my path. On my fourth shot I missed, giving Finney his turn up, and I was surprised to see how clumsily, how unimaginatively he played; when we were young he'd always trounced me handily at this. Now he missed an absolute sucker shot, I took back the table, and I didn't let go of it. One by one the solids disappeared into the pockets as though sucked into black holes, and it wasn't until the next to the last shot—only one solid left before the eight-ball—that I looked up to see the barely concealed rage on Finney's face, the cords in his neck tensed and ropy, his hand fiercely gripping the cue stick. I finally realized the mistake I'd made: just as I'd violated an unspoken agreement when I tried to order scotch, I was now violating another tenet of his and Rick's relationship. This, too, had not changed between them over the years.

But it was too late to do much about it now. I sank my last solid, then the eight-ball, winning the game. I was terrified that my sudden sophistication at the game had made him suspicious, but it quickly became clear that he was too angry to entertain anything remotely like suspicion. Instead of congratulating me, Finney just brushed past and started racking them up again.

"Two out of three," he said tightly. This time I broke, and now, I saw, I had a fine line to tread here. I couldn't appear too suddenly clumsy without making it obvious I was throwing the game. I had to lose just enough shots, by close enough margins, to make it believable. I hated myself for it, loathing the necessity of going back to being the loser, the fraction in this pathetic equation. I tried to convince myself it didn't have to go on like this indefinitely—that eventually I could work my way up to where he and I could play honestly and equally—but as I watched him miss easy shots and sink others more by luck than by skill, I realized bleakly that that day would never come. Thirteen years of honing my game had made me a better pool player than Finney would ever be; and ironically, it was Finney's own fault. I'd never realized it before, always just looked on pool as a pleasant diversion or a way to hone my actor's reflexes, but I knew now that that was all facade: I'd become a good pool player to make up for all the humiliations, all the whippings Finney had put me through in our youth.

I lost that game, and the next as well, by which time Finney—with the help of two more bourbons—was in fine fettle; fine enough that when a burly construction worker challenged him to a game, Finney accepted cheerfully. And the construction worker then proceeded to whip the living daylights out of Finney, even as I had in our first game.

Living in New York, you become hypersensitized to any potential violence around you; your peripheral vision expands, and that drunk just ahead of you or that wild-eyed proselytizer on the corner, all the borderline weirdnesses around you are processed automatically and examined in terms of possible physical threat. Maybe living in Appleton these past weeks had dulled my instincts; or maybe I was just so relieved not to be playing, not to have to take any more dives, that I didn't see the danger signals until almost too late. As the construction worker sank ball after ball—using an impressive array of bank shots, three-cushion shots, and combination shots—Finney's bright mood eclipsed. His face darkened, his eyes took on a hooded aspect, the cords in his neck stood out again. After every missed shot—and the more he drank, the worse his playing became—he took to hurling his cue to the floor with a shout: *"Shit!"* "Son of a fucking *bitch!*" "Cocksucking *bastard!*" I couldn't tell if the epithets were directed at himself or at the other player; by the end of the game, neither could his opponent, who was casting surly looks in Finney's direction.

Finney took the loss of the game even less well than he had with me; he demanded, rather belligerently, a rematch, and when the construction worker declined Finney came just short of questioning his manhood. Stonily the construction worker acceded, snapping up the balls, then racking them up; but as he went to chalk his cue stick, Finney began circling the table, and with the quarts of pure trouble he'd been drinking all night slurring his words, he suddenly yelled, "You bastard! This is a fucking whorehouse rack, you cocksucking pussy!"

A whorehouse rack is when the balls have been loosely packed, so loosely that when a player breaks, the cue ball absorbs all the shock, robbing the player of a full break. I'd watched the rack, and it was definitely not loose. But Finney needed some excuse for his inevitable loss.

Before I could even move, Finney's opponent hurled his cue stick violently onto the table, its tip making a jagged tear in the green felt. "Jesus Christ!" he yelled, bearing down on Finney. "*You* are the pussy around here, man, you know that?"

"The *fuck* I am," Finney snapped, facing him off. They were both roughly the same height, but the other guy had at least ten, twenty pounds on him, and Jimmy the Greek would not have given Finney very high odds. I hurried over and grabbed him firmly by the arm. "C'mon, Fin, take it easy," I said, trying to pull him away. "The rack looked fine to me—"

"What the fuck would you know about it?" he snapped at me; then, turning back, pushed the construction worker in the chest with the flat of his hand. "I'll show you how fast this 'pussy' can tear your fucking face off, asshole!"

"Go ahead," and the other guy pushed back, hard

enough to send Finney sprawling backward into the pool table. Finney lunged forward, but then I jumped in, leading with my shoulder, knocking Finney backward and to the left; he gave the table a glancing blow before sprawling onto the floor.

I stood between him and his opponent, looking down as Finney drunkenly tried to scramble to a squatting position. "Okay, that's *enough!*" I yelled—shocking him, I think, with the steel in my tone. "You've got no beef with this guy, he wasn't cheating, he beat you on the square and you damn well know it!"

Finney got to his feet, swaying as he tried to lunge forward again, but I was even more ready now and when he was just inches from me I pushed at him with both hands, hard—not hard enough to fell him, but hard enough to shake him with the knowledge that I could stop him cold if I wanted.

He swayed there a moment, taking this in, and then I said, "Okay. You're going home now."

I turned to the construction worker behind me. "Sorry," I said. "He won't be bothering you any more tonight."

The guy just shook his head and sighed. "You his keeper, or what?" I scowled, not at him, not even at Finney, but at me. "Yeah," I said quietly. "I guess I am." Taking Finney by the arm, I guided him out of the bar. His steps were rocky, uncertain, and just before reaching my car he stooped suddenly and vomited into the gutter. After he'd finished, he squatted there, breathing in fits and gasps, for some moments. I gave him a minute, then said, half impatient, half bemused: "You all done? I mean, it may be just a box on wheels, but it's got genuine leather upholstery." He laughed raggedly—the first hint of the old, good-natured

Finney I'd seen in hours. "Keep the window rolled down," he suggested hoarsely, "and I'll turn at appropriate moments." I helped him into the Volvo and within minutes we were threading our way through Manchester's back streets toward the nearest entrance to Route 3.

Halfway home, Finney leaned his head back on the headrest, tilted his face toward me, and smiled a strange, weary smile. "Came in a bit late this time, didn't you, Cochrane?" he said, the words a bit thick, but the thought alarmingly clear.

If this was a joke, I was in no mood for it. "I saved your goddamn ass, Finney."

He nodded. "Granted, granted. It's just that you usually step in before I'm stupid enough to make the first move."

Good Lord, what *chutzpah*. It wasn't enough I pulled his stupid neck out of danger—he had a specific routine all laid out for me. I thought back to the similarly averted—and sometimes not so averted—brawls of our youth, then multiplied them by all the scrapes and arguments Rick had doubtless broken up since then. "Maybe," I suggested, an edge to my voice, "I'm getting tired of having to do it. Maybe I wanted to give you a little more rope this time, to see how you might like it."

"Ah," he said, head tilting away from me again but still with that damnably irritating smile on his lips, "like the time you walked out on me in Concord, and that large black gentleman broke both my kneecaps? The time I couldn't walk for a month?"

I said nothing for a long while, feeling chilled despite the heat blowing full blast from the air vents, till Finney finally looked over at me again, his expression now more bemused than taunting. "Quite a shove you gave me back there," he said, part appreciative, part quizzical. "Where'd you get arms like that, Cochrane?"

From learning to juggle for a production of *Barnum*, I wanted to tell him; from going three days a week to the gym, because you need physical strength as much as intellectual skill as an actor. I gave him a mysterious look. "Maybe I'm a costumed adventurer," I said. "Maybe I have a secret life."

He laughed quite a bit at that, then fell silent the rest of the way back to Appleton.

I got him up the front steps to his house, supporting him as best I could, fishing around in his pocket for the house keys. Somehow I got him upstairs, by which time he seemed to have developed something of a bladder problem; I propelled him into the nearest bathroom, then after a decent interval, pried him off the toilet seat and guided him toward his bedroom, where he sprawled on his back in the bed. His eyes closed as I switched off the lights—I thought he'd passed out—but as I started to leave the room I heard his voice behind me, slurred but still comprehensible. "Cochrane?"

I turned.

"Thanks," he said into the darkness. "I'm lucky . . ." He paused. "It's lucky that jerkoffs like me have friends like you."

I didn't know how to answer, and after a moment the sound of his shallow, steady breathing told me that he had, indeed, passed out. I shut the door behind me, heading down the upstairs corridor to the staircase, but passing the door to what had once been Martin Finney's den I stopped and lingered in the doorframe. In the light of a small desk lamp I could see the heavy walnut desk, the comfortable leather recliner Finney's dad had always sat in, and the bookshelves that lined three sides of the room. Empty bookshelves. A few chemistry texts lay on their sides, untouched, no doubt, since Mr. Finney's death, but other than that, no books. I switched off the desk lamp and hurried down the stairs, locking the front door behind me and leaving the keys under the doormat. I backed out too fast from the short driveway, spraying gravel across the dead lawn, feeling more than wind at my back as I hurried away, hurried home.

I got in around eleven-thirty to find Paige planted sullenly in front of the living room TV, not really watching whatever screeching cop show was playing, headphones on as she studied—with something like a scowl—a textbook in her lap. Mine was the first generation able to simultaneously watch TV and read, or listen to rock and study, but I noted Paige's peers had taken the genetic mutation one step further. Paige was up a little later than she should have been, even for a Saturday, but oddly I was the one who felt he'd been out past curfew. I went into the kitchen, after the last four and a half hours desperately needing a nightcap, but one lingering flash of Finney, his head hanging out the side window as we raced along Route 3, was enough to switch my choice to a Polar raspberry-lime soda.

I joined Paige on the living room couch, surprised to find that the text she'd been so aggressively frowning over was, in fact, *Romeo and Juliet*. "Hey, great stuff," I said. She read my lips, I guess, and removed her headphones. "Yeah," she said sourly, "except you've gotta go to the glossary for every third word. I mean, how're you supposed to remember that back then, 'an' meant *if,* and 'list' was another way to say *please,* and—" She flipped to a page with particular agitation. "Get this: 'I'll look to like, if looking liking move.' Why did these people *talk* like this?"

"Just to annoy us," I smiled. "See, that's a great moment there: Juliet's just been given this long harangue on why she should love Paris, not Romeo, and she's asked, 'Can you like of Paris' love?' And Juliet, contemptuously, says in effect, If the mere sight of him is enough to make me love him, fine, but otherwise, 'No more deep will I endart mine eye/Than your consent gives strength to make it fly.' Meaning he's not going to get much more than the courtesy you obligate me to give him."

Paige sort of gaped at me, her mouth open as I recited the lines. "You—you remember all *that?*"

"I did my share of Shakespeare," I said, "in college."

Looking utterly forlorn, Paige slapped shut the book. "Oh God," she lamented. "I'm never going to be able to play this."

I straightened a little, my interest piqued. "You mean you're doing a scene from it in some class?"

Paige suddenly looked as though she'd spilled the H-Bomb secret to the Russians. "Well . . . actually," she admitted, clearly uncomfortable, "we're sort of doing the whole thing. In closing assembly, end of term."

"And they've cast you?" I said in surprise. "Which part?"

She looked utterly morose. "Juliet, the little wimp."

"But that's *terrific,*" I said, and my delight seemed to genuinely startle her. "Honey, it's a great part, you're going to love it! When did this all happen?"

She looked downward, at the closed book in her hands. "Yesterday," she admitted.

"Why didn't you tell me sooner?"

She looked up at me, visibly distressed: not knowing how to answer this, not wanting to dredge up things best left forgotten. My tone quickly sobered. "Right," I said. "Wrath of the Father-Thing, Part Two. Got it." She smiled a little bit at that, and I laughed and put a hand to the back of her head, ruffling her shoulder-length blonde hair. "That was a different guy," I said, knowing she couldn't suspect how much truth there was to the joke. "A pod-person. I'm happy for you, honey, really I am."

I wasn't sure if she believed me or not, but in any event her mood didn't improve. "Well, I'm glad *you* are," she sighed, "'cause I'm halfway through this and already I want to jump off an overpass. I mean, God, I can't even understand half these funny old words—how am I gonna *play* them?"

"Well, that's your director's job; he'll help you with that."

She looked at me with amazement. "Mr. *Conover?*" she gasped. Teenage girls, I was discovering, do gasps very well. "Weren't you the one who told me what a stiff he was?"

"*Frank* Conover?" I said, remembering suddenly the only actor in my college stagecraft class—possibly the only one in the history of the stage—to read Macbeth's "Tomorrow and tomorrow" with the same inflections, the same trenchant pauses, as William Shatner at his most excessive. "Tomorrow ... and to*mor*row," I began to recite, falling into the Shatnerian rhythms, "creeps in its...petty pace...from day to day...to the last *syl*lable of...recorded *time*..."

Paige was in hysterics, giggling uncontrollably the more I went on, and the more she laughed, the harder it became to keep a straight face; eventually I gave up, the two of us collapsing into helpless laughter. I wiped a tear from my eye. "You mean that Frank Conover?" God, I couldn't believe it—not only had the lummox actually graduated from the theater program, he'd become a teacher. And the wafflecone was teaching *my* daughter!

"Okay," I said, sobering up, "I'll coach you. We won't mention this to Mr. Conover, of course, but we'll work on it together, you and me—okay?"

Her expression was equal parts astonishment and a small, secret pleasure. "Really?"

"Really. When you played Peter Pan—ten to one he showed you tapes of Mary Martin in the role, am I right?"

"Yeah," she confirmed, "she was great."

"Yes, she was. And William Shatner can be a pretty good actor, too, with the right director sitting on top of him, but the point is, Frank Conover doesn't have the vaguest inkling of a personal acting theory—all he ever did in college was mimic other actors, and it sounds like as a teacher all he does is give you examples on which to model your performance. Good models, maybe, but that's not all there is to learning to act." I put my hand to her back, rubbed it reassuringly. "Don't worry, kiddo, we'll get you through this alive."

"You mean my Juliet won't come out sounding like

Captain Kirk?'" she said, grinning wickedly, and then we were both in hysterics again—"Romeo," Paige intoned, "wherefore... *art* thou... Romeo?"—until the commotion brought Debra downstairs in her bathrobe, looking understandably puzzled: "You guys on drugs, or what?"

"Dad's gonna coach me in my Juliet," Paige said, excited now, all her doubts and disbelief gone. Debra looked stunned, but covered it with a joke. "I remember your Juliet," she said dryly. "Sexy décolletage."

"She scoffs," I said, standing, "but we'll show her. Meantime, kitten, you better read through the play; we'll talk it over tomorrow over brunch, in general terms, then get down to the nuts and bolts later." I kissed her on the forehead. "Night."

"Night, Dad."

Night, Dad. I liked that. More and more, I liked the sound of that.

Debra and I adjourned to our bedroom, where the CD player was playing a track from a George Winston album—*Winter into Spring,* I think it was—and I started undressing. "So how was your heavy date with Finney?" she asked.

"Fine," I said. "Fine."

Whether she believed me or not, she propped herself up in bed and returned to the book she'd been scanning: the latest auction catalog from Sotheby's. As I crossed over to the bed, in fact, I noted a whole stack of similar art catalogs—three-inch-thick volumes from Sotheby's, Butterfield & Butterfield, and Christie's. I flipped the pages of one phone-book-size catalog. "A little light reading before bedtime?"

She seemed to weigh something in her mind, carefully.

"I've been thinking," she said finally. "Jeffrey's ready for day care, but instead of putting him in full-time, I thought"— she eyed me cautiously—"I thought maybe instead of going back to the gallery, I might try my hand at art appraisal . . . work here, out of home, and only have to put Jeffrey in daycare a couple days a week—whenever I had to schedule appointments or view paintings. I'd like to be able to spend more time with him than I have with Paige, because of that crazy schedule we were on when we were first married, you know?

"Of course," she added quickly, "even though the rate can go as high as a hundred an hour, all told I won't be making nearly as much as I did at the gallery—at least at the start." She hesitated. "Do you think we can manage it? Financially?"

"If it makes you happy," I said, "we'll find a way to work it out." She looked both relieved and surprised; maybe Rick would've grated about having to shoulder more of the financial burden. "It is funny, though, thinking of you as an appraiser. I mean, God, remember how in college you never even wanted to *know* from pricing—appreciation—any of that 'bourgeois artifice'?"

She winced a little at that. "Well, it wasn't till I left the museum, and started working in small galleries, that I began to see things differently. I mean, here you are in the Rose Art Museum, and you see this piece of tripe by Warhol valued at five gazillion dollars and you can't help but think, come *on*, this is all a crock. Or you see a Wyeth priced at six figures and you think, how can anyone put a price on anything as sublime as this? It's absurd. It's crass, it's—God help me—*bourgeois*."

She laughed, closing her catalog. "But then you go to

work in a small gallery in Hanover, and one of the local artists comes in—some guy who lives on ten thousand a year,
just scraping by, even with a little commercial work on the
side—and you tell him the piece you sold for him six months
ago has appreciated ten percent since then..." She
smiled, looking at once embarrassed and pleased. "It's
not like he's getting any more money for that particular
piece, he's already sold it, but—it does something for him,
you know? You can see it in his smile, in the way he walks
out of the gallery—it tells him that someone values what he
does, that he's not just working in a vacuum, that he's making progress.

"And," she conceded, "it makes me feel like I've had
some part in it, too. That's one of the things I envied
about you, when we first met—you were studying something you loved, we both were, but you could practice it.
You could get up on that stage and act, but all I could do
was study. Analyze and admire. Give me a pen, I'm lucky
to manage my own signature."

She hesitated, then gave me a slightly disbelieving,
slightly pleased look. "You're really going to coach Paige
on this Juliet thing?"

"*You* remember Frank Conover," I said, slipping into
bed beside her. "You don't mind, do you?"

"Mind? No, of course not. If anything"—she put her
Sotheby's catalog aside, snuggling closer—"I find it kind
of a turn-on."

"Really?" I said hopefully. "Maybe you'd like me to recite one of Petkoff's speeches from *Arms and the Man*?"

She gave me a playful kiss. "Just the arms and the man
will do fine right now," she said. We embraced, kissed,

long and lingeringly... but after a moment I felt her stiffen, start to draw away, and I let go, wondering what I'd done wrong. "Deb?" I said uncertainly, looking suddenly into eyes clouded by doubt and apprehension. Had I made some ghastly mistake, fallen horribly out of character? "Did I... do something wrong?"

Debra frowned and shook her head. "No, that's just it," she said quietly. "You've been perfect. Too perfect."

I felt the tightness across my chest again; I struggled to stave off the anxiety, to keep my expression mild and puzzled when inside I was terrified, panicked that somehow she knew, somehow she suspected—

"I'm just afraid..." She stopped, her voice quavering. "Rick, forgive me, but... I'm just so frightened that all of this—you and me, you and Paige—it's all just a..." She looked down. "An act. A pretense. That underneath, nothing's changed, and one day—"

She began crying softly. I reached out, put a hand gently to her chin, made her look up at me. *Stage gesture,* I assailed myself. *Can't you do better than that?*

I looked her in the eyes and said, as plainly and truthfully as I could, "I swear to God, Deb... *this* is not an act," and I leaned in and kissed her again, more hungrily this time, as though by joining my mouth with hers I might, by sheer force of will, bind myself to her—forge a covenant that could convince her of my love and sincerity, despite the great falsity, the unvoiced lie, that separated us. It was an impossible task, I knew, but for the moment, we both wanted to believe, and she returned the kiss just as hungrily, entered the covenant just as willingly. Our bodies pressed close, the flesh making real the faith—the faith that what we felt was real, and that nothing else mattered. It was a contract written on air and upheld only by love; I think both of us knew it, and both chose not to care.

CHAPTER TEN

RICK

They were going to find me out. The thought haunted me, taunted me, all the way back from that first, shattering run-through. I cursed myself for a fool to think I could pull this off—for allowing my ego, my macho pride, to convince me that I was Richard's equal. I was a reflection, not an equal; a counterpart, but not a peer. In my own deluded mind I'd been competing with Richard from the moment our lifelines crossed, but for the first time I saw that there was no competition here—that I was barely in the race at all. And I saw, finally, that this silly, one-sided rivalry—this jealousy—was utterly pointless. The stakes had suddenly changed dramatically for me. In the space of one afternoon my ambitions had gone from proving I deserved the kind of success and respect Richard had attained, to simply *getting by*—to somehow struggle through the play, to perform at a level not so far below the rest of the cast as to make an idiot of myself, or worse.

I tried to reassure myself that I wouldn't, couldn't be exposed for what I really was; hurrying back to my apartment, I even made, in a fit of paranoia, a thumbprint with an old ink pad and compared it with prints I found on one of Richard's wineglasses. They were identical, of course. But my confidence was short-lived: I kept thinking of all sorts of subtle physical differences that could be just as damning—a broken bone, say, that could show up on an X-ray, a scar, an appendix or set of tonsils removed or not removed.

Dammit, *no.* I had to stop this. I had to concentrate on one thing and one thing alone: the play. The part. I took out my playscript and began going over it again, reading aloud the lines, hoping to make them familiar and comfortable. But the more I read the more I heard myself as though from a distance—and what I heard was just as stiff, forced, and artificial as it had been at the runthrough. I hurled the goddamn script into a wall, the brads popping, the pages scattering. *Damn* it—what was I going to do?

As I sat on the couch, staring at the pages strewn across my living room, the phone rang. I had a brief paranoid fantasy that it was my agent calling to tell me I'd just been fired from the production, and I was ashamed at the relief I felt at the idea. Picking up on the third ring, I heard instead Catlin's bright, cheery voice: "Hi, it's me. How'd it go today?"

My bleak mood lifted; all at once the depression was forgotten. "Fine," I said, almost believing the lie myself. "Great. How about yourself?"

"Well, one week in town and I am already *besieged* with offers," she said in a tone so exaggerated with false airs that I had to smile. "So many, so numerous, so copious that I couldn't—I'm sorry, I know this is gonna break your heart, but I can't, I just can't—I couldn't possibly make time for you tonight. No, really, don't even ask. I *can't* go out to dinner with you. I could *not* be coerced into a few hours of crazed dancing at the Tunnel, followed by several hours of debased, animal sex, and I *certainly* can't squeeze in that twenty minutes of prolonged fellatio you seem to enjoy. I'm sorry; I feel terrible about it, but I just *can't.*"

"Oh," I said, playing along. "Are you sure?"

"God, I love to hear a man beg. Pick me up at seven-thirty." And she hung up. I laughed, the bleakness and fear now completely dispersed by the prospect of seeing, touching her again. It was just after six; I showered and dressed in record time, picked Catlin up at her fancy but funky SoHo apartment, and from there it was on to dinner at Lutece, and later, dancing at the Tunnel. True to our agreement, Catlin didn't mention anything about our "marriage" all night long; she might've mentioned friends or acquaintances "we'd" known during that time, but I recognized most of the names from Richard's journals and her mention of them was always in the context of, "Did you hear what Marcy is up to now?"—always focusing on the present, never the past.

The insecurity I'd felt that afternoon seemed just as far in the past. Around Catlin I felt confident, secure, excited; she accepted me as Richard, and any differences she might've perceived, far from making her suspicious, actually pleased her. And none more than the biggest risk I was to take, later that night—after we'd danced for hours at the Tunnel, then, happy and exhausted, cabbed it back to SoHo. The elevator was out, so, arms wrapped around one another, we climbed—a bit wobbly, considering how much we'd had to drink—the six or seven flights up to Catlin's apartment.

It was only once we were inside, as Catlin went to freshen up in the bathroom, that it all abruptly caught up with me: the nerve-racking tension of the read-through; the panic afterward; the manic swing in the opposite direction, all the drinks, all the physical exertion, the erotic suspense of the past few hours. I was suddenly exhausted; drained. I had to brace myself against the couch to keep from dropping on the spot. When Catlin came back out—now wearing only a silk robe and slippers—it took all my energy just to smile, to kiss her, to walk with her arm in arm to her bedroom.

As I took off my clothes, Catlin did a line of coke. I slipped into bed and immediately she was at me, mouth pressed hungrily against mine, fingernails crisscrossing my back. I responded in kind, for a moment—but the exhaustion took hold again and Catlin sensed my lassitude at once, though misinterpreting its cause. "Richard? Is something wrong?" Her eyes narrowed worriedly. "Oh, God. Is this the second thoughts part? And after I finally convince myself I'm not crazy to—"

"No, no, no," I said quickly, putting a hand to her cheek. "No way. I'm just—I'm fucking exhausted, that's all. The run-through today, all that dancing... all those drinks..."

She regarded me cautiously; perhaps skeptically. "Well, if that's all it is," she said, "I have a quick fix for it." She reached over to the nightstand, picked up her snuff tin—her stash box—and held it in her palm. "Why do you think I'm so bright-eyed and, pardon the expression, bushy-tailed?"

I wanted to make love with her so badly, just then—needed to make love with her, to affirm that someplace in this world I could be what I was supposed to be—that I barely hesitated, surprising myself as much as Catlin.

"What the hell," I said. "Let me give it a try."

She looked shocked—and, a moment later, pleased. A slow smile came to her. "My Lord," she said, popping open the stash box, reaching for her mirror, "we certainly *have* changed, haven't we?" She grinned as she cut me first one, then two lines of cocaine, and showed me how to use the coke straw. I watched, listened, nodded, then—ignoring a small voice inside urging me not to—I took the first hit, then the second.

The thing that surprised me was how cold it felt—a cold that numbed my sinuses for a few moments, a liquid, fluid kind of cold. At first I felt nothing else, then I noticed that I no longer felt quite so groggy as I had before, nor so tired. Catlin came to me, gripped the shaft of my penis in her long-nailed fingers, and began stroking, firmly but gently. "Feeling better now?" she asked, and as my cock stiffened, my energy came back to me in a rush. I took her face in my hands, kissed her long and hard, and suddenly we were all over one another and my exhaustion, like our discarded past, was long behind me. Whether it was the cocaine or the wicked thrill of *using* the cocaine, I don't know—but suddenly sex had never seemed as vital, as vibrant, as dynamic as it seemed that night, and I had never felt as vigorous, as passionate, as alive as I did at that moment. I liked the feeling—I liked Catlin, fierce and hungry below me—and I wasn't about to give up either.

We went at it till three in the morning, falling asleep quickly, but some internal alarm clock—perhaps the last, waning vestiges of my common sense—woke me a little before seven. We had another run-through at nine a.m. sharp, and allowing for an hour to get dressed and back to my apartment, another hour to shower, change, then cab it to the rehearsal hall—I simply couldn't afford the luxury of further sleep. I forced myself to sit up, swinging my legs off the bed, then bending to search, groggily, for my socks on the floor. Catlin stirred beside me.

"You're not getting up at this hour, are you?" she said disbelievingly, eyelids half closed.

"Rehearsal," I said, yawning. "Nine o'clock." I got to my feet—and suddenly it was all back, all the exhaustion of last night, with one mother of a headache thrown in for good measure. "Oh Christ," I said, falling back into bed. "I can't even find my goddamn socks, how the hell am I going to read my frigging lines?"

"Here's your big chance," she said, grinning dreamily, "to see if you really *can* do it in your sleep."

"Dammit, Catlin, I'm serious! I'm fucking exhausted—what am I going to do, call in sick the second day of rehearsals?"

Catlin sighed as though at a backward child, reached over and retrieved her stash box again. "Lines to take care of lines," she said, handing it to me.

I hesitated, but Catlin just rolled her eyes and sighed.

"Oh, for pity's sake Richard, it's the equivalent of drinking about twenty cups of coffee, you know? Except," she added, "you won't have to get up every twenty minutes to pee."

I thought of yesterday's run-through—of how, even wide awake and sharp as a tack, I had struggled just to keep up with the rest of the cast—and of how horribly worse it would be in this condition: frazzled, burnt-out, hung-over. My hesitation was brief. I did the coke.

By the time I reached my co-op, I was no longer groggy, just a little drowsy; by the time I reached the rehearsal hall I was not only awake, I was alert. As I joined the rest of the cast around the conference table, I felt at least on an equal footing with them—until we started, that is.

Jonathan opted for another couple of read-throughs before blocking the play out—actually getting it up on its legs, as it were—and I couldn't help but wonder if his motivation was apprehension over my performance. This time I think I held my own with Mary Sue/Beth in the opening scene, but the following one with Larry tripped me up again, and though I might've been awake, I was far from confident as I headed into the pivotal first scene with Phoebe, referred to Steven by Larry's wife:

STEVEN. So you met Katie at—

PHOEBE. The Club Med, in Cancun. We were both parasailing. *(Off his blank expression)* There are these enterprising Mexicans with powerboats, see, and they sort of go up and down the coast, looking for *turistas* from the various resort hotels. On the beach they strap you into this parachute harness, and it's attached by ropes to the speedboat, so that when the speedboat zaps out to sea, the parachute catches the wind and up you go, two hundred feet over the ocean. It's cheap, too, about twenty bucks, and lasts for almost—

STEVEN. Wait a minute. This is not some sort of terrorist action; this is something you enter into willingly?

PHOEBE. *(Laughs)* It's great! It really is. The boat takes you in this slow, graceful arc around the bay—so slowly you barely feel yourself moving—except at the start, when you're yanked into the air like a lost balloon, and you suddenly say to yourself *(in a tone of utter panic),* "Oh, shit! What have I done?!"

STEVEN. *(Laughs despite himself; then, scanning her résumé)* It, ah, says here you speak fluent French, German, Swedish, Italian, and . . . Mandingo? *(Eyes narrow)* This is a joke, right? A trashy paperback?

PHOEBE. *(Laughs)* No, no . . . the Mandingo are a very real, very ancient people, on the West African coast. One subgroup, the Kangaba, is one of the oldest ruling dynasties on earth—thirteen centuries and still going strong.

STEVEN. And they teach Mandingo at Mount Holyoke College?

PHOEBE. *(Smiles)* I only learned French and German in school. The others I just . . . picked up while traveling. I'd stay awhile, maybe get a job as a tour guide in Lisbon, or a waitress in Oslo . . . maybe not a formal education, but a practical one.

STEVEN. *(A little dazed by this)* You do a lot of . . . traveling.

PHOEBE. Well, I'm sure you've seen your share of the world.

STEVEN. Oh, I've seen . . . my share of it.

Before we'd even finished the scene, Jonathan leaned in and interrupted. "Richard, when Steven says he's seen 'his share' of the world, I'd like to hear a hint of irony in there, some sad irony, because he's *standing* in 'his share' of the world; we should see him look around, take it in, and see the pathetically small scope of this man's world. Let's try it again, with that overlay of irony, all right?"

"Sure," I said. "Fine." I smiled and nodded, even as I castigated myself for missing an obvious interpretation. We went back and did it again, and this time I stole a quick, furtive glance at Jonathan, to gauge his reaction—and thought I detected a glaze of disappointment to his eyes. Disappointment and... worry?

That was enough for me to lose my balance again; I didn't regain it the rest of the day. Like yesterday, I was struggling, grasping to discern meanings and interpretations to the lines that were obvious to the others. Jonathan seemed to interrupt every other line with a suggestion, an interpretation; I tried to give him what he wanted, but as he smiled and nodded and said, "Better. Better," I knew full well it wasn't better—just a different shade of bad.

I left hurriedly at the end of the day, calling Catlin as soon as I got home. We didn't go dancing this time, just dinner—and tonight, when I took a couple hits of cocaine before having sex, I didn't even think twice about it.

A day or two later, Catlin landed a guest role on one of the few hour dramatic series currently being shot in New York, and her agent had already lined up an impressive volume of commercials to follow that, so it became apparent that the only way we'd be able to see as much of each other as we wanted was to move in together. Sort of. We decided to split our time between our respective apartments, half the week on the West Side, the other half in SoHo. We each transferred half our wardrobe to the other's closets, purchased a duplicate supply of toiletries so Cat would never be without a makeup kit at my place and I'd never be without a razor—not pink, nor one recently used on legs—at hers. So busy were we that about the only times we saw each other were late night or early morning, at which time we'd order either pizza or Szechwan, take a few hits of coke, and screw like rabid bunnies.

By the end of my first week of cohabitation with Catlin, Jonathan Lawlor decided it was time to get the play up on its feet. Still insecure about my line readings, I could now add to that the terrors of blocking. I arrived one day to find the floor of the rehearsal hall crisscrossed with beige masking tape: a small rectangle represented Steven's desk and computer; rough circles delineated the various pieces of furniture in his apartment; and three folding chairs side by side stood in for his sofa bed.

Some directors—not the kind, I understand, that actors particularly like to work with—give an actor explicit instructions on where, when, and how to cross upstage or down; they give you bits of business and expect you to follow them to the letter. Jonathan wasn't like that at all—he encouraged his actors to work out their own blocking, whatever felt right for them, with minimal interference—but halfway through the first day I began to wish he were that other kind of director. I must have committed half a dozen stupid moves—crossing or turning in ways that, in an actual theater, would swallow up my lines, or worse, accidentally upstage the actor I was playing opposite. I always apologized, but what were they to think? Either the renowned Richard Cochrane was an overrated fuckup, or the renowned Richard Cochrane was a brazen scene-stealer. Some choice.

By lunch break I was so embarrassed and self-conscious I hurried out, barely able to look my fellow actors in the eye. Now they probably thought I was an uppity snot, as well. I waited in the men's room until I believed the last of them had left for lunch; but as I waited for the elevator, as I stood in front of the small violin shop, admiring the grand old Stradivarius in the display case, I suddenly heard—down the hall and around the corner—the fall of footsteps, and a too-familiar voice:

"... surface. It's all surface stuff, he's not hitting on any of the deeper levels ..."

It was Evan Hazlett. But worse than the dismay and anxiety I heard in his tone was the too-hearty optimism in his companion's, Jonathan: the hopeful sound of a man not as convinced of what he's saying as he'd like to be. "Look, I talked with Dick Lonigan, he's worked with him before; says he always starts out slow ... needs a little time to work things through. He'll be fine."

"Maybe," Evan's voice came back, dubious and a few steps closer; "but maybe not." They were almost at the end of the corridor now, and already cringing at the unpleasant scene I could envision as soon as they turned the corner, I dashed back into the men's room—hiding out until I heard the elevator arrive, the ding of the doors closing, and the creaking of the old car as it descended the shaft.

What little confidence I had in myself evaporated; I had no reserves of strength left. My only sources of self-esteem were those which I drew from Catlin—and from cocaine.

Catlin couldn't be here with me, at rehearsal . . . but the cocaine could.

That night in bed when I handed her the money and asked her to buy me a couple of grams of coke, Catlin looked at me a long second with those big hazel eyes of hers, and I thought I detected a real ambivalence on her face. "You sure you need this much?" she said, as though she felt obliged to say it. "I mean, if all you're gonna use it for is sex and a little pick-me-up now and then, we can share, you know that . . ."

"That's not fair to you," I said, closing her hand around the folded bills. "And I don't 'need' it," I lied, "I like it. There's a difference."

Catlin put the money aside, lit a cigarette, took a deep pull on it, and let the smoke out slowly. The ambivalence was gradually fading from her face.

"There's this nice Baptist girl in me," she said, "who thinks I'm a sinful little devil leading you astray. And I probably am, and I probably have. Trouble is—" She grinned, leaned in, and nipped playfully at my earlobe. "—it's the nice Baptist girl who's also turned on by it."

Our sex was hotter and fiercer that night than it had been yet; I took a hit of coke before it, I took another when I got up that morning, and I took a third in a stall in the men's room just before going into rehearsal. And, goddamn, it worked this time: I felt up, I felt confident, I felt terrific. I launched right into it, no hesitation, no doubts. I was solid and self-assured in the scenes with Beth, Larry, and Phoebe; but I really started to take off in my scene with Sydell, the exterminator. This was the penulti-mate scene of Act One: the roaches have gotten so far out of hand even Steven can't ignore them any longer. Worse, they're terrifying Phoebe as they had Beth, and Steven finds himself not wanting—not daring—to lose Phoebe, to whom he is increasingly drawn. Enter Duane Sydell of Sydell Exterminations of Brooklyn, "Premier Bug-Buster of the Tri-Borough Area"...played to perfection by Tony Campos, a short, rough-at-the-edges type who'd done stand-up as well as straight acting:

DUANE. *(Having completed his survey of the apartment, he makes his way down the winding spiral staircase, carrying a flashlight about as long as his arm and a plastic Zip-Loc pouch. Steven hangs back, afraid of what he is about to hear.)* Well, you got 'em, all right.

STEVEN. Yeah, well, I think that's obvious, don't you? They've practically set up a miniature Friars Roast in the kitchen—they've got the dais, they've got the tables, they're starting to tell scatological bug jokes. I mean, they *own the room.* What else can you tell me?

DUANE. *(Holds up plastic pouch; inside it are some vaguely repugnant whitish lumps)* Know what these are?

STEVEN. *(Pales)* Very small matzohs or very old beluga?

DUANE. Roach eggs.

STEVEN. That would be my next guess.

DUANE. Found 'em in the closets, in the walls, under the sinks, everywhere. I could spray in here for the next eight months and I'd still miss some nest, somewhere. *(He settles himself on Steven's couch, shakes his head.)* I'd recommend a bomb. Diethyl O-phosphorothioate, open all the closets and cabinets, let that juice seep through the wood, the carpets...wipe 'em out and sterilize the eggs. Twenty-four hours and you're roach-free—guaranteed.

STEVEN. (Nervous) These gases...they only affect bugs, right? I mean, I could stay here the whole while, couldn't I?

DUANE. Sure. If you were from Pluto. *(He leans forward, puts a penny in the gumball dispenser on Steven's coffee table, pops a red one into his mouth.)* Lemme tell you about bugs, Mr. Lindstrom. Everybody's got 'em. You live in an apartment, you got roaches; you live in a house, ants. Me, I've got a nice place in Brooklyn Heights. Woke up one morning to find a whole stream of ants marching in and out of the microwave, collecting little scraps of food left over from dinner. I figure, what the hell, I'll just nuke 'em. I set the power on high, I set the timer for one minute, and I press the Big Red Button. You know what happened? *(Steven shakes his head, dully. Duane leans in; fervently:)* Nothing! Nada. Oh, they scurried around for a while—like the heat kinda annoyed them, a little—but they might as well've been to a goddamn tanning booth. *(With an almost religious fervor)* You talk about your nuclear war, you talk about your hole in the ozone layer—lemme tell you: ain't gonna make no difference to them. Darwinism, Mr. Lindstrom. Them and us, we're climbing the same evolutionary stepladder, but only one of us is gonna reach the top. For now, we got the advantage—a few chemicals they haven't adapted to yet—but you gotta move fast, and you gotta be prepared to escalate. *(Slides contract over to Steven)* Sign here.

STEVEN. *(Takes all this in; starts to put pen to paper, then hesitates; a beat, then:)* What if I wore a gas mask? Or used an Aqua-lung. Would that work?

DUANE. *(Blinks once)* Maybe you *are* from Pluto. Will you just sign the fucking contract?

I felt great—I got just the right comic timing on each line, I knew just where the emphases fell, found just the right inflections to make the jokes work. The high carried me through the rest of the run-through; but when we broke for coffee, Jonathan took me aside and said, "You've got the comic rhythms down fine, Richard, but I'm afraid you're submerging the character's fear at the expense of the laugh—especially in the scene with Duane. I'd like to see more anxiety, and less manic humor, if you see the difference?"

I wanted to deck him, right then and there, so help me— I'd been perfect, spot-on all the way through, and I knew it. But I just nodded tightly and excused myself to go to the bathroom. I took another hit of coke and it worked its magic again: I no longer cared about hitting Jonathan, because what did Jonathan matter, anyway? Maybe I had never been as bad as I thought I'd been. Maybe this asshole had never liked Richard's work, maybe he'd had me forced on him by the producers—maybe no matter what I did, I couldn't measure up. And if that was the case—fuck him. I'd do the part my way, follow my instincts, and we'd see which one of us was correct on opening night.

We went back and ran through some of the blocking again, and when we got to the scene with Duane, I did it *exactly* the way I'd done it before. And Jonathan didn't say a word. Not a goddamn word.

As the weeks went by, my confidence soared and peaked; I couldn't believe what a wimp I'd been. Now that I knew in my own mind that I was finally on the right track—now that I had the self-assurance that what I was doing worked—I determined not to stray from my vision. I went ahead and did what I wanted, and if Jonathan objected to a reading or a bit of business, I didn't just roll over and do what the Great God Director wanted me to do—I fought. And most of the time, I won—because I was the one who said the lines, in the end; I was the one, ultimately, with the power.

I felt so primed, so ready, that even after a full day of rehearsals I was still pumped up with energy, ready and eager to take the town with Catlin—dinner, dancing, premieres, parties. Oh yes: parties.

It was at a party for one of Catlin's friends in SoHo that I ran into Ray Perelli. I'd just come out of the men's room for a quick freshener and was making my way through the crowd when he spotted me, flagged me down. We met, shaking hands, in a quiet corner of the rather pretentiously decorated co-op. "Been a while," Ray said, and immediately I could tell there was something odd, something strained in his voice; I was glad I'd just taken a hit, glad I was sharp enough to spot the trouble early on.

"Well," I said, "there's the play. It's keeping me busy."

He hesitated a moment. "Yeah, I imagine. I, uh, hear it's been kind of a stormy ride for you and Jonathan."

"Jonathan's an asshole," I declared bluntly. "He's hopeless. Incompetent."

Ray was looking at me with a slightly incredulous expression. He laughed nervously. "Richard. Come on. That simply isn't so. Jonathan's a talented director; maybe not inspired, but a clever, inventive man."

"Maybe he saves his invention for others," I said mysteriously, then, more explicitly: "The bastard's got it in for me, Ray, I swear. Whatever I do, however I play a scene, he's all over me. I can't do a goddamn thing right in his eyes, and you know what?" I turned, took a drink from a nearby tray, turned back to him. "I've stopped trying. Screw him. Let him run his little vendetta, see if I—"

"Vendetta?" Ray was wide-eyed. "What vendetta? Why do you think he's prejudiced against you?"

"I don't fucking know," I snapped, "but he *is.*"

Ray tried for a small laugh to defuse my anger. "Sounds a little paranoiac to me, buddy. Give the guy a chance, okay?"

I could feel myself tense at that word—*paranoiac*—hearing in it Debra's accusations of months ago. But I forced myself to remain calm, I took a silent swallow of my drink, and after an awkward pause Ray decided to change the subject. "I was . . . surprised to hear about you and Catlin getting back together," he said. He tried to make it sound casual, but I could read the meaning, the disapproval, behind the words.

I shrugged. "Surprised us, too," I said. "But we're giving it another try."

Ray was silent a long moment. I looked up from my drink, acutely aware of what was being unsaid here, and I locked eyes with him, defiantly. "Go ahead. Say it," I urged. "Get it out of the way."

"Okay," he said. "I will." He stole a glance to make

sure no one—one person in particular—wasn't within earshot, then, in a hard but muted tone: "Are you out of your fucking *mind*? You forget what she did to you last time?"

"Maybe I have," I said. "Refresh my memory."

"Richard, don't pull this shit on me. I was the one who picked up the pieces, remember? I *saw*. Yes, I know, she's bright, she's funny, she's sexy—but she's also selfish, and self-centered, and..." He paused, gathering his thoughts, shook his head. "You become obsessed with her, man, you try to fit in with her lifestyle—the parties, the credit binges—Jesus, have you forgotten the debts you and Cat piled up in two short years of marital bliss?"

"I'm handling it, Ray, really I am."

"Yeah," he said. "So I hear. I hear how you've been handling it."

Now all pretense at civility disappeared from my tone. "And what the hell is that supposed to mean?"

"It means what it means," Ray snapped back, then put one finger to the side of his nose and inhaled quickly. His voice grew softer but no less urgent: "Are you *crazy*, man? You've never gone this far with her before—maybe a hangover now and then, but this—"

I took a step forward, glared at him. "I don't think," I said, my voice growing slowly, gradually louder, "that this is any of your goddamn business."

He held up a hand in a make-peace gesture. "Hey, c'mon—cool down, okay?" he said. "I'm not saying I don't understand. Your Mom's death was a shock, I know that, and going back to an old relationship, a familiar relationship—like going home again, when home's no longer there—I understand all that, but—"

"If I want a character profile," I said, even louder now, "I'll go to a better fucking director than you!"

He reacted to that as if to a punch in the stomach. Around us, people were starting to listen in, but he paid them no mind. He looked me square in the eye and said, unknowingly, the one thing that would bring my anger to fever pitch.

"You're not Richard," he declared flatly.

I flinched. My heart was pounding; I was suddenly finding it difficult to breathe.

"You're some ... bizarre *distortion* of Richard," he went on. "I won't dignify that remark with a reply, because I know it's not you, it's not the real Richard talking, it's that shit inside you."

Suddenly I lunged forward, pushed at him with both hands, sending him staggering backward. He looked stunned; too stunned to react in any way. "Shut up!" I found myself screaming. "Shut the fuck *up!*" The party turned very still around us; out of the corner of my eye I could see Catlin making her way hurriedly toward me, as the other guests watched with a mix of embarrassment and delighted voyeurism. "Why don't you just mind your own fucking business!"

I wanted him to scream back, wanted him to lash out as I had ... but he wouldn't even give me that; didn't look at me with anger, but with sadness. Before I could do anything more, Catlin was at my side, looping an arm through mine, pulling me away.

"Whoa. Down to Earth, Space Ranger," she said, stroking my face as though calming some dumb animal ... which, at that point, I suppose I was. She looked to Ray. "You okay?"

Ray nodded. "Yeah," he said tonelessly. "I'm okay."

"Too much excitement for one evening, *compadre*," she said to me. "Let's go home."

I shrugged off her arm; if I had to walk away from this, I'd walk on my own. But my anger was still there, bottled up, with no channel out. I glared at Ray as I brushed past him. "Just mind your own damn business," I tossed off, then, with Catlin right beside me, I made a mumbled apology to the host and hurried the hell out of there.

In the cab, Catlin slammed the door, gave the cabbie her address, turned to me, and exhaled with great exaggeration. "What in the *hell* was that all about?"

I wouldn't say. I shrugged it off with some ambiguous remark, but the rage inside me, far from dissipating by the time we reached Catlin's apartment, actually intensified. I hadn't felt this furious, this enraged, since—since New Hampshire. I threw off my coat as we entered, tossing it onto the couch without much regard for whatever was in its way; an ashtray skidded across Catlin's coffee table, fell onto the floor. "That son of a bitch," I ranted, not giving a damn for the bloody ashtray, obsessed with my anger and my anger alone. "Who the fuck does he think he is, lecturing me like a frigging—"

"Richard, for God's sake, calm down," Catlin said, putting a hand briefly to my arm. "Let me fix you a drink."

"I don't want a drink," I said. "I just want to kick his fucking balls inside out. I want to smash his fucking *face* in."

"For a moment there," she said, "I thought you might." She regarded me curiously. "I don't think I've ever seen this . . . particular side of you before, Richard."

No; few had. Debra and Paige, they'd only glimpsed it;

now, exaggerated by the cocaine, it was magnified beyond all reason. I knew this—knew what I was saying, knew what I was feeling—and didn't care. I took out my stash, did a line or two. "Yeah, well, get used to it," I said offhandedly.

Catlin smiled a small, enigmatic smile.

"I believe I could," she said quietly.

There was something maddening, teasing, about that smile. I took a step forward.

"You like this. Don't you?"

She stepped forward, slipped her arms around my neck. "I like *you*, like this, if that's what you mean."

I felt both disgusted and aroused; it was impossible to tell where one began and the other left off. I kissed her, hard, then brought my hand up her back and tore a hole in the back of her silk gown. She shuddered, pressed closer. I pushed her away, grabbed a handful of silk at the neckline, and tore that, too. Knowing just what to do to further inflame me, she lashed out with those long fingernails of hers and swiped at my neck, drawing blood. Instinctively, I raised my hand to swipe back—

But didn't, somehow; instead I cupped my hand around the back of her neck and pulled her to me, roughly. And then we were kissing again, nothing loving in our embrace, nothing tender in the joining.

In bed, I went into her in short, hard strokes, hammering away with the same violence I wanted to do to Ray. Catlin moaned with each stroke, as though at a physical blow—perhaps that was what she was fantasizing—but my erection was partial, hard enough to perform but not enough to come. My frustration mounted: twenty, thirty, forty minutes of it, nonstop, and I couldn't reach orgasm. What the hell was going on?

Finally I withdrew, cursing, Catlin quickly surmising my problem. "Don't worry," she said, leaning over to grab a cigarette from the nightstand. "Common side effect of coke usage: you can get it up, but you can't get it out."

I threw her a sharp glance. "Not a bad deal for you, though."

She lit the cigarette, smiled. "Nope," she said. "Don't work the same way for girls, luckily enough."

I looked at her, realizing just how right Ray had been. She was selfish, she was greedy, she had more than your average number of kinks—but I didn't care. I was both repelled and transfixed by her; repulsed by my own attraction for her darker aspects, aroused as much by them as by my own weakness for them. Arousal, though, without culmination; my cock may not have been hard, but it felt as though the rest of me was. I reached for my stash, rationalizing that if I couldn't get off, I could at least get high.

When I'd finished I turned back, straddled her again, saw again that teasing, selfish little smile.

"Cunt," I said.

"It's still there," she challenged. And on we went with our voracious, angry sex, our nasty, endless dance—filling me, more and more, with anger and frustration and unquenchable desires, all the things I imagined I'd left behind in New Hampshire, in that other world. I thought briefly of Debra, but then, feeling as though I were soiling her memory by invoking it now, like this, I quickly shunted her out of my mind. After she'd been satisfied, Catlin lost interest and we came apart; we rolled over on our sides, backs to one another, barely touching, as I fell almost instantly asleep. In my dream I was sleeping, too—but not here, and not beside Catlin.

I took my frustration and anger with me into rehearsal the next day; the worst day, as it turned out, to do so. We were concentrating on the pivotal scene in the play: Steven, forced from his apartment by the exterminators, is shepherded by Phoebe to her Village flat, where he has agreed to crash on her couch for the night—*one* night. It was, in fact, the only way to get him out of the apartment. Phoebe has become the only person in the world Steven truly trusts, and he won't be abandoned to the germ-ridden anonymity of a hotel room. She practically has to drag him out of his apartment moments before Duane Sydell gleefully sets off his bug bomb, and after an unseen, but harrowing, cab ride downtown, the two are alone in Phoebe's engagingly messy flat. Being inside, Steven feels safer than he did out on the streets; but he is still terrified, and after they've eaten dinner, after he's had a glass or three of Chablis to calm his nerves, Phoebe broaches the subject neither has ever discussed before.

PHOEBE. Steven? How did you... *(A beat)* How did you become so—afraid? Of the outside?

STEVEN. *(Immediately defensive; scoffing)* I'm not afraid of—

But his denial turns bitter in his mouth as he looks up at her and sees the knowing look in her eyes—knowing but not judgmental. He looks down, stares at the wineglass in his hand, rotating it slowly between his palms. His voice is soft.

STEVEN. It...starts small. Like first you're afraid of catching a cold, or flu, because you've got a deadline coming up or a big deal about to go through; so you avoid crowds, especially in enclosed areas, like shopping centers or movie theaters...yeah, I'd say movie theaters, they're the first to go. *(A long beat)* Then when you do have to go out, you find that since you've been away, things have gotten noisier and grimier and...bigger, somehow...you go into the A&P to buy groceries, not quite sure what you want, fretting over what to buy for dinner as though deciding on a new car...nothing seems right, somehow, everything you toss into the basket isn't really what you wanted...until finally you find they don't have your favorite brand of apple juice, and something inside you—*(Amends; quietly:)* Something inside *me* just snapped...and I...I pushed my cart into a wall...abandoned everything I'd spent the last hour fussing over...and stormed out of the place in a huff. *(A long pause)* That's how it starts, I guess.

PHOEBE. *(A moment as she considers this; then:)* And how does it end, Steven? Where does it end?

Steven does not look up. Despite his best efforts, he finds that there are tears in his eyes.

STEVEN. I don't know...

She goes to him, embracing him, holding him as he cries...her hair brushes against his face, her cheek touches his...the tears stop; he looks at her, and she at him; and slowly, cautiously...but not fearfully...they kiss...

It was the scene with the most punch, the most emotional juice in the whole show, and I played it all at a high pitch, at the same manic level I had maintained for the last three weeks. Halfway through Steven's speech Jonathan interrupted, his patience now worn completely thin. "Richard, bring it down! You're supposed to be frightened, we're supposed to see that fear, that vulnerability—"

I was immediately on my feet, the words seeming to come of their own volition: "You don't want him vulnerable, you want him weak! I'm trying to preserve the strength of the character!"

"The strength of the character," Jonathan insisted, "is in his *overcoming* his weakness. You're not giving him anything to bloody overcome!"

But admitting to Steven's fear and weakness was tantamount to admitting to my own, and I was not about to do that; I was too far gone.

"Look," Jonathan said, trying to be conciliatory when he no doubt really wanted to punch me out. "Just *try* it my way, let's see how it plays, and then—"

"Your way is shit!" I was screaming at him now. "Why the *fuck* should I take direction from an incompetent traffic cop like you?"

The rest of the cast flinched in the way onlookers to a ten-car pileup might flinch, yet not look away. But Jonathan didn't flinch a bit; he met me toe-to-toe. "If you stopped stuffing your head with nose candy for a few moments," he said evenly, "perhaps you might learn something. Even from a 'traffic cop.'"

That did it. I stormed over to the coatrack, recovered my jacket, yelling and cursing all the way: "When you decide to fucking get serious," I ranted, "call me! Don't waste my time with this bullshit, okay?"

I slammed out of the rehearsal hall and down the stairwell, taking the whole eleven flights in one crazed, manic trek. I flagged a cab on Lexington, fuming all the way, certain—absolutely, unequivocably certain—that when I got back to my townhouse there would be a sheepish, plaintive message on my machine from the producers, begging me to stay on, inducing me to stay with the dismissal of the asshole director. I knew it, knew it for a fact; after all, wasn't I Richard Cochrane, for Chrissake? Wasn't I their fucking star, weren't they goddamn lucky to get me in the first place?

I returned home, and sure enough, the message light on my answering machine was blinking feverishly. I took the time to do a couple lines before playing it back; and when I did, I heard not a message from the producers, but from my agent, Joel—informing me, quietly and professionally, that the producers of the aptly-titled *This Way Out* were, effective immediately, terminating my services.

CHAPTER ELEVEN

RICHARD

In early May, Debra, the kids, my mother, and I drove down to Connecticut for my cousin Diane's wedding—the one my own mother, in my other world, had never lived to see. That was my secret pleasure, as well as my secret sadness: seeing her there in her blue dress, smiling as Diane, grown from a chubby young girl with a mop of dark brown hair into a tall, slim beauty, walked up the aisle on her father's arm, to join her husband-to-be, John, at the altar. Edgar and Charlotte had eight children, and I had frankly lost count as to how many marriages and offspring they had among them; but Mom knew every one, as she had known in my other life.

I thought about that later at the reception in Ed and Charl's big suburban house outside Hartford, as I watched her play with Gail and Lee's daughter Kimberly, with David and Feli's two kids, Jennifer and David, Jr.—with all of Edgar and Charlotte's grandchildren. But in between each she always came back to Jeffrey: holding him, rocking him when a sudden burst of laughter frightened him, singing him silly little songs I'd forgotten she ever knew, songs I'd probably heard as an infant but could no longer remember. And Paige, too: she never neglected Paige, now or on our Sundays together, always remembering to stock her favorite diet drink or presenting her with a charm for her charm bracelet, something she'd picked up in a mall somewhere. They were the grandchildren I'd never given her in that other life. I remembered how in that world she used to shrug pragmatically and say, "I'm not counting on anything anymore," though not without a whisper of regret and a trace of hope that maybe, some-day, she might be proven wrong.

So I watched her play with Jeffrey and Paige and was glad for the happiness they seemed to bring her, at the same time not feeling as though I could take credit for it.

We'd been visiting my mother at least once a week for the last several months and I spoke with her, however briefly, every day, though the conversations were usually of a piece, the dialog varying little from day to day. "Hi," I'd say. "What's new?"

"Oh," she'd say, "Jessie's not feeling too good. We were going to go out to Bingo, but she's not feeling up to it."

"So why don't you go by yourself?"

"Maybe."

Sometimes she went; sometimes she didn't. She used to be a demon when it came to Bingo, going out three, sometimes four nights a week. It used to drive my father nuts, he'd complain about her being out all the time, but I knew why she went: when she stayed home they might sit and watch television for a while, then Dad would lose interest, turn on his side on the couch as though turning his back on the world, and fall asleep. Or he'd fixate on some physical complaint for days on end, until she took him to the doctor and he was told there was nothing wrong, it was all just stress and nerves. Her Bingo nights were her only refuge, her only escape. I wondered now if her reluctance to go out was a self-inflicted punishment for all the times she'd gone, all the lost hours and nights she might've spent by his side, however silent or tedious or maddening they might have been.

"So what did you do today?" I'd ask, and she'd make a little sound on the other end and say, "Well, I watched my stories," recounting some details of the soap operas she faithfully followed. Back in my old world, I at least had some common ground with her from my work on the soaps—she loved to hear about the backstage gossip, who was really sleeping with whom, and she never tired of telling me how much *Guiding Light* had gone downhill since I left. I remember her shock and disbelief when I told her one of the more macho players in one of her stories was, in fact, gay: "No, no, no," she'd insist, "the way he kisses that girl in the story, you can't tell me he's gay!" I argued with her for ten minutes on that one: "Mom, trust me on this, I've met his roommate, I've been to their apartment, there's only one bed, you know what I mean?" I remember the time she came to New York and I took her to the studio, introduced her around; she was dazed, star-struck, for months after, and whenever we talked on the phone after that she'd ask, "How's Laurie? She's such a sweet girl. I haven't seen much of her on the story lately, are they trying to write her out? Should I send a letter to the network?" I think she liked being a little bit on the "inside"; I think she used it to impress her friends at Bingo.

In this world, paradoxically, I found myself with more time to talk with her but fewer things to talk about. She'd ask about the kids, I'd tell her about Paige's current heartthrob or the new play she was doing; she'd ask about me, but what was there to say? "Our doctors say Mr. Fergusson is P&S, his doctors claim a functional overlay—I don't know, Mom, what do *you* think?" Nope. I'd hang up, wishing I'd spent more time on the line with her, knowing there really wasn't anything more to be said; feeling guilty for it nonetheless.

A day or two after the Hartford trip, Deb and I were sitting out on the back porch, a half-moon trickling light over the various plastic toys strewn across the backyard, a rustling of raccoons in the woods just beyond. Debra was leaning on my shoulder, looking as I was at the thin, fast clouds scudding across Orion's belt, as though bearing the stars away, briefly.

"Know what we should do next month?" Debra asked.

"What?" I rejoindered smartly.

God, this was all so banal. I loved it.

"Prescott Park," she said. "They start up around June, don't they?"

Prescott Park was a harborside park in Portsmouth, noted as much for its lovely gardens as for its stage—an open-air amphitheater that hosted singers, dancers, mimes, even old Broadway musicals, all of it for free, at all hours of the day and night. In the evenings you brought along a blanket or a sleeping bag, a boxed dinner or one purchased from nearby vendors, and curled up under the stars to listen to John Hartford or Emmylou Harris, local groups or touring artists; the park also made itself available to any of a dozen university or repertory theater groups, students and senior citizens alike gathering round under clear skies to watch an unpolished but earnest revival of, say, *Carousel.*

"Great," I agreed. "I bet my mother would love it. They're bound to do a production of some old musical she'd—"

I stopped as I caught Debra looking up at me, awkwardly.

"Actually," she said, "I was thinking more of you and me, snuggled up in an old sleeping bag, listening to bluegrass like we did back in college. Remember?"

"Oh," I said, feeling like an idiot. "Yeah. Sure. Of course." I thought back to one of those nights: a light drizzle fell unexpectedly from a thick cloud cover, but the crowd didn't care, they just draped their blankets over their heads like rain ponchos and happily took in the rest of the concert. "God," I said wistfully, "do you remember Joe Val and the New England Bluegrass Boys?"

"Yeah," she smiled, a bit sadly. "Poor Joe. I miss him."

I nuzzled her gently on the neck. "So . . . regarding this proposed sleeping bag. Do I get to second base, the way I did back in college?"

She laughed. "I'm not sure second base is even there anymore. I'll have to go check."

We both laughed, I drew her closer to me, but could tell, just in the way she held her arm around me, by the subtle change in her breathing, that there was still something bothering her. Oddly, I felt neither worry nor fear, but a kind of unruffled pleasure in the comfortable, nonverbal rapport we shared.

"Rick . . . all these excursions you keep planning for your mother. Don't you think you're getting a bit carried away with them?"

"You're right. I'm sorry. I guess we do wind up seeing her more than we do your folks, but—"

"No," Debra said quickly, "it's not that. I mean, after all, your mother lives in the same town we do, my parents are down in Rhode Island, there's bound to be an imbalance—what I mean is—" She sighed. "It's like she's at summer camp and you're her activities director. Dinners in Boston, movies in Nashua, taking her along with us to Benson's Animal Park—I mean, even Paige is too old for Benson's, your mother must've been bored senseless—"

Suddenly defensive, I said, "She's been lonely, Deb. She and Dad were married forty-five years. Can you imagine what it must be like, living with someone for nearly half a century, and then one day he's gone, and there's nothing to fill that vacuum?"

Debra thought a moment, with that look on her face I'd come to know as one of delicate contemplation, how best to say something without offense. She was a lot better at this than I, doubtless the result of living all those years with a loose cannon—with Rick. Did she still think of me, I wondered, as a loose cannon? Was she still afraid I was going to blow up at her at the wrong word, the hasty phrase?

"Rick," she said finally, "did your parents ever do much traveling?"

"Uh . . . well, the Catskills when I was a kid, sometimes Maine, or Vermont—"

"No, not with you—later, after you'd moved out. Did they travel anywhere together?"

"Only to—" I almost said, *Only to New York, when I was in a play,* but caught myself just in time. Damn; how did I answer this, anyway? I really didn't know every detail of my parents' life in this world—I could only speak for what it had been like in mine. But everything else being equal, all I could do was speak from that other, parallel experience, and hope Debra didn't spot any major discrepancies between the two.

"No," I said. "Not really. They talked about going down to Florida for a visit, but never quite got around to it... I was always trying to convince them to go somewhere... Europe, California, Hawaii... but they just never seemed very interested."

"Did they visit friends a lot?"

"Well, most of Dad's co-workers from the textile plant moved away when it closed... New York, New Jersey... it always seemed too big a deal for them, I guess, driving all that distance."

"Any hobbies?"

Why was she asking me this? Was she testing me, did she suspect something? "Well, my Dad used to be a pilot... owned a light plane, but sold it when he and Mom got married. Photography—he loved his old Minolta—but after I grew up he stopped taking so many pictures..."

"I never saw many books at your folks' place, when I was over."

"No. No, they weren't much for books," I admitted. Uncomfortable now, I said a bit irritably, "Look, I must've told you this a million times before, haven't I?"

"Yes," she said, "but I don't think you've told it to yourself lately." She turned a little in her seat, fixed me with a sober look. "Rick, you've said it yourself: your parents never really did much even when your Dad was alive. They stayed at home, they watched television, Sol and Jessie were the only real neighbors they were close to and even that was, what, maybe once a week, dinner at the King George—"

"What are you trying to—"

"Honey," she said gently, "they never really did anything, but what they didn't do, they didn't do *together.* There may be a vacuum in your Mom's life now, but there was one then, too; she just never noticed it before."

I looked down, thinking of something my mother told me just after Dad's funeral. "She never imagined, you know, that...that he might die first. Or that she might. She always assumed, naively, that they'd go together, somehow."

Debra put her hand on mine. "It's well and fine to want to make her less lonely...to bring Jeffrey over for a while, or invite her out to dinner...but you can't live her life for her, Rick. If she'd wanted that kind of life"—she hesitated—"she would have made one for herself. They both would have."

Intellectually I understood what she was saying, but emotionally I fought it.

"I...can't help it, Deb." How did I explain? That this was my second chance—that I'd traveled a different road, made a different turn, seen a different ending? "I have to try," I said, and I knew as I said it that there was no way to make her understand—no way to communicate the loss I'd experienced, nor the guilt I was trying so hard to atone for. Still another unwritten, unspoken clause in our silent covenant, but worse, another part of me I could never share with her. Just as I couldn't tell her, when we made love, why I so cherished holding her—because I'd once lost her. It was a small thing, perhaps—I had the love, the life, I'd let slip away once before, I just couldn't tell anyone what it meant to me. A small thing, but it was starting to eat away at me—as small things inevitably did.

A nd then there was work.
Years ago, when I made the transition from junior high to high school, the hardest thing to get used to was the earlier start of classes: having to be in homeroom at eight o'clock meant getting up at six-thirty, showering, breakfasting, then walking the mile or so up Manchester Avenue to school. Later in life, of course, I would frequently have to get up even earlier—four a.m. to be in makeup by six, on the set and shooting by seven or eight, and not off call sometimes till eight or nine at night—but somehow I never minded that much. I was doing something I loved, and in any event wasn't on call every day (if I'd been a big star it might've been different) and had a finite shooting schedule, after which I could sleep in for the next three weeks if I chose.

But after a month and a half at State Mutual, I found myself waking, tensed, half a minute before the alarm clock went off: lying there feeling each of the next thirty seconds slip away, savoring them before the alarm razzed me from bed and I forced myself into the shower. Every day I told myself, You elitist ass, the majority of the world does this every day without complaint; stop being such a bloody *artiste*. So I'd pump myself up with enthusiasm, charge into work—and after the first hour of approving or disallowing liens, I was already glancing at the clock, anxiously anticipating coffee break. That held me over for an hour, then it was another two, two and a half till lunch . . . and so on through the day, until the magic hour of five. It occurred to me one day that I was suddenly, horribly, back in high school—stealing glances at the clock, jumping up as the bell rang, taking a few extra minutes at lunch and hoping I wouldn't need a hall pass if caught being late.

And there was Finney, calling on an average of twice a week—or sometimes just dropping by unannounced on his way back from work at seven a.m., just as I was getting ready to go in to work; frequently, even at that hour, there was a whiff of scotch on his breath. He'd invite me out—bowling, drinking, a game of eight-ball in the rec room at the Colony Inn—but somehow I found myself putting him off, feeling awkward and uncomfortable around him even when he'd just stopped by for a few minutes. Because when I looked at him I didn't just see him, I saw the other Finney, *my* Finney, transposed over him like two badly developed photographs; and I'd invent some perfectly plausible excuse for not joining him, for getting him out of there as subtly but quickly as I could. "Sunday night? There's a new club over in Manchester I'd like to check out," he'd say, and I would demur yet again, trying not to see the hurt and somewhat baffled expression on his face as he shrugged and said, "Okay, Cochrane, later"; trying not to acknowledge the relief I felt when he ambled out the front door.

More and more I looked forward to my coaching of Paige as a respite from the tedium of work or the worry that Finney engendered in me. Our first few sessions we simply read and reread the play; most important, I thought, was that she had an overview of the entire story, understood the other characters and their motivations as well as her own. Too often I saw actors who had memorized their own part and no one else's; they knew their cues, but if another actor suddenly went dry and started improvising (easy to do in Shakespeare: in a moment of blank panic I once lifted a short passage from *Richard II* while performing *Richard III*, one critic commending me for "bold and original transposition")...well, the actor who knows only his own part, faced with another desperately spouting improv, is about as naked and helpless as it's possible to be on stage. If, however, you know the sense of the other actor's speeches, you can feed him the lines, you can improvise your way along until the other actor can find his way back.

Paige's biggest worry, of course, was the language. Every student doing Shakespeare for the first time is terrified of all those archaic words, that baroque syntax and blank verse. At first she simply wanted to go through the text, memorizing one footnote after another; I tried to convince her that this would be a waste of time. "First you find the sense of the line," I told her, "and all the rest will follow." She looked dubious, but since this was more than Mr. Conover had yet offered, she withheld judgment, at least for the moment.

I had to wait till a Saturday for our first run-through. Paige was puzzled when I told her that morning to put on her grungies—jeans, tennis shoes, an old denim jacket— while I loaded a backpack with cheese sandwiches, a bag of Granite State potato chips, and a six-pack of Cherry Coke. We piled into the Volvo, looking more as though we were headed for a picnic than a rehearsal. I drove through the center of town, then took steep, winding Mohegan Pass to a thick stand of woods half a mile outside town, finally parking on the shoulder of the road. "Here we are," I announced, swinging the backpack out of the car.

Paige looked around skeptically. "Which is where, exactly?"

I smiled enigmatically. "There's a trail over here," I said, stomping into the woods, pack slung over my shoulder. "Just follow me."

Paige grimaced as she stepped over the fallen branches and rotting leaves that had obscured parts of the old trail. "This is great," she said flatly. "Listen, I hate to tell you this, Daddy, but they eventually did find a Northwest Passage, you know?"

We broke through a thick knot of undergrowth that had appeared in the years since I'd last been in these woods, finding ourselves in a small clearing near the base of a low cliff. I dropped the backpack and looked around, a smile coming to me as I surveyed the familiar terrain, so little changed since my childhood. We were standing in a patch of rye grass, directly in front of a great slab of granite that stood about three feet high, ten feet wide, and eight feet deep. Backing it was a cliff, angling steeply upward, with hand- and footholds sufficient to take an adventurous (if stupid) young boy to the top of the cliff, maybe twenty feet above. That steep climb had first drawn me and my friends here, twenty-five years before, but its real allure, the thing that made me smile and tingle a bit with remembrance, was the wide, flat slab at the bottom—about three feet high, as I've said, bracketed on either side by two six-foot pillars of granite.

"Jack and Denny and Dave and I used to come out here when we were eight, nine years old," I said, craning my neck to look at the summit, "scale the cliff, somehow scramble down again without breaking our necks, and then—"

I jumped up suddenly onto the granite slab and, to Paige's great chagrin, began bounding and skidding across the granite surface, wielding a make-believe weapon, slashing it vigorously back and forth, up and down.

"We'd make cutlasses out of old branches...you had to find just the right kind, curved, not straight...jury rig a hilt out of hollowed-out old pinecones"—I was starting to get a bit out of breath with all this lunging and swinging and lopping off of limbs—"and play pirate for hours on end. Then, when we finally got tired of that, it was Legionnaires, with sabers instead of cutlasses."

I stopped, tossing aside my mimed sword, and looked down at my puzzled daughter. "This was our stage, you see? When you're nine years old, it's okay for a guy to pretend—not like girls pretending their dolls are babies, of course, but *manly* pretense, *aggressive* pretense." Paige laughed at the macho emphasis; I jumped down and sat on the edge of the "proscenium." "Unfortunately," I went on, a bit wistfully, "there's some vague line of demarcation along about when you hit puberty, when that kind of pretense— that kind of playacting—becomes uncool. Worse than uncool—abnormal. So whenever my guy friends would catch me in the backyard fencing with Tybalt—oh, yeah, I'd discovered Shakespeare by then; eighth grade, Miss Hughes' English class—they'd do their best to make me feel like a fruit. They didn't actually believe I was, of course, but it's a favorite fallback position for adolescent boys: anyone who does anything they think is unhip or weird is a fruit."

"Boys," Paige agreed, boosting herself up to sit beside me, "can be such dorks."

"That's where the term comes from, kiddo," I said— embarrassing her a little, I think, unwittingly. "Anyway, when I got into high school I found the Drama Club, so at least there was a clique of us bizarros, you know, and if a guy still razzed me I could always tell him it was a good place to meet girls. But between the time I stopped playing pirate with the guys, and joining the Drama Club, this"—I gestured, taking in the arena behind me—"was my secret stage. The one place I could come, read aloud Prospero's speeches from *The Tempest,* confront the Specter at the Banquet . . . anything." I shrugged. "I just thought this might be a nice place for us to rehearse," I said, and Paige I think knew it was not as offhanded a gesture as I made it out.

She looked around, sizing up the locale, then nodded judiciously. "Sure," she said. "This'll do." Then, with exaggerated impatience: "Now are we going to talk about the words?"

I sighed, flipping open one of the paperbacks of *Romeo and Juliet.* "Like I've been telling you," I said, "you can memorize the glossary all you want, but what you need is the sense of the line, first.

"See, honey, those words that baffle you will probably be equally unfamiliar to the majority of your audience—who's not going to have a glossary readily at hand. The syntax may be strange—archaic—so what you have to communicate to the audience is the underlying emotion; so that even if they don't get every word, they understand the sense of what you're saying. You see?"

I flipped through the play till I found what I wanted. "Let's start with the funny stuff; it's easier. Act II, Scene V, line 30."

"Funny?" Paige looked at me incredulously. "God, it's all so slow, so ponderous—"

"No," I corrected her, "an interpretation can be slow and ponderous. What you mean, I think, is that the lines are wordy. It's your job to make them seem *not* wordy." I held up the book. "Okay. Juliet has been waiting frantically for her Nurse to return from her rendezvous with Romeo. The Nurse clumps in, exhausted, and Juliet says, 'I pray thee speak,' to which the Nurse"—I fell back, feigning hot flashes—"says, 'Jesu, what haste! Can you not stay a while? Do you not see that I am out of breath?'"

I nodded, cuing her, and Paige began reading her lines carefully, ponderously, flatly: "'How art thou out of breath when thou hast breath to say to me that thou art out of breath? The excuse that thou dost make—'"

I held up a hand. "Okay, hold it. Let's contemporize this passage. If Juliet were saying this today, she'd say, 'What the hell do you mean, you're out of breath? How can you be out of breath, you bimbo, when you've got breath enough to say you're *out of breath*?!'"

Something glimmered in Paige's eyes. "But that sounds like...I don't know, Neil Simon."

"It's called comedy, dear heart," I sighed, "and Neil didn't invent it. Come on, let's stand; maybe it'll loosen us up." We stood up on the stone slab and I felt an odd thrill, a familiar pleasure, being back here. "Now take that cadence I just used and lay it over the words you just read."

I swayed, fanning myself with the book like the Nurse trying to regain her energy after a long journey. "'Do you not see,'" I cued her, "'that I am out of breath?'"

"'*How* art thou out of *breath*,'" Paige said, and now her arms shot up in exasperation, "'when thou hast breath to *say* to me that thou art out of breath?!'" She looked to me for a signal; I smiled, nodded. She consulted her lines, then went on in the same fast, frantic cadence: "'The excuse that thou dost *make* in this delay,'" she said, circling round me, arms flapping impatiently at her side, "is longer than the tale thou dost *excuse!*'"

"Meaning what?" I asked, stepping out of character.

"Meaning in the time it's taken you to tell me you're too tired to tell me," Paige said, "you could've *told* me, for Chrissakes!"

"Exactly," I said. "And even if there's someone in the audience who doesn't know what 'dost' means, he can't help but know what you're saying, because of the way you're saying it."

Paige looked up, pleased and relieved. "You mean I did it?"

"It's a good start," I allowed. "Now let's try it again, but this time, dial the franticness down a notch or two, and easy on the hand motions. Okay?"

We spent an hour or so on that scene and one other, going over the text, contemporizing it so she could get a handle on the underlying emotion, and of course occasionally going over a definition of some obscure word; but by the end of all that, not knowing that 'jaunce' meant 'rough journey' didn't frighten her the way it might've at the start. She just nodded, stored the definition away in some corner of her brain, and went back to the business of playing the line. As I knew—as I'd hoped—she would. She had the talent, and she had the flexibility to learn; and I discovered, with quiet surprise, that I was as proud of her that day, taking her first few faltering steps into the profession, as I was of any performance of my own. I began to realize that of all the things in this new life, Paige was the only one I could say was truly mine.

Because it was Debra and I, not Rick, who had concei-
ved her, fourteen years ago: it wasn't till two months later
that the split, the divergence between worlds occurred,
but at the moment of conception it had been me, before
Richard and Rick became two people, taking two different
paths, living two different lives. Paige had Debra's sense of
humor and Debra's disposition, but I saw much of myself
in her as well, even as I was helping to awaken more. We
sat there eating our cheese sandwiches and potato chips
and I stole wondering glances at her, awed and delighted
that I could, truly and honestly, call her my daughter, and
myself her father. And as with Debra, there was no way I
could explain just how or why, in that moment, I loved her
as fiercely, as strongly as I did; no way at all.

It was too early for Prescott Park to start its thriving
summer activity, but toward the end of May, Deb and I
left the kids with my mother for a day, took the Volvo,
and drove to Portsmouth anyway. It was a cool, breezy
afternoon as we walked hand in hand along the water-
front, watching the fishing boats entering port with their
nets full of haddock and cod; the wind ripping across the
water made tall, turbulent whitecaps on the Piscataqua
River. We stopped in each of our favorite bookstores from
our college days—eating up our book allowance for the
entire month—then, to satisfy Debra's craving for bluegrass, took an early dinner at a little place on Bow Street,
listening to Tony Trischka and Skyline perform "Late for
Work" and "Stranded in the Moonlight." Afterward we
walked along the harborfront at sunset, the darkening
silhouette of a lighthouse standing against an orange sky.
I don't think we said more than five words in half an

hour, but it was one of those nearly perfect moments that come so rarely in a person's life, and even more rarely with someone to share it with, someone with whom you can summon up the memory again years later.

We drove back to Appleton and at the sound of our approach my mother suddenly appeared in the doorway of her home, her face unreadable in the darkness but her stance visibly tense. My first thought was, Oh my God, the kids—something's happened to the kids. But as I brought the car to an abrupt halt I saw Paige, shouldering a sleepy Jeffrey in his blue pajamas, safely standing behind Mom in the doorway, and I relaxed a little.

"Now don't get upset," my mother said—in that tone of cool and reason I'd heard so often before, the one called upon in emergencies or worse—"but it's Dave Finney. He's in the hospital up in Manchester, and he needs you to come right away."

My heart pounded as I got out of the car. "Oh, Jesus," I said softly. "Is he all right? What happened?"

"Some kind of auto accident," Mom said. She padded down the walkway in her quilted bathrobe, taking Debra aside as soon as she got out of the car. "You'd better go directly from here," she said, taking charge, as usual, thinking clearly when those around her were too shocked, too confused to think at all. "I'll get dressed and drive Debbie and the kids home. He's in Elliot Hospital—the Trauma Center. I looked up the address—955 Auburn. You know where that is?"

"I'll find it," I said.

"Rick," Debra said, "do you want me to come with you?"

"No. No, I'm okay," I said, slipping behind the wheel again, fastening my seat belt.

"Go," said my mother. "Don't worry, everything's taken care of here." I looked at her thankfully, backed out of the narrow driveway, made an illegal U-turn in the middle of Lochmere Street and broke all records getting to Route 3. I forced myself to remain calm, but all I kept envisioning was an image I'd never actually seen in reality: the twisted wreck of Finney's old Chevy Nova wrapped around a telephone pole, state troopers using acetylene torches to free him from the driver's seat, his legs pinned and crushed beneath the dashboard. Oh God, I kept thinking, oh Jesus, I failed him, I failed him again. I was able to blink back the tears only because I had to see to drive. After twenty minutes at sixty-five miles an hour, I hit the outskirts of Manchester, crossed the Merrimack River at Queen City South, finally locating Auburn Street and Elliot Hospital.

I found the Emergency Department/Trauma Center with little trouble. It seemed to be a relatively slow night in the waiting area—one young man with a bandage on his left hand, an elderly man in pajamas and a bathrobe—but behind the admissions desk things were considerably more hectic. I saw interns and nurses pushing gurneys and crash carts laden with medical trays. I stepped up to the desk, leaning in to get the nurse's attention.

"Excuse me," I said breathlessly. "I'm looking for a—a David Finney? I'm his friend, Richard—Rick—Cochrane; he called me from here?"

She scanned a clipboard on her desk, then nodded. "Yes, he's with Dr. Adelman right now. Let me see if you can see him." She went away for what seemed like ten minutes but was probably closer to two, then opened the door to admit me. "He's in first-aid bed two," she said, guiding me past exam rooms and E.R. beds. "That one there."

She pointed toward a curtained-off area, one of several in a row, but in front of this particular one stood a uniformed police officer looking very much on duty. The nurse explained who I was and the officer—tall, late twenties—just nodded and said, "I'll have to search you, I'm afraid," and as he patted me down, starting with my jacket, I asked, "What—what is he being charged with?"

He pulled my jacket pockets inside out, finding nothing, of course, but lint. "Aggravated DUI. 'Aggravated' as in second offense."

"Oh, Christ," I said.

He worked his way down to my pants, saw I wasn't concealing any gravity knives in my shoes, then straightened. "Sorry about that. You can go in now."

I turned, steeling myself for what I was about to see—for what I hadn't seen thirteen years ago—as the nurse parted the curtain and admitted me into the room.

Finney was sitting upright on the bed, his shirt off, a few scrapes and cuts on his chest as a doctor was gingerly stitching a large gash on the left side of his face. He looked up happily at my entrance.

"Rickie!" he said, and immediately winced as the sutures pulled at his flesh. "Let's keep the facial motions to a minimum, shall we, Mr. Finney?" the doctor suggested, and Finney, chastened, complied by speaking very slowly and without undue lip action. "Thanks, man," he said to me. "Thanks for coming." He looked vaguely embarrassed. "I—I didn't know who else to call."

I stared at him—at his legs swinging jauntily off the bed, at the minor laceration the doctor was sewing up—and all my tensed muscles went limp. I had to sit on the small stool at the foot of the bed, I was so weak with relief.

"You're okay?" I said disbelievingly. "Really okay?"

He looked suddenly troubled, tense. "Not with a second DUI facing me," he said darkly. "Jesus, man, they could pull my license for this. And I can't even make the bail." He eyed me hopefully. "I was kind of hoping you could—"

He didn't need to finish. "No problem," I said. "Whatever you need. Jesus, Fin, just as long as you're okay, physically."

His eyes clouded over. The doctor was using some sort of suture that ran beneath the skin; the knot he tied off at the end was the only thing visible.

"Yeah. Well," Finney said, in a much more subdued voice than I had yet heard from *this* Finney, "I was a lot luckier than the other driver."

I felt myself go cold. "What—other driver?"

Finney looked down and away, facing neither me nor the doctor who was now bandaging his chest cuts. "I . . . I ran a red light on Harrison," he said, "and there was this car, turning right onto it from Maple, and I . . ." He paused. "I hit her left front side . . . she spun out . . . smashed into a parked car at the intersection . . ."

" 'She'?"

He nodded. "Woman. About twenty-five. That's all I know about her."

All the relief and happiness I'd felt turned to ash. "So . . . so how is she?" I asked, afraid for the answer. Finney shrugged helplessly. I looked to his doctor; he frowned and said, "You'll have to ask her attending, not me. Dr. Rinaldi."

I nodded.

I sat there a long moment, then stood mechanically as

I spoke: "When they're done with you here," I said tonelessly, "I'll follow you down to the cophouse and take care
of your bail. Okay?"

If he heard the coldness in my voice he ignored it.
"Thanks, man," he said. "What would I do without you?"

I parted the curtain and exited, pausing a moment just
outside. I felt as though I were inside one of Sylvia Plath's
bell jars, all the sounds of the E.R. ringing hollow around
me, all the shouts and cries of pain blunted and unreal. I
looked at the uniformed officer standing watch. "The other
driver," I said quietly. "Where is she?"

He nodded to the adjacent first-aid area. In contrast to
Finney's, this one was swarming with activity, muffled
voices from within, curtains parting every few moments
to admit or release a nurse or intern. In one of those moments I glimpsed medical personnel clustered around a
woman lying in bed, tubes running into her arms, nose,
and abdomen; EKGs and EEGs tracing irregular lines on
the monitor above her, bags of blood hanging from I.V.
stands pumping life into her. It was the scene I expected
to see, coming here tonight; but so different, so awfully
different, that I could barely absorb what I saw.

A short woman with dark hair, wearing a white doctor's smock and name tag, emerged from the E.R. area. I
stepped up to her as she paused to make notations on a
chart. "Dr. Rinaldi?" She looked up. "Excuse me...my
name is Cochrane, I'm a friend of..." I was loath to say it.
"...of the other driver. I just wanted to know...how is
she?"

I must have looked haunted or worse, because instead
of declining comment she said simply, "She's had some
internal injuries...a little bleeding...but we think we've

got that under control. Mainly we're concerned about concussion, about possible neural damage and loss of motor coordination. But we won't know about that until she regains consciousness." She fixed me with a sober look, adding, "Mr.—Cochrane, is it?—if you really are that man's friend...you'll get him some help." A call from another exam room took her away and I went to the waiting area as Finney was readied for transfer to the Manchester police station.

I followed the patrol car to the main station on Chestnut Street, where formal charges of Aggravated DUI were made against Finney and where the bail commissioner set his bond: the high end of a sliding scale, five hundred dollars. I'd left my checkbook at home and all I had on me was a little more than twenty dollars, so they had to put Finney in lockup while I went in search of ATMs to gather the remaining cash. Finney was taking it all stoically but looked as though he could use a pat on the arm or a firm handshake; I gave him neither.

Once bond had been posted, Finney was given a date for arraignment and the two of us gratefully took in the cool night air as we left the police station and began walking down Chestnut toward my parked car. "Jesus, man," Finney was saying, "you're a lifesaver. I don't know how I can make it up to you."

I stopped, turned, looked at him. I tried to temper the anger I'd been feeling toward him all night. "Dave," I said soberly, "if you really want to make it up to me—please get yourself some help. Now."

He stiffened, suddenly defensive. "What, like traffic school?" he said derisively. "It was an accident, man, it could've happened to any—"

"You were drunk, Finney! You jumped the light, they say you were too loaded to even retain control of your car—"

"I wasn't drunk!" He was shouting at me now. "I'd had a few Beams, okay, but by the time I left the bar I was fine, I was—"

"You need *help*, man," I shouted back at him. "You need to go to AA, see a shrink—"

He had that same hooded look to his eyes I'd glimpsed in the poolroom, the same tight cords standing out in his neck. "The only goddamn help I could've used," he yelled raggedly, "was from *you*, man! If you'd been here tonight, if you'd been driving back, maybe this whole thing wouldn't never have hap—"

He didn't get a chance to finish. I don't know what came over me; suddenly enraged, I grabbed him by the collar, thrust him violently against the wall of the building, felt the jolt pass through his body and into my arms, and didn't care.

"You son of a bitch!" I screamed at him. "Don't you dare say that to me! Don't you dare!" He was staring at me, stunned more, I think, by my strength than by my rage. "*If* I'd known you were going to get so blasted you could barely drive, and *if* I knew you were gonna run that red light, *then* maybe I'd be responsible! But I'm not, goddammit! I'm not responsible for your life, Finney! I'm not responsible for *you!*"

I let him go, stalked over to my car, and yanked open the passenger door for him. Shakily he climbed in, I keyed the ignition and pulled away from the curb; we rode in silence down Chestnut, over Bridge Street, to Route 3. We didn't utter a word to one another all the way back to

Appleton—me out of anger, Finney out of shock and apprehension. And as I drove I found myself thinking about his other self, a world removed; about the woman lying unconscious in the Emergency Room in Manchester, and about her counterpart on that other earth, as well. And for the first time I dared admit to myself that perhaps Rick had not done Finney such a great favor, that icy night thirteen years ago; and that this world I had so coveted was not, in fact, a perfect world, but merely a different one—in its own ways, just as sad, and just as fragile.

CHAPTER TWELVE

RICK

F*ired?*" I was screaming at Joel; it was a testament either to his professionalism or to his friendship that he didn't hang up on me. "They *can't* fire me! I have a contract, a fucking pay-or-play contract!"

"Yes," Joel agreed calmly, "and they've elected to pay."

I didn't know whether I was more angry or astonished. "They're paying me off? All because of that asshole director?"

"Richard," Joel said, the strain starting to appear in his voice, "calm down and listen to me. You're in trouble here, you need help–"

"From who?" I snapped. "From you? Can you get me back the part?"

"No, I can't. That's not–"

"Then what the fuck *good* are you?" I shouted. "You're supposed to be my agent, you're supposed to handle these things–"

"Forget the goddamn part," Joel said, finally raising his voice. "It's you that's the problem, not them! You need–"

I screamed an obscenity and hung up on him. I threw the phone across the room and into the entertainment center, gutting the CD player in the process. Not content to limit the destruction to that, in my rage I turned to the most breakable things I could find: I put a foot through one of the nine-hundred-dollar stereo speakers; I snapped up a heavy ceramic ashtray and hurled it into a framed Harrill print, shattering the glass, a volley of splinters erupting outward and draping the carpet, the couch, the coffee table. When the phone, off its hook, continued its insistent wail, I yanked the cord from the wall and sent the whole thing flying into the kitchen, where it bounced off a cabinet and into the sink, smashing the half dozen wineglasses and coffee cups left in the basin.

I stood there amid the carnage, taking it in with perverse satisfaction. I wanted to do more, but I was breathing raggedly, my energy lagging far behind my rage. I went to my stash for a quick hit, but it was empty—only the merest grains sticking to a corner of the tin. I became still angrier at that, but now the lassitude, the exhaustion was really taking hold of me. Bitter, angry and frustrated, I slumped into a chair—one not covered with glass, or torn and grazed by flying objects—and closed my eyes, my jaw tight, my hands balled into impotent, useless fists. That bastard, Jonathan; *he* did this to me. He'd been out to get me from the start. I'd kill him, I'd tear his fucking balls off. As soon as I could find the strength to get up out of this damned chair; as soon as I could stop my goddamn hands from trembling.

I sat there for—I'm not sure for how long; I was aware only of my trembling, of my anger, and of a change in the light in the room. However long it was, there finally came the click of a key in a lock. I looked up as the door opened, as Catlin entered the apartment, breezily at first—then stopped dead as she saw the shambles around her.

"Oh, my heavens," she said, softly. "Oh, Lord."

She surveyed the damage with horrified disbelief, saw me sequestered in my little corner of the room, clutching a pillow against my chest as though to ward off God knows what. "Richard?" she said uncertainly. "Are you all right?"

My voice, I found, was hoarse and scratchy. "I need a hit," I said, ignoring the concern in her voice, ignoring her, really; only one thing mattered just then. But Catlin didn't take out her stash; she dropped her purse at the door, walked slowly across the room, crouched down beside me. "Richard, what *happened*?"

She paled as I told her about my fight with Jonathan; flinched when I related the message from Joel and the conversation that followed. When I'd finished she let out a long, sad sigh, silently went back across the room to recover her purse, then sat down in the chair opposite mine and shakily lit a cigarette.

"I'll be fine. Honest," I said in a tone that belied the words. "All I need's a couple lines to get me past this."

She took a deep pull on her Salem, then shook her head slowly. "No," she said. "I think you've had enough."

My anger flared again, and briefly I had some energy. I tossed aside my pillow and stood. "*You* think? Who gives a flying fuck what you think, just give me a lousy hit, for Chrissake!"

She stood, meeting my gaze coolly, evenly; she put her hands on my shoulders, trying to calm me down.

"Honey," she said, "you're out of control. We've got to bring you down, okay?"

I shook off her hands. "Just give me the goddamned coke!" I screamed. I lunged for her purse, snapped it up and open. As I fumbled through it, searching for her stash box, she grabbed the purse away from me, yanking it so hard that its contents went flying, scattered across the living room floor. I fell to my hands and knees, rummaging for the stash; but Catlin found it before me, snatched it up, and bolted out the living room and down the hall.

"Catlin!" I yelled, running after her. "God damn it!" She dashed into the downstairs bathroom, slamming the door—and by the time I forced it open I saw, to my horror, that she had emptied the entire contents of her coke tin into the toilet, flushing it just as I entered. I watched, aghast, as the white powder dissolved on contact with the water, then in a cloudy spiral was sucked down the drain.

I stood there, stunned, lost, and betrayed. She saw the betrayal, I know, because I saw the guilt reflected in her eyes; she rinsed the stash box of any remaining particles, then headed back down the corridor to the living room. I followed her, hearing an unwelcome catch to my voice. "Why?" I asked her, hating the plaintive, pathetic way I sounded, even to myself. "Catlin, for God's sake—"

She started moving toward the kitchen. "Come on, we'll fix some coffee and—"

The anger suddenly flared back, fierce as ever.

"You fucking bitch!" I yelled at her, so loud it made her jump. "Isn't this what you wanted? Isn't this what you were so turned *on* by?"

She stopped; turned, slowly. She looked at me, and now the guilt in her was nearly palpable; she looked tired and sick, in a way I had never seen in her.

"Sex is one thing," she said flatly. "Career is another.

That's where I draw the line." She moved closer, putting a hand briefly to my arm. "You lost a job, honey. You stepped over the line."

I shook off her touch. "And you never have?"

"No," she said. "Never. Because I can handle it, and . . ." She took another cigarette from her discarded pack, lit it. ". . . and you can't."

"Oh. Well. That explains everything, then," I said coldly, pacing back and forth as she sat back down in her chair. "You're Supergirl, and I'm a mere mortal."

She took a deep drag off her cigarette, tossed back her long blonde hair, and sighed. "Richard, I do maybe two hits a day; some people *can* do only two hits a day. Lots more can't. You're one of them. My trouble"—she frowned, took a pull on her cigarette—"was in not seeing that, soon enough."

I fixed her with an icy look, my thoughts starting to coalesce again. "No," I said coldly. "Your trouble was see-ing, but not caring—until I crossed this invisible line of yours you never bothered to tell me about."

She considered that a long moment, then nodded slowly.

"Yes," she said, very quietly. "That's quite right. I de-served that." She stood, stubbing out her cigarette.

"I'll be right back. Then we'll fix you up that coffee, and a sandwich, too, maybe, okay?"

She went down the hall to the bathroom, I thought, then some minutes later returned to the kitchen. She put the coffee on, rummaged about in the refrigerator, then—after carefully disposing of the shards of glass in the sink, not to mention the dismembered telephone—improvised a lunch for both of us. I was starting to feel tired again and felt a mother of a headache coming on, but my head was clearing enough to feel a creeping dismay come over me as I surveyed the ruined apartment. Good God, what was I thinking of? What had I done?

By the time Catlin came back with the coffee and sandwiches, I had regained enough of my sanity and worked up enough of my nerve to say, "Okay. So I've got to get off this stuff. What do I do, check myself into the Betty Ford Clinic or what?"

"A bit dramatic," she said, taking a swallow of coffee. "You'd only need that if you'd been at this for months. You've just been on a binge, that's all. Four or five days should be all you need to clean out your system." She put down her cup and looked at me. "But, hon, they're not going to be four or five *easy* days."

I nodded, my headache almost obscuring the sense of her words. As though feeling it herself, Catlin fished out a bottle of Advil from the scattered contents of her purse on the floor, handed it to me. "Here," she offered. "You're gonna need plenty of this to get you through the next few days."

I took them gratefully, downing three caplets with a swig of coffee. I looked up. "You'll be here, to help me through them. Won't you?"

She looked away, put down her coffee, got up and went to the window. "I'm not sure you would get through them with me here," she said quietly.

I was alarmed by the resignation, the finality, in her tone. I joined her at the window; she was standing, arms folded across her chest, looking down at the street below. "All right," I said. "I'll do it alone. I'll kick the stuff, then we'll pick up where we left off, but at a saner pace, okay?"

She sighed. "Richard—you still don't get it, do you,

honey?" She looked at me sadly. "You see in me everything you can't be, and I see in you something I can't be. If I were a nicer person, maybe, I'd try to be more like you—but I'm not, so I let you go ahead and try to be something you're not."

She shook her head. "The second take didn't print any better than the first," she said with a cheerless smile. "What say we just burn the negative, okay, hon?"

I started to argue—wildly improvising all the reasons we should stay together, knowing they had a hollow, desperate ring to them—when the buzz of the door intercom interrupted me. Catlin turned expectantly and hurried to the intercom. "Yes?"

"A Mr. Perelli here to see you," came the elderly doorman's voice, made raspy by static. Across the room I twitched in response to the name, my pulse beginning to race.

"Send him up," Catlin said. "Thank you."

"So that's what you were doing—" I began, but she ignored me, heading down the corridor to the bedroom. I followed her, stopping short as she took out the clothes she'd been keeping in my closet and began draping the wardrobe bags, one after another, over her arm. I was so distressed at this that I didn't have time to worry about who was coming up on the elevator. "Catlin—can't we work this out?"

She snatched up the last bag, fixing me with a fiery gaze. "Richard, if you keep this up, you are going to up and throw away your whole damn career," she snapped. "I will not have that on my conscience, Richard. You understand? That far I *will not* go." She hurried out of the room, down the corridor, just as the doorbell was chiming; wardrobe bags still slung over one arm, she opened the door to admit, to my great chagrin, Ray Perelli.

I retreated to a corner by the window, too ashamed by my behavior toward him to even speak. Catlin looked relieved at his presence. "Thanks for coming, Ray," she said, then, with a rueful smile: "We really have to stop meeting like this."

Ray regarded her with a combination of weariness, resignation, and dismay. "Last time, Catlin. Absolute last time." Then he looked past her to the ruins of the apartment and his eyes widened. "Jesus H. Christ."

"I warned you," she said, slipping past him into the doorway. She handed him her set of keys, then looked across the debris of the shattered living room to me. "Take care of yourself, Richard," she said softly. And then she was gone, and I was alone with Ray.

He stood there on the threshold for a moment, seeing the trouble I was having meeting his gaze. "You okay, man?" he asked, stepping down to cross the room.

I turned away at his approach, looked out over the Hudson. It was a bright, sunny June day, yachts and sailboats dotting the river; little wonder I hadn't noticed before, but it felt good, seeing it now. I thought of Uncle Nick for some reason, I thought of the Merrimack and Aunt Eleanor and my parents.

"You didn't have to come," I said, as Ray joined me at the window. "After what I said at that party, she shouldn't even have called you."

"Don't be a putz," Ray said amiably. "I've been here before. I know the terrain. Who else should she have called?"

"Ray . . ." My voice was shaky. "I am so sorry—"

"Like I said at the time," Ray said gently, "that wasn't Richard. That wasn't Richard at all."

He had no idea how right he was. His simple, unadorned forgiveness made me want to cry—not just for what I'd said to him at the party, for the hurt I'd caused both him and Joel, but for the senseless havoc and destruction I'd wrought on Richard's life and career. *I have things I cherish in my life, too,* he'd said to me. *Friends. Lovers. I'm trusting you to take care of them.* And this was how I repaid his trust. Not with betrayal so much as carelessness; not conscious treachery, but reckless stupidity. I hadn't just violated the trust he'd placed in me—I'd neglected it, and somehow that seemed a thousand times worse. I wanted to cry, but couldn't: the tears were bottled up inside me and all I could do was tremble as the first of many chills ran through me. Ray led me to a chair, and as I grappled with demons and struggled with guilt, a man who thought I was his friend went through a closet he assumed was mine, packing clothes he thought I'd earned for a trip he mistakenly believed I deserved.

Ray and Melissa owned a small beach house in East Hampton, Long Island; it was there that Ray took me, and it was there I spent the next week. Ray had known enough ex-users to warn me of what cocaine withdrawal would be like, but nothing he said truly prepared me for the reality of it.

After the long drive from the city, I dragged into Ray and Melissa's guest room in late afternoon, lay down with the intention of getting a few moments' rest—and fell immediately asleep. When I woke it was four in the morning, yet somehow I was still tired, wanted to sleep even longer. Every muscle, every bone in my body ached: a deep, throbbing ache that even three Advil did little to relieve. It was like the worst day of the worst flu I had ever had: headaches, bodyaches, chills, and night sweats. I fell in and out of a fitful sleep; my underwear, the sheets, the pillows, all were drenched with sweat. Too weak to even change the sheets, I settled for searching out dry spots and curling up atop them.

In some ways the physical parts of the withdrawal were more tolerable than the psychological ones, and I can't be sure even now how much of my physical pain was magnified by my mental state. I wrestled with depression and anxiety, doubt and desperation. When you're hooked, your brain starts running sneaky little mindfucks on you; you find yourself thinking, Jesus, if I could just have one line, just one line, I could handle this. Then you start thinking, if I can't handle *this* without coke, how will I ever handle anything without it? You convince yourself you'll never be able to deal with the real world without it; you tell yourself that, well, maybe you'll be able to use it only recreationally in the future...

Dissident voices waged war inside my head—Ray told me later they were usually referred to, collectively, as the Committee—and if there had been coke anywhere in that house, I can't say for certain I could've resisted the temptation. Fortunately the physical discomfort helped me ignore the harping of the Committee: most of it was just chills and a dull soreness, except for my sinuses, scraped raw by the white blade of cocaine—so chafed and inflamed, it felt sometimes as though the front of my face were going to fall off, and the only thing that relieved it, the only balm, was, of all things, Preparation H. Imagine the indignity, the humiliation of stuffing that up your nose, three, four times a day—and happy to do it, too. A quick fix to whatever delusions of grandeur the coke had given me.

Over the course of the next several days I lay in bed, or sat in a chair in the living room overlooking the surf, or hunkered down outside on the sand—arms wrapped around myself, too weak or anxious or depressed to do much of anything. Once, on the beach, Ray and Melissa had to carry me in off the sand, where I'd fallen asleep and collapsed in on myself like a spider-crab in hibernation, as my body recovered the rest that I lost when I'd been cranked up for weeks on end.

And through it all, Ray and Melissa were there: watching over me as I slept, keeping me company when I was awake, doing their best to keep me occupied—playing Scrabble with me, or bridge, watching television or movies. One night I awoke after fourteen hours of fitful sleep, suffering such chills that all I could do was lie there shivering, waiting for it to pass. Melissa must have heard me rustling about, because she knocked politely on my door and entered to find me curled in a tight little ball of pain—sweaty, chilly, bones aching. Wordlessly she came over, sat on the edge of the bed, and put her arms around me...and at last I let myself go. I wept in her arms, wept for all the mistakes I'd made and the people I'd hurt. She stayed with me for the better part of an hour, letting me know I wasn't alone, until I finally drifted back to sleep; the last thing I remember is her putting a pillow on my chest, and my hands atop that, so I would have something, in her absence, to hold on to. And the next night, when the chills and anxiety sent me wandering restlessly through the house, it was Ray who got up, feigning insomnia himself, and sat with me as we watched a rerun of Robert Riskin's *Magic Town* on Channel 2's Late Late Show.

After four or five days, as Catlin had predicted, the aches and chills began to subside, the depression lifted, and I began to feel less like a wounded animal than a man—a foolish but very lucky man. On the fifth day—a hot, balmy summer's day—I sat on the beach watching the sailboats, the windsurfers, the yachts and the cabin cruisers, and I decided to join them. Crazy, maybe, but the water looked enticing and irresistibly near. I was still a little achy, but not enough to prevent me from wading into the cool Atlantic. I winced a little as I made my first stiff, tentative strokes, but I kept at it and it wasn't long before I was swimming without any apparent discomfort—my muscles actually feeling better as I swam out to the nearest buoy, then back again. It became a routine for the next several days: breakfast, then a morning swim, twenty or thirty laps to the buoy, maybe twenty yards out; then lunch, and another swim, this one just playful, diving and rolling underwater, sometimes catching a wave as it rolled in, riding its crest or being dumped onto the sandy bottom.

I'd always loved swimming; loved it ever since I was five years old, when my parents took me to the Catskills for our annual vacation and checked into a small resort with housekeeping bungalows clustered around what for me was the main attraction—a big blue swimming pool. It was there that I learned to swim from a lifeguard who coached me one morning, showing me kicks and strokes which I faithfully imitated, kept afloat by my water wings.

That afternoon, when my parents took me back to the pool and the lifeguard tried to put the water wings on me again, I promptly announced, "I don't need them. I can *swim*"–and as the lifeguard cautiously stayed with me in the shallow end of the pool, I proceeded to swim exactly as he'd shown me, back and forth, kicking up a monster of a spray on my trek from one side of the pool to the other. The lifeguard was stunned–"I just showed him this morning"–and my parents were pleased and proud; soon, as soon as years pass, my father was snapping photos of me frozen in midair as I leapt off the diving board to do a bellywhopper into the water.

I'd forgotten how much I enjoyed the water, the movement, the freedom of swimming. Debra and I took Paige to Weirs Beach several times each summer, but I had never recaptured the feeling I'd had as a child–until now. It helped restore me to sanity, to health, and to myself.

I'd just come in from my afternoon swim, moving up the beach to find Ray–in cut-offs and an old t-shirt–sitting on the sand, smiling. I joined him, toweling off my hair, wiping the sand and salt from between my fingers. "You looked pretty good out there," he said. A short pause. "You feeling as good as you look?"

I nodded. "Yeah. Finally. Thanks to you and 'Lissa."

He shook his head. "We handled the easy parts. You got through the worst on your own."

"Which I never would," I insisted, "if not for you."

"Six of one," he said. "You've done your share for us, too."

I felt a jab of guilt. No: *I* hadn't; Richard had. My conscience reminded me that they hadn't been helping an old friend, they'd been helping a stranger; but along with the guilt I felt a gratitude and an affection for Ray and Melissa that I knew I would never be able to explain to them.

"So," Ray said into the short silence. "You think you've finally got her out of your system?"

His words made me see Catlin again in my mind, and though I felt a certain stirring at the image of our bodies locked together in bed, it was more than outweighed by the vivid memories of pain and failure and humiliation that had followed. I looked out at the sailboats riding the horizon and smiled. "Yesterday," I said, "I thought about something Catlin said to me. At your party; as she was lighting her cigarette. She quoted this line from *Crimes of the Heart*, about smoking—"

Ray nodded, recognizing the line: "'Taking a drag off Death. What power! What exhilaration!'"

I laughed, a bit sheepishly. "I guess that's what I was doing, all along, with Catlin: taking a drag off Death. I'd never done anything like it before. Never gotten that close to the edge. Cat—or Beth Henley—was right; it *is* exhilarating. Addictive."

He looked at me soberly. "You think you've had your fill?"

I laughed again. "Oh, yeah," I said, standing. "My fill, your fill, and the guy down the block's. I'm ready to take a few drags off Life for a change."

Unfortunately, it was not going to be that easy. At the end of the week I returned to Manhattan, and before I even called to arrange repairs to the townhouse, I rang up Joel. I was a little amazed that he even took my call, but Ronni put him on the line right off, and his first words—which I expected to be hard, and hurt—were instead muted and concerned: "Richard! You okay? You still over at Ray and Melissa's?"

I hadn't realized he'd known where I was. "No," I said hesitantly. "No, I'm home. And I'm okay."

I apologized for what I said to him the week before; he didn't exactly wave it away, but he genuinely sounded more concerned than offended. "You were going through a bad time, with your mother passing away... people turn to strange things when they're going through strange times."

I felt another stab of guilt: dammit, everyone was being so bloody understanding, and it was all founded on a false assumption, a bogus mourning I never actually felt, not in the way Richard had felt it. It was at once a convenient excuse and a nagging lie; even so I grasped at it, because I had no other choice.

"Yeah," I said. "Very strange, sometimes."

Joel hesitated a moment before going on. "If I were you," he said, "I'd be less concerned with what you said to me or Ray than what this has done to you professionally. Word travels fast in this town; we've got some rebuilding to do, you understand that?"

I girded myself for the worst. "What are they saying about me?"

A brief pause, then, with a sigh: "That you're a user; that you're arrogant, temperamental, abusive; that at best, you're emotionally unstable after your Mom's death, and if you turned to coke once in a crisis, you might do it again." He paused again. "I'm sorry, man. You asked."

"Of course," I said numbly. I looked around at the ruins of the apartment, realizing that it was going to be far easier repairing the damage to the townhouse than the damage I'd done to my—to Richard's—career. "Okay," I said, taking a deep breath. "Where do we begin?"

We began with me writing a letter of apology to Jonathan Lawlor, Evan Hazlett, and the producers of *This Way Out:* not contritely asking for my job back, but a simple, sincere apology for unprofessional, uncalled-for behavior. At Joel's urging I alluded to my mother's death, but I felt somehow as though I were defiling her memory by invoking it and so limited myself to a vague reference to "emotional turmoil" and let it go at that.

Second step was to send me out on auditions: everything and anything that Joel could think of, even parts he knew I was wrong for, just to get my face seen, to show the casting directors and the producers around town that I was whole and well and clean. Or at least as whole and well and clean as you can impress upon them in a ten-, fifteen-minute reading. I auditioned for commercials, radio spots as well as TV; for guest shots on sitcoms; for plays that were so off-off-off-Broadway they might as well have been in Newark. Five weeks, eight hours a day, five days a week, rushing crosstown from one appointment to the next, from a casting office on Seventh Avenue to a sound studio on West 44th. I shook a thousand hands, smiled a thousand smiles: "Hello, nice to meet you," "Hello, how are you," and if I inadvertently said "Good to meet you" to someone with whom I—Richard—had worked with before, it became not just an innocent flub or a lapse of memory. I could see the uneasy flicker of their eyes, the wrinkle in their forehead, the worry: Is he all right? Is he still having problems? And when I didn't get the job, I never knew whether it was my reading or my reputation which had lost it for me.

I did, at least, get something I'd lacked before: practice. Short bursts of practice, to be sure—pacing in a waiting room, going over the "sides," then putting my all into one or two readings within the space of ten minutes or so; then off to the next one, a different script, a different character. It was like a scene workshop from college, though incredibly compressed and accelerated. But it was precisely what I needed to get my bearings, my confidence back again—exactly what I should have done when I first arrived in New York, but how was I to have known? For all the frantic rush and the numbing tedium of meeting and greeting innumerable people, I felt good: I may have started out shakily at first, but by the fifth week I knew I was delivering, I knew the readings were always solid and sometimes exceptional. I was improving steadily, going from rusty amateur to polished professional. And the best part was that I knew it—I felt it—without the illusive ego-boost of cocaine.

And in those five weeks, how many jobs did I get from—conservatively estimated—the hundred-odd auditions I went on?

One.

Un. Uno. Eins. A thirty-second radio spot for a local appliance chain. *"Find more at Fillmore's! In Brooklyn on Empire Boulevard, on Staten Island off Hylan Avenue, and in Morris Park at Atlantic and Lefferts. Fillmore's—find more, spend less!"*

Such was the extent to which my talents were being exploited. And damn it, I was beginning to believe again that I did have talent: that maybe I would never be as good as Richard, but that I might, possibly, be worthy of leading his life. And no one would hire me. Leads in plays went to actors I'd never even heard of; guest shots on TV eluded me, just as vexingly.

"Am I doing something wrong?" I asked Joel. "I try to sound interested, but not desperate; together, but not arrogant—"

"You're coming across fine," Joel explained. "They call me and say you're looking good, that they hope you've licked your problems." I could almost see Joel's frustrated grimace. "They just don't want to be the ones to bet their shows that you have."

What could I do? I kept at it. Kept getting better, with no outlet for my improving skills. Until, early in July, I found a message from Joel on my machine: "Call me. We've got something to discuss." There was a funny tone to his voice, and when I called him back he said, "Listen, I'm about to turn something down but I thought I should run it past you before I did."

"Turn something down?" I was appalled. "Jesus, Joel, what is it? Whatever it is, I'll do it!"

"Check your enthusiasm at the door, okay?" he said soberly. "It's some *pitzel-cocker* dinner theater, some little town in Massachusetts. They're doing a production of *The Odd Couple* and they want you to star. As Oscar. Three weeks, three-fifty a week."

Dinner theater. Even I knew what that meant. With few exceptions, dinner theaters were boneyards for ex-movie and TV stars of dubious celebrity, trotted out and propped up in indifferent productions of aging, former Broadway hits. Even I knew that any actor of Richard's caliber would never even consider doing dinner theater. Never think twice about it. A short step from that to *I'll take Richard Cochrane to block, please?*

And despite this I found myself saying, "Take it. Take the offer. I'll do it."

Joel was aghast. "Richard, this is not even remotely a horizontal career move—this is vertical, this is decaying orbit, you get what I'm saying?"

"The way I see it," I said, "I don't have much of a career at the moment, so any move is a good career move."

"You're in a slump, man, that's all; it doesn't mean you just woke up and discovered you've turned into Jamie Farr, for Chrissakes—"

"Joel, I need to work," I said imploringly. "I need to *do* something. I can't just take meeting after meeting and not use my skills! Please, Joel? Please, will you just accept it?"

There was a long silence at the other end.

"Okay. But there's more," he said. "Your reputation has preceded you even to the wilds of Massachusetts." He hesitated, as though loath to speak the next words: "They'll pay you a per diem to foot your bills during the run, but they want the option to withhold your full salary until after you've finished. In the event—"

He didn't finish, but I did: "In the event I fuck up?"

What could I do? I wanted to work—needed to work. Even if it was in Frostbite Falls, Minnesota. Even if it was dinner theater. And now this. Could I really say they were wrong, asking for such a hedge, given my recent behavior? I thought: Well, I've already humiliated myself to this extent; what's one more indignity suffered along the way?

"Take it," I said sharply. "Just *take it.*" I hung up, angry at myself for giving in, but knowing I'd be far angrier at myself had I not. For now, I tried to console myself with one thing: I had a job. Maybe not the best of all possible jobs, but compared to the alternative—voice-overs for Fillmore Appliances—it was practically Joe Papp.

I kept telling myself that a week later as I disembarked my train at the Amtrak station at Route 128 in Massachusetts; feeling, as I trundled down the steps and off the train, as though I had somehow regressed simply by being back in New England. Luckily I didn't have much time to brood. I heard my name called out and caught sight of a young woman—twenty-one, twenty-two years old—with long blonde hair, making her way through a small crowd toward me. "Mr. Cochrane!" She greeted me with a shy, formal handshake: "I'm Bettina Norris. With the Wyndham Dinner Theater. I'm so pleased to meet you." There was a bright, genuinely star-struck quality in her eyes and in her tone that disarmed me; the last time I'd seen it was my final night in New Hampshire, the clerk at the Colony Inn. She made a grab for one of my bags. "Here, let me help with that," she said, and before I could protest we were heading down the steps of the station toward the parking lot.

"Really," I said, "I can handle—"

"We would've sent a limo," she went on, guiding us toward a battered brown and white Ford station wagon, "but I thought that was too impersonal. And," she added with a sheepish smile, "because I saw you in *House of Blue Leaves* when I was in high school and I thought you were terrific."

It was a twenty-minute drive to Wyndham, Massachusetts, a small town—not much larger than Appleton—south of Boston. Bettina, it turned out, was a lighting operator at the theater, one of a small number of nonunion crew mixed with union members. I don't know what I expected to find—I'd always thought of dinner theater as kind of shlock commercial ventures, I suppose—but the staff I met was as professional and competent as any New York crew, though perhaps not as jaded. In New Hampshire I'd never thought of the Theater as anything but New York, Broadway, London. But for these people, *this* was the Theater—it was their way of being a part of it, and the fact that *The Odd Couple* had probably been staged a few hundred thousand times before didn't diminish their enthusiasm. They were taking their shot at it, and none of those other productions mattered; it didn't deter them any more than I'd been deterred, back in college, from doing *Hamlet* simply because a few other chaps like David Garrick, Edmund Kean, Olivier and Gielgud had taken a fly at it before me.

I saw at once how important all this was to them—not just the resident production staff, but the cast as well. I was the "star" name in the production; the rest of the company was filled out with local actors. At our first rehearsal I was impressed to learn how many of them struggled to make a career in regional theater—how many had day jobs to pay for their true love, and how others tried to make a go of it full-time, rooming in cheap apartments or co-ops with other actors. I'd always looked down on local theater as amateur, bush-league; only New York was professional, only New York—distant, unattainable New York, glimpsed jealously from my small-town exile, my mundane insurance job—only New York was real. Could I really have been that stupid and condescending . . . or was there some other reason I had kept away from regional groups like this back then, in my other life? The thought eluded me; I pushed it aside as rehearsals began.

Quite a difference between this read-through and my first, back in New York: the five weeks of auditioning had helped bolster my confidence, to be sure, but the truth is that I felt more on a par with these people. Most had graduated from the same kind of small, local school I had, and one had actually gone to New England College itself about five years after I graduated. They weren't as polished or practiced as my fellows from *This Way Out*, but then, neither was I, was I? I didn't feel threatened or in over my head; from the very first scene, the card game with Oscar and Vinnie and Murray and Roy and Speed, I felt at ease, I felt secure and comfortable and relaxed.

Playing Felix was Gene Symington, a local actor of some repute—a veteran of New England repertory and community theater—and when I first met him he seemed a bit nervous, uncertain, I suppose, whether or not I would try to run away with the show. In *The Odd Couple* either Oscar or Felix could walk away with it; both were great parts, and for a properly balanced production you needed a balanced cast—you needed Matthau and Lemmon, or Klugman and Randall—it couldn't be lopsided, one actor stronger than the other. Gene was a good actor, but not a "name"; I guess he had a certain justifiable apprehension that because I was the "draw" in the cast, I'd steal the play away from him. But after we finished that first read-through, he came up to me at coffee break and the tenseness was gone—because he saw that I wasn't, in fact, going to trample all over him. I suppose he thought I was holding back, trying to maintain that balance between the two characters, and he seemed both impressed and relieved.

I have to be honest: I wasn't holding back. I wasn't trying to balance the production. If I'd been able, who knows, maybe I would have tried to run off with the show; but as things stood, I couldn't. Gene had the edge on me in experience; I think I had the edge on him (he said, immodestly) in talent. So despite our disparate backgrounds, we were fairly evenly matched. The rest of the cast could attribute all the noble motives to me that they wanted, but the blunt truth was I was vastly relieved to be among equals here, and not to be the runt of the litter, as I had been in New York.

Finally I began feeling what I'd remembered feeling on the stage, back in college: that sense of excitement, of energy, of fun. It was quite a rush, throwing that plate of spaghetti onto the kitchen wall, even with rehearsal props; quite a kick when a certain delivery of a certain line brought a laugh from the other actors. It was an ideal working situation for me: I could flub a line or blow a piece of business and not be worried that the rest of the cast thought I was an amateur—far from it; they seemed impressed that I wasn't pulling any star trips, that I could shrug and say, "Well, I sure screwed that up, didn't I?" then go on and get it right next time. And I did get it right next time, because I wasn't terrified, as I had been in New York, of showing myself to be a poorer actor than they.

I made several friends during rehearsals—Gene, for one; Denise Hallyn, who played one of the Pigeon sisters, Cecily; Bob Fryer, who played Murray the Cop—all of us, and others from the cast, getting together for dinners, local restaurants during the week, Boston on weekends, or just hanging out around Wyndham.

And as much as I hated to admit it, Wyndham was one

of the reasons I felt so comfortable and relaxed. It was, as I've said, not much larger than Appleton, and in many ways felt just as familiar. There was a crossroads at the center of town, a Mobil station on one side of the road, a Richmond convenience store on the other; a little farther down there was a Wendy's, a red brick courthouse on Main Street, and an IGA market, its windows plastered with homemade posters advertising yard sales and crafts fairs and the steak and lobster dinner at the Masonic Temple that Saturday afternoon, 1:00 to 7:00 p.m., sixteen dollars a person.

All of the characteristic aspects, in short, of a small, suburban New England town; all the things that had once driven me crazy with claustrophobia, but none of which, oddly, now seemed to bother me. Perhaps because I was here as a visitor, they didn't threaten me as they once had; perhaps because I knew this was a temporary sojourn and not an incarceration for life, I could go to the Sunday morning Swap Meet with Gene and Denise and not feel as though I'd slipped back into that other, drearier world I'd escaped after so long.

But after the Swap Meet we drove south on a lazy, aimless summer's drive, winding our way along rural roads, and it wasn't just novelty that drew my gaze to the landscape rolling past. There were old saltbox-type farmhouses with lean-to roofs, tucked away an acre or more behind slide-rail fences; old churches with wooden spires and clock turrets, each of them about a minute off, as though they hadn't quite been synchronized with the present day; tranquil, sleepy little towns that all tended to look alike, and yet different if you took the time to look. I observed it all partly with the avid interest of a tourist passing through ... and partly with the quiet recognition of a longtime resident, an unvoiced, almost unarticulated pride in one's roots, one's home.

Except this wasn't my home anymore, and I *was* a tourist now. Still, it was all right, wasn't it, to take comfort in something familiar, especially after what I'd been through the past month? Nothing wrong with that, as long as I kept my perspective—right?

The play opened in mid-July to a sold-out house. I was both startled and thrilled at the burst of applause—of recognition and welcome—that greeted me on my first entrance. I held for the applause perhaps a second or two longer than I should have—I think I can be forgiven for that—and then launched into it. It was the first time I'd been up in front of an audience in thirteen years, but at the first laugh I got from the crowd, it felt remarkably as though no time at all had passed; as though I were simply picking up where I'd left off years before.

The cast clicked as we'd clicked in rehearsals; we were in excellent form, a true ensemble. At the curtain call, the actors ran one by one from the wings up to the edge of the stage and took their bows—starting with the lowest-billed players, some of them coming onstage in tandem, and culminating with me because I was the star, the name, the draw. But as good as the swell of applause at my entrance felt, I knew I was no star, just another player—and when the cast, according to tradition, joined hands for their final bow, it felt somehow more just, more equitable.

Mixed with the satisfaction of each succeeding performance, however, I discovered a strange kind of melancholy, as well; as we slowly neared the end of our three-week run, I began to dread, more and more, that final performance.

Gene, Denise, Bettina Laurel–these people had saved me, in a way; had given me safe harbor at a time I needed it most; had provided me with confidence and security in a way they could never know. And the town–Wyndham. I told myself its quiet and solitude was comforting in the way Ray's beach house had been comforting: a breather, a refresher, a pause after stormy times. But was that all that made me sorry to leave its narrow paths and cobbled walks, its suburban monotony that seemed not so tedious, not so restrictive as it once had?

Yes. That was all it was: the contrast between the chaos of Catlin, New York, and cocaine, and this safe, restful interlude. It was exactly what I'd needed, but now it was time to move on; back to New York, back to the auditions, back to building, or rebuilding, my career.

I'd just about convinced myself of that, the next to the last night of our run; had basked in what I knew would be the penultimate curtain call, had gone back to my dressing table to take off my makeup, when I heard from behind me something even more familiar than the town and the countryside; familiar, and far more intimate.

"Richard?"

I recognized the voice at once, but dismissed it as impossible. I started to turn around in my seat, expecting to be reassured by the sight of some stranger who merely sounded familiar–but no. I turned, and saw her standing there behind me, wearing a light summer dress, smiling hesitantly at me.

It was Debra.

For an instant I thought the two worlds, Richard's and mine, had somehow converged again; that this woman I was staring at in surprise was my wife, who'd tracked her runaway husband to this tiny dinner theater in this small suburban town and had come to reclaim him. But as I stood up—the smile on my face not betraying, I hoped, my astonishment and anxiety—I noted the tall man standing beside her, his arm around her waist, and I realized that all that was just daydream or nightmare, I wasn't sure which.

"Hi," she said. "You remember Mark?"

Not my Debra; the other Debra. The one who'd never given birth to Paige, never married me, never mothered Jeffrey. A different person entirely, but—Good God, so much the same, too. Her hair was styled differently, a little longer, a little more fashionably; she wore her makeup a bit differently too, and her glasses were a tad more stylish. But the face, the eyes, the body—all that was the same; impossibly, paradoxically, she was different and yet not different, another woman entirely and yet the *same* woman. Jesus—was this how Richard had felt, standing outside my house in Appleton, seeing my Debra?

"Mark. Of course," I said, shaking her husband's outstretched hand. Debra stepped up, gave me a polite hug; I tingled, strangely, at her touch. "You were terrific," she said, separating too soon. "Great show."

"I'm flattered," I said. "You guys came all the way down from"—I almost said *Appleton,* but caught myself in time—"Concord? Just to see me?"

"Well," Debra admitted sheepishly, "I did have some gallery business in Boston today, so we thought we'd make a weekend of it. We don't make it down to Broadway very often, so we thought it was damned nice of you bringing Broadway up here, just for us."

I laughed. The same Debra: same candor, same sense

of humor. The humor that toward the end had seemed to me mocking and contemptuous; the candor I had never wanted to hear. But now, here, it seemed charming and sexy, the way it had when I first began falling in love with her, years and worlds ago. I was alarmed at what I was feeling now, at the stirrings inside me, the sense of loss I suddenly found there.

"If you're not busy," Mark said, "maybe you'd like to grab some coffee across the street?"

What could I say? "Yes," I said, wanting it and not wanting it, "that would be nice. Let me just get myself together." I finished removing my makeup and the three of us crossed the street to the Minuteman Cafe. If I had any remaining doubts that I was, in fact, a good actor, they were erased by that simple half-hour conversation. I smiled, I laughed, I listened to stories about their ten-year-old, Eric, as I in turn regaled them with showbiz anecdotes, most of them stolen from Ray—and it was torture, all of it. Every minute was agony, seeing her again—her and yet not-her—seeing her with this amiable stranger whom I rather liked, hearing about the child she'd had with someone else, about the life she'd forged without me. The similarities were haunting, the differences somehow enticing: the perfume she wore, the subtle but unaccustomed shade of eyeshadow, the way she held her coffee cup. God help me, I wanted her: I wanted her badly. But was it love, or loss, or merely a desire to mark this Debra as my own—to both embrace and wipe away the differences, to make her mine just out of jealousy or envy? I didn't know. It didn't matter. We talked, we laughed, and after we finished our coffee they had to hit the road—not to Concord, it was too late to drive all the way back to New Hampshire, but to their hotel in

Boston. I thanked them for coming, shook Mark's hand again, bussed Debra nervously on the cheek, then walked back to my own hotel, along a street that might've passed for Schuyler Street, back in Appleton. Back to a room where, as I lay naked in bed, I masturbated fiercely for half an hour, seeing her face, her body, remembering her scent, remembering what it felt like being inside her—except that the face kept changing, ever so slightly, and even as I came, even as I whispered her name in the dark, I could not tell which Debra I had been fantasizing; nor which woman I was longing for.

The final performance came and went. At the cast party we said our farewells, cried our tears, promised to stay in touch though somehow I knew we never would. I took the night train back to New York, thinking of the events of the past month: of Ray and Melissa's care and concern; of the friends in Wyndham who had given me more than they could ever suspect; of last night, and the strange feelings developing within me.

I thought of my rage after being fired in New York and the devastation I had wreaked on my apartment. I tried to use it to frighten myself out of what I was feeling, but it didn't work: I'd been alone in the apartment and the damage I'd done had been merely to furniture or belongings. I kept thinking about that one night with Catlin, when she had lashed out at me with those long, sharp fingernails, drawing blood, and of how I'd raised my hand to hit her . . . but didn't. Even when I wanted to—even when she wanted me to—I couldn't do it.

And now I found myself wondering: if I couldn't do it then, to Catlin . . . could I ever really have done it Debra?

CHAPTER THIRTEEN

RICHARD

A y,'" said Juliet, rubbing her hands together uncon-sciously, nervously, as she entered the bedchamber with her Nurse, "'those attires are best; but, gentle nurse, I pray thee leave me to myself tonight; for I have need of many orisons'"—and here she closed her eyes briefly, her nervous hands knitting together in something like a prayer—"'to move the heavens to smile upon my state, which, well thou knowest, is cross and full of sin...'"

I smiled. She did the business with her hands perfectly, just as we'd rehearsed it; making it seem like a spontane-ous movement, and not a subtle but artificial way to define *orison* for the audience. I stole a glance at the rest of the crowded high school auditorium; was it just fatherly pride or did they seem as absorbed in Paige's performance as I was?

After the exit of Juliet's mother and nurse, Paige lin-gered at the doorway, looking wistfully after: "'Fare-well,'" she said softly. "'God knows when we shall meet again. I have a faint cold fear thrills through my veins, that almost freezes up the heat of life...'" This was the scene in which Juliet contemplates taking the poison that shall render her seemingly lifeless, as per the Friar's plan. Now she begins to have second thoughts, mood swinging back and forth between hope and fear, anticipation and premonition—not the easiest of shifts to pull off, but Paige handled it beautifully: "'What if it be poison,'" she said, fearfully, "'which the Friar subtly hath ministered to make me dead, lest in this marriage he should be dishonored—because he married me before to Romeo...?'"

I felt as excited, as exhilarated as I had on any opening night I could remember: that familiar first-night enthusiasm, trying to get the sense of the audience, trying to feel its mood, its responses to a line, a movement, a silence... but it felt strange as well, because suddenly I was on the wrong side of the proscenium. There was no smell of greasepaint or spirit gum, of fresh lumber or newly painted sets; there were no footlights at the edge of my vision, no dim parquet beyond; no wings to my left nor flies above, and the spotlights were not blazing suns shining from on high, but shafts of light that passed above my head, just out of reach.

"'O, look!'" Paige said, in a soft, wondrous tone we had practiced long to achieve; "'methinks I see my cousin's ghost seeking out Romeo, that did spit his body upon a rapier's point.'" She raised the vial of poison with one hand, holding out the other as though to ward off the errant spirit. "'Stay, Tybalt, stay Romeo, I come! this do I drink to thee.'"

She'd learned, she'd learned well and quickly; she was better than anyone else on that stage and the audience knew it. From her first, faltering steps weeks before, coping with cadence and syntax, she had grown into her role—not always an easy task, as on the day she threw her copy of the play to the granite floor of our secret stage in exasperation, cursing the play, cursing Shakespeare, cursing Juliet. "She makes me want to *scream,*" she said, sitting on the edge of the 'stage,' popping open a can of soda. "I mean, she is such a wimp. Why don't she and Romeo just up and leave? To heck with the Capulets, to heck with the Montagues, why all this plotting and scheming and wailing?"

I sat down beside her, stealing a swallow of her Coke. "It was a different time," I said, "and running away wasn't as easy as it is now. Especially not for the offspring of two noble houses."

She frowned, looking a little desolate. "How do I play someone like that? Someone so different, from a different time?"

"Well, there are two schools of thought on that, each valid. One would have you find something in yourself that you can relate to the role—go in, inside yourself, to find the character. The other would have you reach out— that is, if you're playing someone so far outside your experience you can't find any parallels inside you, then you simply...extend yourself...to *become* the character."

She looked at me hopelessly. "Dad, I'm thirteen years old. No way can I do that! Not yet."

I considered a long moment before replying.

"Juliet feels...trapped. Trapped between her family and Romeo, between Romeo and her intended groom, Paris. So trapped that she's willing to take the most desperate measures to get out." I looked at her. "Are you sure you've never felt that trapped? That desperate?"

She looked at me for an instant, then glanced away. "No," she said quickly. "Never."

"Not even," and I proceeded cautiously, "the night your Mom and I were fighting—and you came down the stairs, and said—"

"I know what I said." She stared down at her sneakers. "Daddy, I . . . I don't like thinking about that, okay?"

"Neither do I," I said gently, "but it's okay to think about it, 'cause it's not going to happen again. And because what you were feeling that night—that's Juliet. She's there; she's inside you. It's all right for you to use her."

She was silent a moment, then looked up, her face torn with conflicting emotions. "It hurts to think about it," she said. "Do I have to?"

I touched her cheek, then shook my head. "No. Not if you're not ready to. But if you're really serious about being an actress, you will have to confront this someday. Acting does hurt, sometimes. If it's good . . . if it's true . . . it does hurt."

She didn't speak any more of it that day and hadn't since. But sitting here tonight, watching her perform, I knew—in a way no one else could know or see—that she was using that Juliet inside her. She was using the pain, using it to create something beautiful; rough and unpolished, perhaps, but true, and because it was true it did have beauty. She might not have realized it . . . might not realize it for years to come . . . but here, tonight, is when she first became an actress. And when the curtain fell, when the applause began, I clapped longest and loudest of all—because alone of the hundred or so people in that room, I knew what it had cost her.

"God, isn't she wonderful?" I said, turning to Debra as we both applauded. "Wasn't she terrific?"

There were tears round the edges of Debra's eyes—tears for Paige or tears for something else, I couldn't tell.

"Yes," she said, smiling. "She *was* wonderful."

Afterward we went backstage and I hugged her long and hard. "Honey, you were great. I'm so proud of you."

We separated and she looked at me with quiet delight and a hint of amazement. "I was worried about the poison scene . . . I wasn't sure if—"

"Are you kidding?" I said. "You were perfect. That can be the hardest scene to pull off, sometimes, for an actress, but you handled it like a real pro."

And now, suddenly, tears sprang to Paige's eyes too, and she hugged me again, her voice wavering between happiness and disbelief. "Oh God, Daddy," she said, "thank you. Thank you . . ."

Debra gave her a hug, offering her own plaudits, and as she did I noticed someone off to my right, a familiar stance at the periphery of my vision. I turned to find Frank Conover beside me, a smile on his face, a hand extended toward me. "Hello, Rick."

I took his hand and smiled. "Frank. Good to see you." He'd changed little since college: tall, lanky, his hairline receding somewhat, dressed in a tweedy sport coat with patches at the elbows, pleated pants, rep tie. When he was a boy, Frank's family lived briefly on Nob Hill, but though their fortunes declined, Frank's pretensions, alas, did not.

He turned to Paige, shaking her hand as well. "Very nice, young lady, very nice indeed. Congratulations."

"Thanks, Mr. Conover."

Another cast member swooped down on Paige, bearing her off momentarily, and meanwhile Debra had begun talking to the mother of the girl who'd played the Nurse, leaving me off to one side with Frank. "You have good reason to be proud of her," he said, with what seemed genuine pleasure. "She's a natural. In rehearsals she'd come up with all sorts of ideas, bits of business, line readings I wouldn't have expected of someone of her age and experience. I helped her shape them, of course, but her instincts are good, very good..."

Helped her shape them. I kept a pleasant smile on my face. "Yes," I agreed, "I think so."

"Good genes, maybe," Frank said, taking me by surprise. "You showed a lot of promise yourself back in college."

He said it in the same schoolmasterish tone he used when speaking of Paige. I fought to keep my smile in place, as his own smile became a bit wistful and not a little patronizing. "Seems a shame you never did anything with all that training. You ever regret it?"

My expression turned sober; I hoped he took it for quiet contemplation and not the wounded pride and stifled anger it really was. "Sometimes," I said. I considered adding, *Do you ever regret, Frank, teaching drama at some jerkwater junior high, instead of, say, Dartmouth or Yale?*—but thought better of it.

"Well," he said, "maybe your daughter will go on to do what you didn't. I do hope you encourage her, Rick. I mean, granted, it's none of my business, you're her father, but she has talent. It would be a shame to waste it."

Waste it. Like me. I wanted to bludgeon him with my Drama Desk Award, but instead I just smiled and nodded. "I have every intention," I said, as congenially as I could manage, "of encouraging her, if it's what she wants to do." I shook Frank's hand again, thanked him for his support of Paige, and made my way through the room crowded with student actors, friends, and parents, until I was at my wife's side. Suddenly it was stiflingly hot in here. "What's the plan, Sam?" I said, trying to keep the tenseness and irritation from my tone.

"Same sad tale," she sighed. "Cast party. Parents left out in cold. Tragic, really."

"In that case," I said, leaning in to murmur in her ear, "what say we find an old sleeping bag somewhere and see where second base has gotten to?"

She laughed, put an arm around me as I did her, and after congratulating Paige one more time, we left—skirting, on our way out, the wings of the stage. We passed by for no more than a few moments, but in those moments I took it all in: the fresh smell of new lumber; of makeup and wig paste; even the lingering heat generated by the now-extinguished footlights and spots. We were gone soon after, into the warm June evening, but those moments stayed with me for hours—even while making love, even as I drifted off to sleep—stayed with me longer than I'd expected, and perhaps longer than I'd wished.

At Finney's arraignment in Manchester he was charged with Aggravated DUI, reckless driving, and at least one moving violation I'd never even heard of. With his Jag in the shop, I felt obliged to take the day off and drive him to court, not passing up the opportunity to continue pressing him to join AA; but though he apologized for saying what he had to me that night outside the police station, he was as hard-assed as ever about getting help or about needing help. "No way, man," he said, "no way am I getting together with a bunch of gimps. Forget it."

I sat with him through the arraignment, my anger mounting as, after two and a half hours of waiting for his case to come up, a court date was finally set and we were out of there, both feeling drained and dry. I suggested we grab some lunch at the McDonald's down the street, Finney preferring a small restaurant on the corner. "C'mon, man, no McShitburgers, okay?" But no sooner had we slid into one of the restaurant's red vinyl booths when I came to realize Finney's true preference for this place. A waitress approached and Finney immediately ordered a beer.

I looked at him in stunned reproach. He gave me a long-suffering look. "What? What now?"

I stared at him a moment, then shook my head. "Jesus Christ, Finney," I said. "You are some piece of work."

"C'mon man, it's just a Budweiser. And anyway, you're driving."

"That's not the point!"

"It's just a goddamn beer," he persisted, stubbornly. "Stop making a Federal case out of it."

I could see he wasn't going to budge; as if he didn't drink this beer, he'd be tacitly admitting that he had a problem. I sat there fuming as the waitress came over and planted a tall beer glass with a thick head of foam atop it in front of Finney. And as soon as she did, I found myself sliding out of the booth.

"Cochrane? Where you going?"

I started walking away, toward the exit. "Home," I said. "Enjoy your Bud."

His beer not yet touched, he scrambled out of the booth after me. "Oh, for Chrissakes, man, don't—" He grabbed at my arm, stopping me—though part of him knew, I think, that I had stopped of my own volition. "How the hell am I supposed to get back to town?"

"You can walk back," I said tightly, "for all I care." I shrugged off his hold on my arm, continued threading my way through the tables in the dimly lit restaurant. He stared after me a moment, torn and indecisive, then, huffing back to the table with a great show of exasperation, slapped some bills down, left his drink behind, and hurried to catch up with me. "All right, goddammit, all right! You satisfied?"

The drive back to Appleton was as tense as the last, though not as silent. As we passed Pine Island Pond, and the southern outskirts of Manchester, I said—in a very deliberate, very flat tone of voice—"I called, a few days ago, to ask about Miriam Cooperman."

"Who?" Finney said, blankly.

I felt a sudden stab of anger, fought it back, giving him merely a pointed glance. "The woman you ran into," I said evenly. "I called the hospital to ask about her condition." Suddenly quiet, Finney looked down as I kept my eyes forward, on the road. "I lied and told them I was a cousin of hers, calling from Florida. Wanted to know how she was doing, whether I should fly up and see her."

"And they bought it?"

I nodded. Finney forced a small smile. "You always were a pretty fair actor," he said. I didn't reply. Didn't say anything, purposely—wanting him to ask the next question. Finally, he did. "So how is she?" he asked, his face turning toward the side window.

"She's conscious," I said slowly, "and the internal injury—the bleeding—is under control. But as they'd feared, there's been some neural damage." I watched him twitch, his face still turned away, his reflection lost in the bright sunlight. "They likened it to the kind of motor impairment people suffer after a stroke. She can barely walk; can't hold a pen, or a fork, can't do anything with her right hand. She's going to need months, maybe years, of retraining; learning to use those parts of her body, all over again."

He looked back, a tentative relief on his face. "But she will get it back?" he said. "Some of it?"

"Enough," I allowed. "Eighty, ninety percent. Enough to function."

Finney, the idiot, actually smiled with relief. "Well, that's great," he said. "That's terrific. She'll be okay."

I turned, fixing him with a disgusted glare. "You don't get it, do you?" I said. "She's lost a year of her life—maybe more—and maybe twenty percent of her potential. She was an electronics technician—worked in computer mainframes. Very delicate work—you actually go in, work with the circuit boards—"

I turned back to the road. "In insurance we have a ratings manual for what we call 'residual disabilities.' Minimal, slight, moderate, severe. Even with 'moderate' disabilities, people sometimes can never go back to their old line of work." I glanced back at him. "What if she has to find a new career, Finney? What then?"

Finney shrugged. "Then she'll find a new one. The insurance'll take care of retraining, right?"

Angrily I said, "What if she likes what she does now, Finney? What if she loves what she does? Christ, man— some people have careers."

He threw me a sullen look. It was a cheap shot, I knew, but I didn't care; because it was true and it was germane.

Finney seemed to care for so very little in his own life, he couldn't imagine anyone else having anything valuable or perishable in theirs; so anything he did to them couldn't matter, because he couldn't imagine it mattering.

He swallowed his anger and his pride and said sharply, "So what the hell do you want from me, man? You want me to go to fucking AA, is that it?"

"Finney," I said, trying somehow to get through, "I understand what you're going through—this compulsion, this—"

"How the hell," he shot back, "would *you* know about what I'm going through? Give me a for instance, Cochrane, okay?"

I couldn't answer. How did I explain that I did understand what addiction was like—maybe not alcohol addiction, but compulsion, obsession, oh yes, that I knew all too well from my brief, turbulent marriage to Catlin. I understood addiction because I'd been addicted to *her*, to the kind of sex I had with her that I had with no one else before or since. I understood compulsion from two years of trying to hold on to her by adopting her lifestyle—pissing away my money as fast as I made it on upscale clothes, expensive restaurants every night of the week, extravagant gifts that I somehow thought might buy Catlin's devotion, might appease her for my not indulging in the rest of her vices—the booze, the drugs. It had taken me three years to dig my way out of the debt I incurred in that short, disastrous marriage; yet even now, thinking of Catlin, I felt a hint of familiar arousal, a temptation I simply had to ignore. Yes, I understood addiction very well, but none of this, or anything like it, existed in Rick's experience—how did I explain any of it to Finney?

Very simply, I couldn't. "If you're convicted," I said lamely, "the courts will make you go into rehab."

"Fine," he snapped. "I'll deal with it then. And in the meantime, get off my fucking case."

I was silent a long moment, then nodded, slowly.

"Fine," I said, stonily. "I'll stay as far off your case as possible. I don't want you calling, I don't want you dropping by with liquor on your breath, I don't want to see your goddamn face until you're ready to get help. When you are, I'll be there. But until then, I don't know you—I don't *want* to know you."

He was half angry, half astonished. "You're serious... aren't you?"

I don't know if Rick would have reacted this way, and right now, I didn't care.

"Yes," I said. "I am."

And true to my word, I kept away from Finney those next several weeks. He didn't call, he didn't stop by, and I didn't seek him out. I couldn't force him to go to AA or to a shrink, all I could do was wait until he was ready, or until the courts made him ready. And I got on with my life.

Debra made her first tentative inroads into art appraisal; through a contact in the gallery she used to work in, she was hired to assess the value of an old Turner found in the effects of a recently deceased dowager in Milford. I came home from work to find her still hard at hers, poring through catalogs from Sotheby's and Christie's, reading and rereading passages from half a dozen art history books that obviously hadn't been taken off the shelves in years... and as I watched her polishing her glasses in the bright fluorescence of a desk lamp or intently flipping through pages, I caught a glimpse, I think, of the Debra that Rick had told me about. The one who stood up before her night classes, pointer in hand, passionate about Goya and *kouros* statues, light playing on her hair and in her glasses ... and I felt sorry for Rick that he couldn't be here to see it.

Toward the end of June the first of the summer's stage productions began at Prescott Park: a local theater group, the Pennacook Players, were doing the old Comden and Green musical *Wonderful Town*. Debra was busy with her work and Paige found my description of it a bit too creaky and old-fashioned for her taste, but my mother remembered with fondness the old Rosalind Russell movie *My Sister Eileen,* which shared the same source material as the musical ... and so I succeeded in prying her from her house for an evening. The two of us drove to Portsmouth, bought a bucketful of fried shrimp from one of the many vendors, then settled down on a blanket on the warm summer grass with a hundred or so other spectators gathered round the open-air amphitheater. I brought along a folding canvas beach chair for Mom and made sure she packed a sweater and a coat, in the event a cool wind blew in off the water; but the breezes were light and warm and she barely even needed the sweater, even after the sun went down.

I lay easily on my side, propped up on one elbow, as a cast of enthusiastic local singers and dancers launched into the opening number, "Christopher Street." A few minutes later, I suddenly sat up, startled at the entrance of the actress playing Ruth, the star role. "I'll be damned," I said softly, more to myself than to my mother. "It's Susan DeVries." Off my mother's blank look I added, "I went to college with her. We were in a production of *Tartuffe* together."

We watched as "Ruth" and her sister "Eileen"—two naive young girls, fresh from Columbus, Ohio—contended with typewriter thieves and assorted 1930s Greenwich Village eccentrics, all on their first day in the Big City. Ruth had the best lines, the kind of smart, fast, Thirties dialog that wore as well today as it did then—Ruth identifies her stolen typewriter by the missing "W" key: "It fell off after I wrote my thesis on Walt Whitman"—the audience laughing in all the right places. After Susan, as Ruth, got off a particularly good line and the actors held for the laugh, my mother turned and tapped me on the arm. "She's good, isn't she?"

I nodded. "Yes. She is. Nice timing." And she was good; no Meryl Streep, certainly, but a talented light comedienne. I was pleased and surprised to see one of my classmates on a stage after all these years; the only other being Gary Kohler, who moved to New York a little after I had, did a few one-line roles in a few off-off-Broadway plays, then vanished, presumably back to New Hampshire. Or maybe not; I'd done my share of touring, but that was with national companies, and chauvinistic as it sounds, it hadn't occurred to me that some of my classmates might be practicing their craft a bit closer to home.

Home. I had occasion to consider that word, in the next few minutes, as Ruth and Eileen—both of them horrified at New York, yearning for safe, comfortable Columbus—sang the plaintive duet "Ohio":

> *Why, oh why, oh why, oh—*
> *Why did I ever leave Ohio?*
> *Why did I wander to find what lies yonder*
> *When life was so cozy at home?*

Wond'ring while I wander,
Why did I fly,
Why did I roam . . .
Maybe I'd better go home.
Maybe I'd better go home.

The song evoked in me an odd reaction: in its wistful longing I felt echoes of my own yearning, back in New York, to escape to that lost home I'd left behind; but what I was feeling now was more than just an echo. I felt suddenly as the characters did on the stage; I wanted to go home, wanted it so badly, if only for an instant, that I could join them in their lament. But *this* was home—the home I'd longed for, the life I'd let slip by once, reclaimed only by a twist of time and chance. I didn't miss New York; it wasn't that simple. Somewhere inside me something was mourning, for what, for where, I didn't know; or perhaps I just didn't want to know.

The song ended and the mood passed as the musical barreled along. Susan was excellent, she really carried the show, though the other players were perfectly competent, too. When it was over we applauded, the cast took their curtain call, and I helped my mother to her feet. "Come on," I said, collapsing her canvas chair, tucking it under my arm, "let's go backstage. I want to say hello to Susan."

"Oh, no—I wouldn't feel right, intruding."

"Mom," I said patiently, "it's okay, people do it all the time, even on Broadway—"

"No," she insisted, "you go. She's your friend. I'll wait in the car." Resigning myself, I gave her the car keys, told her to turn on the heater, and made my way backstage alone.

I wandered back to the rather improvised dressing

areas, where a small knot of well-wishers had gathered around Susan. I held back until they had all had their turns, then stepped forward. "Susan. Hi. It's—"

"Rick?" She broke into a startled smile. "My God! How *are* you?" We hugged briefly; she half turned to a beefy man with thinning hair standing beside her and introduced me. "Ted, this is Rick Cochrane—we were classmates at NEC. We did *Tartuffe* together. Rick, this is my husband, Ted Hanley."

We shook hands, saying our hellos, and then I noticed two smaller figures lurking behind Ted and Susan. "And these," Susan said, "are Samantha and Ted, Jr." Samantha looked to be about eight, Ted, Jr., maybe a year older. They smiled a little shyly and hung back as I congratulated their mother. "You were great out there," I told her, "but then, you always were the best comedienne in class."

"That's sweet," she said. "Thank you. I was just relieved we got through it at all—our assistant stage manager left us a few weeks back, moved down to Providence to work for Trinity Rep... God, it's been a nightmare. I'm glad it didn't look like one."

"Not in the least," I assured her. "Have you been with this company very long?"

"About five, six years. Once these guys"—she nodded toward her kids—"got out of the Terrible Twos, I had the time again."

"And your theater is—?"

"Over in Exeter. We do a little bit of everything—classics, light comedy, a few new plays by local playwrights... in the last year we've done everything from *As You Like It* to *American Buffalo*."

I don't know why I should have been as surprised as I

was, but I hope I didn't show it. Then, just as I was tempted to ask Susan, Why didn't you ever have a go at it in New York? she preempted me with: "So Rick—what have you been doing since graduation?"

My lofty chauvinism promptly burst, pricked by a single innocent question to which I could give only one answer. "Well," I said, "you, ah, remember Debra Aversano... we got married... two kids, Paige and Jeffrey..." All at once I felt ill at ease, defensive. Why the hell had I done this? Why was I suddenly embarrassed and ashamed of things I'd spent years dreaming of, longing for? "We live over in Appleton, and I'm in... insurance... down in Nashua..."

"Keeping your hand in acting, at all?"

"Ah... no. No, I'm afraid not."

She looked surprised. "Really?" she said, sounding genuinely disappointed. "Why not?"

I didn't know what to say. It was a question that only Rick could answer, and one—in my zeal to trade places with him—that I'd never thought to ask him, one that, until this moment, had never even occurred to me. I looked at Susan and her family; even if she didn't have a day job, raising two kids was probably more than the equivalent of one... and still she'd managed to find the time to practice her craft. Why hadn't Rick?

At a loss to explain "my" self, I just shrugged. "Just never seemed to find the time," I said lamely.

"But you—" Susan hesitated; then, forcefully: "You were so *good*, Rick. Really good." I felt like I was hearing my own postmortem. This was worse than the condescension I'd gotten from Conover because Susan obviously cared and I found myself feeling guilty—feeling as though I'd let her down, somehow. God, if only I'd been able to tell her the truth.

"Look," Susan said, pulling a card from her purse, "we're not a very large company—just a little community theater—but why don't you come over, meet some of the people, and maybe try out for a show? Lots of our people have day jobs, we've got flexible rehearsal periods—nights, weekends—"

Reluctantly, I took the card. "I appreciate the thought, but . . . I'm really not sure."

"Well, give it some thought, okay?"

Trying to bring the subject—and the conversation—to an end, I glanced at my watch. "I'd better let you go. I brought my mother up to see the show, she's waiting for me. Congratulations again, you were super."

She hugged me once more, kissed me on the cheek. "It was good seeing you again, Rick," she said. "And think about what I said, okay?"

I shook Ted's hand again, made my goodbyes, and got out of there, fast—my mind a tangle of emotions I could barely sort out. I hurried back to the parking lot, where my mother sat in the Volvo—engine idling, heater on—looking up as I opened the driver's door and slid inside.

"You talk with your friend?" she asked.

I keyed the ignition, flipped on the headlights. "Yes. Very nice. I met her husband, her kids . . . it was—nice."

We drove down Marcy Street, through downtown Portsmouth, picking up I-95 at Woodbury Avenue; from there we'd connect to the 101, the 102, and eventually back to Appleton. My mother was silent for a while, but about the time we hit I-95 she spoke up, in a quiet and dreamy sort of voice. "It was a lovely show, Rick. Thank you for taking me."

I smiled. "I enjoyed it, too."

She paused briefly; then: "Your father and I saw the movie years ago, on television. You know how obsessed with old movies he got, later on... looking up the names of character actors from the thirties, the forties, in that book you got him—what was it—?"

"*The Filmgoer's Companion.*" Rick had obviously gotten him the same book as I had my father.

"God, yes. He used to drive me crazy, sometimes, asking me out of the blue, 'Do you remember that girl, the one who starred in *Broadway Melody*?' Or, 'What was that movie Wallace Beery made, the one with Enid Bennett?' A day didn't go by that he didn't dredge up some old movie I barely even remembered, asking me about some dead movie star I couldn't care less about—"

"He was just trying to...recapture something. His youth, his past, the world that was..." I considered what I'd just said. "You know, I never really thought about it before, but...your generation was probably the first to have its past preserved like that, on film. Different from having it written up in books, or captured in still photos... forty years later, the whole world as immediate, real, as alive now as it was then...but dead. Gone." I thought about films and TV shows from my own youth, how odd it sometimes seemed even to me—the world outside altered in some ways beyond recognition, but the world the shows depicted, unchanged and immutable... "It must have been strange for him," I said quietly. "Comfortable, but—strange."

Mother looked at me sadly. "He wasn't always like he was, at the end—he was a good man, Rick. A good provider. He always saw to it we had everything we needed."

"I know," I said.

"When the hurricane flooded the house, you remember how he moved as much of the furniture as he could to the second floor, all by himself...he was always so thin, you know, but when he needed to be, so strong..."

I nodded. "He was a tough old bird."

"When I think of him, I see him as he was when I met him," she said softly. "Dapper. Wiry. That thin mustache. Not...not that old man lying on the couch; a young pilot in his Cessna, wearing his flying goggles." She paused. "Sometimes I wish he hadn't sold it when we married..."

Something vague moved restlessly within me, but before I could put a name to it, it was gone, lost in my memories of Dad. "I remember him in the Catskills," I said, "diving into the pool, like he used to...he couldn't swim, could he? But he dove right off the diving board, through the deep end, into the shallow..."

"Like me," she said. "Neither of us could swim."

I turned to her. "What do you mean, you can't swim?" I said, taken aback. "You were always in the pool with me, when I was little."

"In the shallow end," she said. "It was that lifeguard who taught you to swim, remember? Your father and I were both terrified of the water. His mother'd thrown a scare into him about it when he was little; he never got over it. Mine did the same thing."

"But we used to go to the shore...and on Uncle Nick's

boat... and when we went on vacation, you'd always take me to motels with swimming pools."

She nodded. "Your father and I," she said, "were determined we wouldn't do to you what our parents did to us. We wanted you not to be afraid of the water; we didn't want to pass on our fear of it to you." She smiled proudly. "And we didn't. You took to it right away."

For the second time that night, I didn't know what to say. Somehow you never think you're going to discover major revelations about your parents when they're in their sixties; you think, smugly, that you know all there is to know about them. But clearly I didn't.

"I..." Nothing I could say seemed adequate. "Thank you," I said quietly. "I had no idea."

She said nothing, just smiled and patted me on the arm; and all the long drive back to Appleton, I began to see my parents in a different light. For years I had been baffled and aggravated by their provincialism, their reluctance to go new places, try new things; but that was only part of them, the part easiest to discern. For years I'd thought that I'd struggled to overcome the inertia that seemed to rule their lives and break free on my own; but now I knew that in at least this one thing, they had given me a hand up and out, without me even knowing it. I felt ashamed. Ashamed because in this way and in others—during that terrible hurricane; that last day in the hospital, before my father went in for surgery; at all the funerals for all the relatives Mom had buried over the years; in God knows how many other ways I was still unaware of—they had put aside their fears and done what was needed, because it was needed. And I could only hope, should I someday be called to account, that I could say the same; that I could acquit myself as well as they.

Some weeks later, in mid-July, Finney called again, this time to ask if I would drive him to his court date in Manchester. "I could go with my attorney," he said, "but I'd rather ride with a friend." He sounded frightened and alone, and more important, not afraid to admit it. I took a day off from work, swung by Finney's house around eight, and we were in the Manchester courthouse by nine. On the way up he talked about sports, about the Red Sox victory over Milwaukee the night before—but distantly, as though hoping the sound of his own voice might distract him from himself. Looking at him—at the tenseness in his shoulders, at the way he stared constantly out the side window, afraid to meet my gaze—my anger at him dissipated, but it was more than pity that dissolved it. No matter what he'd done, I was still his friend; his only friend, perhaps, in many ways. In the courtroom I sat directly behind him but slightly to the right, far enough so that he could catch sight of me with a sideways glance, hoping my presence might bolster him through what was to come.

Because this was not a trial, but a sentencing. Finney had retained a sharp local lawyer to defend him, but the case against him was so open-and-shut, the evidence so overwhelmingly negative, that even Perry Mason would've balked. Three people had seen Finney run the red light on Maple; Breathalyzer tests had shown a .20 alcohol content in his blood. Waiving a jury trial—the last thing Finney needed was Miriam Cooperman, laden with prostheses, limping up to the witness stand—the attorney had plea-bargained, got the best deal he could under the circumstances, and Finney pled guilty.

The sentence was not lenient but not unfair, either: three years' suspension of license, a mandatory ten days in jail, and compulsory enrollment in an alcohol abuse program. I saw Finney flinch at each count as it was read, but after it was over he stood straight and composed as officers took him into custody for his downtime. Before they did, he turned to me and shook my hand. "Thanks, Cochrane. Thanks for coming," he said, trying to sound offhanded. "Give me a ride home in about a week and a half?"

"Sure. Of course," I said. And then he was led away, and I didn't see Finney for the next ten days.

Now, I know the city jail in Manchester, New Hampshire, is not exactly Leavenworth, but it couldn't have been very pleasant nonetheless. I never did find out how unpleasant, because Finney wouldn't talk about it. Not when I picked him up the following Wednesday, not that night when Debra and I took him out for dinner (but no drinks)—not even as I drove him the following week, to his first AA meeting in neighboring Derry.

The local chapter held its meeting Thursday nights in the basement of a small church. It was roomy, warm, with thirty to forty folding chairs and a coffee machine serving up a never-ending supply of caffeine, dozens of ashtrays, and a single podium at the front. As we entered there were already a dozen or so members working the Mr. Coffee, but Finney steered clear, taking a seat near the back and off to one side, with me beside him for moral support. He looked tense, anxious; he looked as though he hated being here and he might bolt at any moment. I chatted with him about the Mets game that weekend, occupying his thoughts until the room finally filled up and one of the members—a short, stocky man built like a small retaining wall, with crewcut graying hair—stood and took the rostrum.

"Welcome," he said, "to a fellowship of those who share certain problems. Tonight, we will tell each other our experience—how we came to be here; our strength—how we got safely through it; and our hope—how it is for us now."

He turned to a small table, picking up a large leather volume and placing it atop the podium, and began to read from what he called the "Big Book," which included the twelve steps to sobriety. "One," he said. "We admitted we were powerless over alcohol—that our lives had become unmanageable.

"Two: Came to believe that a Power greater than ourselves could restore us to sanity..."

At first I balked a bit myself at this "greater power" business, wondering if this was going to turn into a revivalist meeting. But when I spoke with some of the members later on, I learned that a "greater power" didn't necessarily mean God—although for some, of course, it did—it could mean Fate, Destiny, Love, Human Contact, Moral Support, anything outside the self in which power could be vested, in which trust could be laid and drawn upon as needed. Finney sat there stonily through the first few "commandments," a deepening scowl on his face as it progressed.

"Eight: Made a list of all persons we had harmed, and became willing to make amends to them all."

Finney stiffened, shuddered. He stared straight ahead, lips tightly together.

"Nine," the man continued. "Made direct amends to such people wherever possible, except when to do so would injure them or others..."

I looked at Finney and saw that his hands were trembling. I put a hand atop his; they seemed to shake a little less, and by the time the man had finished reading I was able to take my hand away. But Finney continued to stare ahead, the words having taken their toll on him.

The blocky man addressed the group: "Is there anyone here with less than thirty days' sobriety?" he asked. "If so, will you please stand and state your disease. We say this not to embarrass you, but to welcome you."

A moment's silence, then up in the third row a tall, well-dressed man in sweater and glasses stood, looked around him, took a shallow breath and said: "My name is Andrew, and I'm..." He hesitated a second. "...an alcoholic."

"Thank you, Andrew," the man at the podium said. "Welcome."

Another silence, shorter this time, and then a teenage boy—couldn't have been more than sixteen—in jeans and a light summer jacket stood. "My name is Pete," he said, "and I'm a drug addict."

And so on like that, three or four more people rising in turn... until Finney finally stood, his hands trembling just a bit but his voice not shaky at all.

"My name is Dave," he said quietly, "and I'm an alcoholic."

I was proud of him; prouder still when the floor was

open to members' relating their experience and after three or four others, Finney stood and told—in a flat, toneless way—about the accident, about the woman he had hit, about the sentence and the jail time. There was no cross-talk, no questions or advice from others—that came during coffee break and after the meeting itself, when new members were pounced upon by older ones, congratulated, welcomed, and given phone numbers. "Can I have your word," one would say, "that you'll remain sober till the next meeting?" "Will you promise," another would ask, "to call me if you feel the need to take a drink?" A lot of it felt formal—ritualized—but I guess that was the point: to give a ritual, a structure, to people whose lives had none, who'd spiraled out of their own control.

By the end of the meeting Finney had exchanged numbers with several others, and when I dropped him off at his place he turned and smiled before getting out. "Well," he said, "that wasn't half as awful as I thought it'd be." I asked him if he needed another ride next week, but he just shook his head: "I'll get a ride with one of the other guys." He rapped his knuckles, lightly, on my shoulder. "Later, Cochrane."

Driving home, I felt happy and proud. Maybe this Finney would grow up, after all; maybe I had helped him to grow up. I arrived home a little after nine to find Paige engrossed in some sitcom in the living room and Debra in the den reading a novel and listening to Mark Isham on the stereo. I was just settling down with a cup of hot tea and a Walker Percy novel when the phone rang. "I got it," I sighed, pushing myself out of the comfortable easy chair, snapping up the receiver. "Hello?"

"*Rick*—thank God—"

It was my mother, and immediately I knew something was wrong—her voice was strained, she sounded breathless and frightened. My heart suddenly began to pound.

"Mom?" I said. "What is it? What's wrong?"

She didn't answer at first, as though gathering breath and strength to tell me. "I...I started having the chest pains again, about an hour ago? So I took a nitroglycerin tablet, but after half an hour they still hadn't gone away, so I took another, but—"

Oh, God; oh, Jesus, no. "Mom, listen to me: have you called the paramedics?"

"Yes...yes, a few minutes ago, but—"

I was already halfway across the room, cradling the phone on one shoulder as I put on my shoes with my free hand. Debra, too, was on her feet, hurrying into the next room to get my coat. "Okay...take it easy. You're going to be fine, just lie down and *rest*—I'll be over as fast as I can, okay?"

"Rick, it *hurts*...it hurts and it won't go away—"

I'd never heard her like this, so helpless, so much in pain. She'd always been the anchor, the strength in the family, and to hear her like this—

"It'll go away. It'll pass," I said, forcing myself to sound calm, trying to do as she would. "Just stay calm, okay, Mom? Go lie down. You're sure you called the paramedics?"

"I...yes, I think so, I..."

"Mom, I'm leaving. I'll be right there. You're going to be fine." I wanted desperately to add *I love you*, but didn't dare alarm her any more. "You...you hang in there till I get there, okay? I'll be right over."

"I'll wait for you," she said, but her voice sounded, if anything, weaker. I didn't want to hang up, but I had to, had to get there. "I'll be there, Mom, fast as I can. See you in a few minutes." It took all my strength to hang up, but once I did I was racing out of the den and down the stairs, Debra right behind me.

"Call the paramedics," I yelled behind me to Deb, "just in case. Then call her back, keep her on the phone—don't let her talk too much, just talk *to* her, let her know everything's going to be all right—"

Debra immediately went to the phone, punched up 911. Paige jumped up as I passed her, her face white. "Is it Grandma?" she said. "Is something wrong with—"

But I was out the door and down the walk before she could finish. The Nissan was parked at the curb; I fumbled with the keys, scrambled in, not bothering with the seat belt, just gunning the engine and taking off down the street, zero to fifty in about twenty seconds. I drove like a madman, running yellow lights and jumping stop signs; it was a miracle I didn't kill myself, or someone else, as I sped through Appleton's sleepy streets. And I had the nerve to condescend to Finney. At the intersection of Thornton and Woodbine a red light, and opposing traffic, brought me to a reluctant halt. I cursed and sweated the two, three minutes it cost me, until the light changed and I took off, doing sixty in a thirty-five-mile-an-hour zone.

When I finally careened around the corner onto Lochmere Street, I saw, in the distance, red flashes down the block, coloring the trees from summer to autumn, from green to scarlet—as an ambulance, siren wailing, began pulling away from the curb in front of my mother's house. Damn it! It had a good half-block lead on me, one that widened as it took the corner and picked up speed; all I could do was follow in its wake as it raced up Route 102, helpless to know what was happening inside its red and white shell, as distant from her now as I had been in New York. The tears were flowing now, despite the necessity of driving, and at times all I could see ahead of me was a blurred strobing red; cars all along the way stopped as the ambulance sped past, then, just when they began to move again, along I came in the backwash of its light and sound, forcing them to swerve and weave away from me. It was a wonder I lived to follow the ambulance into the E.R. entrance of the Parkland Medical Center.

By the time I screeched to a halt inside the garage, paramedics were taking a stretcher out the back of the ambulance; my mother lay on that stretcher, eyes closed, connected to both I.V. and EKGs. I wasn't two seconds out of my car when one of the paramedics was all over me, blocking my way as the stretcher was transferred to a gurney, and the gurney loaded up a ramp into the E.R.

"What the fuck were *you*–?" the paramedic was shouting at me, but my attention was not on him but on the gurney.

"She's my *mother*," I shouted back at him, more desperately than angrily; he was unprepared for this. "Please, I'm sorry, but I had to, I have to *see* her–" I watched her disappear through the sliding glass doors of the E.R., I hurried after, the paramedic now pacing me, his attitude entirely changed. "Take it easy, okay?" he said reassuringly. "Give me the keys to your car; we'll have it moved for you." I tossed them to him on the run, and as the glass doors slid open he gave me an update: "She's unconscious– she started fibrillating in the vehicle, we used the paddles on her and she's got a normal sinus rhythm now, but–"

We raced inside; the paramedic talked quickly with the E.R. nurse. He had sounded hopeful, but by the time I entered her exam room her EKG was erratic again, a keening noise sounding and quickly muted by one of the nurses; a doctor was again using the defibrillator on her. I winced as the electricity jolted through her, making her body jerk and convulse, giving it the impression of motion, if not life. I could see that the upward deflections of the EKG were gradually becoming shorter, the pauses between them longer—until suddenly the vertical deflections ceased completely. "She's flat-lined," someone said, the doctor applying the paddles to her again, but to no effect. I watched in numb, horrified silence as a scalpel appeared in someone's hand, as a quick, careful incision was made in my mother's chest and the doctor actually reached inside my mother's frail, helpless body and began open-heart massage, trying to coax the blood through its arteries, the dark red tissue squeezed between his gloved fingers, here and there a white or blue vein visible beneath a purplish membrane. I wanted to run, but couldn't; wanted to look away, but didn't. I gazed at her face—so calm, so impassive, showing no traces of the battle being waged inside her body—and knew, somehow, that it was over; that there was no trace of my mother remaining there, no reflex left in that bruised, fragile heart, her spirit long since surrendered. The nurses exchanged looks, coming to the same conclusion, as someone switched off the EKG; the doctor withdrew his hands—gloves stained bright red, too red, almost unreal—and took a long, deep sigh. "I'm sorry," he said to me, as a sheet was drawn up over my mother's body. I went slowly to her side, lifted the sheet from her right hand, and put mine atop it. *Mama, my poor Mama*, I thought again, as I had once before, in a different life; wondering if she was with her Bert now, not the old man lying dreaming on the couch but the young, dapper pilot with his goggles and thin mustache. She'd been through too much, suffered too many losses, grieved too often for too many; she deserved, at least, that much. I withdrew my hand, replacing the sheet; and then, all at once, I was weeping uncontrollably, a nurse leading me out of the exam room, into...

Into Debra's arms. I wept like a little boy, taking in big, ragged gulps of air, holding on to Debra for all the world. "I couldn't save her," I kept saying—baffled, confused, betrayed. "I should've been able to save her." She held on to me for long minutes and then took me home, where I cried most of the night, as did we all, Debra and Paige and myself; only Jeffrey too young to understand, too near the beginning to comprehend the end. I got a few hours' sleep; fitful, half-conscious dreams of riding a train in the dead of night, that left me more exhausted than rested. And the next day, I set about the terrible business of burying my mother for a second time.

CHAPTER FOURTEEN

RICK

I woke, my first morning back in New York, with the sudden and certain knowledge that my mother was dead.

I had my first intimation of it the night before, on the train from Massachusetts. We left Route 128 about ten p.m., due to arrive at Penn Station a little before three. I spent most of the first couple of hours wrapped up in my thoughts of Debra, of her counterpart in this world... wondering, God help me, at the choice I'd made, the bargain I'd struck with Richard. But it had been a long day—packing, preparations, the cast party—and after two hours of soul-searching and sudden misgivings, I nodded off to sleep, along with the half dozen other passengers sharing the car on this red-eye special.

I dreamed of Debra, of course, both my Debra and the other; dreamed of making love to her, as I'd fantasized the night before. Then, as dreams do, it fragmented—one moment I was with Debra, the next sitting on the beach with Ray—suddenly on stage in Wyndham, and just as suddenly watching Paige in a green leotard, flying across a stage as Peter Pan—then outside my mother's house, watching as an ambulance pulled away from the curb, lights flashing, siren wailing—me following it at breakneck speed through the streets of Appleton, then to a hospital—

I was only getting bits and pieces, flashes and images, but even asleep, a part of me sensed something odd, something subtly wrong: because as fragmented as the images were, they were occurring in sequence, not jumbled or scrambled in time—and because they were terrifying, ghastly images at that. My mother in a hospital bed, electric paddles on her chest, her body heaving reflexively—suddenly a terrible cavity in her chest, gloved hands reaching in, blood splashing on doctor's whites—the awful banshee of the electrocardiograph—

I woke with a start, the wail of the EKG now the screech of brakes as the train slowed for its stop in Providence. I was trembling, sweating so hard I could feel my shirt soaked beneath the light summer jacket I was wearing. Jesus God—what was *that* all about? I tried to dismiss it as a nightmare, triggered by seeing Debra, fed by my creeping doubt and anxiety over what I'd done; but even so I didn't allow myself to fall asleep again, forcing myself awake the remaining hours till we reached Manhattan.

I took a taxi home—the townhouse had a musty but welcome smell upon entry—then, my exhaustion catching up with me again, I didn't even bother unpacking, just stripped off my clothes and collapsed into bed, falling almost instantly asleep.

And I dreamed of Debra again, of holding her—but no joy or lust in it this time, only grief and pain—standing with her in an emergency room, weeping helplessly—at home in Appleton, Debra and Paige and I holding one another and crying, united in a common sorrow. Other images too, but none as immediate, more like memories—can you remember things in a dream?—a sheet drawn up over my mother's body, a hand, my hand, resting atop hers—but all the while I saw it, I was also sitting on our bed with Debra and Paige, a nightmare recollected within a nightmare.

I woke a little before eight and knew in my heart that my mother—not Richard's mother, but mine—was dead.

It had been too real for a dream; too logical and self-contained. Sitting on the bed, one arm wrapped around Paige, the other around Debra—the love and mourning uniting us in our sad bond—these were feelings too deep to be dreamt, too remote from the life I'd left to be fantasized. That kind of love, that common anguish and support—when was the last time I'd felt something like that, in my old world? When Dad died, two years ago? It seemed further back than that, estranged by months of sniping and fighting, frustration and jealousy.

But of course it wasn't me they were holding, it was Richard. Somehow he had repaired the damage I'd wrought to my family, mended the wounds, restored the love—and even through the anguish that began to descend on me, I was jealous of him yet again. Not only for doing what I couldn't do—for what I'd lacked the courage, the resources to do—but because he'd been there, at her side, when she died, while I was impossibly distant. He had the consolation of family, at least, while I sat alone in this apartment, unable to see her even one last time, unable to attend my own mother's funeral, unable even to share my grief with anyone in this world. Richard's mother had passed away four months ago, I'd been consoled and

comforted many times over for a loss I hadn't actually suffered. Now I needed that consolation desperately, but I'd
already used the death as an excuse for my foolish flirta-
tion with Catlin and cocaine—if I broke down now, to Ray
or Melissa or anyone else, I'd seem even more unstable,
I'd undo everything I'd worked the past two months to
overcome.

As I sat there alone in the apartment, sobbing to myself, I thought of Richard and how he must have looked
much like this when his mother died; how he, too, had
not been with her when she'd gone, perhaps only miles
and not worlds away, but still apart. And I began to feel
ashamed of my sullenness, my jealousy. It hit me, then,
that Richard—dear God, Richard had had to go through
this *twice*...and here I was, envious because he had
someone to weep with. Jesus. What kind of selfish, self-
involved shit was I, anyway? He'd earned that comfort
and consolation; deserved it, if only because he was taking on the burden a second time.

The last, mean vestiges of my jealousy began to dissi-
pate and die that morning, as I sat mourning a loss I could
explain to no one, bearing up as Richard had borne up to
it—and understanding, perhaps for the first time, the forces
and feelings that had driven Richard to my world in the
first place...

I got a few hours' sleep, at last, toward late morning, and
when I awoke that afternoon my melancholy had
turned to a kind of numbness, as I found some solace in
the ritual motions of unpacking and checking the accumulated messages on my answering machine. Of the dozen or
so calls, two stood out: one from Ray, left yesterday, asking

me to call as soon as I got back into town; and the other from Libby Sherwin, a tentative, hesitant just-called-to-say-hello message, sounding as though she might have heard of my recent problem and wanted to see how I was doing. I was still leery of meeting her, but the concern in her tone was as clear as it was when we'd spoken after Richard's mother's death. Despite their breakup she obviously still cared for him, and I was beginning to feel guilty for avoiding her. Putting aside my fears I called her, and confess to relief when I got her machine; I left a message, then called Ray.

"Richard," he said brightly at the sound of my voice. "How'd it go up in Massachusetts?" God bless him, there was no condescension in his tone; he might as well have been asking about a Broadway opening as a dinner theater in New England.

I was still feeling numb, but I managed to mask it with a false enthusiasm—or perhaps not so false, because as I related how well the show had gone, I was far from lying.

"Great," he said, when I'd finished. "Sounds like it was just the sort of depressurizer you needed." A pause, then: "So—you ready to leave the decompression chamber and get back into the real world?"

"Ray," I said, laughing at the strained metaphor, "what the *hell* are you talking about?"

"Meet me for lunch tomorrow," was all he would say. "Carnegie Deli, twelve-thirty. We have things to discuss."

The next day, over a pastrami sandwich and a Dr. Brown's Cel-Ray soda, Ray asked offhandedly, "So. How'd you like a job, Cochrane?"

My BLT got about two inches off its plate before I put it down again, taken off guard by the question. "What?"

"I'm doing a special for PBS," Ray went on, chewing around his words, "on the life of Christopher Marlowe. Kind of a free-form, dream-play biography, interpolating what little we know about his life with scenes from his plays; one minute he's at Rheims, or Rome, doing whatever skullduggery he did in his youth for the Queen, the next he's Faustus, pondering the fate of his soul." Ray swallowed, shook his head. "He's a great character: a poet, a scholar, but also reckless, impulsive, violent—we're calling the show *A Small Reckoning*, after Shakespeare's line in *As You Like It*."

"'A small reckoning in a little room,'" I said, recalling Shakespeare's memorial to his friend from my drama history courses in college. "He was killed in a tavern, wasn't it? When he was barely thirty?"

Ray nodded, took a swig of his soda. "Twenty-nine. And we see that death scene play out different ways, because there are all these byzantine theories about why he was killed and by whom. I mean, he's in a room in this tavern with some pretty scuzzy characters: Robert Poley, a double agent; Nicholas Skeres, fine fellow, a notorious cutpurse; Ingram Frizier, the guy who supposedly did him in, a servant or something for Thomas Walsingham—"

"Sounds interesting," I said, trying to contain my excitement—God, this was just what I needed, work, something to take my mind off the grief and loss and longing that were threatening to consume me. "So which part did you have me in mind for? Poley? Walsingham?"

Ray just scowled at me. "No—Queen Elizabeth," he said with mock derision. *"Marlowe,* you asshole, who else?"

I started. "Me?" I said disbelievingly. "Ray, last time I looked, I was colder than yesterday's sushi in this town. PBS is never going to approve me!"

Ray took another bite of his pastrami. "They already have," he said.

I just stared at him, dumbfounded. He shrugged: "I'm the director," he said, "and you're the best choice for the role. A little old for it, maybe, but I'd rather fudge the age than go for someone younger and less experienced—this could be a tricky piece to pull off."

Less experienced. Jesus, if only he knew.

"It can't have been that easy," I said, "to get me approved. Ray, I appreciate this, but I don't want you to get into a firefight with the network over—"

"Richard," he interrupted me, "does the part interest you?"

"Of course it—"

"Do you have any doubts that you can play it?"

Strangely, my reply was an immediate, "No. I *want* to do it. But I—"

"What I told PBS," Ray said, "was that you were one of the best actors I'd ever worked with; that you'd be perfect for the part; and they had my personal assurance that you would be nothing less than professional in your conduct. That's all it took."

That's all? Ray was staking my reputation with his own; I was touched, flattered, and grateful. But I also felt the weight of my own responsibility to him—to earn the faith he'd placed in me. After the breach of trust I'd made of Richard's life, could I risk letting Ray down? And yet could I turn him down and still pretend that I was worthy of leading Richard's life?

If I was any kind of *mensche* at all, there was only one answer, really, I could give.

"Okay," I heard myself saying. "You got me."

"Great." Ray grinned, pushing aside the remains of his sandwich. "I'll have business affairs call Joel this afternoon. We're shooting it one-camera tape, two-week shooting schedule, one week's rehearsal—but if you're willing, I'd like you involved from the start, on a conceptual level. Like, for instance: did you know that nobody knows what Marlowe—or Morley, or Marley, or however he felt like signing himself that day—nobody really knows what he looked like? So how—"

I missed Ray's next words, because suddenly I heard: from behind me, it seemed, from somewhere in the crowded deli:

"*—oh, and Rick? Peter Klein, is he permanent and stationary yet, or still—*"

I spun around in my seat fast enough to whiplash myself, and for an instant I actually expected to see her, the face matching the voice I'd heard every weekday for the last three years.

"Amy . . . ?"

But she wasn't there, and in the next instant I knew, of course, that she couldn't be there, and I heard Ray's worried voice: "Richard? Something wrong?"

I searched the room one last time—a futile gesture, but I couldn't help myself—then turned back to Ray and forced myself to laugh with what I hoped was an offhanded chagrin. "Sorry," I said. "Just thought I heard someone I knew." I leaned in, not giving him a chance to have second thoughts: "So. You were saying?"

"Well, I was saying that since we don't know what Marlowe looked like, we have some latitude in creating an appearance, and I was wondering how you'd like to handle it?"

I didn't have the vaguest notion, but fortunately neither did he; we bruited about a few ideas, finally deciding I'd do a little background reading before coming to any firm decisions. Ray picked up the check, shook my hand vigorously as we left the deli—"Okay. Let's do it. Let's make the movie"—and caught a cab, leaving me to walk alone down Seventh Avenue, alone with the thoughts I hadn't dared dwell on back in the restaurant.

Had I really heard Amy's voice back there, or was I still shaken from last night's dreams? Was I longing to be back there at my mother's side so badly that I was deluding myself into thinking it was starting all over again?

Yet the dreams were more than dreams—something *was* happening, some kind of overlap between Richard's life and mine. Was it starting all over again? And if it was, should I have been terrified or relieved, angry or glad? I didn't know. I didn't know how I felt: I was still numb, dazed from the multiple shocks of the dream, Mom's death, Amy's voice, and now this job—this wonderful, unexpected act of kindness and loyalty from Ray.

I came to an abrupt stop at 53rd Street and thought suddenly: Screw it. Screw what might or might not be happening; screw how I felt about it. What happened, happened; what was important right now was the trust Ray had placed in me. What was important was that I live up to that trust. That was what Richard would do; that was what I had to do. Turning aside everything but the task ahead of me, I now had a direction to walk in: down Seventh Avenue to the Drama Bookshop, to pick up the collected works and selected biographies of Christopher Marlowe.

And as I walked, the full implications of this job finally sank in. I had no doubt that I could play the part—I'd done *Faustus* in college, if anything I was stronger in the classics than in contemporary theater—but like an idiot it hit me, for the first time, that this was television. What the hell did I know about hitting my marks, about playing for the camera, about projecting for the microphone instead of the balcony? I fought back a momentary wave of panic: two-week shooting schedule, one-week rehearsal; these were generous working conditions compared to what I understood was the norm for television. There'd be plenty of time to learn, I had a sympathetic director—and the Drama Bookshop was bound to have dozens of books on the subject of TV acting technique. Somewhat reassured, I climbed the creaky, musty stairway to the bookstore, entering near the bulletin board on which were posted notices of casting calls, part-time jobs, and roommates wanted; I passed the cash register up front, my nose pointed toward the film-TV section.

"Mr. Cochrane. Hello." The clerk behind the counter was smiling at me. I froze. I smiled a stiff but, with any luck, not too unnatural smile: "Hi," I said. "How've you been?"

"Fine. Haven't seen you in for a while. Been on the road?"

"Matter of fact, yes." Well, now, this was just swell. What was this clerk going to think of Richard Cochrane, formerly of *Guiding Light*, bearer of some three dozen episodic series credits, buying a beginner's guide to television acting technique? "Ah...I'm looking," I said, stalling for time, "for some biographies of Christopher Marlowe. Where could I find them?"

"That would be over here." The clerk led me to the proper section, directing my attention to a book by Charles Norman. I scanned and selected two or three more books, found a nice copy of the *Collected Works*, but was no closer to figuring out how I was going to swing the rest of this until I looked up, saw a young woman about nineteen years old avidly flipping through a copy of Matson's *The Working Actor*, and inspiration struck.

I turned to the clerk and said, "I have a nephew in Connecticut who's thinking about a career in acting—I'd like to get him a few books on TV acting techniques. Can you recommend something, something current?"

Indeed he could, and five minutes later, to my great and profound relief, I was leaving the shop with all the necessary research—which my "nephew" devoured over the course of the next several weeks. Alone in my apartment, I could practice hitting my marks—strips of tape on the carpet—but there was other advice in the books that I would only be able to put into practice later: don't blink as much on camera as you would in real life; don't let your gaze, when you're looking at someone, flick back and forth from eye to eye, because it makes you look shifty-eyed; if you're crying in a scene, make sure to tilt your head to allow the light source, wherever it is, to catch the tear...

New lessons, to be sure, back to kindergarten in many respects, but I was determined to learn them; and if Ray detected any hesitancy or lack of confidence on my part, he ascribed it to the wringer I'd been through of late and was always supportive and accessible. I could see why Richard, in his journals, had spoken so highly of him as a director. Early on, at a preproduction meeting with Ray, me, the play's author and various production personnel, the question came up again of what kind of physical appearance we wanted for the mysterious, faceless Marlowe. The makeup man found one supposed picture of him in an encyclopedia, "a presumed portrait by an anonymous artist," but there was no hundred percent certainty that the portrait *was* of Marlowe—and indeed, part of the point of the play was that Marlowe eluded definition, defied easy scrutiny, the visionary poet living in the same body as the reckless, sometimes violent young man.

It was with this in mind that I spoke up, albeit a bit nervously: "You know, since part of the point of all this is that we can never really fully know Marlowe—that much of his motivation, even his life itself, will always elude us—I thought it might be interesting if—" I hesitated, but their attention was on me now, so there was no turning back. "—if every time we see Marlowe, his makeup, his appearance, is just a little bit different. Maybe in one scene he has a fuller beard than he had in another; in the next, his hair color is half a shade darker; maybe we could even use different-colored contact lenses. Keeping the central figure sort of... out of focus. Out of reach. I mean, isn't that the point?"

They all just looked at me for a long moment, and I thought: Oh, Christ, Cochrane, you've blown it now; but then the author, James Hauser, broke the silence. "Damn," he said softly. "Wish I'd thought of that."

"Everybody will think you did," the makeup supervisor said with a smile.

"God damn," Ray kept saying, "God *damn,* that's good, that gives us all sorts of new textures to work with—"

"Textures, my ass," said the unit production manager. "How the hell are we going to effect all these makeup changes with a character who's on camera ninety percent of the time? Where do we find the air in the schedule to do his makeup while we shoot something else?"

"We'll find a way," Ray said, his mind already made up. "We'll make it work."

"They don't have to be—they shouldn't be—*large* changes," I pointed out. "No fake noses or anything like that, just wigs and beards and—"

"I think we can do it," the makeup woman said, consulting some notes. "Here, look at the schedule . . ."

From then on, it was all like a dream: it was everything I'd imagined this craft could be, a true collaboration. Rehearsals were held at the WNET studios on West 58th, where all my practice at home began to pay off. I was determined, even if I missed my mark, *never* to look down for it—the sign, I knew, of the rank amateur. I knew enough, too, to tone down my performance from what I might do on stage—abandoning larger gestures for the more intimate camera, not trying to project to the galleries, allowing my voice to lower to a whisper if necessary. And I soon picked up from watching the other actors how this varied even from shot to shot: how one actor was looser and more laid-back in the long (or master) shots, but became subtler, more intense, as the camera moved close in, television acting being played more with the eyes than with the body. I also discovered, unexpectedly, that playing to a camera was like playing into a mirror, because with those big lenses you could actually catch your reflection in the glass—and I had to fight the urge to glance at myself, as people naturally do when they pass a mirror or a window.

If I seemed a bit clumsy at first, Ray and the others attributed it not to inexperience, thank God, but a bit of rustiness and perhaps anxiety after what I'd recently been through; and the confidence and trust they all placed in me made it easier to overcome that clumsiness, to get the minimum technical proficiency I needed and concentrate on the performance itself.

No; if I had any problem, it was not with the medium, but with Marlowe. James Hauser had captured the dichotomy of the man on paper, but it was up to me to somehow emotionally reconcile those two parts of him for the audience. Marlowe was both a poet capable of penning, "Come live with me,/And be my love,/And we will all the pleasures prove"—and an impetuous young man who could drunkenly attack two constables, or engage in a swordfight with a man not because he had any quarrel with him, but on behalf of the brother-in-law of a friend of his.

The closer I studied him, the more frightened I became: frightened that in finding Marlowe, I would have to tap that inner violence of my own, violence that had seemed dormant in me ever since I hit bottom and destroyed half the apartment. The structure of the play forced it on me: one moment I was Marlowe in Hog Lane, brandishing a sword against one William Bradley, falling back and allowing Marlowe's friend, Thomas Watson, to kill Bradley; then, in the same makeup and costume, I

bounded into another scene, and I was now power-mad
Tamburlaine, proclaiming:

> *"Our quivering lances, shaking in the air,*
> *And bullets, like Jove's dread thunderbolts,*
> *Enroll'd in flames and fiery smouldering mists,*
> *Shall threat the gods more than Cyclopian wars;*
> *And with our sun-bright armour, as we march,*
> *We'll chase the stars from heaven, and dim their eyes*
> *That stand and muse at our admired arms . . ."*

One moment I was Marlowe, reeling drunkenly home
and assaulting, God knew why, two constables whom he
has just bumped into; the next, I was Tamburlaine again,
and boasting:

> *"So shall our swords, our lances, and our shot*
> *Fill all the air with fiery meteors.*
> *Then, when the sky shall wax as red as blood,*
> *It shall be said I made it red myself,*
> *To make me think of naught but blood and war . . ."*

The more I played the scene, the deeper I probed inside
myself, trying to tap that anger, that wellspring of violence I knew to be there . . . and the more I searched, oddly,
the more it eluded me. Hating the idea but acknowledging
the necessity of it, I forced myself to remember that awful
night, six months ago—hitting Paige as I had, wanting to
hit Debra—

And thought again of Catlin and of how I hadn't hit her.

I thought of the frustration of working at Mutual, of a
job I'd come to hate, of denying myself the life I'd longed

for—and though I remembered the anger and the frustration, I no longer felt it as I had then. It was as though it were tucked away in one of my own insurance drawers labeled FILE INACTIVE—and I was examining it with the same sort of detachment I might have Peter Klein's ENT report. At first my doubts surfaced again—if I really were a good actor, I told myself, I should be able to tap into those feelings, as afraid as I was to relive them, to God forbid revive them—and then I realized something that probably should have been obvious but for my pressing need to identify with Marlowe.

There are different kinds of violence, and my kind—a rage born of frustration and repression—was not Marlowe's. His was a reckless violence, an impulsive disposition toward what he saw as bold, valorous action—witness the duel in Hog Lane; he had no quarrel with Bradley, but his exaggerated view of honor made the grievance of a casual acquaintance, several times removed, his own. He fought not, most times, out of anger, but daring and adventure...the same sort of recklessness that would later lead him into trouble with the Queen's Privy Council for his boastful jests denying Christ's divinity or "esteeming St. Paul a Jugler," at a time when others were being burned at the stake for such "blasphemies."

My kind of violence was not his, and the more I reached inside to explore it, I began to realize that it was no longer mine either. Take away the frustration, you take away the anger; take away the anger and the violence follows. I was doing, here and back in Wyndham, exactly what I'd always dreamed of doing. I was happy. And happy men are rarely violent men. The image I had held of myself as a loose cannon, a tragic accident waiting to happen, was slowly being erased—thanks, ironically enough, to Marlowe.

Which is not to say that I didn't find Marlowe's kind of violence inside me to tap into. I hadn't thought of it in years, but midway into rehearsals I suddenly remembered my old "stage" off Mohegan Pass: the slab of granite in a clearing where my friends and I used to parry at one another with fake sabers or slash at the rigging of imaginary pirate ships with our makeshift cutlasses. It was the childish view of violence and fighting as great battles to be won and victories to be savored, and I used that in creating my Marlowe—not the real Marlowe, necessarily, but a credible Marlowe, a product of his times. A brash, rash young man with the confidence of fame and talent and the bravado of most young men of his era—a bravado he would no doubt have outgrown, had he not been cut down by it in a tavern in Deptford.

During rehearsals Libby Sherwin finally called me back—she'd been in L.A. at a recording session—and we arranged to get together after my show was done. Once more I had put off the inevitable, though this time with a decent excuse—the show was all-consuming. I thought of it twenty-four hours a day, sometimes waking in the middle of the night with ideas for readings, for interpretations, for bits of business, culminating finally in the taping in mid-August.

They'd arranged the schedule so that my makeup changes could be done during set changes; we'd decided to change the makeup only in Marlowe-as-Marlowe scenes, not when he shifted from Marlowe to Faustus, or Tamburlaine, or Edward II. Thus, when we first meet the

young Marlowe—or Marley, as he also signed himself
back then—he is a divinity student at Cambridge. We see
him growing bored and skeptical of his divine studies;
then, in a speculative scene taken from mysterious allu-
sions in public records, we postulate that young Kit went
to the Catholic seminary at Rheims as a spy ferreting out
enemies of Queen Elizabeth. The lights dim on one set as
I walk onto another, this a study lined with books and
curios, and suddenly I am Faustus:

> *"Had I as many souls as there be stars,*
> *I'd give them all for Mephostophilis.*
> *By him I'll be great emperor of the world,*
> *And make a bridge through the air*
> *To pass the ocean ..."*

And then the duel with William Bradley, and Marlowe
is consigned for a time to the darkness of Newgate prison;
yet out of that darkness we hear Tamburlaine's words, glorious words from a most unglorious source, celebrating all
that human beings can be:

> *"Nature, that fram'd us of four elements*
> *Warring within our breasts for regiment,*
> *Doth teach us all to have aspiring minds:*
> *Our souls, whose faculties can comprehend*
> *The wondrous architecture of the world,*
> *And measure every wandering planet's course,*
> *Still climbing after knowledge infinite,*
> *And always moving as the restless spheres,*
> *Wills us to wear ourselves and never rest,*

Until we reach the ripest fruit of all,
That perfect bliss and sole felicity,
The sweet fruition of an earthly crown . . ."

How many "elements," I wondered, had warred within Marlowe's breast to take him from the heights of his art to the low places he often frequented . . . and in which he would ultimately die?

Finally—for we were shooting in chronological sequence, unusual but not unheard-of in television—there was that tavern in Deptford where Marlowe met his end, killed in a room he'd taken with Poley, Skeres, and Frizier, supposedly in a dispute over a bar bill. Frizier, the unsavory servant of Thomas Walsingham, claimed later that Marlowe had taken Frizier's own dagger and hurled it at him, forcing Frizier to plunge the blade into Marlowe's skull in self-defense . . . questionable, since Marlowe couldn't have overpowered the other two men in the room. Had Marlowe really been killed at the will of other, absent forces—Walsingham, Kyd, Sir Walter Raleigh—who feared his implication of them as fellow atheists before the Privy Council's inquisition? Or was it the government itself—for which Marlowe, as well as Poley and Skeres, on occasion worked—whose hand was on the dagger that day?

No one can say which, and so we shot the scene in *Rashomon* fashion, alternate versions of what might have occurred: once it is Frizier with the dagger, acting in self-defense as supported by Skeres and Poley's testimony; then it is Poley with the dagger, acting to eliminate Marlowe on behalf of the Privy Council; then Skeres, silencing Marlowe before he can implicate Raleigh; and finally back to Frizier, but this time Poley and Skeres are restraining Marlowe, al-

lowing Frizier to do his ugly deed. In between each ver-
sion, the players rushed, fell, or rolled into adjoining sets,
and now the struggle was of Tamburlaine with Mycetes, or
Edward II facing his assassins, Lightborn, Matrevis, and
Gurney; until we are back in the room in Deptford, and the
dagger is about to be plunged into Marlowe's skull.

Later, when the film is assembled, the image will freeze,
the blade just inches above Marlowe's right eye; and
through the miracle of backscreen projection, I—Marlowe—
am in the scene as Faustus, speaking not his part but that
of the Chorus announcing his death; though, with two
small emendations, not his death at all:

> *"Cut is the branch that might have grown full straight,*
> *And burned is Apollo's laurel bough,*
> *That sometimes grew within this learned man.*
> *Marlowe is gone. Regard his hellish fall,*
> *Whose fiendful fortune may exhort the wise*
> *Only to wonder at unlawful things,*
> *Whose deepness doth entice with forward wits,*
> *To practice more than . . . heavenly? . . . power*
>   *permits . . ."*

The question mark was ours. Faustus moves off screen,
the frame begins to unfreeze, the dagger starting to plunge
downward just as the picture GOES TO BLACK.

And then it was all over, as quickly as it had ended in
Wyndham. We had our wrap party, drank our toasts,
and Ray went away to edit the show, the cast scattering to
other assignments. Once again I understood the feelings
that had driven Richard away from here, to another life:

these brief whirlwinds of activity, drawing people together into a kind of heat-and-pressure-forged family, and then the pressure is suddenly released and you're alone again. I had never really been alone, in this way, before. I went from living with my parents to a college dorm, then sharing a small flat with Debra, and finally to marriage. I'd never felt what I was feeling now: a loneliness and longing that even the presence of friends could not appease.

As for the show, it was hard to predict how it would come out when assembled, but for my part I'd felt confident and proud of my performance. I'd watched dailies at first and was satisfied with what I saw, but there was something unsettling about seeing yourself doing the same shot, over and over—it reminded me, a bit too much, of the artifice involved in what I was doing—and after the third or fourth day I stopped going, not wanting to become too self-conscious.

I must have done something right, though, since after *A Small Reckoning* wrapped, the job offers began to trickle in. Word had presumably gotten out that Cochrane was "clean" again, and little by little people seemed willing to take a chance on me. Estée Lauder invited me back for another voice-over audition, and this time I got the job; Joel got an offer for me to do a guest shot on a sitcom, which I'd start rehearsals on next week; slowly, it seemed, my reputation—Richard's reputation—was being restored. Now all I had to do was follow through and not screw up again, and I needed no prodding for that.

It was between jobs and I was getting ready for my long-postponed lunch date with Libby—almost out the door, in fact—when the phone rang. The machine picked up, but I intercepted: "Hold on, I'm here, I'm here," and when I switched off I heard a woman's voice I didn't recognize: "Richard? It's Meredith. Meredith Holt."

For a moment that familiar panic gripped me: who was this? How did "I" know her? I started running down the list of names and faces I'd committed to memory while studying Richard's journals and the old *Theatre World* volumes. "Meredith," I said happily, as though I actually knew who the hell I was talking to. "Hi. How are you?"

"I'm fine," she said, "but I'm afraid I'm calling with some bad news."

Now I recognized the voice: it was the same one I'd heard—albeit touched with a Scottish burr—out of nowhere, back in my office at Mutual; she was one of Richard's fellow cast members from *Brigadoon.*

"It's John Danker," she went on, her tone grim. "He's in the hospital. With full-blown AIDS."

"Oh, my God." I didn't have to know the man personally to feel shocked. A moment later I placed his face—the face I saw that very first time, the man in makeup and costume who'd suddenly been sitting beside me.

"He's just been admitted and a bunch of us from the old company are going over tomorrow to visit. Can we count you in?"

I hesitated. I didn't know this man from Adam, yet I was being asked to pay him what sounded from Meredith's tone like a deathbed visit. But I was Richard now, and Richard would not have hesitated; so I had no choice but to say, "Of course. What time tomorrow? What hospital?"

"One o'clock, at St. Vincent's in the Village. We'll meet in the lobby, okay?"

"Fine," I said. "See you there."

I hung up, feeling oddly detached; sorry for this man

but not entirely comfortable with what I'd agreed to. I reset the machine and was out the door before another call could come in.

I got to the restaurant early and got seated well before Libby. I wasn't sure I'd be able to recognize her from the one or two snapshots Richard had of her, so rather than try to pick her out of a crowd, I figured to leave that to her. Damn, but I was growing tired of all this planning and forethought, just to go to a goddamn lunch. I felt as though I were in a play, one for which I was constantly having to do intense, ongoing research. Which, I suppose, I was.

In any event, the plan worked. I looked up after about five minutes to find a tall, slim, dark-haired woman waving at me from the maître d's station, smiling as she made her way across the room. She was attractive—an oval face framed by straight brown hair, brown eyes, sharp, distinctive features. She was wearing a red blouse, jeans, and was carrying a large purse—or perhaps it was a manuscript pouch, considering her profession—slung over one shoulder.

"Richard," she said, giving me a brief hug. *"Finally."*

"Libby," I said, hugging back. "Nice to see you."

She sat down, dropped her purse or pouch or whatever it was to the floor, then looked across the table and caught me totally off guard: "I don't know if you're aware of this," she said matter-of-factly, "but I am really pissed off at you." She took a deep breath, exhaled quickly. "There. I said it. I've almost blurted it out half a dozen times before, but it's not exactly the kind of thing you want to do over the phone."

Oh God; my worst fear. What was it in their shared past I didn't know about? What was I going to say? Well . . . what else could I say? "Why?" I asked, not having to feign, at least, my puzzlement.

"For shutting me out," she said, meeting my gaze. "Ever since you got back from New Hampshire." I relaxed a little, and now I could see that there was more hurt than anger in her face. She leaned in, lowering her voice a bit. "We may no longer be lovers, Richard, but I thought we were still friends. And after your Mom's death—"

"After my Mom's death," I said, "I went through some bad times."

"I might've helped. I offered, on the phone, but you gave me the runaround, remember?"

I winced a little inside, trying to formulate some explanation for what I'd done. (No: not explanation. Lie. I was trying to formulate a lie, damn it.)

"Libby, I . . . I got a little crazy, after New Hampshire . . ."

"Yes, well, you once said you'd have to be, to take up with Catlin again."

"You, uh, know about that?"

Libby rolled her eyes. "Richard, they know about it in *Bolivia.* Word travels fast. About everything." Her tone softened. "What hurts most," she said quietly, "is that when you needed someone, you turned to Ray and Melissa, not me. I know that sounds childish—but dammit, Richard, we were close for a year and a half. I wanted to help."

Unable, of course, to tell her the simple truth, all I could do was invent a plausible lie.

Thinking fast, I said, "I was just too damned embarrassed. What was I going to do, call you up and say, 'Libby, honey, I just went through a destructive affair with my ex-wife, would you mind coming over and picking up the pieces?' What kind of crass, manipulative jerk would do that to his former lover?"

She leaned back in her seat, the idea taking her by surprise; she was silent a long moment, her expression now more thoughtful than troubled.

"I...guess I never thought of it that way," she said. "From your side, I suppose it would sound kind of tactless." She sighed, leaned forward again, resting her elbows on the table. "Richard, why did you ever get involved with her again in the first place?"

Again, I couldn't tell her the truth, but I remembered something Richard had said about another woman he'd dated, Lana, something that might serve as well. "I don't know. Maybe as a kind of—punishment," I said, shrugging. "But I didn't mean to punish you, too. Libby, I'm sorry if I shut you out. It wasn't deliberate"—the words burned in my mouth as I said them—"and it won't happen again." That much, at least, I could promise.

She nodded once, smiled tentatively. "Okay," she said. "Apology accepted. Let's order. *Sturm und Drang* always makes me hungry." I laughed, we ordered, and our conversation loosened up, at least outwardly. For me, every topic was still a perilous one, each in my ignorance holding the potential for disaster. I steered the conversation toward her work—always a reliable gambit—and she spoke briefly about her recording session in L.A., the pop star recording it who had an ego the size of Dodger Stadium, and the book for an off-Broadway musical she was collaborating on for the Actors' Collective.

Soon the subject drifted to music in general and I was

surprised and pleased to discover how similar our musical tastes were. She admired the early (pre-Bacharach) Carole Bayer Sager, the sad, quirky, funny songs like "Come in From the Rain" and "You're Moving Out Today"; she thought Harry Chapin was as unto God, as did I, revering not just the oft-heard "Taxi" and "Cat's in the Cradle" but more obscure songs like "Better Place to Be"; and we shared a fondness for composers ranging from Rachmaninoff to John Barry.

But instead of discovering all this with delight, as one should when encountering someone for the first time, I gleaned it mostly from context. I couldn't just blurt out, "You like Billy Goldenberg's film scores, too?" because chances were that ground had been covered before, long before, by her and Richard. I had to be very careful in how I framed every sentence, making them ambiguous enough not to assume that she knew or didn't know my taste in something. On the one hand, I was as pleased as anyone discovering a rapport on a first date; but on the other, this wasn't a first date for her, and I couldn't let my pleasure of discovery show. It was as tense and frustrating as it was exciting.

As we finished lunch, Libby mentioned that she had passes to a new musical that had opened a few weeks ago; would I like to go see it next Thursday? After the way I'd snubbed her the last several months, I couldn't very well say no; nor did I want to. I liked her, I enjoyed her company, but I knew I was letting myself in for more of this edgy, cautious conversation, this tightrope I was desperately afraid of falling from. "I'd love to," I said, and we parted with a peck on the cheek and a hug.

As I walked home, perhaps a little smitten despite myself,

I found myself wondering why she and Richard had broken up in the first place. She was smart, funny, talented, in the industry but not directly competitive with him as, say, Joanne had been; and their temperaments seemed similar. How had Richard put it, that rainy night in my garage, in Appleton? *And Libby, who grew too close, I think, and so I set about frightening her away*... But why?

And then I thought of something I'd said over lunch— the lie, the excuse I'd made for being with Catlin—but it was founded on a truth: how Richard had taken up with that woman, Lana, as a kind of self-punishment for letting go of Joanne. Had he also been punishing himself when he drove Libby away? And Joanne, and all the other failed relationships he'd lamented? Punishing himself—but for what? For daring to think that an actor might have both family and career?

For leaving Appleton?

For not marrying Debra?

Jesus, could that be it? Had he felt such guilt, deep down, for taking the path he'd chosen, that he set about sabotaging all his subsequent relationships?

No. No, that was part, but not all of it. That was too facile, too noble a face to put on it; the truth, I think, was more self-serving than that. Yes, he was punishing himself for leaving Debra, for rejecting a home and family; but every relationship he sabotaged, every affair that ended badly, he could use to assuage his guilt: *Actors can't have homes and families* and *careers*. A bit of show-business homily that was doubtless true of many, but hardly axiomatic; look at Paul Newman and Joanne Woodward. But Richard held that adage up like a shield, using every failed relationship to justify his breaking up with Debra. Punishment, yes, but sweet punishment, palliating his guilt, mitigating his culpability while at the same time allowing him to wallow in remorse.

By the time I got home to Riverside Drive I was feeling pretty smug about my sharp analysis of Richard's psyche, until slowly it sank in, over the next few hours, that the psyche I had analyzed had also been my own. We weren't so different, Richard and I, in other ways; could we be alike in this as well? I tried not to think about it, turned on the television to drown out my own thoughts, but a door had been opened, a light spilling in from a room long left closed. I began to think more about punishment, rationalization, and my own life—and began to realize that Richard and I were not so very different in this, either, in the end.

The next day I met Meredith, Keith Greenwood, Sally Marsden, and a few others in the lobby of St. Vincent's Hospital. Sally seemed especially nervous, smoking one cigarette after another; most of the others had been through this before with other friends, but this was, I gathered, Sally's first time. Those who'd been through this previously told of the friends—actors, writers, dancers, composers—they'd lost to AIDS in recent years. I thought of Marlowe's time, of the black plague forcing the closure of the London theaters for fear of infection, and I wondered if this plague would do the same to our stage—not through fear of public contamination, but simply by the merciless and indiscriminate slaughter of some of our finest talents.

We went up to a private room where a man lay in bed watching the overhead television jabbering away with some too-loud game show. At our entrance he turned, and his face lit with a weak but glad smile. It was the same face I'd first glimpsed across the gulf of worlds... but it was shockingly different, as well. The cheeks were sunken, the eyes receded; he looked at least thirty or forty pounds lighter. His bony, emaciated arms, resting at his sides, were covered with purple lesions, and he was connected to a respirator; but there was that glad smile when he saw us enter, a glimmer of life in a pale death mask of a face.

"Meredith," he said. "Richard..."

We went to his bedside, someone switching off the TV so we could talk. Or rather, that the others could talk: I kept my silence for the most part, not knowing what to say, wishing to God I did. Richard would have had things he'd wanted to tell him, memories he would have invoked. I thought of my mother, of the things that had been left unsaid between us, of Richard there in my world perhaps not knowing what I'd wanted said...

Finally, John turned to me, and between coughs—deep, racking coughs; you could hear the rattle of fluids in his lungs—he started to say something—

But suddenly, I was no longer in the hospital room, no longer looking into the dying eyes of John Danker. I was in the nursery—*Jeffrey's* nursery—looking down at my infant son in his crib. He raised his arms, his hands danced in little circles; he gurgled happily, as though with recognition. Giddy with wonder and delight, I reached out to touch him—to hold him—

And found my hand touching instead John Danker's bony fingers. His body was wracked by another cough, and a nurse came to his side, telling us we'd best leave and come back a little later. Still dazed by the brief journey I'd just been on, I trailed the others, listening numbly as John's doctor spoke of pneumocystis pneumonia, talking in terms of weeks rather than months.

I stood there wishing I could feel more but knowing in my heart he was a stranger to me. I thought of the image I'd so briefly seen, of Jeffrey, of my son, and I wondered: Was it happening all over again? Was the pendulum swinging back? Or was it just a trick of time, a torment to remind me of what I'd given up—"deprived," like Faustus, "of the joys of heaven"?

Was this what it was going to be like, for the rest of my life? Living a lie, trying to comfort strangers while those I loved died a world away from me?

Why this is hell, nor am I out of it. I followed the others to the hospital coffee shop, where we sat and ate and talked, cheerlessly, about the man in the room above. But Jeffrey lingered in my thoughts, so near I'd almost touched him, though I'd been drawn away before I could. Having made the choice I did, I wondered, did I deserve even that much?

CHAPTER FIFTEEN

RICHARD

I wasn't alone, this time, when I returned to my mother's house the morning after her death. Debra was with me, for which I was more grateful than I could say, but all the rest was brutally familiar. There was no faint, lingering scent of smoke because there had been no abortive move to Long Island, no moving van engulfed in flames; but the orange recliner was there in the same corner, the marble coffee table, the couch, all the furniture in their usual positions. There were different pieces of flatware lying askew in different ways in the sink, but it was their very randomness that seemed to mock me: as though even randomness itself had been duplicated, repeated, in this supposedly different world.

And in the bedroom, the same haunting mix of identical images and arbitrary changes: the bed was unmade, as before, but the containers for her nitroglycerin tablets—three in all—were scattered farther about the room, two amid tangled blankets, one on the floor near the far window. Debra winced as we entered, seeing, I knew, my mother's last moments, even as I had seen them once before; but I moved less aimlessly, going immediately to the walnut dresser across the room, drawn to what I knew I would find there, wishing to God I was wrong.

I picked up the small slip of paper from the dresser and read:

My dearest Rick,

> *If I should die please don't let them do an autopsy on me.*
> *Buy me a metal coffin like the one I got for Dad.*
> *Call Memorial Arts and have them put my name on the plaque in the cemetery.*
> *Lay me out in the blue dress I wore at Diane's wedding.*

Love, Mom.

The differences were there, but small enough, random enough, to be no difference at all. No: it was *I* who made no difference. I read the note and my hands began to tremble; and even as I had the first time, even knowing what words I'd find there, I began to cry. Debra read it with me and her eyes filled with tears as well. I sank onto the edge of my mother's bed and I wept, Debra holding me, comforting me but unable to guess the true horror of the situation; unable to understand how deep my sadness truly ran. Not just the sadness of a son who's lost his mother; that I'd known, and even in that grief there had been a certain cold balm—my guilt. Telling myself, if I'd done this for her, if I'd tried that, maybe things would have been different, maybe she'd still be alive. It was that

I wept for now, as much as for Mom. I'd done it all differently, I'd done everything I could—and it hadn't mattered, in the end. It hadn't mattered at all.

And yet a part of me couldn't accept this; a part of me was still seeking penitence and would not let go. Why had I found my way to this world, it asked, if not to make a difference? All right—perhaps my mother, in her loneliness and need, had been fated to join my father all along, no matter what I did. Perhaps the mistake I made was not before her death, but after. And so I sought my atonement in other ways.

At the funeral home, I deliberately set out to alter each decision I'd made the first time around, except when those decisions conflicted with my mother's wishes. I'd eschewed the viewing period the first time, remembering the long, enervating hours spent by my father's casket, waiting with my mother for people to drop by and pay their respects—and a sizable number had. But with Mom's death I hadn't been up to facing that ordeal alone, even with Edgar and Charlotte's support, and I'd been disappointed with the number of people who turned up for the morning service—would more have shown up if I'd had the viewing period? This time I opted for it—four hours in the afternoon, four at night. Certainly that would make a difference, wouldn't it?

And so Debra and Paige and I sat there for those eight hours, accompanied largely by Edgar and Charlotte and their eight children, watching my mother's still, peaceful body as it lay in state in its bright copper coffin, the one she'd requested. In the afternoon we were virtually alone, just the family; in the evening, some of Mom's neighbors and Bingo friends showed up. I kept careful note, comparing the turnout to that of the single morning service in my other world; some people showed up who had not appeared at the other, but others who *had* been at the service oddly never turned up now. It was a toss-up, in the end, as to whether more people attended these services than the last; again, the vagaries of chance seemed to mock my best efforts to overcome them.

The mockery turned my grief aside, gave it an angry, frustrated edge. Perhaps I simply had cried all the tears I had to cry for my mother once before, or perhaps some wiser part of me knew that to mourn so again would be unbearable—whatever the reason, after that time in Mom's house, reading the note, I didn't cry again. I was too angry for that. Angry at the fates that had led me here, given me the opportunity to make amends for the mistakes of my past, only to taunt me now by having the path end exactly where it had before.

Debra saw the tight mask of suppression I showed to the world and was rightly worried for me. "Rick, you've got to let it out," she said to me gently as we lay in bed the night before the funeral. "It's okay. It's necessary."

How did I tell her I'd already let it out once before? That what I was really struggling to keep in was my rage at God, at Destiny, at this cruel joke They were playing on me? That I didn't dare let *that* out, even in some muted, disguised form, because that would be too much like the old Rick she knew and feared?

"I'm dealing with it," was all I could say, in the end. "Honest, Deb. I'm dealing with it."

And so again the flowery Episcopalian ceremony at the funeral home, the kind my mother had requested for my father, the kind I knew she'd have wanted for herself;

again the short but slow drive to the Cemetery on the Plains, where she was lowered into the earth beside my father, beside her mother and sister and my Uncle Nick, where once again I castigated myself for all the things left unsaid.

Except there was one thing that *had* been said—wasn't there? That night driving back from Portsmouth, when she had told me of the fear she and Dad had never passed on to me—the insight I had never had, in that other life—and I'd said, "Thank you . . ." in stunned, wondering tones.

Thank you. Had I ever said it to her before? To either of them?

We put her to rest, then, but my own rest was still distant. Hunt Bailey had given me a week off; he'd been at the funeral too, he and Amy and Karen and a few of my other co-workers, along with Bill and Louise Cohen, Susan and Dennis McCardle, in fact most of the people I'd grown up with in this town . . . with one significant exception.

It wasn't until the next morning, around eight a.m., that he showed up: announcing himself in his usual manner, a manner that seemed horribly inappropriate just now. I was sleeping lightly—I didn't remember my dreams, just the tenor of them, tense and anxious and troubled—lightly enough so that the moment I heard the first knock on the window, I was instantly awake. The second knock came, and with it, a reflexive anger; I tossed off my covers, went to the window, yanked the cord raising the blinds.

It was Finney, of course. Teetering on his ladder, looking properly abashed. "I'm sorry, man," he said, voice muffled through the glass. "I should've been there. But I—"

Debra came awake in time to hear me say, tersely, "Finney, if you've got something to say, just come to the goddamn front door like an *adult*, will you?" I yanked the cord again, the blinds clattered down onto the sill, and I snapped my robe up off the chair I'd left it on last night. Debra looked at me worriedly as I shrugged it on. "Rick," she said, "I know this may sound strange, coming from me, but—take it easy on him, okay? In a lot of ways he's just a kid, still, you know?"

I didn't reply. I padded down the stairs in my robe and bare feet, just as a quiet, sheepish knock came to my front door. I opened it; Finney stood in the doorway, looking chagrined and repentant. "I'm sorry," he repeated. "I should've been there, I know, I just..." He shrugged helplessly. "I just couldn't make it."

I glared at him. "You 'couldn't *make* it'?" I repeated derisively. "You mean like you were on special mission in Beirut, that sort of thing?"

He stepped inside, and as he drew up close to me I recoiled at the reek of booze on his breath—and the rage inside me redoubled.

"I tried to make it," he started to say, "but I—"

"God *damn* you," I said—feeling hurt, feeling betrayed, feeling used. "You've been drinking again?"

He held up a hand, in a combination mea culpa and makepeace gesture. "Just a few," he said. "Don't make a Federal case of—"

It all became very clear to me then. "You couldn't make it," I said evenly, "because you were out on a bender somewhere. Or sleeping one off. Weren't you?"

"Rick—"

"Weren't you?" I shouted.

He winced, then reluctantly nodded. "All right. I fell off the wagon, okay? I admit it. I couldn't help it, man.

When you called and told me about your Mom, I felt so awful, I–"

Suddenly furious, I lost control; taking myself by surprise as much as I did him, I took a swing at him, my right fist connecting with his nose, blood spurting upon impact. Finney staggered back, more shocked than hurt, swaying for a moment as he stared at me in stunned silence.

"You *bastard*," I hissed at him. "You have the gall to use that as an excuse? To dishonor my mother's memory that way?"

He took a step forward. "Cochrane–c'mon–"

"Get out," I snapped. I went to the door, yanked it open so hard the doorknob took a piece out of the wall behind it. He took another step toward me, hands held out in supplication, but it was too late, he'd finally gone too far. "Rickie–please–"

"Get out!" I yelled.

He hovered there a long moment, not wanting to leave but afraid to stay, fearing the unaccustomed fury in my tone. Finally he turned without a word and left. I slammed the door behind him with as much force as I could muster– wishing, God help me, that I could have applied as much force to Finney.

I staggered into the living room and sank into a chair, putting my head in my hands. Jesus God–I'd never struck anyone in anger before in my life. Was I more like Rick than I'd ever imagined . . . or was I just becoming more like him?

Debra had been watching all this from the top of the stairs; now she came down, came up behind me, and put two hands on my shoulders. Her touch was a light one, as though afraid anything more might trigger something she'd rather not see again. "Rick," she said softly, "it's not your fault."

Debra's touch had the calming effect she intended. I shook my head helplessly. "I thought he was growing up," I said, more sad than angry now. "I thought I was—" Making a difference? Again? "At the AA meeting, I thought he was starting to understand about what he did to that woman, about responsibility—"

Debra gently kneaded the muscles of my neck, trying to work the spasms from them. "Some people don't grow up until they absolutely have to," she said. "There are times I think Finney would have to be run over by a truck before it'd make any difference."

I tensed all over. Debra felt it, sensed it, but didn't know—couldn't know—why.

"Look," she said tentatively, "I've got an appraisal this afternoon, but I can reschedule if you'd like me to."

I stood, put my arms around her waist, smiled, and shook my head. "That's very sweet of you, but—no. I'm okay. And anyway, I've got an appointment this afternoon myself, with our lawyer. Mom's estate."

"I could come with you."

I gave her a small kiss, lips just brushing hers, and stroked her back with my hand. "What are you appraising today?"

"Frederick Church. Family in North Hampton's donating it to the Freer. Juicy little tax deduction."

"We may be able to use a few of those ourselves, if you keep picking up referrals like this," I said with a smile. "Who was it who said she might not make much of a go at it, financially, at first?"

She grinned, clearly proud of the progress she'd made

in the last few months. "Wouldn't have happened but for one person."

I nodded. "That curator at the Fine Arts. That referral he gave you really started the ball rolling, didn't it?"

She laughed. "No, you maroon," she said, "not him. You."

"Me? What did I do?"

She looked at me a long moment, as though searching for something in my face, something elusive, something quicksilver.

"You made me feel," she said quietly, "like I did back in college. Back when we first met." A small smile. "You made me feel like new things were possible."

Touched, I put a finger tenderly to her cheek.

"Thank you," I said softly. Then, with a sheepish smile: "We maroons can be a bit slow on the uptake, sometimes."

She kissed me lightly on the lips. "Don't let this thing with Finney eat away at you, okay?"

"I won't," I promised. And I might even have been telling the truth.

Debra went to her appraisal; I to the attorney. My mother had left behind the house, her car, and my parents' accumulated life savings—somewhere in the upper five figures. I filled out the necessary forms, mechanically, as I had once before, resisting the temptation to tell the lawyer what he was about to tell me a second before he actually said it; when he did speak, the words seemed to echo in my thoughts and I only needed to half listen, because I knew this all too well. It didn't take long, and leaving his office I felt restless, deciding on a whim to take a drive—no particular plan, no particular destination; up the 111, through Londonderry, Derry, past the Robert Frost farm, then circling back to Appleton; thinking of Finney, of Mom, of roads not taken ...

And as I drove, the anger that had consumed me the past five days, the rage that had culminated in my ouster of Finney from the house this morning ... the anger cooled and the frustration eased, leaving only a hollow shell of remembered guilt.

I thought I'd failed them, both of them. And that guilt had driven me here, to this other road, this second chance—only to discover that whatever I did or failed to do for my mother didn't really matter much in the end. The cold balm of guilt is this: it gives you a power over loss and life, over tragedy and circumstance, that you never actually possess. At a time when you feel utterly powerless, it gives you the illusion of control—the comforting mantra of *if, if, if*—making you the center of the universe, giving you ultimate responsibility over everything you've loved or lost. Sometimes, maybe, it's even true—sometimes it is your fault, and you indeed might have made it different—but even when it's not, you take the guilt to heart, you embrace it eagerly, a black solace that imparts you with power when you're most powerless, and grants you control when you're most helpless.

But my mother would have died in either world, and Finney—Finney, God forgive me, was actually better off without me there that icy night years before. So what was I to conclude from all this? To hell with responsibility, to hell with obligation, because it doesn't matter anyway?

No. Because it did matter. I returned home to find Debra, fresh from her appraisal, buried in art histories and auction catalogs; and Paige in the living room, simultaneously listening to her Sony headset and reading *A Midsummer Night's Dream.*

I *had* made a difference to them. Helped guide them to paths they might otherwise have passed by. I went to bed that night for the first time without the comforting mistress of Guilt; without hearing her seductive litany of my failures, her accusations and succor. Because I'd finally reached a kind of peace, and found a certain truth: that you *can* make some difference to some people; but you can't make *all* the difference to everyone.

So why did things still feel unresolved to me? I had a wife, a family, I loved . . . yet that ache was still there, that sense of loss I first began to feel at Susan's play. Now as then, I knew what it was, but chose to deny it; so much so that I returned a few days early to work, to keep my attention off that gnawing sensation at the back of my mind. This didn't sit well with Debra—who, still fearing I was bottling up my feelings, was growing increasingly worried for me—but I went anyway, forcing myself to drive to Nashua that Thursday morning.

I returned to my desk to find a pile of bills, liens, doctor's reports, and lawyer's letters, not unlike the one that had greeted me on my first day here. Back then the mountain of paper had invoked terror in me, by dint of my ignorance; now, knowing full well what each sheet of paper meant, it inspired merely apathy. I sighed, settling in behind my desk as Amy came round the corner from her cubicle, looking surprised and concerned.

"Rick. Hi," she said. "I . . . wasn't expecting you back till Monday."

"I wanted something," I answered truthfully, "to occupy my mind. Keep busy, you know?"

She nodded. "Sure. I understand."

Trying to forestall any possible condolences, I said, "You, uh, want to give me an update on all this delightful paperwork?"

"Let me grab my notebook." In a moment she was back, rattling off names, figures, facts: "Mr. Ribiero's attorney is claiming severe psychological trauma, citing those surveys that claim Hispanics—and presumably other Latin minorities, like Portuguese—due to cultural differences, *machismo* and all that, can suffer impotence even after the loss of a finger—'not being a whole man,' that sort of thing..."

I nodded, head down, already making notes of my own, but more out of reflex than real interest; and in a pause between Amy's words there was suddenly a change in the ambient sound of the room—less the clatter of keyboards and the ringing of phones, more the clink of silverware and the murmur of cross-talk, as in a restaurant—and in the next moment I heard, or thought I heard:

"—how do you want to play him? Physically, I mean. They wore beards more often than not in those days—any appliances, makeups that come to mind...?"

I looked up sharply.

Ray? I thought. The gravelly voice, the Bronx accent—it couldn't be anyone else.

"Richard? Is anything...?" The words grew faint, like the ocean heard in a seashell, and then were gone.

Amy saw the tense, shocked expression on my face and stopped reading from her list. "Rick?" she said. "Are you all right?"

The ambient sound was normal again, no more restaurant chatter, no more tinkling of glasses. No more Ray. I looked up at Amy and tried to dispel her worry with a wave. "I'm fine," I lied. "I . . ." Damn—I didn't want them to start doubting me again, what else could I say? "Maybe I'm still just a little shaky, after all."

"Rick," she said gently, "go home. Get some more rest. No one here will think the less of you for it, believe me, you've—" She lowered her voice slightly. "—you've been so on track the past few months, and everybody here's lost someone, they understand what you're going through. You don't have to worry about appearances any longer."

I stood and pecked her on the cheek; I think it both embarrassed and pleased her. "You're right, as usual," I said, forcing myself to sound casual, controlled, despite the panic welling up inside me. "Maybe I was trying too hard." I shut my briefcase, started out. "See you Monday, okay?"

Minutes later I sat in my car in the parking lot, grateful that Amy hadn't noticed my hands trembling as I picked up the briefcase. I pressed them against the wheel to steady them, taking deep, regular breaths to calm myself. Ray; it *was* Ray, no question about it. I'd heard him as clearly as I'd heard Hunt Bailey's voice, that night on stage during *Brigadoon;* that first night, when all this began . . .

Sweet Jesus—was it happening again? It couldn't be—all those years of wondering *what if,* of wondering how it might've been, and then this second chance, this miraculous, inexplicable second chance—and now to see it snatched away, taken back, like some cruel trick? Why? Despite Mom, despite Finney, I loved this life; there was more good here than bad, I was satisfied, I was content.

No. No, that was a lie. I had to own up to it, at last: the

feelings that had been stirring, really, long before that musical in Portsmouth...as early as when I was coaching Paige, as I stood once more on my secret stage. I missed it, damn it: I missed acting. I missed my craft, I missed the highs and I missed the lows; Mutual was steady, invariable, boring. And however much I liked Amy and Hunt and my other co-workers, there was nothing to compare to that sense of camaraderie you felt in a show, players forced together like particles in an atom chamber, forming a nucleus, creating something new and different and unique. I missed my family—*that* family.

Maybe I ought to go home. That was what the song had meant to me: not that I wanted to go back to New York, but that I wanted to go back to my other home. Back to the stage.

I didn't know if my paranoia was justified—if the worlds were in fact converging again—or if it was just my suppressed longing for the stage that made me hear Ray, or think I heard him. But if it was real, if it *was* happening, perhaps it was precisely because I was dissatisfied in some ways with my life; wasn't that what triggered it the first time? Maybe I could forestall it. Maybe, by satisfying those desires I'd been suppressing, I might be able to stay.

I felt my hands stop trembling and slowly took them off the wheel of the car, reaching into my back pocket to get my wallet. I took out the small white business card I'd been handed weeks before—PENNACOOK PLAYERS, EXETER, N.H.—with the phone number scribbled on its face; and within minutes I was calling Susan DeVries.

I don't think I've ever been so nervous at an audition—not even my first, back in New York, over a decade ago. Back then I thought the whole world was at stake at that one audition—but this time I *knew* the whole world, my whole world, was at stake. I'd studied my audition scene at home, furtively, for days before this appointment—it was a scene I'd performed before, but I went over it again and again, desperately memorizing every phrase, every nuance.

I entered the .tiny lobby of the small community theater and I thought: This is crazy, I've been on Broadway, for God's sake. This should be a walk. But the minute Susan appeared, all enthusiastic, and led me into the auditorium to introduce me to the company's artistic director—suddenly Broadway was a memory, and this stage was as daunting and forbidding as that of the Brooks Atkinson or the Mark Hellinger.

We all chatted pleasantly for a while, me talking about my college experience, Susan laying it on a little too thick about how good I was in *Tartuffe*. "And you've done nothing since then?" the director asked. I hesitated, then reluctantly shook my head and shrugged a small shrug. "No. Not really," I said. "Ah," he replied. "Getting your sea legs back, then, eh?" Was I getting paranoid again or did I detect a thin membrane of skepticism fall across his eyes, a faint hint of condescension in his voice? Was he thinking: Wonderful, an old college friend who hasn't been on the boards in years—how long is this going to take, what time is lunch?

Real or imagined, that condescension abruptly reminded me of who I was and what I'd accomplished: so when I took the stage to read, the nervousness was gone, I was calm, I was confident, I was at my ease as I launched into Aeneas' farewell to Carthage and the Queen he loves:

"Carthage, my friendly host, adieu!
Since destiny doth call me from the shore:
Hermes this night, descending in a dream,
Hath summon'd me to fruitful Italy..."

The artistic director leaned forward in his seat a bit, intrigued, perhaps, by the choice of material. I went on, the soldier torn between love and duty:

"Yet Dido casts her eyes like anchors out
To stay my fleet from loosing forth the bay:
'Come back, come back,' I hear her cry a-far,
And let me link my body to thy lips,
That, tied together by the striving tongues,
We may, as one, sail into Italy..."

I did some condensing here, omitting the dialogue of Aeneas' shipmates, going directly into Aeneas' parting anguish:

"To leave her so, and not once say farewell,
Were to transgress against all laws of love.
But, if I use such ceremonious thanks
As parting friends accustom on the shore,
Her silver arms will coil me round about,
And tears of pearl cry, 'Stay, Aeneas, stay!'
Each word she says will then contain a crown,
And every speech be ended with a kiss:
I may not dure this female drudgery.
To sea, Aeneas! find out Italy!"

Why I chose Marlowe for my material, and this scene in particular, I didn't know; any more than I knew why there were tears, real tears, in my eyes, as I finished. I looked up to find Susan beaming proudly at me, while beside her the director seemed more than a little stunned. There was a short silence, punctuated by the clearing of his throat, and then he said, "Well. That was ... quite impressive, Mr. Cochrane."

"Rick," I said, feeling emboldened.

"Rick. Yes." He glanced at Susan, a silent question seeming to pass from him to her; she nodded, then he nodded once himself and turned back to me, his tone firm and decisive.

"Rick," he said. "We're going to be staging *Twelfth Night* for our next production ... rehearsals beginning in about four weeks. Would you be interested in playing Antonio?"

I glanced at Susan, allowing myself a small, pleased smile, then back at the director.

"Yes," I said quietly. "I'd be very interested in that."

All the way back from Exeter, pleasure competed with apprehension. The thought of working again, of practicing my craft again, delighted me more than I ever imagined it would. But it wasn't going to be easy juggling my schedule at State Mutual to accommodate rehearsals, and it was certainly going to be exhausting doing both jobs at once—though probably no more so than taping a soap opera in the morning and afternoon, then performing off-Broadway in the evening, as I'd once done for six straight months. I knew I could handle it; what I wasn't as sure of was what Debra's reaction would be.

Alone in the den with her, I told her about the audition, about my need to do this, one she could understand without me telling her the full truth because that need had existed in Rick as well. "I know it sounds like a strain," I said, anticipating her reservations, "handling two jobs—and I know it'll mean more time away from you and the kids, but—"

"It does sound like a lot," she agreed, her face unreadable.

"I can handle it."

"Working eight hours at Mutual, then rehearsing four, five hours in the evening; more, on weekends?"

"Deb, I swear, I can do it. I *have* to do it."

"It's too much, Rick. So soon after your breakdown, your mother's death . . . I hate to see you under that kind of pressure."

My hopes plunged; then suddenly she was saying, "So why don't you quit State Mutual?"

I did, probably, a classic take. Had I heard her correctly? "Uh . . . come again?" I said in a small voice.

Debra sounded quite matter-of-fact about it. "I said, why don't you quit Mutual? You know you want to; you've wanted to get out of there for years."

I sat down beside her, a bit taken aback. "Honey, if I quit, I'm committing myself to trying to make a living as an actor in regional theater. The pay is modest at best, I can't even guarantee continuous employment—"

"I'm doing pretty well," she said, unruffled, "better than I did at the gallery. We may not live like kings, but we won't exactly be serfs, either. We'll get by."

"I can't take a risk like that. Can't let you and the kids take a risk like that, just for me—"

"There's always your inheritance...your parents' estate...to fall back on, if need be."

Startled, I didn't know what to say at first; I hadn't even thought of the inheritance. There was enough there, by itself, to support us for maybe two years; supplemented by Debra's income, probably a lot longer. But why did the thought make me so uneasy?

I frowned. "I...I don't know, Deb. That was my parents' life savings—if I use it to support myself while I get established, it could be gone inside of a couple years. It doesn't feel right, squandering everything my parents earned in their lifetime."

"Rick," she said gently, "they'd want you to use it to be happy; to do something they couldn't. Just like they wanted you to learn how to swim." She saw the indecision in my eyes. "Okay: worst-case scenario. My business falls off, we have to live off the inheritance for a couple years. By the end of that time, you're either able to make a living as an actor or you're not. If not, you go back and get a day job—not insurance this time, something you *like*. And if you do make a go of it in the theater—" She squeezed my hand. "Think of it," she said, "as using their inheritance to create something beautiful in their memory."

I kissed her tenderly, then brushed aside a strand of hair from her forehead. "I love you," I said.

She kissed me back, smiled. "I love you, too," she said. "And I'm glad that you've decided to stop...punishing yourself."

I blinked, confused. "What do you mean?"

"You know what I mean," she said quietly. "Why did you go into a field—insurance—you had no real interest in? Why not teaching drama at a local college, or working as a stage manager at a dinner theater—something, anything, that was closer to what you loved?"

Not being Rick, I had no answer; in recent weeks I'd even asked the same questions. Debra looked me calmly in the eye: "Whenever I'd suggest anything like what you're doing now, you'd dismiss it out of hand so vehemently it became obvious what you were doing. You were punishing yourself for marrying me."

A chill ran through me and I quickly tried to deny what I suddenly knew was true. "Deb, no—I could never—"

"Oh, maybe not for marrying *me*, per se, but for giving up on New York, on that whole dream—I was the one, remember, who was willing to go to New York with you, but—"

"That would've been no life for either of us," I said, and all at once it was as though we were picking up where we had left off thirteen years before. "Struggling to make ends meet, a working mother and an aspiring actor—" In fact, my first five years in New York had been just that: a struggle, living in a one-room apartment on East Fifth, bussing tables for minimum wage, sometimes eating macaroni and cheese three times a day because it was filling and you could stretch it out for a couple of days—lean times, when a splurge was buying a pint of the cheapest ice milk the grocery had in stock, when a quarter dropped and lost on a busy street could bring me to the verge of tears because that meant no bus fare, that meant walking all the way from Times Square to the Village... "I couldn't have asked you and Paige to suffer for my art," I said.

"So you did the noble thing... married the girl, raised the family... and punished yourself for it for years after," she said, no trace of anger in her voice, just sadness at the wasted years, and I couldn't say she was wrong. Everything she said made sense, answered all the questions about Rick I'd had since that backstage meeting with Susan. If he couldn't go to New York—if he couldn't be a star—he wasn't going to be anything at all. But he'd revel in it, in the suffering, the self-denial, the martyrdom...

"Maybe I *was* punishing myself. But I don't regret marrying you, Deb, so help me God."

She smiled. "Maybe not now." She stared into my eyes—that same searching gaze, looking for that elusive thing that would explain away all the difference in our lives—and before, perhaps, she had time to reflect, she blurted out: "What happened, Rick? Was it really just hitting Paige—the collapse—is that really what turned you around?" She said it as though she dearly wished to believe it, but couldn't. "Or was there something more to it?"

And so our silent covenant was breached, as I suppose it had to be, sooner or later. What could I do? I wanted to tell her as much as she wanted to know—but would she ever accept the truth? And if by some miracle she did believe it—would she resent me for it? Would she hate me for taking her husband's place—or hate herself, for having loved me?

I kept my expression carefully neutral, thoughtful but not guilty, and hated myself for what I did next. I smiled, put a hand to her neck, and stroked her smooth dark hair.

"Like you," I said, "I suppose I finally realized...that new things were possible. That's all."

She smiled, relieved, and kissed me—but the kiss tasted bitter to my lips, spoiled by my deliberate and calculated use of her own words to allay her suspicions. Before it had merely been an unexplored mystery, an unspoken question between us; now it was a lie. A lie I had no alternative but to tell, but for me, as adulterous an act as any affair. It would be there, in my thoughts, every time I held her, even as it was there later that night, when we made love—a black badge of duplicity casting its shadow over what had been, for a time, a perfect relationship. I lay beside her, listening to her shallow breaths as she slept, the same moonlight spilling across our blanket as before, the same chirp of crickets outside our window—but somehow, everything was different.

I lay there feeling like an intruder in what I had come to think of as my bed, my home—my thoughts drifting, for the first time in a long while, to my old life, my old world, the choices I'd made. And slowly, I began to realize that perhaps Rick wasn't the only one who'd meted out punishment to himself—nor the only one to revel in his martyrdom...

The next day over breakfast Debra and I made the mistake of telling Paige about the changes that would soon be taking place in our lives. I was enthusiastically telling her about my audition, about the role I'd been offered, the players and the theater; so enthusiastically, in fact, that I failed to notice the glaze that had come over Paige's eyes, or the rigid line of her mouth. When I got to the part about me quitting my job, she finally couldn't contain herself any longer; she spun round in her seat, looking to Debra for support.

"Mom," she said, "this is crazy! Tell him this is crazy."

I started. Debra, too, was taken aback, but managed to

say matter-of-factly, "Honey, it was my idea. It's not crazy, it's—"

"*Your* idea?" Paige looked aghast. "But he, he can't quit his *job*, how will we live, how will we—"

"I'm making good money now," Debra explained calmly, "and your Dad's got some money coming from Grandma's estate—"

"Don't *I* have some say in this?" Paige demanded. "I mean, this is my life, too, we're talking about."

"Honey," I said soothingly, "your Mom and I would never do anything we thought might hurt you or Jeffrey. We're not going to starve; this is just a sort of experiment. If I can't make a go of it after a couple of years, I'll find other work...maybe as a stage manager or theater administrator or—"

Paige sprang to her feet, throwing down her napkin with a dramatic flourish, but despite the theatricality of her gestures there was real pain in her face. "You're just being *crazy*," she shouted, tears suddenly welling up in her eyes. "Both of you!" She ran from the table, bolted out of the house. As Debra and I got to our feet we saw her through the window, taking off down Schuyler Street on her bicycle.

Debra looked at me worriedly. "I think," she said, light dawning for both of us, "we should have expected that."

I nodded, starting toward the door. "I'll go talk to her."

"You don't even know where she's headed."

I knew where. I gave her a twenty-minute head start, recalling how long it had taken me to ride there on my bike when I was a kid; then I took the Nissan and drove through Appleton, up Mohegan Pass, parking the car at the shoulder of a road I'd come to know quite well these past few months. I made my way through the undergrowth, following the old worn trail, until I spied Paige's bicycle propped up against a tree—and as I pushed through the last stand of shrubbery into the clearing, I saw her there, sitting cross-legged on the slab of granite at the base of the cliff, her head bowed. She must have heard me making my way through the woods, but didn't look up; at first I thought it was for dramatic effect, but as I drew closer I realized it was to give her time to stop crying. Her cheeks were streaked with tears, her eyes red. I had an inkling then of what Rick had felt when he'd hit her—was there any greater pain than to hurt your own child, even accidentally, without thinking?

I sat down beside her on our 'stage,' my legs dangling off the edge. "I'm sorry, honey," I said softly. "I should've realized." I made an unhappy smile. "What a maroon, huh?"

She didn't reply. Didn't even look up. This wasn't going to be easy.

"Paige . . . I'm not trying to compete with you. Really."

She looked up sharply at that, fire in her eyes. "No?" she said, voice dripping with sarcasm. "What *do* you call it?" She looked down again, her face taut but her lips quivering. "The way you coached me—all the time you spent with me, how happy you seemed at the play—I really thought you'd"—she had trouble getting the last part out—"you'd changed."

"I *was* happy for you, honey. And I have changed."

"No, you haven't."

"No?" I paused. "Well, I'm not the one," I said, gently but pointedly, "who's jealous now. Am I?"

She looked up sharply again. "Yes you are! You're doing all of this because you're jealous of me, just like before!"

I tried to put a hand to her back; she shrank away. I sighed. "Honey, I'm doing this because I have to. I'm doing it to help me, not to spite you. I'll still be there to coach you and help you; but I have to do this for me, too."

"Why now?" she demanded. "Why all of a sudden now?"

"It's got to happen sometime."

"Why?"

"You want the old Dad back?" I asked her. "The Father-Thing, you want him?" She glanced at me, the words finally hitting home. "I was sick for years and years, honey," I said slowly. "I made myself sick by denying myself something I wanted, and I took it out on you, on your mother, on myself. You understand?"

She sniffed back some tears, but kept her silence. I looked around us at the secret stage, bright and hot in the August morning. "This place . . . helping you . . . brought it all back for me. Reminded me of how much I missed doing something I used to love. And—"

I hesitated; this was something I had barely articulated to myself, something that had floated at the periphery of my thoughts last night before I finally drifted off to sleep.

"Something else, too," I said. "I was so proud of you, honey, on that stage—using that Juliet inside you, bringing her out, using her." She squirmed uncomfortably. "I told you that acting could hurt, that sometimes you had to use that pain, dredge it up and make it work for you. But it works both ways, honey. You use the pain to create your art, but you also use the art to cope with the pain. It gives you someplace to *put* the hurt, you understand? It lets you work it out." I paused, feeling confident for once that I could speak for Rick in this. "For years, I didn't have anyplace to put the pain, any way to let it out, and it just made me angrier and angrier. Then your Grandma died...and I didn't have anyplace to put that pain, either."

She looked at me; her eyes brimmed with tears; and her voice trembled. "Neither do I," she said, and suddenly she was in my arms and I was saying, "Yes, you do. Yes, you do," and pretty soon we were both crying, as we had that first night my mother passed away. And I realized now that I did still have tears to weep for her—but I didn't want them to be futile tears, I wanted them to have some meaning and beauty; something that would honor her, as Debra had said. Even if no one in the audience knew the wellspring of those emotions, I would know, and maybe, somewhere, Elsie would as well.

Finally, our eyes dry, I looked at my daughter with a small smile and said, "The sad fact of the matter, my love, is that we're both actors. A common affliction, for which there is no known cure." We got down off the 'stage,' walking with our arms around one another through the clearing and down the path to her bicycle. I lifted it onto the bicycle rack on the roof of the car and we rode home...and for a time, for a few hours, I was able to believe again that it *was* home...the doubts of the previous night, as well as the breach in the covenant with Debra, momentarily forgotten.

Debra had to go out on an appraisal, so when Jeffrey started crying around one in the afternoon, the ball was in my court. As I stripped off his Pampers and replaced the diaper I felt a certain contentedness, a quiet satisfaction in the proficiency with which I did this. Even after he'd been changed, though, he continued crying. I gave him his bottle, but he just pushed it away. I held him, rocked him, made soothing little noises, but nothing I did seemed to quiet him; nothing I ever did, come to think of it, seemed to quiet him. I lay him down in his crib again, intending to go downstairs to get some baby food, thinking perhaps that would help.

But before I could make a move, I was no longer in Jeffrey's nursery; no longer staring down at my infant son. I was in a hospital room, looking into the hollow, sunken eyes of—oh, Jesus—it was John Danker. I almost didn't recognize him—he was so thin, so frail, his bony arms mottled with—oh God, Kaposi's sarcoma? He was staring up at me, starting to say something—"Richard," and his voice was raspy and sore, it hurt me to hear it; "dear boy"—but before he could finish he collapsed in a fit of coughing, a horrible rattling cough that spoke of pneumonia, of lungs filled with fluid.

I reached out and put my hand on his. Tears welled up in my eyes at the sight of this sweet old man, once strutting so powerfully across the stage, voice booming in his best villain's timbre, now unable to speak more than three words without pain.

"John," I said. "John, I have to tell you—"

But as suddenly as I was swept away, I was pulled back to the nursery, back to Jeffrey, and away from John. *No!* I found myself crying soundlessly. *Please . . .* But it was over, John Danker was again no more than a memory from another life, and Jeffrey—

Jeffrey was no longer crying. He was gurgling happily, in fact—almost as he did when his mother held him. I reached in to pick him up . . .

And once again he started to cry.

Numbly, dazedly, I went downstairs, picked up the phone and called New York information, getting the numbers for most of the major hospitals in Manhattan; then I called each one in turn, asking if they had a patient named Danker, John Danker. Finally, the patient information line at St. Vincent's confirmed that, yes, Mr. Danker was a patient there; would I like to be connected to his room? "No," I said quickly. "No, thank you." And hung up.

As I'd suspected: the only differences between this world and my old one were those caused by my decision thirteen years before. John Danker had lived much the same life in both worlds, with the sole exception that he'd never performed with an actor named Richard Cochrane. So the man dying in the small hospital room in New York would never recognize me; never know what his friendship, in another life, had meant to me; and yet despite this, I knew I had to go to him. Even if he didn't know me, even if I had to pretend to be merely a fan, an admirer who'd seen him years before on stage and had come to offer my respects and thanks; even so, I had to see him one last time.

But I was afraid, too: afraid that I might instead see a glimmer of recognition in his eyes as I entered the room. Yet would that really be so awful? Part of me wanted it; and part of me wanted not to go, not to budge from this room, this house. I could no longer delude myself that nothing was happening here; events were moving me along familiar tracks, or perhaps I was moving events, I didn't know which. I was numb as I called Logan Airport to make plane reservations for the next morning, and as I told Debra, later, that an old college friend—I invented a nonexistent classmate from some acting course—was in the hospital in New York and I had to fly down to see him...

But that night, making love with Debra, the numbness wore off and I was gripped with the fear that I might never hold her like this again. I made love to her fiercely but tenderly, and for a moment she seemed alarmed by my sudden passion—sensing, perhaps, my desperation and fear—and so I had to pull back, be more playful, try not to frighten her with my need. All I could do was lie there afterward, her head resting on my chest, and try to stay awake for as long as I could—try to savor the warm breeze drifting through the half-open window, try to memorize, in every detail, the feel of her skin against mine, the rhythm of her breathing and the beat of her heart.

The next morning the fear was almost overwhelming; it took all my control to keep the desperation from my voice as I hugged Paige goodbye. To her, to Debra, I was just flying down to New York for a day to visit an old friend; any trenchant pauses, any tremor in my voice, could only alarm them. So I kept my tone bright and cheerful, my smile casual. I kissed Debra goodbye at the door, my mouth lingering only moments longer than it should have.

Each word she says will then contain a crown,
And every speech be ended with a kiss...

I was out the door before my heart could betray me; and before my flesh could bind me.

CODA

RICK, RICHARD

"—that's an awkward transition there, we'll smooth it out in post—don't pay any attention. And this one coming up, the one between Hog Lane and Tamburlaine's chambers, we're going to goose it up a little, do an optical fade, it'll play much better—"

I was sitting on a stool in an editing bay at WNET, watching a rough cut—not Ray's director's cut, but the editor's preliminary assembly of footage that Ray would use as the blueprint for his cut, rearranging, modifying, adding or deleting shots. It was a sweet gesture on Ray's part, inviting me here; although he'd been careful never to say anything, all through the shoot he'd known I was anxious and a little rusty—attributing it to the coke withdrawal, never guessing the truth—and now he wanted to bolster my confidence by showing me that even at this rough stage, even without slick editing and fancy underscore and color-correction, we'd actually pulled it off.

I sat there, transfixed, never having seen myself on anything but a home video before. Ray kept apologizing for the little glitches—the lighting effects that hadn't quite come off on the stage and would have to be enhanced optically; the light bars that ran across the screen from left to right, indicating where dissolves would be placed—but it was still as close to magic as I'd ever seen. I nodded and smiled with the restraint of a man pretending to be a blasé professional, but inside I was fairly bursting with wonder and excitement at that figure on the monitor, that man who looked like me, but so much more than me as well.

"Ah Faustus," he said now, despairingly, "Now hast thou but one bare hour to live...

"Stand still, you ever-moving spheres of heaven,
That time may cease and midnight never come.
Fair nature's eye, rise, rise again, and make
Perpetual day..."

On stage I had always been able to tell when it was working, when an effect I was going for registered with the audience, but this was different. I was the audience *and* the actor, I saw the bits of business I was using, remembered how they felt at the time... but I was seeing them rather than feeling them, watching, not intuiting. And as Faustus and Marlowe plunged toward their twin dooms, I found myself feeling sorry for the poor bastard on screen, found myself actually moved, in a way I'd never experienced on stage.

Amazingly—miraculously—the man on the screen was good. Not great, perhaps, no Emmy winner—but *good.* Professional, competent, and at times even inspired. I saw all the clumsy moments, all the awkward beats... but I also saw what not to do next time, I saw the potential as well as the reality. And every once in a while—in an offhand gesture, an inflection of a line, a reaction in the eyes—I saw something spontaneous, something true, something that even Richard might have been proud of.

"Marlowe is gone. Regard his hellish fall,
Whose fiendful fortune may exhort the wise
Only to wonder at unlawful things . . ."

The matte hadn't been made yet, and so I saw only a freeze frame of the dagger above Marlowe's head, and my voice—Faustus as Chorus—over it:

"To practice more than . . . heavenly? . . . power
permits . . ."

The frame went to black; color bars filled the screen. Ray looked at me. "Well?" he said. "What do you think?"

"I think," I said, "that I had a damn good director."

"Well, yes, there is that," Ray grinned, "but taking that as a given . . . are you satisfied with it?"

I stared at the color bars on the screen, remembering my face filling that frame, thinking of how, in just a few months, a few million people would be watching me as I just had . . . being moved, perhaps, affected even briefly, by what I'd done. Satisfied? More than that: I realized with pride and a trace of amazement that I had nothing more to prove. To myself, or anyone else.

I slid off my stool, extending a hand to Ray. "More than satisfied," I said, wishing I could say more, knowing I never could. "And thanks. For taking a chance on me."

Ray shook his head. "You take a chance betting on roulette," he said, "not on Richard Cochrane."

I got out of there before I could burst into tears.

As I walked out onto 58th Street, however, I felt suddenly off-balance—as though I'd just missed an extra step I hadn't known was there. In the hour and a half I'd been inside, the hazy sunshine of early morning had turned into a cloudy iron sky, a particularly New York kind of sky that I'd noticed once or twice before, these past months. There's the most peculiar quality of light in Manhattan just before a cloudburst: a flat, dim light, with a kind of stillness in the air despite the shuffle of pedestrians up and down the street. The clouds, more black than gray, seem closer, nearly touching the backs of the tallest buildings, but it's the light and the stillness that's most unnerving, foreboding. The light is the kind of light I imagine I'd see in the moments before death: a becalmed silence, a dimness before the final dark.

I took a cab uptown and tried unsuccessfully to concentrate on the various offers Joel was fielding. Maybe it was just anticlimax after viewing the show—maybe I was still thinking of Jeffrey, of yesterday's brief, teasing glimpse of him. Or maybe I knew that, having proved to myself all I ever needed to prove, that all the rest of this life I had so coveted *was* anticlimax.

I thought of Libby and our date next week. I was apprehensive, not just because of the necessary pretense when I was around her but because I found her attractive and the idea of embarking on yet another of Richard's old relationships did not seem the wisest of courses just now. No, I was going to have to start a new relationship—someone not from Richard's life, someone with whom I could start fresh—but when I tried to conjure what I wanted in a woman, why did my thoughts keep circling back to Debra?

Gradually I became conscious of a dull staccato sound above and beyond the surrounding traffic. I looked up and realized that it was the sound of wiper blades ticking back and forth across the cab's windshield. It was raining, but in the cab, with the windows rolled up and the sounds of traffic buffeting us, I hadn't even noticed the light drizzle that had begun to fall around us.

Raining. It was *raining* . . .

I rolled down the side window, straining to hear the sound of the rain on the pavement, but it was drowned out by the blare of car horns and the roar of a bus trying to cut us off on our right. My driver, as territorial as the best of them, gunned the engine and swept ahead of the bus, swerving just enough to avoid colliding with it as he passed— and through it all, all I cared about, all I strove to do, was to hear the rain, damn it, just to hear how it sounded . . .

I chafed and fretted all the way to Riverside Drive, though it couldn't have been more than a five-minute trip. I handed the driver a ten for a four-dollar fare, burst out of the cab, onto the sidewalk in front of my building— and realized that even now I couldn't hear the sound of raindrops on the street. This wasn't New Hampshire, it was New York; something about the concrete and the macadam and the ambient traffic noise seemed to filter out the finer sounds you could hear more easily in a small, quiet town. What I did hear was the sound of rain on the roofs of cars and the spray of water as a car drove through a large puddle in the road.

But there was something odd about that, too; instead

of a wet, sloshing sound, it had a faint ring to it, a hollow, glassy sound—a sound as familiar as it was dissonant...

I stood there, immobile, my heart beginning to race. I was getting soaked but barely noticed—all I could think was, What did I do, what *should* I do, where did I go? I spun round desperately, pedestrians with umbrellas and rain hoods jostling me in their rush to pass me, to get out of the rain. I looked up and down Riverside, I looked under the awnings of nearby buildings, I looked across the street—

And then I saw him.

He was standing on the fringes of Riverside Park, wearing my old wool coat, the rain coming down so hard I almost couldn't make him out; he seemed to be staring at me, though at this distance and through the rain I couldn't make out his expression. But he must have seen me notice him because he turned suddenly and started walking away, into the park.

I rushed into the street, dodging and weaving amid angry motorists, ignoring the nasty bleat of car horns, until I reached the other side. He was still walking away and so I began running, tramping through the wet grass to catch up with him.

Without looking back he started slowing as he reached the arched walk-bridge near the esplanade overlooking the river; and as he gained its dry sanctuary he stopped, turned, and stood waiting for me to join him. Behind him, on the Hudson, small pleasure craft caught in the sudden summer squall tacked toward shore; but even the whitecaps on the river looked strange, moving in odd ways, seeming at times to overlap like multiple images off a bad TV antenna...

I slowed as I approached the bridge; the rain was now a torrent and we were virtually alone in the park, with only the occasional jogger skirting the esplanade, hurrying home. I came to a halt about three feet away from him, and now I could finally read his expression: somber, impassive, cheerless.

I paused to catch my breath, and in that pause he spoke up.

"I went upstairs," Richard said soberly, nodding across the street, "but I didn't have a key, didn't want to risk staying there and then having you come up, and the doorman see me going up twice. So I came down and waited over here."

"How did you know?" I asked. "To come here? To New York?"

He smiled, a bit ruefully. "I was coming on ... other business. It started to rain when I hit Manhattan, so I ... just had the cabbie take me here."

He hesitated, as though something was weighing on his mind. "I have something to tell you," he said finally. "About—"

"I know," I interrupted him; trying to spare him, I suppose, the necessity of saying it. "My mother is dead." Off his baffled expression, I explained, "I saw parts of it. In dreams. An ambulance ... paramedics putting paddles on her ... then—"

I winced and looked away. "I saw it. I wasn't there, but I saw it." It all started to come back now: the frustration, the impotence of being so distant, so powerless ... "I wasn't there," I repeated softly, helplessly.

He looked at me a long moment. "Do you remember putting your hand on hers? When it was over?"

I thought back, not really wanting to summon up those images, yet clinging to them as the only memories, the only goodbye I would ever have. "Yes," I said, feeling the tears welling up, not caring if he saw. "I think so."

"Then you were there," he said gently. "Who's to say whose hand it was?"

We were silent for a long while after that, the rain not slackening at all, the sound of the surf on the Hudson jarring and dissonant. Finally I worked up nerve enough to say, "I have some things to tell you, too." And in a flat, toneless voice that belied my shame and fear, I began to recount what had happened to me since taking over the life he'd entrusted to me. When I got to Catlin, to meeting her at Ray's party, to our first night in bed together, his eyes widened a bit, but he was otherwise impassive; then, feeling almost as though I were talking about someone else, I related the whole sordid, pathetic story. I left nothing out: the cocaine; the obsession with Catlin; the play, and how I'd fucked it up. I told him about Ray and Melissa, about their help during the withdrawal, and about the damage I'd done both to his apartment and his reputation. I assured him I was clean now, told him about Wyndham, about the PBS special, about the offers that were starting to trickle in... but somehow, hearing myself tell it, it seemed inadequate recompense for the trust I'd violated, the faith I'd breached. I told him about my meeting Libby—about the date we'd arranged for next week—but that, too, could hardly atone for the mistakes I'd made.

I told most of it with my head down, staring at the concrete pathway, but occasionally stole glances up at him, his eyes growing wider, his face paler, the further I went on. I couldn't read beneath the shock, couldn't glimpse the anger and betrayal hidden behind it, but I was prepared to take it—to accept it, when it came—as my due. I deserved whatever came next.

I stood there listening, feeling increasingly dizzy as he went on, as though someone had just dropped me down an elevator shaft and I just kept falling and falling, with no bottom in sight. The hell of it was, I could understand it, everything he was saying I could comprehend: Catlin certainly, I could see how susceptible he might be to her allure, and even the coke, given his insecurities, even that I could understand. If this had been his life, I could well have patted him on the back, nodded consolingly, and said, *These things happen. Don't look back, just move on, move ahead,* or some similar bonehead platitude.

But it wasn't his life, damn it, it was *mine.* It was me who all my friends thought went on a coke binge; it was me who acted like a temperamental asshole with a respected director; it was me with his career in disarray. Good God—could I face all that? Could I ever face my friends, my colleagues, my peers, after all that?

"Excuse me," I said, sinking onto the dry sidewalk beneath the bridge. "I think I have to sit down a moment."

He sat down beside me. I listened to the rest of it, finally starting to feel an anger building up inside me. God damn it, how dare he screw up my life like this? What gave him the right to make everyone I knew think I was unstable at best and a drug addict at worst? Who appointed him the arbiter of my—

I stopped; caught myself.

Me. That's who. I had given him the right: I had appointed him executor of my life, as he had done me in return. And as I started thinking about what I had to tell him, my anger dissipated and turned to chagrin.

I suddenly became aware that he had stopped talking, though for how long I wasn't sure. He looked tense, uneasy, as though awaiting a coming blow. I shook myself out of my reverie, spoke up.

"Okay," I said. "Anything else?"

"Isn't that enough?" His face contorted in reproach and regret. "I'm sorry," he said, almost a whisper. "I know that's not enough—I know how I've betrayed you, I know I can't make it up to you, but—"

"Rick," I said.

My use of his name took him off guard. I reached over, laid a hand atop his wrist.

"We made an agreement," I said. "I trusted you with my life; you trusted me with yours. We both knew what we were doing. We had no illusions about that."

He seemed confused, not knowing how to respond to this. "But what I did to your life—"

"What you did," I said evenly, "you did to *your* life. I gave it to you. That was the agreement: neither of us thought we were going to be giving them back, we both thought they were ours to keep, to do with as we will. I understood that, going in; did you?"

He nodded, a bit dazedly.

"Good," I said. "Because I've done some things in your life that you may not be too crazy about either."

He straightened. "They can't be as bad as this," he said obstinately.

"Well, which would you say is worse?" I asked, deliberately setting out to puncture his self-reproach. "Having the reputation of being an ex-coke fiend or of being not too tightly wrapped?"

His eyes widened. His face went white.

"What?" he said.

The rain ran off the arch of the walk-bridge above us, making a kind of curtain of water on either side of us, obscuring us from whatever passersby there might be on the street; but the downpour was already lessening and I could sense our time was growing short as I began to tell him my story.

I told him about my—his—"breakdown," how I had used it to explain away the gaps in my memory, and how, serendipitously, it had eased the tensions in his family—making a clean slate of things, as it were, for me to write a new life, new relationships, onto. He paled a bit at the idea of the entire town, his friends, his co-workers, all thinking him some sort of emotional basket case. He looked, for a while, as shocked as I had been moments earlier—but the shock gradually turned to relief as he realized that we had both done some major reconstruction on each other's lives and reputations and that we were, perhaps, more even on that score than he had imagined.

I told him about his mother; about some of the things I'd learned, some of the things we'd spoken of that we'd never spoken of before. He looked happy to hear them. He'd never known about the swimming either, and I saw in his eyes the same surprise and reevaluation I had gone through. I told him about Finney and the accident, and the falling-out between us, though he didn't seem too surprised by any of it—if anything, he seemed relieved that he didn't have to go back to that old role, Finney's keeper again. I started to tell him with some trepidation about Paige: about my coaching her, encouraging her, about her Juliet and what it had cost her. I wasn't sure what his reaction would be—I was nervous, afraid that the old envy might show itself again.

But as I told him about her performance, a smile lit his face: a proud, fatherly smile. And he began to ask me questions. How did she handle the balcony scene? Was she uneasy with the blank verse? Did she seem nervous? How did the audience like her?—and in that moment I saw clearly, for the first time, the change in him. No longer the embittered husband and jealous father, he seemed genuinely pleased at Paige's progress and grateful for what I'd done for her; there was a calmness to him now, a self-assurance, that I'd not seen in him before. And I realized, with a shame I hated to acknowledge, that a part of me—a mean, small, selfish part of me—had been hoping not to see that.

I didn't want to dwell too much on my relations with Debra, as much for his feelings as for mine, for what I wished to keep my own private memories—all I would have left, when this was over—but what could I do? I had to tell him as much as I could, so that when he...took over again...he wouldn't make any mistakes, wouldn't "forget" something that couldn't be explained away by his "breakdown." In the end, then, I even had to give him my memories; my only keepsake of my other life.

So I told him. Everything. I told him about the second spring in his marriage; about the renewal of affection, of passion, between Debra and—him; and as I did, as I related our trip to Portsmouth, her decision to go into appraising, our joint decision regarding the future and my audition at the Pennacook Players, I saw what I feared seeing most: I saw longing and loss and desire. Not just for Debra, not just for Paige and Jeffrey, but for the new life I'd built for him—for *me*, though I wouldn't get to live it now—and I knew then that I could hardly deny him his rightful due. That small, selfish part of me had hoped that I might—hoped that he had not changed, that he wasn't deserving of it—but it seemed that we had both emerged from this, in many ways, as different men.

He must have seen some hint of this in my eyes because as I finished—as I looked up into the lightening sky, the slackening rain—he studied me closely for several moments, then said quietly: "You didn't want to leave, did you?"

I hesitated a long moment, but there was no anger, no hostility in his gaze—just understanding and compassion.

"No," I admitted. "But I couldn't keep living a lie. Couldn't keep sleeping next to someone, knowing that I wasn't who she thought I was . . ."

He nodded, as though he knew exactly what I meant. He looked out at the Hudson, the whitecaps smaller now, the water calmer. "Pennacook Players, you say?" he asked quietly, his gaze unfocused, as though staring at something very far away.

"That's right," I said. "In Exeter."

He nodded to himself and smiled.

Finally I stood; someone had to bring this to a close. The rain was quite light now and the curtain of water falling off the bridge was not as concealing as it had been. "Time's running out," I said, but he didn't stand up; he remained sitting, staring off into the distance, and when he spoke there was still a measure of guilt and remorse in his tone. "Doesn't seem fair," he said quietly. "You leave me with a new career... a mended family... and I–" He looked up at me ruefully. "I leave you with less than you started out with."

I was surprised by how quickly, how vehemently, I disagreed.

"No," I said. "That's not true. You gave me–" The skies were clearing; the rain abating. How did I tell him, in the brief time remaining, everything I'd learned, everything I'd felt? How did I fully explain about Mom, about Finney, about guilt and release? About Debra and Paige and living the life I thought I'd never know—only to discover, in the end, that the only thing that was preventing me from living it was me? No matter what he'd done to my career, it paled beside what I'd gotten from him—from the brief gift of his life. But how did I compress all that into the few short seconds left to us?

He stood, faced me, demanding an answer he was convinced did not exist.

"What?" he asked. "What the hell did I give you?" The past six months flashed through my mind: all the things I'd done, the people I'd touched, the lessons I'd learned. But only one thing, in the end, seemed to truly matter.

"You gave me," I said softly, "the chance to say 'thank you.'"

He smiled at that, nodded wordlessly; both of us looked up into the sky at the same moment and realized that the time had come. It wasn't practical, or necessary, to exchange clothes again. I slipped off my—his—wedding ring and handed it back to him; we exchanged wallets and watches, and in less than a minute it was done. He held out his hand; I took it. We both searched for something to say, but everything that came to my mind, at least, seemed inadequate, so we simply shook hands and he turned and started out from under the shelter of the walk-bridge. And it occurred to me then that we had not, as I supposed, emerged from this as different men—but as whole men. Where before we'd been, each in our own way, half-men, living half-lives.

I watched him walk away; the rain had fanned out into a gentle spray that hung over the park like a Scottish mist. I stepped out from beneath the shelter of the bridge and saw that I was still almost alone in the park—alone but for Rick, walking off, and one sad and stooped old man, making his way slowly along the winding path. I looked into the sky, briefly, then back again.

And for a moment—only a moment—I thought I saw more than just one old man ambling through the park. I saw, trailing behind him like a procession of ghosts—each dimly seen, each receding one more transparent, more diaphanous than the last—a succession of old men, all the same but all different. One walking with a cane, another without; one wearing threadbare clothes, another smartly dressed in a Brooks Brothers suit; one walking alone, and the one behind him strolling arm in arm with an elderly woman, the two of them talking and laughing. I watched, transfixed, realizing that I was standing at a kind of crossroads—all the roads that never were, all the roads that always are, all the roads of time and chance converging briefly in this place, at this moment—

I turned away, looking for Rick ... but he was nowhere in sight. I turned back to the old man.

And there was just one of him, now—stooped, sad, and slow, making his way through the park, alone ...

Later, there would be time to consider what changes my other self had brought to my life; time to think about Libby, about things I'd held true for so long which now seemed palpably false. For now, I needed to do what I'd come here to New York to do. I hailed a cab at the corner, giving the driver the address for St. Vincent's Hospital, telling him to hurry. All the way down to the Village I thought about John, about the things I wanted to tell him, the answer to that question I'd asked of him months before. When we arrived I pulled out my wallet to pay the fare... and something dropped out of one of the sleeves, a slip of paper that fell to the floor of the cab. I paid the fare, then reached down to pick up the fallen paper.

Slowly, tenderly, I put the snapshot of Paige back in my wallet, then headed into the hospital, hoping that this time I would not be too late.

Q: The premise of this book is very unusual—how did it come about?

A: I think all of us at some point have wondered "What if?"—what would my life have been like if I'd taken that job, stayed in that town, married this person or that. I was in my early thirties, and like Richard I was fairly successful in my career—as a writer-producer for television—but hadn't yet married. Sometimes I'd find myself wondering what might've happened had I not moved to California but remained on the East Coast, settled down, maybe wrote for the theater, which had always been an interest of mine (as an aspiring writer I was influenced as much by playwrights like Robert Anderson and James Costigan as I was by authors of prose fiction). So for me, the "what if" of the story encompassed both Richard and Rick's lives—I was daydreaming, on paper, about both a career in theater and a fulfilling marriage in a small town.

Q: Have you ever been an actor, like Richard?

A: My acting experience is limited to a single course I took in college—I reasoned that if I wanted to write for actors I should have some idea of what their job was like. I played a scene from Samuel Beckett's *Endgame* (nothing like starting out with something easy). It was an instructive experience and it gave me great respect for actors, but I never had the slightest desire to be on the other side of the camera, even as a cameo in one of my own shows. But I do have actor friends, one of whom, Anne Twomey, took me around to various actors' haunts in New York when I was researching the book. In fact, the rehearsal hall for *This Way Out* is identical to one Anne took me to, right down to the violin shop on the same floor and the Stradivarius behind glass.

Q: Nevertheless, it sounds like the story has some basis in your own life.

A: In some ways it's one of the most autobiographical stories I've written. Richard's parents are essentially mine. When he gets the call telling him that his mother has died, that was how I got the news that my mother had died. What he sees when he walks into her house is exactly what I saw when I entered my mother's apartment after her death. The note he finds is word for word what my mother wrote to me. But it's not just tragic similarities: the story Richard's mother tells him—about how she and his father were terrified of the water but determined not to pass that along to him—my mother told me before she passed away, and I was as surprised by the revelation as Richard is. Writing *Time and Chance* was actually a tremendously cathartic experience, helping me come to terms with my parents' deaths.

There are other true-life aspects to the book too, not the least of which is that I watched a good friend of mine nearly destroy his career because of a cocaine addiction. So there's a great deal of observed life in this book.

Q: You eventually got to experience what it was like to work in the theater, didn't you?

A: Yes, ironically enough, right after I wrote this book I was approached by Alan Menken and David Spencer about adapting one of my stories into a stage musical (which ultimately became a show called *Weird Romance*, still being performed to this day). So strangely enough, I soon found myself living in New York City for seven weeks as I worked on a musical, living the dream I wrote about in *Time and Chance*. And to complete the circle, while I was living in Manhattan I had my first date with the woman who would, a few years later, become my wife.

Q: On the literary side, what were the influences on your story?

A: I've always admired the work of writers like Robert Nathan, who's probably best known today for his book *Portrait of Jennie*, and Jack Finney, author of the classic novel *Time and Again*—sound familiar?—and a charming alternate-world novel called *The Woodrow Wilson Dime*. The New England setting was inspired by the work of a wonderful writer named Jonathan Strong, specifically his novel *Ourselves*, which I first encountered when I was in college. It's a lovely coming-of-age story set in Boston, with immensely likable characters and sweet, clear, evocative prose. For years afterward I would periodically go back and re-read the book, each time holding it up to myself as a standard of excellence against which I judged my own work.

Q: How did the process of writing *Time and Chance* compare to that of writing the historical novels you're now known for?

A: When I'm writing a historical novel, I'm trying to plausibly re-create a past world. In *Time and Chance*, I was creating instead an alternate, or parallel, world, but it had to be depicted just as plausibly, with the same attention to detail I would use when evoking a past milieu. That's really the job of any novelist: to create a world in which your readers can believe, peopled with characters you come to care for. I hope the readers who came to care for Rachel in *Moloka'i* and Jin in *Honolulu* will also find that true for Richard, Rick, Debra, Catlin, and the world—or worlds—they live in.

For more information about Alan's work, or to contact him about speaking to your reading group, visit his website at www.alanbrennert.com.

1. The author introduces Richard and Rick through alternating first-person chapters. How do their voices, the way they express themselves, differ? How are their personalities different? Did you relate more to one than the other?

2. If you had to choose between Richard's life and Rick's, which would you choose? Or do you find both lacking?

3. Was the concept of parallel worlds familiar to you before reading this book? Did you find it clearly and plausibly presented?

4. Do you have a moment in your life about which you think, "What if"? Would your life be much different had you made another decision at that turning point? Do you regret the choice you made or the choice you didn't make?

5. What did you think of Richard and Rick's decision to switch lives? If you had been in their position, would you have considered such a drastic move?

6. Compare and contrast the world each man lives in—small town versus big city, workaday job versus glamorous showbiz—and the positive and negative aspects of each. How do these relate to the positive and negative aspects of the characters themselves?

7. If you were Debra, do you think you would have known that Richard was not your husband?

8. Can you see the qualities in Debra and Catlin that both Richard and Rick are drawn to? Did you find Catlin sympathetic or not?

9. What do you think will become of the Dave Finney of Rick's world? Would you have reacted as Richard does the last time he sees Finney?

10. Discuss the narrative resonances found in many of the quotes from Marlowe.

11. At the end of the book, how have Richard and Rick evolved as people? Have they changed enough to overcome their flaws and mistakes? What do you see happening in their lives beyond the end of the novel?

12. Dave Finney's name is obviously an homage to author Jack Finney. What author of another classic parallel worlds story (hint: do a random search) is being homaged in the town of Wyndham, Massachusetts?

Alan Brennert was born in Englewood, New Jersey, to Herbert E. Brennert, an aviation writer, and Almyra E. Brennert, an apartment rentals manager. Since 1973 he has lived in Southern California, where he received a B.A. in English from California State University at Long Beach and did graduate work in screenwriting at UCLA.

In addition to novels, he has written short stories, teleplays, screenplays, and the libretto of a stage musical, *Weird Romance,* with music by Alan Menken and lyrics by David Spencer. He has developed screenplays for major studios as well as miniseries, pilots, and television movies, and earned an Emmy Award for his work as a writer-producer on the television series *L.A. Law.* His short story "Ma Qui" was honored with a Nebula Award in 1992.

His novel *Moloka'i,* about the forced segregation of leprosy patients to the settlement of Kalaupapa in Hawai'i, won praise from *The Washington Post,* the *Chicago Tribune,* and *Publishers Weekly,* and became a national bestseller in paperback as well as a favorite selection of reading groups across the country. His most recent novel, *Honolulu,* was named one of the Best Books of 2009 by *The Washington Post.*

He is currently at work on a new historical novel.

Experience the "dazzling historical novel" *(The Washington Post)* that has become a reading group phenomenon.

Young Rachel Kalama, growing up in idyllic Honolulu in the 1890s, is part of a big, loving Hawaiian family— but at the age of seven her world is shattered by the discovery that she has leprosy. Forcibly removed from her family, she is sent to an isolated settlement on the island of Moloka'i. From then on, her life will never be the same....

"Brennert's compassion makes Rachel a memorable character, and his smooth storytelling vividly brings early-twentieth-century Hawai'i to life."

—PUBLISHERS WEEKLY (STARRED REVIEW)